PRAISE FOR THE MYTHS OF AIRREN

"This whimsical and enchanting tale, filled with poisonous injustice and seductively forbidden romance, will sink its claws into you and have you falling for the monsters."

— Nicole Fiorina, Author, Hollow Heathens

". . . a fast-paced adventure story about prejudice and its consequences, the beauty of trust, and forbidden love."

— Natalie Murray, Author, The Hearts & Crowns Trilogy

"A dash of darkness, a seductive romance, and a quest that promises death. A Cursed Kiss is a one-of-a-kind adventure in a mystical world you won't want to come back from.

— Kristen Kruse, Reviewer, Lady of Bookshire

A CURSED HEART

Myths of Airren
Book Two

Jenny Hickman

Midnight Tide
PUBLISHING

Publisher's Note: This is a work of fiction. Names, characters, places, and incidents are a product of the author's imagination. Locales and public names are sometimes used for atmospheric purposes. Any resemblances to actual people, living or dead, or to businesses, companies, events, institutions, or locales is completely coincidental.

Published by Midnight Tide Publishing.

www.midnighttidepublishing.com

Book Title / Jenny Hickman- 1st ed.

Paperback ISBN: 9781953238627

Hardcover ISBN: 9781953238634

Cover design by Cover Dungeon

Character Art by Lauren Richelieu

AUTHOR'S NOTE

This book has scenes depicting grief and loss, violence, sexual assault, and contains some sexual content. I have done my best to handle these elements sensitively, but if these issues could be considered triggering for you, please take note.

Pronunciation Guide

Gancanagh-(*gan•cawn•ah*)

Padraig- (*pa•drec*)

Tadhg- (*tie•g*)

Rían- (*ree•un*)

Fiadh- (*fee•ah*)

Ruairi- (*ror•ee*)

Áine- (*awn•ya*)

For every woman
told to bite her tongue

Part One

1

Choosing a husband was like selecting the weapon for your execution: your life was forfeit either way. I had been lucky enough to have avoided both until today. If only I had gotten out of bed instead of staring at the canopy for the better part of an hour, not had to slather on cream after cream to hide my freckles, or skipped the toast and sausages cook had served for breakfast.

Then my father wouldn't have caught me and ruined a perfectly good morning with his nonsense.

"Did you hear me, Aveen?" My father braced his hands against the leather-topped desk cluttered with ledgers and books, his tone that of a man not to be trifled with. He'd slicked his thick chestnut hair back from his forehead with pomade. The man was always dressed in the height of fashion—breeches, shirt, waistcoat, and cravat—even though he spent most of his time alone in this office.

I'd never understood his need for all the pomp. Waste of time and effort, that's what it was.

"I heard you, Father." My nails bit into my palms when I squeezed my hands into fists behind my back. "You believe it is time for me to marry."

His mouth flattened beneath his trimmed mustache. The kind and gentle man I had known as a child had died alongside my mother, replaced by a dictator who refused to listen to reason. He wanted neither input nor conflicting opinions, only someone to parrot his words back in a feminine voice. "That's correct. You need a husband."

"I thought I was here to collect funds. Not a husband."

The following Saturday was my little sister's birthday party. Every last coin would be spent on her. Keelynn would love a new frock—something bright and festive for the start of spring. With her rich, dark hair, she looked good in almost any color. Except black. She was far too lively for the color of death.

I'd always been envious of the flawless alabaster complexion she'd inherited from our mother, rest her soul. I took after my father's side. Pale and fair, with freckles I painstakingly covered every morning. If I didn't spend so much time outside, the freckles would've faded. But if I didn't spend so much time outside, I would've faded as well.

"You've had almost twenty-one years to make a match." My father's eyes narrowed over the rims of the spectacles he refused to wear in public. "I don't understand why no one has asked for your hand. You're a comely woman. What is wrong with young men these days?"

Everything.

That was the problem.

None of the suitors who'd called had been worth forfeiting my life, my freedom, or my happiness.

Why would a woman in her right mind want to tie herself to some man anyway? Storybooks spoke of love that transcended time and death, and kisses that stole one's breath. If love like that existed, I hadn't experienced it. And as far as kisses went, they were fine.

Chocolate cake was better.

In the window between the massive mahogany bookshelves,

ominous clouds rolled in from the sea. If I didn't leave soon, I'd end up a drowned rat by the time I reached town.

"Can we discuss this at dinner? I was just on my way to the market to pick up Keelynn's birthday present."

"We will discuss this now."

Men were more likely to listen if you appeared pleasant so I pasted a placid smile on my lips. "I have already told you that I am perfectly content to remain on my own. I know how to run a household, do the finances, and manage the gardens." The other day, I had helped our coachman Padraig birth a foal. Not that I'd ever tell Father that. With proper guidance and training, I could do anything as well as—or better than—any man. "I do not need a husband."

There were fates worse than matrimony. The plague. Being hung, drawn, and quartered. Being buried alive. Although, one could argue that marriage was its own brand of death. It certainly was more drawn out.

Thick, dark eyebrows slammed down over faraway blue eyes. "I've indulged that fantasy for long enough."

He thought living in this mausoleum until the day I died was my fantasy? The place could burn to the ground, and I would dance around the flames. This house meant nothing to me, and if marrying was the only way for me to keep it, then someone else could have it.

"If you didn't think I could do it, then why did you teach me?"

"Your mother died before she could give me a son. And when your husband inherits my fortune, he will need a partner to help keep this place afloat."

My husband would inherit, not me. Women were pawns in a game of wealth and power. And yet without us, there would be no men.

"We both know Keelynn has no head for such things," he went on, "and she is nowhere near ready to settle down."

Keelynn. A beautiful wildflower, growing free, whimsical and full of dreams. She had hope for love. For the future. For happiness.

I had learned a long time ago that there was no point in wanting any of those things. What a woman wanted played no part in what she received.

Still, I owed it to myself to try.

"I'm not ready either." I'd spent the last eight years taking care of Keelynn, making sure she experienced the childhood I didn't have. I wouldn't change it for the world, but now it was my turn to live. And he wanted to take it away.

"Nonsense. Do you really want your cousin Willard to inherit all of this when I die?" He waved a hand toward the coffered ceiling, shelves of books, and vast expanse of gardens below the window.

Willard Cartwright was the only male cousin on my father's side, so far removed we were barely related. The last time I'd seen him was at my mother's funeral. The only thing I could remember about him was that he had the personality of a plank.

Still, if handing over this house to an obscure relative was the price of my freedom, I'd gladly pay it. "I'm sure he would make a fine heir."

My father's reddening face and the vein bulging in his forehead weren't nearly as menacing as the creak in his jaw as his teeth ground together. "You have a duty to this family, Aveen. To marry and marry well. Think of your sister." He paused, letting the words sink in.

Marrying well would ensure Keelynn continued to enjoy a carefree life full of parties and dresses and all the other frivolous things she loved. And it would release my sister from the responsibility of having to provide an heir.

Although I'd known my fate since I was a child, I hadn't anticipated time passing so quickly.

"I expect you to find a husband by the end of March," he finished.

He couldn't be serious. *The end of March?* "That's in seven bloody weeks!" I immediately bit my tongue. I never spoke to him like that. I never spoke to anyone like that.

"Watch your mouth. You are a lady and will act like one."

Act like a lady.

Bow and scrape and do as I was told. Keep my thoughts and opinions and feelings to myself. I was good at "being a lady." Perhaps too good.

Showing emotion would only make me look weak and irrational. I swallowed the retort on my tongue, silently vowing to come up with a rational solution even a man like my father would accept.

"I'm sorry." I wasn't. "I understand your urgency." I didn't. "I will find a husband, but I ask that you give me at least until the end of the summer. This is an important decision and shouldn't be made in haste." The milder months brought visitors from the neighboring island of Vellana. Perhaps I could find one that wasn't awful.

"Enough!" His fist slammed against the desk, rattling the glass decanter on the corner. "This matter is not up for discussion. If you do not find a husband by the thirty-first, then I will find one for you."

Useless tears burned the backs of my eyes, but I refused to cry in his presence. Refused to beg for something that should have been my right. Refused to let him see how weak I really was. My skirts swirled about my ankles as I turned to leave. The sooner I escaped this hell, the better.

"Aveen, wait."

Hope warmed my core until I twisted back around and saw the five coins in my father's extended palm.

"Take these. Buy something nice for yourself."

If only five pieces of silver were enough to purchase an honorable man.

Resisting the urge to tell him exactly what to do with his coins, I took the silver and slipped it into my purse with the rest of my weekly allowance that I'd scrimped and saved for the past six months.

My father picked up one of the loose pages from a pile to glare at the missive. "That is all."

Dismissed like a servant, I turned on my heel and didn't stop until I reached the bay window outside my father's study.

Lifelong commitment. Till death do us part. Rings and promises. I didn't want any part of it.

Think of your sister.

I didn't want any part of it, but I'd do this for her.

I'd do anything for her.

The sky outside darkened to match my black mood. The hedges around the garden could do with a trim, and the hellebores were getting out of control. From the looks of the sky, I'd have to wait until tomorrow to deal with them.

My boots slipped across the pristine marble tiles as I made my way down the long hallway to the curved staircase. If this had been a normal week, I would've used my money for a new trowel and some dahlia bulbs from Farmer Warren. But I needed to find my sister a gift.

And myself a husband.

My fingers smoothed down the mahogany bannister as I descended. Maids nodded as they passed, toting buckets and rags. One of our footmen, perched atop a tall ladder, used a feather duster on the chandelier in the entry hall.

Two heavy chairs held open the wide double doors, letting in a cool, salty breeze as more maids scrubbed the black and white tiles.

I found Padraig waiting for me in the stone driveway with my horse saddled and ready for town.

"Milady." When he bobbed his head his woolen flat cap slipped, revealing thinning white hair. "Best be on yer way. 'Twas a fine mornin', but I'm afraid the same won't be said fer this afternoon."

I felt what he said on a much deeper level.

I thanked Padraig and mounted before my father caught me riding instead of taking the carriage. He thought proper ladies of our social standing should ride in carriages like pretty little porcelain dolls.

So I rode whenever I had the chance.

The road rose and fell, stretches of fields waiting to be planted on either side of high bramble hedges. In a few months, they'd stink of slurry. Today, all I could smell was the salty breeze rattling through a few stubborn brown leaves, the leather saddle and the horse beneath me.

Who was I going to marry?

Callum McNamara had wed this past spring. His brother Liam was too fond of the drink. Michael O'Donnell had left to serve in the king's army in Vellana. Lord Donnelly was too old. Sir Roger Quinn was rumored to have done away with his first two wives. Thomas Mattingly was kind enough, and he made me laugh with his irreverent sense of humor. But there was no way my father would approve of a miller's son.

My father.

What would he do if I flat out refused? Likely keel over from shock.

Hedges eventually gave way to low stone walls and grazing cattle. The few travelers I passed waved but no one tarried. Black clouds on the horizon edged closer to the small town built on a height, overlooking a port filled with merchant ships.

What if I skipped town altogether, went straight to the docks, and used my savings for passage on one of them? I'd entertained that foolish notion a few years ago when I'd met a handsome sailor. We'd made plans. Silly, naïve plans.

Plans that ended the night he sailed away.

I passed the sign welcoming visitors to Graystones, an apt name for a town devoid of all color beyond the daffodils blooming around the central square.

The plaster buildings, cobbled streets, and limestone cathedral were all varying shades of gray. Even the signs swinging from the shops remained unpainted and unadorned with decorations.

I tied my horse outside the milliner's and made my way through the lively crowd of gentry and commoners toward the daily market. I probably should have been smiling at the eligible men who passed, trying to catch their attention. Instead, I glared at them.

No one told a man when he should marry. Being a bachelor wasn't frowned upon. If anything, it was regarded as a badge of honor. A man could ride his way through the entire female population and still be considered a catch if he had any wealth to speak of.

If I was caught having a conversation with a man in a room without a chaperone, I'd be ruined.

So bloody unfair.

Skirting around a wide puddle, I stalked toward Dame Meranda's shop at the far side of the square, the only building in Graystones owned by a woman. When she'd first opened five years ago, the locals had shunned her until it became clear that none of the other seamstresses could hold a candle to her talents. And then Graystones' elite had changed their tune. What took others a fortnight would take Meranda a few days. And her stock of fabric remained unmatched on the east coast of Airren.

This trip should've been the highlight of my week. Today, I couldn't wait to return home. And just when I thought the day couldn't get worse, I caught sight of Lady Freya Goodman strolling toward me on Robert Trench's arm. I didn't give a whit that he couldn't pull his gaze from her abundant chest being strangled by her too-tight corset.

The cad had been dead to me for years.

It was my sister's heart I needed to protect. If Keelynn had come along, she could see first-hand the way he acted around other women and save herself a good deal of heartache.

When she caught sight of me, Lady Freya waved her handkerchief in my direction. "Lady Aveen? Is that you?"

I stifled an unladylike groan.

Robert's hazel eyes went so wide, it looked like they could pop out of his skull. And if they did, I'd stomp them flat on the cobblestones.

"Lady Freya, it's lovely to see you." I reluctantly returned the wave. "And is that Robert Trench?" His shins deserved a good dent. My boots ached to give it to them. "Robert, it's been ages."

A lie. Two days ago, he'd swung by to take my sister on a picnic. She hadn't stopped smiling since.

Freya looked between us, her thin eyebrows pulling together.

"A pleasure as always, Lady Aveen." Robert slipped a finger beneath his cravat, loosening the knot at his neck. It would be unladylike to grab the ends and pull until it choked him. Wouldn't it?

It would.

I hid my hands behind my back in case they got any ideas of their own.

How had I ever been attracted to someone so awful? Sure, he was handsome, with trimmed blond hair and a strong jaw, but beneath it all, he was vapid and hollow. "I'd love to chat, but I'm afraid I'm in a bit of a hurry. It's my sister's birthday next week, and I still need to pick up a few bits for her. You remember Keelynn, don't you, Freya?"

Robert stiffened, and his Adam's apple bobbed when he swallowed. The sheen of perspiration at his hairline was more thrilling than a second helping of dessert.

No-good, lousy, two-timing wretch.

"How could I forget darling Keelynn?" she sniffed, her painted lips turning down in a frown.

I'd caught my sister kissing Freya's brother at the Samhain festival a few years earlier.

Keelynn was so desperate to find love that she sought it out at every opportunity.

I knew there was no point.

Love was used to trick women into giving themselves away. In my social circles, it rarely factored into a marriage transaction. The most I could hope for was finding someone likable and kind, and most importantly—at least according to my father—a man who could manage the estate without gambling it away.

That was my fate. The curse of being a nobleman's first-born daughter.

I swore after the first time I saw Keelynn cry over a boy that I would do everything in my power to ensure that she married the man she loved. I hadn't accounted for the fact that the man would be a philandering wastrel.

"Is she still off chasing faeries," Freya asked with a grating giggle, "or has she finally grown up?"

It was one thing to look down her upturned nose at me but another thing entirely to speak ill of my sister. "Perhaps that's something you should ask your escort."

Freya whipped toward Robert, eyes narrowing into slits. Robert's mouth opened and closed like one of the gaping salmon displayed on the fish stall.

"Enjoy your day, Freya. Goodbye, Robert." I offered a false smile and danced around a young woman pushing a pram along the uneven cobblestones.

Salesmen called from their stalls displaying pottery, fruit and veg, and handmade jewellery. The spools of ribbon were pretty, but ribbons as a birthday present ceased being acceptable after Keelynn had turned ten. The bolts of fabric would make for a fine dress, but even Meranda couldn't hope to finish something from scratch on such a tight deadline.

The bunches of daffodils tied with twine at Farmer Warren's stall used to be my favorite flowers. Now they seemed too cheerful.

Beside the daffodils, the bundles of dirt-crusted bulbs, which would bloom into stunning dahlia and echinacea come summer, called my name.

Gardening took patience and cooperation from the elements that remained outside human control. And people loved control. I'd put my faith in the earth over a person any day. At least I knew its betrayal wasn't personal.

Farmer Warren nodded when I passed, and I told him I'd be back tomorrow for some bulbs.

A few ladies milled around the "fortune teller's" booth. I wasn't sure why. It wasn't as if the old crone was a real witch practicing real magic. That sort of thing had been illegal in Airren for centuries.

Still, the soldiers who kept a close watch on the town let the harmless old woman sit at her booth and exchange her false second sight for coin.

An act of charity.

The woman dressed the part perfectly, with long, snowy hair unbound, a bronze circlet across her forehead, and two milky eyes searching the sky for lies to tell her "clients."

As if she knew I was thinking of her, the woman's eyes landed on me from across the square. She had enough people paying her today, unlike the dark figure begging on the cathedral steps behind her. Most of the creature's grotesque features remained hidden beneath a threadbare brown robe. Everything except gnarled hands covered in red hair, holding a tin cup.

A grogoch.

Since he'd arrived three months ago, I'd seen him spat on, kicked, and jeered. Told to go back to where he belonged—to Tearmann—but he never did. Even if he wanted to leave, how could he get all the way to the creatures' haven on the west coast with no funds?

He sat there every day, without fail, and I had never seen anyone else give him so much as a copper. Whatever I had left after my visit to the modiste would go to him.

In order for the creatures to remain in Airren, they had to follow laws that were far harsher than the ones humans were meant to keep. They were taxed for magic they weren't allowed to practice. Ridiculed, hated for being different.

When I'd first seen the man, I'd been wary. According to the books in our library, grogochs were known to be fond of drink and mischief.

But the poor creature never seemed to move from the cathedral steps, and any time his sorrowful brown eyes had met mine, he'd look away as if ashamed.

My situation was nothing compared to his, but I felt he and I were kindred spirits. He wore his pain on the outside; mine remained hidden inside. Humans ruled his world; men ruled mine. Neither of us were free to do as we wished.

The bell above the modiste's door jingled when I opened it. A few dresses had been pinned to dress forms right inside. Small tables jammed between larger ones overflowed with spools of ribbons and lace, beads and feathers. There seemed to be no rhyme or reason to the place, and yet if someone asked for a specific item, the proprietor would know exactly where to find it.

At the back, I spotted a woman bent over a table, feeding black fabric through a sewing machine.

When she heard the bell, she glanced over her shoulder, and her face broke into a smile.

"Good morning, Dame Meranda," I said with a wave.

The modiste, a few years my senior, had a personality to match the fiery red curls escaping her chignon. The buzzing from the machine stopped. Bunching her flouncy green skirts in her fists, she rose and bustled toward me. "So wonderful to see you, Lady Aveen. I'm afraid the dress you ordered has yet to arrive, but I'll send word the moment it does."

My twenty-first birthday was still three months away. By then, I'd be married.

"I'm actually here to purchase something for Keelynn." A garment the unique shade of rose campion peeked from behind her. "Is that a dress?" I gestured toward the magenta fabric half-concealed behind a velvet curtain.

Frowning, Meranda withdrew the garment. Square neckline. Empire waist. Flared skirt. Stunning. "I'm afraid Lady Freya ordered this a few months back."

Drats. "Has she paid for it?"

"A deposit only. Once she acquires the remaining funds from her father, she will be back to collect the dress."

Buying my sister a stunning dress had been my goal. Irritating Freya would be a happy bonus. I unhooked the purse at my wrist, setting it on the table beside a pair of silver shears. "How much would it take to convince you to sell it to me instead?"

Meranda laughed. "Stay for a cuppa and it's yours."

After tea in her apartments upstairs, I paid for the dress and thanked her again. She assured me she could have it finished in time for my sister's ball.

Outside, rain fell in soft waves. I hurried over to the grogoch. My few remaining coins *clinked* into his empty cup. "I'm sorry it's not much." Something had to be better than nothing though, right? Tomorrow, when I returned for bulbs, I'd bring more.

"Thank ye fer yer kindness, milady," he rasped. "Ye may restore my faith in humanity yet."

If only a few coins could do the same for me.

My horse was tied across the square, past the stocks and ropes swaying from the gallows. I caught sight of the McFaren twins giggling as they huddled beneath their shared parasol, golden curls bouncing free. The last thing I wanted was to get stuck talking to them about fashion or men or some other nonsense, so I ducked behind the butcher's stall overflowing with plucked chickens and sheep parts.

Behind the stall, a small door led to the blacksmith's tool shed. Thanks to my sister's childhood obsession with hide-and-go-seek, I knew there was a second door inside that would spit me out on the other side of the market. I opened the door and slipped inside.

"You're late," a deep, lilting voice said from the darkness.

My hand fell to the empty purse at my hip. If the owner of the voice wanted to rob me, he'd be sorely disappointed.

A pair of hands slid around my waist. Heated breath tickled my ear. My heart hammered when my spine met the hard wall. A pathetic whimper escaped when those hands slipped to my backside, and yet I couldn't find my voice to demand he stop as warm, soft lips grazed down my neck toward the hollow at my throat.

The man smelled sweet, like cinnamon and honey and something more. Something darker.

Something like . . .

Magic.

2

THE MAN JERKED AWAY, RIPPING THE AIR FROM MY LUNGS AND leaving my chest with a dull, hollow ache. Something crashed to the ground and shattered. "You're not Eithne," he snarled.

The only Eithne I knew was married—and not to this man.

"Why have you come?" he demanded. "Who sent you?"

I scrubbed at my tingling neck, searching for my missing voice. "No one sent me." I didn't want to be affected by *anyone* like that —much less by a man having an affair with a twit like Eithne. "Next time, plan your trysts someplace with a little more light."

Orange light flashed, and I found myself squinting at a ball of flame in the palm of the man's hand, a pair of piercing cerulean eyes staring back at me.

The owner of those eyes had dark hair and high cheekbones, a small, silver scar across his straight nose, and a rigid jaw that came to a stubborn point at his chin. The looks of a devil with lips of flame. Dark and dashing, daring me to close the distance between us with his hypnotic gaze.

"Who are you?" I whispered.

The corner of his mouth lifted. "I am whoever you want me to be."

Brilliant. Another man who believed himself irresistible. "The only thing I want you to be is gone."

His eyes widened, reflecting the flame in his palm and revealing a thin ring of gold around his pupils. "I was here first."

He had a point.

"Fine. I'll go." Pushing away from the wall, I stalked toward the exit. Dust motes spun in the shaft of light illuminating a broken clay jug.

A shadow crossed the entrance. "Oisin? Are you in there?"

Eithne.

The stranger grabbed my cloak, dragging me behind a wooden bench and forcing me to the floor where the rest of him hunkered. "Not a word," he warned, a finger pressed to his lips.

Lips that had tasted my skin.

I resisted the urge to scratch at the spot where he'd kissed me, my nerves still buzzing.

Eithne whispered his name again.

The bloody gossip, she'd tell everyone if she caught us together.

She'd delight in seeing me ruined.

Why did this man have to be having an affair with Eithne of all people?

Five years ago, she'd shown me the type of man Robert was beneath all his pretty lies.

I shouldn't hate her for what had happened.

I hated her anyway.

Oisin didn't look the least bit concerned about getting caught. Didn't bother glancing toward the boots tiptoeing through the sawdust. Didn't blink or wince or react at all when she drew closer and closer and closer still.

All the man did was stare at me.

"Eithne? Where did you go, pet?" a man called from outside, his voice gruff and stilted. Was it her husband? Did he know she was having an affair?

Cursing, Eithne stomped to the door. The hinges whined, and

the voices from the market grew louder, then muffled by the closing door.

"That was close," Oisin said with a deep, rumbling laugh.

Close? What did it matter to him? He was the one having an affair with a married woman. If he'd been caught, nothing would've happened. But my life would've been over.

I shoved to my feet.

He clambered after me, knocking into the bench with his hip and cursing. "You're leaving?"

The question didn't deserve a response. Why on earth would I do anything but leave? I slipped through the door and sprinted to my horse, splashing my skirts with mud and muck, praying the man didn't follow.

My bloody boot slipped in the bloody stirrup, and it took three bloody tries to get myself into the bloody saddle. I glanced toward the shed, expecting to see Oisin, only to find a crooked wooden door staring back.

I turned my horse toward the only road leading out of town, urging her to pick up the pace once we passed the town limits.

The mist turned my curls to frizz, growing heavier and more insistent as I finally reached the small forest before our estate.

If only I could tell my sister what had happened without having her romanticize the encounter. She'd be unbearable, asking for all the details, making more of it than it was.

A simple instance of being in the wrong place at the wrong time.

That was all.

Nothing to get worked up over.

And certainly not worth dwelling on.

Dampness seeped through my cloak and skirts. A few sheep munching on clover beside a stone fence glanced my way as I flew past. The left turn up ahead would lead to my father's estate. If only I had it in me to go right. To escape this fate. To leave and never come back.

My mare came to a neck-breaking halt, sending me careening

into the saddle horn. Hair slapped over my eyes. I shoved the sopping strands back from my forehead.

The beast's ears twitched from side to side, then flattened against her brown head. When I tried to nudge her forward, the stubborn brute refused to budge. What was she so afraid of? The trees creaking in the breeze? The steady pitter patter of rain on the puddles?

The booted foot dropping from the branch above my head?

Bloody hell.

I grabbed the horn to keep from toppling headfirst out of the saddle.

Oisin had his long, lean frame draped over a low hanging branch. Black breeches hugged his thighs as he swung his leg back and forth.

"You never told me your name," he drawled, smoothing his thumb over the shiny buttons on his gold waistcoat. Thick, mahogany hair fell to the tops of his ears, swept to the side by careless fingers. Although it continued raining, he remained dry, like the rain knew better than to dampen his white shirt.

He'd sought me out? For my name? "You never asked."

A grin played on his full lips. Dimples. Of course. Deep obnoxious ones. "My mouth was otherwise occupied."

Not what I wanted to think about at present—or ever again. "My name is Lady Aveen Bannon, daughter of Lord Michael Bannon."

Plucking a tiny bud from the branch, the man traced a finger along its edge. The bud unfurled, growing to a brilliant green beneath his touch. "Radiant beauty."

He was good. I'd give him that much. Still, a handsome face and a few parlor tricks wouldn't be enough to impress me. "Do you say that to all the women?" He looked like the type of man who used such silly lines.

"Only the ones called Aveen." He rolled onto his side, propping his chin on one hand as if he were lying on a bed and not on a thin branch twenty feet in the air. "It's what your name means."

"And what does Oisin mean?" *Worthless cad?*

"Oisin means 'little deer.'" A wink. "But that's not my real name."

As much as I wanted to know his real name, a stranger who sought to have affairs with married women was not the sort I needed to know. It didn't matter that hearing his voice sent shivers down my spine and made my stomach flutter like leaves in a breeze. He could take his grin and his dimples and jump off a cliff. "It was a pleasure meeting you, not-Oisin." It wasn't. "But I'm afraid I must be on my way." I kicked my horse forward; she took off at a brisk canter.

The stranger appeared on the road, startling my bloody horse and blocking my path with his broad shoulders and lean waist and smarmy smile. "Where are you off to in such a rush?"

My fingers tightened on the reins, and I resisted the urge to groan. Couldn't he take a bloody hint? "Home. It's getting late, and I don't want to miss dinner."

Something tickled against my throat like a feather. I brushed my face, but there was nothing there.

I tried to urge my horse around him. He blocked me again, catching the bridle to scratch the patch of white hair between the beast's eyes.

"If you'll kindly get out of my way, I'm soaked to the bone and would hate to catch a cold."

He peered up at me from beneath dark lashes, glinting eyes full of secrets. "Aren't you even a little bit curious as to who I am?"

I was. Very. But it was much safer for me if I didn't know a thing about this man. Because if I knew a little, I'd want to know a lot. And knowing a lot about someone so lacking in morals, whose smile made my heart race and who clearly had no regard for Airren's laws about magic, wouldn't end well. "Not curious enough to miss dinner."

This time, when I tried to pass, he let me go. The delays forced me to push my horse to make up for lost time. Hooves pounded through the puddles, splashing mud up my back. When my father's home came into view, my stomach sank. Deep red ivy crawled toward the pitched roof along the high stone walls of my beautiful cage.

Padraig hobbled out of the stables. The poor man could barely move, and yet he insisted on coming out to collect the horses instead of letting us bring them to him.

"Best be quick, milady. Yer father's in quite a temper." He offered a hand for me to dismount. I was always afraid I'd knock him over but didn't want to slight him either. So I let him help me to the ground.

"He's always in a bloody temper."

Padraig chuckled, giving my hand a pat before leading my mare toward the stables.

I took the stairs two at a time, unhooking my cloak as I climbed. Before I could reach for the handle, the door flew open.

"Where have you been?" Keelynn hissed, dragging me inside by the wrist and closing the door with a quiet click. Lacing her warm fingers with mine, she tugged me into the coat closet. "Father is in one of his moods again. You being late will only add to his ire."

Why did his ire matter more than my own? I could guarantee every bit of irritation he felt, I felt tenfold. "There was a delay at the market." *An irritatingly handsome delay.*

"The market?" Her gray eyes gleamed when she grinned. "Did you see Robert?"

Hearing his name made me want to spit. "I caught him escorting Lady Freya."

"Lady Freya?" Keelynn's hand flew to her throat. "He was meant to call on me this afternoon."

Could it be more obvious that Robert Trench was a damn liar?

Keelynn shook her head. "There must be a good explanation. I'll ask him when he arrives."

Then Robert would talk his way out of it, and she'd forgive him.

Keelynn deserved someone who doted on her, not a fool who sowed his seed in every field he came across.

Biting my tongue, I removed my cloak, hanging it next to the others. Yet another reason to avoid love: it blinded people to the truth.

"Hurry up," Keelynn whined. "I'm starving."

"You go on ahead. I need to change." If Father was already in a mood, me showing up with my boots and hem caked in muck and hair a mess wouldn't help. I could hear the conversation now.

He'd say I'd never capture a man's attention looking so disheveled. I would want to ask why it was a woman's responsibility to catch a man's attention in the first place. We weren't worms dangling on a fishing hook. Why couldn't the men be the ones parading around in finery, nibbling their dinners to keep from appearing gluttonous, smearing creams and rouge and kohl on their faces to make themselves look beautiful?

Instead, I'd end up nodding and apologizing and bowing my head in deference to his greatness as a male, like a "proper lady" should.

Keelynn shoved our father's old coats aside to collect a bundle of cloth at the back. "Nonsense," she said. "We'll face his wrath together."

The bundle included a dress, stockings, and matching slippers. She made short work of the buttons at the back of my dress and helped me into the clean, dry one. I collected my mess of hair and twisted it into a knot at the top of my head, using the hair pins we'd tucked into one of my mother's cloaks for such occasions. If only there were a way to dry it.

Keelynn announced that I looked perfect and took my hand. Our maid Sylvia waited outside the closet, ready to spirit away all evidence of my wardrobe change.

Our heels echoed against the tiles as we flew through the hall. Before we reached the doors to the formal dining room, we slowed, entering in a more ladylike manner.

Our father didn't bother rising from the carved chair at the end of a table with enough room for twelve guests. The parlor had a smaller table, better suited for the size of our family, but he insisted on dining in a cavernous room with vaulted ceilings and portraits of our long-dead relatives staring at us from all angles.

Our father studied me over the rim of his wine glass. "You're late."

"I'm sorry." There was no point giving him an excuse as to why I was late. He didn't care.

He looked me up and down, his expression darkening. "Did you take the carriage to town today?"

I couldn't deny it. I may have changed, but I still smelled like a horse. "No. I took Whinney."

"You will take the carriage next time or you will not go at all, do you hear me?"

"Yes, Father."

His expression warmed when he looked at Keelynn. She hugged his shoulders and kissed his cheek before taking her own seat. Grumbling, he clearly fought a smile.

A steady procession of servants entered through a door concealed in the dark wood paneling, carrying trays and dishes with silver lids. Enough food for at least four meals. So much waste, and for what? Who were we trying to prove our position to? It was just us.

The first course consisted of a small cup of vegetable soup and a crusty brown roll. I ate a few spoonfuls, letting the savory warmth slip down my throat. If only it could reach my toes, which had turned into blocks of ice. As much as I loathed the carriage, it really would've been the better choice today. I set my spoon aside to reach for my wine. A servant had the dishes cleared by the time I brought the glass to my lips.

A small dish of honeydew cleansed the palate, followed by a plate of chicken and mushroom vol-au-vents. Next came a main course of roast duck, steeped in plum sauce. I could've eaten twice the amount on my plate but knew that would only earn a comment from my father. It wasn't my fault food settled on my hips.

"Have you thought about our discussion earlier?" our father asked, slicing himself some more duck.

Keelynn glanced at me from across the table, her dark eyebrows drawing together.

Discussion? Was that what they called ambushes these days? "I have."

"Good. Your husband will be the most important person in your life. Your job is to care for him and support him in all things, including the running of this household."

Why was that my job? Shouldn't it be his job to care for and support me?

Keelynn's wine glass froze halfway to her mouth. "You're getting married?"

I added more wine to my own glass. The more I drank, the easier it was to forget that my life was over. "Apparently so."

Her cup slammed onto the table, sloshing wine over the white tablecloth. "How did I not know you were courting someone?"

"Oh, I'm not," I said, watching my sister dart a confused glance at our father. "But Father has graciously given me less than two months to find a husband."

Keelynn's jaw dropped. "You cannot expect her to fall in love with someone in a few weeks. Father, be reasonable."

Our father sawed at a carrot as though the vegetable had wronged him. "I'll not hear any argument from either of you. As the head of this household, my word is final. Aveen will marry, and that is that."

"Yes, but in under eight weeks? Please, Father." Keelynn reached for his hand. "Give her time. This is the biggest decision of her life, and rushing it will only lead to disaster."

Father slipped his hand from beneath hers to collect his wine. "You women are far too focused on love and feelings." The deep red liquid in his glass swirled as he spun the stem between his fingers.

"Then think about this estate. Do you really want it to go to the wrong man?" Keelynn pressed. "Someone who may let all you've worked to create fall into disrepair or crushing debt?"

The way his eyebrows lowered, as though he were actually considering her suggestion, left hope swelling in my chest. And then he opened his mouth, and it all flew out the bloody window.

"Seven weeks is more than sufficient. You will choose a husband by the end of next month or I will choose one for you."

"Yes, Father."

His chair scraped the tiles when he shoved away from the table. Muttering under his breath, he balled up his serviette, dropped it onto the table, and stalked out of the dining room.

"That explains the mood," Keelynn sighed. "Seven weeks to find love. Impossible."

I couldn't agree more. "Thank you for trying."

"Fat lot of good it did you. How are you holding up?" She nudged the wine bottle until it teased my fingertips.

I tilted it into my glass, filling it to the brim.

Holding up? More like drowning in despair. But this was my problem, and I refused to burden my sister with her birthday so close. She deserved to enjoy what could be her last month of freedom. After our father paired me off, she'd be next. "Do not worry about me. I will be fine."

"I have no doubt you will. You always are." She settled back in her chair, pressing her glass to her chin, deep in thought. "Who are you going to choose?"

I had no bloody clue. John Kelley had eloped to the north with a barmaid, Conor McQueen was off fighting the war in Iodale. All Jim Crawford cared about were his shipping manifests, and Kellen Graham was rumored to spend all his time in the gambling dens in Dreadshire.

"The only good man I know is Padraig."

Keelynn giggled. "If anyone is marrying Padraig, it's me."

3

*T*AP.

Tap.

Tap.

I froze in my bed, afraid to move, afraid to breathe. The stifling coverlet felt like it had been woven with chainmail. Endless shadows shuddered around me, making it impossible to know where the tapping originated.

Tap.

Tap.

Tap.

The window. It was coming from the window.

Slowly, I turned my head toward the noise, certain I'd find some hideous creature staring back at me through the glass.

No creature.

Only darkness.

Even worse.

I knew what lurked in the darkness on this island. Witches and banshee, beings of lore, and monsters without names.

Tap.

Tap.

Something tiny and white collided with the glass before falling away.

Stones.

The legends had never told of a creature throwing stones at windows. If they wanted to come inside, nothing could keep them out. I had read countless fairy tales to my sister, but there had been one book in the library I refused to read aloud. One that held the truth of the creatures and the terrifying power some of them possessed.

More than enough power to enter my room despite the locks on the windows and door.

This person wanted to make his or her presence known. I shoved the heavy covers away and tiptoed across the soft rug, around the chaise, to the window. Three stories below stood a tall figure beside the hedge.

My breathing hitched until the figure stepped out of the shadows, and moonlight struck his blond hair.

Robert.

What was he doing here? Shouldn't he be throwing stones at Keelynn's window instead of mine?

He must've seen me because he started waving his arms. I should go back to bed and let him stay outside in the cold. If I was lucky, a hungry shapeshifting pooka would find him and gobble him up.

Another stone hit my window. He bent and picked up a handful of gravel from the path, making it clear he wouldn't stop until I answered.

I unlocked the latch and lifted the sash. Damp, chilly air smelling of fish twisted my lace curtains. Robert jogged to the trellis attached to the exterior wall, rattling the ivy as he climbed until he reached me, pink-cheeked and winded.

"What are you doing here, Robert? It's the middle of the night."

"I needed to speak with you." He nodded to the dark room. "Can I come in?"

"It's not appropriate for a man to enter a lady's private quarters."

"Don't be such a prude, Aveen. It's bloomin' freezing out here."

He could call me names all he wanted. He wasn't coming in.

Cursing under his breath, he adjusted his white-knuckled grip on the sill. "Did you tell Keelynn that you saw me today?"

"Of course I did." Didn't he realize that she was so in love with him he was the first thing she spoke of every morning and likely the last thought in her head at night?

"Was she upset? I don't want her making more of this than it is. I took a stroll with an old friend and lost track of time. That's all."

"Is that all it was?" I folded my arms over my chest and narrowed my eyes. Did he think I was a fool? "Silly me. I must've imagined your hand on your 'old friend's' backside then."

Wincing, he dragged himself closer, propping his ribcage on the sill with a groan and settling his damp, frozen fingers over mine. "I care for you sister and—"

Had he forgotten that I wasn't a simpleton? Keelynn deserved someone better than a faithless lout who discarded women the moment another pretty face passed by.

I ripped my hand away, scrubbing it against my thigh. "It's time for you to go."

"Aveen, please. I love—"

"If you don't leave, I will scream." He had until the count of three before I shoved him off the side of the building. Hearing his bones crunch when he hit the ground would be worth the repercussions.

When Robert tried to grab my hand again, I stepped away. "One."

"You're such a—"

"*Two.*"

"I'm going, dammit." He removed his hands from the window ledge to clasp the trellis. "No one will ever love you once they meet the miserable woman beneath all those false smiles and feigned manners. You think you know me, but I know you too—"

I slammed the window shut and dusted my hands off on my shift. The nerve of him. Waking me to plead on his behalf.

No one will ever love you.

I didn't need someone to love me.

I needed someone to marry me.

"Lover's quarrel?" a lilting voice asked.

A tingling sensation slipped up my shift as I spun toward the bed. On my mattress, with his ankles crossed and hands behind his head, was the man from the shed.

"How did you get in here?" The door was closed, and he sure as hell hadn't used the window. What if Robert had seen him? Or Keelynn heard us? Or my father? This was my bedroom, my sanctuary. No man except my father had set foot inside this room. And now one was lying on my bloody bed.

"I evanesced," he said.

"Evanesced?"

He rolled his eyes, then disappeared only to reappear at my side, close enough for me to smell his strange, cinnamony magic. I jumped back, ramming my backside against the arm of my chair, knocking it closer to the fireplace.

"Evanesced," he repeated, gesturing toward himself with a wave.

So that's what they called it. He must be one of the more powerful creatures then.

"I had planned on taking the trellis, you see, but it was otherwise occupied," he continued with a smirk. "You really should start locking your door. There's no telling who'll pop in."

"What good would that do?" The door may not be locked, but he hadn't used it. Wincing, I massaged my sore bum. There'd be a bruise by morning for sure.

"You'd be surprised." He wandered around, touching my

belongings. Picking up my perfume and taking a sniff. Trailing his fingers along the tassled canopy drapes.

I should kick him out. I really should. "What's your name?"

"Oisin, Colin, Ciaran, Cian, Liam, Fionn, Dara, Shay. Take your pick or call me whatever you like." He lifted his shoulders in a shrug as he sank onto my chair, bounced twice, made a face, and rose again. "Makes no difference to me."

He probably thought he was charming, with his wicked grin and the mischievous sparkle in his ocean eyes.

I'd been charmed before. Never again. "Whatever your name is, you cannot be here. You need to leave." If he wasn't going to answer my questions, there was no point allowing him to linger.

"First I need a favor." He dragged a long finger across the marble mantle, cluttered with small porcelain figurines and my jewelry box. The embers burst into fresh flames, sending heat slamming into me.

"What sort of favor?"

Ten seconds passed as I waited for an explanation, watching him watch me with an unreadable expression. I didn't have it in me to be polite anymore. "Are you going to tell me or not? It's late, and I want to go to bed."

His eyes darted to the open canopy.

Damn it all if my pulse didn't go berserk. "*Alone*," I ground out.

His black waistcoat and breeches swallowed the firelight, making him look more shadow than man until he stepped closer. Orange light from the flames played on his features, highlighting the scar across his nose. "What's the matter? Do you not find me attractive?"

So bloody attractive. Too attractive. "No. I don't."

He leaned forward, his nose grazing my cheek, and whispered, "Liar."

The timbre of his voice left my insides in knots and heartbeat skittering. Why had my body finally decided to respond to a being who could probably kill me with an errant thought?

Still, no man, no matter how handsome or magical, was allowed to invade my personal space without my permission. He'd caught me off-guard in the shed. Never again. "Get out of my room, or so help me, I will scream." I didn't owe him a favor. I didn't owe him anything.

Although he drew away, the scent of magic lingered, swirling on my tongue. I swallowed it down, intrigued by the way it heated my insides as if I'd guzzled a hot cup of tea.

His shirtsleeve brushed against my bare arm as he stepped past to trace the floral pattern in my curtains. "But if you scream, you'll wake your poor sister."

Building heat became a winter breeze.

He knew about Keelynn? No. No. *No.*

Had he overheard my conversation with Robert, or had he met her himself? The idea left my knees shaking.

"Tell me your favor." Whatever it was, I would give it to him as long as he swore to leave her alone. Keelynn was still so naïve when it came to men. If she met this one, she wouldn't have the good sense to stay far, far away.

He smoothed a hand down his waistcoat, tugging as he adjusted the bottom against his shiny gold belt buckle. "I would like you to kiss me."

The sudden tightness in my chest warred with my fluttering stomach. "Absolutely not."

No way was I going to kiss his perfect pink lips that probably tasted like magic and would be soft and supple and warm and . . .

No. Just . . . no.

"You don't have to look so appalled. It's not like I'm asking for a feckin' ride. It's a kiss."

It may be just a kiss for him, but kisses weren't coppers. I didn't hand them out to people I knew, let alone perfect strangers. "Why?"

"That is none of your concern."

None of my concern? He was talking about my bloody mouth. Still, what choice did I have? If he went to my sister for this sort of "favor," she wouldn't say no. "If I agree, you must swear to go away and leave my sister and I alone forever."

He placed one hand over his heart and raised the other in the air. "I swear on my mother's life that I will leave her alone."

"Fine." I screwed my eyes shut and pursed my lips, tapping my fingers against my thighs to the beat of my leaping heart.

Nothing happened.

My eyes snapped open to find his head tilted, a lock of mahogany hair falling across his furrowed brow. "Well? What are you waiting for?" I clipped.

"You look miserable."

What did he expect? He had broken into my room, threatened my sister, and was blackmailing me for a bloody kiss. "Then tell me how I should look so that I may be rid of you. Should I smile?" I forced a brittle smile to my lips, grinding my teeth for good measure. "Should I swoon?" My hand flew to my forehead as I pretended to faint onto the chaise. "I have it now." I shot to my feet and stalked forward, delighting in the way he retreated a step. "I should flutter my lashes and be grateful that someone so handsome would ask me for a kiss."

The corner of his lips lifted. "So you do think I'm handsome."

Just like a man, listening to only the words he wished to hear. "I think you're irritating."

He was full-on grinning, showing off those deep dimples. "Does that mean you're going to kiss me or not?"

I stomped forward and pressed my lips against his. A shock exploded through my body. White light burst behind my eyes. When they flew open, they met a pair of stunned blue ones. I stumbled back, my hand flying to my mouth as my legs gave out and I collapsed onto the chaise.

"*Shit.*" He swore again, backing toward the bed. "I finally found you."

Before I could catch my breath or ask what that meant, the stranger vanished.

4

WHEN I INHERITED THIS HOUSE, THE FIRST THINGS TO GO WOULD
be the hideous drapes. Burnished gold may have been in fashion
in my grandfather's time, but now they looked gaudy and garish.
This was a respectable manor home, not some medieval castle.

The only redeeming part of this entire room was a large
painting of the seaside done by one of my distant relatives. Turbu-
lent waves crashed against the shore, spraying white foam into an
angry gray sky. If the entire house were burning to the ground,
and I could only grab one thing, it would be this painting.

My fingers found my lips as they'd done a thousand times
today. I wasn't the type of person who kissed strangers in her
bedroom. That sort of recklessness got a woman into trouble.
Now that I was to be married, I couldn't afford to get swept away.

And yet I could think of nothing else.

Something nudged my foot. My sister glared at me, firelight
dancing in her rich brown waves.

"You didn't hear a word I said, did you?" Keelynn muttered,
setting her embroidery on the empty cushion between us.

"Sorry. I don't know where my mind is today."

"Today? You've been away with the faeries all week."

She would've been too if our roles were reversed. The kiss

replayed over and over and over in my mind. If one could even call it a kiss. It had been a mere meeting of lips. What would have happened if he'd given me a proper kiss?

My toes curled inside my slippers.

Not that I'd ever know. The stranger had made good on his promise and hadn't returned. And I'd been utterly useless since.

Knowing a sensation like that existed, and that I would never again experience it, felt like a tragedy.

"I know. I'm sorry." Between compiling a short list of potential husbands and wasting time daydreaming of strangers, I hadn't been myself. "What was it you were saying?"

"Robert asked me to go for a drive to town with him tomorrow."

Much to my dismay, he had called in for her every day this week, bringing presents and flowers. If I didn't know better, I'd believe he was actually trying.

Keelynn had been over the moon, floating around on a cloud of happiness. What would happen when she realized reality wasn't all rainbows and sunshine? "Are you sure that's wise?"

"You worry too much, sister." She gave my shoulder a playful shove. "I assure you, it will be perfectly respectable. His aunt is accompanying us."

On what grounds could I protest if she had a chaperone?

"Robert told me he wished for the two of you to be friends," she added soberly. "I hope one day you'll learn to like him as much as I do."

Robert and I *had* been friends. More than friends. Then Eithne had sauntered across that ballroom and asked him to bring her for a stroll through the gardens. Little did I know, "stroll" was code for "fondle me near the lilacs."

Keelynn's soft hair tickled my cheek when she rested her head against my shoulder. "I don't want the two most important people in my life to be at odds with one another."

It would take a miracle for Robert and me to ever be anything but at odds. Still, there was no point telling her that. She lived in her own fairy tale world, where everything was black and white, while I was stuck in a sea of grays.

This was my punishment for not being forthcoming about Robert. If she'd known the type of man he was, she would've avoided him from the beginning. Now I was in too deep. She wouldn't see the truth as Robert's betrayal. She'd see it as mine.

"You may have to be content with it," I sighed. The unfinished embroidery in my hoop felt too taxing. I set it aside and hugged her close, wiggling my feet to keep them from falling asleep.

How long had we been sitting here? I'd played a few songs on the pianoforte, stared at the painting, poked a few threads through my embroidery . . .

I glanced over my shoulder to the grandfather clock in the corner.

How was it only half one?

I was ready for dinner, and we wouldn't be eating for seven more hours.

There were buns on the coffee table leftover from our tea. The cream on top had melted onto the serving dish. As much as I wanted to eat another, they had been sprinkled with cinnamon.

Cinnamon made me think of strangers and kisses and all manner of dark, forbidden things.

How would I keep myself and my wandering mind occupied for seven bloody hours?

I could go into the gardens but would end up a sopping, muddy mess from the week's worth of rain. My father had been on edge since delivering the ultimatum, and I was too tired to deal with his irritation.

Perhaps Meranda would have Keelynn's dress ready. One thing was for sure, I needed to get out of this house before I went mad. I tapped Keelynn's shoulder, and she raised her head to give me a confused look.

"I need to go." I stood and adjusted my wrinkled skirts where they'd twisted about my hips.

"Go where?"

"The market."

She pushed herself upright, shoving her hair back from her shoulders. "Why?"

"I want to see if Meranda has any new ribbons."

The carriage ride into town took so long, it left no time for me to wander the closing stalls on my way to the modiste. Meranda gave me a peek at Keelynn's dress, and it was even more stunning than I remembered.

Knowing my sister's penchant for flash and sparkle, Meranda had added extra beading to the bodice and dyed ostrich feathers to the hem of the overskirt. Keelynn would look like she was floating on a magenta cloud. Meranda assured me it would be ready the day before the party, and I bought a silver ribbon to embellish one of the dresses I already owned in case Keelynn asked me about my trip.

The bell over the door gave a happy jingle when I left. I wasn't paying attention and ran smack into Lady Eithne on the steps. As always, her makeup was flawless, and the tight curls at her temples bounced like tiny springs. She was the picture of fashion in a dusky blue silk gown. In contrast, her ancient husband was still stuck in the last century, with his handlebar mustache, top hat, and garish gold cane. The man waited at the bottom of the steps, checking a gold pocket watch hanging from a chain.

Lifting her chin, Eithne wiped invisible grime from her deep burgundy cloak. "Why, Lady Aveen. What a surprise meeting you here," she tittered. "I didn't know Dame Meranda carried farm equipment."

"Oh, Lady Eithne, you are too funny." She needed some new insults. That one was getting old. "My sister's birthday is next week. I came to check on her new dress." Not that it was any of her business.

"Can you afford such luxuries? The shop down the road has less of a selection, but their prices are far more reasonable."

Was she implying my family had no money? We may not be as rich as she was now that she'd married a living corpse, but we were still well off.

I wanted to shove her off the top step and watch her land in one of the many puddles, ruining her diamond-encrusted slippers. Instead, I smiled and said, "Thank you. I'll bear that in mind next time."

Her thin eyebrows arched toward her peaked hairline. "How is your darling sister? I hear Robert Trench has been calling to your manor quite often of late." The fan at her wrist banged against her forearm as she tapped her chin with a gloved hand. "Does she mind that the two of you have a history?"

When I stiffened, her lips lifted, revealing slightly crooked bottom teeth. "Oh, this is delightful! Keelynn doesn't know, does she?"

I caught her by the wrist, prepared to beg. My mouth opened, the plea on my tongue . . .

And yet no words emerged. I just . . . I couldn't. If she had been anyone else, I would've grovelled. But not with her. She knew of my past mistakes, that the life I pretended to live was a lie.

I refused to give her the satisfaction of holding this over my head when I had something in my own arsenal to keep her quiet. "Does your husband know *your* secret?" I said under my breath.

Eithne's eyes flashed. "Darling, would you mind if I took a turn with Lady Aveen?" she threw over her shoulder to her husband. "We haven't seen one another in ages, and it would be nice to catch up."

"Of course, pet. Take all the time you need." He gave a nod before limping toward the pub four buildings over.

Eithne's nails dug into my arm as she steered me into the alley between Dame Meranda's and a brick townhouse. Broken glass crunched beneath my boots. The stench of stale alcohol burned my nostrils.

"How dare you speak to me like that in front of my husband," Eithne hissed. "I don't know what secret you think you know, but you'd do well to mind your tongue—and your own bloody business."

I had been minding my own bloody business. She had been the one to antagonize me. "And you'd do well to not plan trysts with strange men in sheds."

Beneath her makeup, her cheeks paled. She flicked her fan, bringing it up to cover the lower half of her face. "You spoke to Oisin, didn't you?"

I smiled. "I did."

Cursing under her breath, she fanned harder, the curls at her temples swaying. "And what did he tell you?"

I dragged my gaze from her too-tight chignon to the heavy pink purse at her tiny waist and the sparkling slippers on her feet, leaving the silence to do my work for me. "What do you think?"

The fan snapped closed. "How do you plan on using this information?"

All I wanted was for her to keep her mouth shut about Robert and me.

She jabbed me with her fan. Hard. "Are you truly so desperate for funds that you would blackmail me? I'll have you know I only receive a small allowance every week."

A small allowance? The purse at her waist had to be at least twice as full as my own.

"Oh, please. I'm hardly going to blackmail you," I snorted, rolling my eyes for good measure. Still, while I had her there, I may as well use her to quench my thirst for answers. "I simply want to know more about your *good friend* Oisin."

She poked me again. "And why is that, pious Aveen? Did the handsome fae catch your eye?"

The man was fae? That couldn't be right. I'd read that the fae of Airren had pointed ears. The man's ears had been rounded like mine.

"Don't be absurd." He'd done more than catch my eye. He'd wheedled himself into my brain like an enchanted weevil.

"Someone is lying," she said in singsong, *jab-jab-jabbing* my shoulder with her fan. "He is rather dazzling, isn't he? And you should see what he can do with that tongue. He is quite wicked, indeed."

Imagining the two of them together left my stomach in knots. How would she feel if I slapped the smirk from her face?

She looked down her nose at me as if I were beneath her, a queen to a peasant. "Although I doubt he'd be interested in a woman with the passion of an icicle."

The passion of an icicle.

Those had been Robert's exact words when I'd asked him why he'd gone off with Eithne. The fact that he had shared such intimate details with another left my face burning. Before Eithne could turn and escape to the street, my hand shot out, catching her wrist.

She glared at my hand, then brought her narrowed eyes to mine.

"You know what? I've thought about it." My gaze dropped to her purse. "And I believe I will blackmail you."

She tried pulling away. "W-what?"

"You heard me." Using my free hand, I gestured to the purse. "How much are the details of your little affair worth to you?"

I left the alley with Eithne's pink silk purse full of coins and a bounce to my step. Hopefully I'd taught her a lesson about the importance of faithfulness.

I strolled straight over to where the grogoch waited on the steps and dropped the entire purse into his cup, then turned and started for the carriage.

Standing up for myself felt invigorating. I'd have to do it more often.

The fortune teller sat behind her dilapidated wooden stall, milky white eyes fixed on me.

A coincidence. Everyone knew the woman was blind as a

mole. I hopped over a puddle, and her head turned with me. When I stopped, she lifted her hand and crooked a gnarled finger.

Bloody hell. She *was* looking at me.

Should I go over?

I had just blackmailed a woman.

If I wanted to speak to a fortune teller, I could.

According to the painted sign leaning against the wooden stall, fortunes cost five coppers. When I sat on the rickety stool in front of the woman, her chapped lips split into an uneven smile.

"I've been waiting fer ye," she said in a voice more gravel than not, wrinkled hands twitching in her lap. Streaks of paint smeared the apron she wore over a gray cotton dress.

It was the sort of thing any "good" fortune teller would say to convince clients they actually had something worthwhile to share.

"And why is that?" I asked, drawing my cloak closed to keep out the sudden chill. It looked as though the break in the weather was about to end as dark clouds rolled in off the sea.

"Cuz ye have questions, and I have answers."

"I have no questions."

A gust of wind tore at my hood, whipping my hair across my eyes.

"His name is Rían," she whispered.

Rían? I didn't know any Ríans.

Her hand fell onto the uneven planks at the top of her stall, palm-up.

I dragged five coppers from my purse and set them in her palm.

"Ask yer questions. Best be quick." She tucked the coins into her apron pocket.

"Who is Rían?" I asked, feeling foolish for falling into this woman's obvious trap.

"The man yer lookin' fer."

Most female clients probably came looking for the name of

the man they would fall desperately in love with. Not me. "I'm not looking for a man."

The scent of thyme and smoke rose with another gust, snapping my skirts. "Are ye not? I heard ye were askin' after a wicked fae."

Bloody hell.

My eyes darted to the alley where I'd been with Eithne, too far away for this woman to have overheard our conversation. "How did you know I was looking for him?" I rushed, my heartbeat picking up.

Her hand fell onto the plank. I withdrew more money and dropped it into her palm. The coins disappeared into her apron pocket.

"The wind tells me its secrets, child."

That answer hadn't been worth the five coins. Still, I dug through my purse for five more. There was really only one other question I needed to ask. The fae's—Rían's—parting words had plagued me nearly as much as his kiss.

"He said he'd finally found me. What did he mean?"

Her hand jerked, closing around mine in a ferocious grip. The coins bounced off of the plank, landing on the cobblestones. I stood, trying—and failing—to pull free from her age-spotted hand. Her spindly arms were like twigs, papery thin skin covering bone. How was she so bloody strong?

Her white hair lifted from her shoulders as if she were floating underwater. "Pity the girl from Graystones who loved a heartless prince. For the only way to save him was at her own expense."

Her hand opened, sending me stumbling into the next stall. The wind continued to rise, tangling hair about her face. Waves crashed over the docks, slamming ships against the wooden planks, testing the strength of their tethers.

The woman rose slowly, her voice growing louder, "Pity the girl from Graystones who loved a heartless prince . . ."

She must have me confused with someone else.

Vellana had two princes. Two princes I'd never met.

"*Pity the girl from Graystones . . .*" The rhyme became a singsong, dancing on swirling gales. Doors on shops creaked. Shutters banged. Over and over and over she shouted.

Two men in red livery burst from the pub, catching their tricorn hats before the wind stole them away. Drawing their swords, searching the dark street. Their gazes landed on the fortune teller, still singing the haunting tune.

I took off, sprinting through the empty streets. Where had Padraig parked the bloody carriage? My heart clattered against my ribs and my lungs screamed as I searched up and down, eventually finding a familiar figure hunched atop the carriage near the mill.

A single clap of thunder echoed over the low buildings.

When Padraig saw me, he made to climb down from his perch. I waved him back to his seat. He was too slow, and I needed to escape.

I launched myself inside, slammed the door, and banged on the ceiling, bellowing for him to go. A whip cracked, and the carriage lurched forward.

I pressed the heel of my hand against my racing heart, trying and failing to calm my ragged breathing. The raging storm left the carriage rocking from side to side like a ship at sea.

The pounding of the horses' hooves grew distant, as if they no longer pulled the carriage. When I shoved the drape aside to look out the window, we were still flying down the dark road.

Heaviness settled over me, as if an invisible fog had descended within the carriage's tufted walls.

And then I smelled cinnamon and spices.

The fae who had invaded my mind appeared out of thin air on the bench beside me, a tilted smile on his full lips and an elbow propped against the dark window.

"*Rían?*" I whispered.

The man's eyes narrowed into slits. "I see you learned my name."

5

RÍAN DRUMMED HIS FINGERS AGAINST THE KNEES OF HIS BLACK breeches, which hugged his toned thighs like a second skin. "Who gave it to you?" he growled.

The carriage lurched over potholes and stones, leaving me gripping the bench's wooden arm to keep from careening into my uninvited guest. "Why does it matter?"

"I need to know who to kill." He said it so blasé, as if discussing his plans for dinner.

The woman hadn't harmed me, and she certainly didn't deserve to die because of my curiosity. "I'm not telling."

"I can think of a few delightful ways to change your mind." His fingers stroked the curtain's tassels. Back and forth. Slow and lazy. Toying with them the way he toyed with me.

I shifted closer to the door, putting as much distance between us as the cramped space would allow. "You said you'd leave me be. You promised."

"Did I?" His lazy glance swung my way, all hooded blue eyes and sardonic smile. "I recall swearing on my mother's life to stay away from your *sister*. Not from you."

Had he made that distinction? I'd been so flustered I couldn't remember.

"But I should probably warn you that I despise my mother." Propping his chin on his fist, he stretched his black boots toward the far wall. "Now, let's try this again. Who gave you my name?"

The smell of cinnamon grew stronger, dancing on my tongue. I shook my head, trying desperately not to inhale. "I'm . . . not . . . telling . . . you."

"All right then." A curved knife appeared in his other hand, silver blade glinting as he tapped it against his thigh. "A different question. Why were you inquiring after me?"

I bit my lip.

He wouldn't use the blade on me.

He wouldn't dare.

"This was a gift from my father." He held the dagger so I could see my wide eyes reflected in the blade. "I like to keep it very sharp. Can you imagine what it would do to your throat?" He pressed the tip to his finger. A bead of dark blood welled from the wound.

"Killing humans is illegal." Not that the law would do much good if I was dead.

All he did was smile.

I darted a glance to the window. We were in the forest now, trees whizzing past. With Rían so close, I wouldn't be able to scream before he cut me.

The answer to his question was simple enough. Certainly not worth being killed over. "I cannot get you out of my head," I confessed, blushing all the way to my toes. It sounded so silly and childish when I said it aloud. Though the dark desire coursing through my blood was anything but.

He inhaled slow and deep, his chest rising and falling. "What did you plan on doing with the information you gleaned?"

Do with it? What could I possibly do with a name? "Nothing. I just wanted to know who you were. I swear it."

He eased forward, leaning his elbows on his knees as he searched my eyes. When he inhaled, I held my breath.

The moment the dagger vanished, I collapsed against the tufted cushions.

Bloody hell.

Rían caught one of my loose golden curls, wrapping it around his finger. "I'm afraid I must beg another favor."

Another favor.

My lips began to tingle. "Are you going to stab me if I don't kiss you?"

He dropped the curl and pushed back against the curtains. "I don't want a feckin' kiss. I want you to break my curse."

I blinked at him, disappointment replacing desire in my stomach. "Very funny."

One dark eyebrow arched toward his hairline.

Oh. He was serious.

How did he expect me to save him from a curse? I couldn't even save myself from my father's archaic demands. I had no magic, no wealth of my own, and no strength to speak of. "I don't know the first thing about curses—or how to break them. You'll have to find someone else."

The thin golden ring around his pupils widened when his eyes narrowed. "I don't want anyone else. It has to be you."

My stomach tightened. The curse. He was referring to the curse. "Let me guess. If I refuse, you'll slit my throat."

His dark chuckle sent a chill through my bones. "If you refuse, I'll ask your sister."

No . . . Not my sister.

I'd break a thousand curses—face a thousand blades—to save her. "What do I have to do?"

He gave my knee a cursory pat. "All in good time, my dear. All in good time. First, we must discuss the terms of our bargain."

Bargaining with the creatures on this island was at the top of the things not to do, right next to kissing them.

"I break your curse, you leave my sister *and* me alone for all of eternity."

Rían crossed his legs at the ankles and went back to playing with the edge of the heavy drapes. The sky outside lightened as we exited the forest. Only a few more minutes and we'd be pulling into my father's estate.

"I'll do you one better. If you agree to help me, then in addition to your demands, I will grant you one wish. Perhaps you'd like a new dress. Or a new horse. How about some diamonds?" His lips pursed. "You women still love diamonds, don't you?"

"I don't want any of those things." I had more dresses than any one person needed; my horse was healthy and strong; diamonds did nothing but collect dust in a box.

"What do you want?"

No one had ever asked me that question so seriously. What *did* I want?

"I . . . I don't know."

His head tilted, sending dark hair falling toward his piercing eyes. "I suggest you figure it out by the time I return."

"When will that be?"

Rían vanished, but I heard him chuckle. "Whenever I feel like it."

The arrogance. The dismissiveness. The *freedom*.

If someone like him couldn't break a curse, what hope did I have?

My knowledge of curses and magic came from storybooks and the tales we were told as children. Where did I even start?

Keelynn.

She'd been obsessed with such things since our mother had read us our first fairy tale.

The moment we pulled up to the house, I launched myself from the carriage, nearly colliding with Padraig.

"Is everything all right, milady?" His light blue eyes darted inside the open door, his expression unreadable. "Ye look as if ye've seen a ghost."

"I'm fine."

"Yer sure? Ye came sprintin' outta town like a host of sluagh were nippin' at yer heels and, yer face is as pale as a banshee's."

"I'm certain. Thank you for driving me to town."

He gave my arm a reassuring squeeze. "'Twas my pleasure."

When he let go, I raced past the potted boxwoods and up the front stairs. Lit wall sconces cast the foyer in an eerie orange glow. My slippers flew across the checkerboard tiles, past the parlor and dining room to the library.

Keelynn was exactly where she always was this time of evening: curled on the leather sofa with a fairy tale in her hands. The fire blazing in the hearth left her cheeks flushed.

When she saw me, she smiled and closed the book. "How was town?"

"Uneventful," I lied, scooting her feet aside and dropping onto the free cushion to collect her in a fierce hug. She smelled of lavender and happiness.

"Are you sure? Because you're squeezing the life out of me."

If anything happened to her, I'd never forgive myself. "I missed you."

"You've only been gone for two hours."

Was that all? It felt like a lifetime had passed since I'd walked out the door. Reluctantly, I let her go. I couldn't afford her getting suspicious. "What rubbish are you reading now?" I plucked the book from her lap, opening to a random passage.

"A beautiful story about a knight who saves his true love from an evil witch."

"Sounds terrible."

She stole it back, hugging it to her chest. "Terribly *romantic*. He loves her so much, he's willing to die for her. You're welcome to borrow it when I finish."

The only person in this world I'd be willing to die for was sitting right next to me. "I'd rather peel the skin from my bones." I glanced toward the walls of books. Where to begin? "Do you have any books on faeries?"

"Yes . . . Why?"

"I'd like to read one." Or all of them.

She rolled off the sofa, crossing to the first of three shelves to withdraw a blue book decorated with golden flowers.

"Here you go." She tossed the book into my lap. "That's the best one I we own."

Keelynn had been collecting reference books on the creatures since she turned thirteen. Although I wasn't sure how accurate they were. This one, for example, had vague sketches and scribbled poems in the margins. All of the faeries depicted were small, roughly the size of a grapefruit, with long, spindly arms, shimmering wings, pointed ears, and humanoid faces.

None of them resembled Rían.

"Apparently, they steal babies and swap them with hideous changelings," Keelynn said, tapping the passage below the illustration I'd found. "They aren't fond of humans either. They'll bring bad luck to any who cross their path. If you're mad, you can summon one by entering a faerie circle with a gift."

Sounded like utter nonsense to me.

Then again, so did being threatened to break a fae's curse.

I closed the book, tracing the embossed daisies on the cover. "There are other faeries though, right? Taller ones."

"Oh, yes." She danced to one of the shelves to pluck a green book from the third row up. "There are quite a few—but they're fae, not faeries. Like the banshee, the pooka, the Dullahan, and the Gancanagh."

Names and stories spoken in hushed whispers.

I knew better than to believe whispers.

Whispers weren't for truths.

Whispers were for lies.

Take banshee. According to the storybooks, they ripped humans from their beds at night, stealing souls for the underworld. Or pooka: shapeshifting beasts who survived on human flesh. I'd heard rumors of people being killed by pooka, sure. But rumors were like whispers, hard to hear and not to be believed.

Then there was the Dullahan. Terrorizing the island on moonless nights, slaughtering humans who crossed its path. According to legends, the thing didn't have a head. That right there was enough for me to dismiss the myths. How could anything survive without a head?

I'd met three creatures myself.

The grogoch? Kind and quiet.

The fortune teller? Admittedly a little scary, but she'd sat at her booth for as long as I could remember, selling fortunes and not causing any problems. Perhaps she'd been boiling humans back at home—wherever that may be. Or perhaps she was more like us than anyone would care to admit.

And finally, Rían.

Chills tingled down my spine as I spied an entry in Keelynn's book:

The Gancanagh.

The last fae Keelynn had mentioned. A mythical creature who terrorized women. *That* sounded like the man I'd met.

"What do you know of the Gancanagh?"

Keelynn opened the book, licked her finger, and leafed through the pages to a story at the back beneath an illustration of a shadowy male figure. "The Gancanagh is one of the most wicked, with poisoned lips. Anyone who kisses him dies. He's irresistible and preys on the women of Airren."

Wicked. Irresistible. Preys on women.

Rían ticked all the boxes except one.

I'd kissed him and survived.

Either the stories were wrong, or Rían wasn't the Gancanagh.

I was no closer to finding the truth than I had been when I'd arrived.

I set the book on the side table, letting my head fall back. "What about curses?"

"I don't have a book on curses specifically. But everything I've read says they're usually punishments for something terrible, cast by witches who practice dark magic."

Punishments for something terrible.

The first piece of information that made any sense. Rían being cursed meant he probably deserved it.

"How do you break a curse?" I asked.

Keelynn toyed with one of her curls, reminding me of the way Rían had played with mine. "The only way to break a curse is with true love's kiss." A shrug. "At least, that's what all the stories say."

True love's kiss?

Was that why Rían had asked me to kiss him?

No. There had to be some other reason. I didn't *know* the man, let alone love him.

It felt like I was missing something barely out of my reach. Something important. Obvious even. What could it be?

"In all your reading, have you ever heard of a fae giving a human a wish?"

She drummed her fingertips against her lips, squinting toward the fire. "I think leprechauns are the only ones who grant wishes. But they're almost impossible to catch unless you have a lot of gold."

Perhaps Rían was a leprechaun then. "Have you read any books on leprechauns?"

"No." Her mouth flattened. "You're never this interested in fairy tales. What's going on?"

"I . . . um . . ." *Think, Aveen. Think.*

Keelynn nudged my shoulder. "Is the husband hunt not going well?"

Husband hunt? That was the least of my worries right now.

"There are better ways to find a good man than to wish for one," she said with a giggle.

A log in the fire popped, sending a shower of orange sparks across the marble hearth.

I couldn't wish for a husband . . . could I?

6

IN EVERY SINGLE BOOK I FOUND IN THE LIBRARY, LEPRECHAUNS appeared as short old men with gold buckles on their shoes and red beards. Rían didn't have a beard or buckles. And he wasn't short or old. Leprechauns must be born like the rest of us, right? They were hardly born as bearded old men. Perhaps they were like us but got shorter as they aged. Rían could be a young leprechaun. He didn't appear much older than me, twenty-five at most, but with the fae, looks were always deceiving.

All the books also said that you needed a considerable amount of gold to catch a leprechaun and only once he was caught would he offer you a wish. I hadn't caught Rían. He'd caught me.

A week spent on research, and I wasn't any closer to learning the truth about Rían, his curse, or how to break the bloody thing.

I closed the tome on my lap and tossed it onto the side table next to the vase of pink roses.

Our parlor had been turned into a bloody flower shop. Smaller crystal vases squeezed onto the mantle between the clock and porcelain figures my mother used to collect. Large bouquets covered every square inch of the pianoforte. The window sills, the floor . . . there were flowers everywhere.

I loved flowers, and even I thought there were too many.

The cloying air didn't remind me of the garden.

It reminded me of a funeral home.

Male voices lifted from the hall, making their way into the room where I'd wasted yet another day.

A footman appeared in the doorway, crushing a tweed cap between his hands. "Milady? I'm afraid there's another one."

Another one. Another suitor.

Blue eyes had plagued my dreams, taunting me, stealing what little peace remained in my life. I had hoped to spend my days abed, making up for lost sleep.

My father had other plans. Every morning, after the servants cleared the breakfast dishes, I'd been forced to receive one gentleman caller after another. He had rightly assumed that I hadn't been searching for a husband and had taken matters into his own hands. And word on a small island spread like wildfire.

There'd been men all the way from the southern town of Burnsley calling, toting bouquets of flowers and small trinkets in hopes of wooing me into accepting their proposals. And there wasn't one of them I'd consider.

Lord Billington had been too interested in staring at his own reflection to look me in the eye. Mr. McNamara had asked four times about my dowry. Three of them hadn't known my name. Another two had come across as unbearably rude. And then there were the men old enough to be my grandfather. Were people really that desperate for companionship, or was I the only woman on this island of marriageable age?

My father checked in with me at dinner every evening, asking if I'd chosen one, as if I were picking a bolt of cloth for a dress. And every evening I told him the same thing: none of them suited.

Sighing, I told the footman to show the newest prospect in. The sooner I met the man, the sooner I'd be rid of him.

When a handsome gentleman with dark curly hair strolled through the door, I rose from the settee. His black boots shined, and his fine clothes had been tailored to accentuate his tall, lean frame.

Finally, someone I was mildly interested in speaking to.

The moment his lips lifted into a cocky smile, his appeal plummeted. Yet another man who thought too highly of himself to be a genuine contender.

"Sir Edward DeWarn," the footman said with a low bow. "His Majesty's Ambassador from Vellana."

I'd been born on the neighboring island of Vellana but had moved to Airren when I was small. Marrying an ambassador would ensure a good deal of traveling and entertaining foreign dignitaries. These days, the idea of escaping Airren appealed more and more. However, if he was as full of himself as he appeared to be, he may as well return to Vellana.

"Good evening, Lady Aveen." Edward lowered his head, but only slightly. "I hate calling this late, but I was anxious to meet the woman who has become the talk of the town."

Forcing a smile, I gestured toward the settee. The talk of the town. Just what I didn't want to be. "And what is the town saying about me?"

"Only that the most beautiful woman on the east coast is in want of a husband." Edward sank onto the cushions, resting his elbow on the settee's tufted arm. He appeared more calm and relaxed than most of the other guests, settling back as if he owned the place already.

"And are you in the market for a wife, Ambassador?" I asked, sitting on the furthest cushion and hiding my clenched hands in my lap.

Sapphire cufflinks at his wrist glinted in the falling sunlight. "No. I'm not."

That was a first. All the others had been almost desperate for a wife. Lord Halpin had brought a stack of love letters he'd been writing me since we were children. Lord Wallsley, a man my father's age, had brought me his dead wife's set of ruby earrings.

Sir Henry Withel had offered me his great-grandmother's engagement ring before the tea had been served.

The ambassador had no gifts as far as I could tell, unless he'd hidden something in the pockets of his fine black waistcoat, trimmed with silver.

"So you've come to see me as if I'm some sort of exhibit at the zoo?"

"Something like that."

I couldn't decide if I respected him for his honesty or despised him. Not that it mattered. I had no intention of marrying Edward DeWarn. Did I really have to choose someone from the list of unimpressive and downright disappointing men who had visited over the last few days?

"Now that you've seen me, you can be on your way." And I could escape to the gardens and trim the laurels. Cutting something sounded rather appealing right now.

Instead of leaving, he settled his ankle across his knee and reached for one of the tea cakes from the tiered tray on the coffee table. "Why is your father so anxious to marry you off?"

"I am nearly twenty-one. It is time for me to marry." I plucked the cake from his hand, my patience wearing dangerously thin. "My apologies, these are for suitors only."

He stole it back and took a massive bite. "I'm intrigued. What sort of trouble would your husband be acquiring?" he asked, his mouth full of cake.

"No trouble at all. I would be the perfect wife. Placid and complacent and completely happy." *To be sold to the highest bidder.*

The rest of the tea cake disappeared into his mouth.

His tongue darted out, catching the icing glistening on his lips. My body swayed toward him, my mouth desperate to meet his.

In a blink, the urge vanished. I pressed a hand to my chest, confused when I found my heart racing. It had been a long day. I was understandably exhausted. I did *not* want to kiss a complete stranger.

"Contrary," he muttered.

"Excuse me?"

"You're contrary, I see." He collected a serviette to dab at his pinched lips. "And stubborn, no doubt. Are there any other short-comings in your character that I should know about?"

Shortcomings in my character? He couldn't be serious. Any bit of remaining goodwill evaporated. I shot to my feet and threw a hand at the door. "Thank you for calling, but I'm afraid I must retire."

"Rigid too."

Robert had called me rigid when I'd refused his advances. I had been too naïve and too nervous to speak my mind back then, afraid he would tell my father that I had agreed to meet him in the garden that night.

Now I didn't have the same reservations.

I glanced toward the open doorway. The footman acting as our chaperone wasn't paying us any attention. "Arrogant," I hissed, lifting a finger. "Vain." Another finger. "Irritating."

Edward's dark eyebrows flicked up toward his curls.

"Are there any other shortcomings in *your* character I should know about?"

He would leave now. No man would stand for a mere woman attacking his pride and character. And the moment he walked out, I would flee to my bedroom and lock myself inside for the next week. Suitors be damned.

The ambassador lifted both his hands and began counting on his own fingers. "Apathetic. Callous. Cynical. Devious. Hypocriti-cal. Impatient. Possessive. There are quite a few more," he said with a careless wave, "but those are the ones I hear most often."

I didn't know what to make of this man. He made no sense. "At least you're honest."

"That's debatable." Blue eyes met mine. "But enough about me. Have you come up with that wish?"

My heart stuttered. It couldn't be . . . could it? "Rían?"

He *winked*. "I'd prefer if you called me ambassador for the time being. Makes it less confusing for any eavesdroppers who may be listening at the door." Tapping his ear, he nodded his chin toward the entrance.

Bloody hell. It *was* him. I ran my fingers along his smooth chin, square where it should have been pointed. It wasn't an illusion. He had turned himself into a different man. "How are you able to change your form?"

"I have my father Midir to thank for that."

Midir. The name sounded so familiar, yet I couldn't place where I'd heard it before.

"May I have my face back?" he asked.

I hadn't realized I was still cupping his chin. I jerked away, scrubbing my hand down my skirts. My skin buzzed as though I'd run my hands through a field of nettles.

Midir. Midir. Midir.

The blue book on the side table. The one about faeries. I'd definitely read something in it about Midir. I flipped through the worn pages until I found the story. Midir had been the ruler of the faeries and otherworldly creatures that plagued this island. *Bloody hell.* Rían wasn't just fae.

Rían was a fae *prince.*

Pity the girl from Graystones who loved a heartless prince . . .

Impossible.

"Now, back to that wish," he drawled, long fingers tracing the scrolling pattern on the settee.

I had tried coming up with a wish but to no avail. Where did one start? Should I wish for something to not only benefit me but my sister as well? Or could I be selfish and wish for something for myself this once? "I haven't decided on one yet."

His fingers stilled. "I've given you a week."

I gestured to the bouquets of flowers surrounding me on all sides. "I've been a little busy."

Rían rolled his eyes toward the chandelier. "Don't tell me you're actually considering marrying any of the pillocks who've called. The last man practically pissed himself when he kissed your hand goodbye." With a flick of his wrist, he was no longer the ambassador but Sir Henry Withel, down to the man's hooked nose and deep-set eyes. "Now, I'm not a woman," he said in Sir Henry's nasally voice, "but I'm fairly certain that is not an attractive quality in a husband."

How did he *do* that? Could he be anyone he pleased? A terrifying thought.

"At least none of them threatened me with a knife." Although at the moment, the prospect of choosing one of them seemed almost as devastating.

He flicked his wrist again and was back to being the curly-haired ambassador. "It was just a little knife." He snagged another cake, a small chocolate one topped with cherries. "And I only showed it to you because you were being contrary."

Little knife, my foot. "So it's my fault you threatened to slit my throat, is it?"

"Did I threaten you?" Powdered sugar dusted his lower lip when he bit into the cake. "I distinctly remember asking if you could imagine what it would do to your throat, not saying I had any plans to do it."

"It was implied." I wet my own dry lips. Rían's lips didn't look dry. They looked soft and supple and would probably taste like chocolate and cherries.

"Implications don't hold up in court, my dear." He grabbed a serviette from the table to clean the sugar and crumbs from his hands. "If you want to kiss me again, all you have to do is ask."

"I'd rather see your dagger."

He snorted. "That could be arranged."

Fairly certain he wouldn't stab me in my own parlor, I slid next to him, bracing my hands on his shoulders as I rose to my knees. Panic flashed in his eyes when I leaned forward until our breaths mingled.

"Rían?"

Hearing his breathing catch did strange things to my stomach. "Yes, Aveen?"

I secretly loved the way he said my name, with the slightest lilt that made my heart stop.

I brushed his soft curls from his ear. "Get out of my house."

He caught the back of my neck with one hand, holding me steady as he grazed a featherlight kiss against my racing pulse. "I'll be back."

He vanished. I fell facefirst onto the cushion.

"What are you doing?" Keelynn said from the doorway.

How long had she been standing there? Had she seen Rían?

"I . . . um . . ." What excuse would explain her finding me with my backside cocked in the air and head buried in the settee?

Something glinted between the cushions. I held the hairpin aloft as if it were a brilliant prize. "I was looking for this."

"You probably shouldn't do that when there are so many suitors about. You look quite silly." She closed the door with a quiet click. Her dark hair swayed as she scanned the room. "Where's the last one?"

"He . . . um . . . he left."

She glanced over her shoulder toward the door. "That's strange. I didn't see him in the hallway."

Stupid bloody fae prince with his stupid bloody disappearing act. "He went through the gardens."

Keelynn's skirts *swished* when she bustled over and dropped onto the settee. "Tell me all about him. Spare no detail. Was he charming? I'll bet he was charming. He was so handsome as well. By far the most handsome of all our visitors today. Probably one of the most handsome men I've seen. Besides Robert, of course."

Bloody Robert.

If the two terrible men were standing side by side, there'd be no contest. Robert was handsome in a generic, safe way. Rían possessed an air of danger that left a woman breathless. Not that I'd ever admit as much aloud.

"I'm afraid he was another pillock," I said, glancing toward the glass doors, hoping the cursed prince was still lurking about so he could hear exactly what I thought of him.

A chuckle lifted on a phantom breeze, leaving my arms covered in gooseflesh.

"A pillock?" Keelynn let go of my hand to give my shoulder a playful smack. "Surely you jest."

"I'm afraid not. He was a pillock without an ounce of charm, and if I never saw him again, it'd be too soon."

Something moved outside on the patio.

I glanced over to find Rían standing there, still pretending to be a Vellanian ambassador, one hand on his hip, the other tucked behind his back, golden sunlight crowning his dark curls.

My damned breathing caught.

Keelynn elbowed me in the ribs. "I heard that," she whispered with a delighted giggle.

"Pardon the interruption." Rían strolled into the room. "On my way out, I saw some flowers in the garden that made me think of Lady Aveen, and I had to bring them to her."

Keelynn-the-traitor swooned.

"You must be Lady Keelynn." He bowed his head. "It is truly a pleasure to meet the woman Aveen holds so dear."

"The pleasure is mine, ambassador," Keelynn tittered.

I bit my tongue to keep from telling him to take his flowers and stuff them up his—

From behind his back, Rían withdrew a fistful of purple and pink fuchsia tied with a blue silk ribbon. The flowers shouldn't have bloomed until summertime. When he held the bouquet toward me, I couldn't bring myself to take them.

Keelynn rammed her toe into my ankle. "Wasn't that sweet of the ambassador?"

"Oh yes. So very sweet. I really appreciate you digging up flowers from the garden I've spent my entire life cultivating. And now that the roots are gone, they'll wither and die." They were gorgeous. The moment he left, I was putting them in a vase and setting them in my bedroom.

Keelynn rolled her eyes. "Don't listen to her. She loves them. They're her favorite, you know."

His head swung toward me, a smile dancing on his lips. "I didn't know that. Isn't that a coincidence? Some might even say it was fate."

"Those people would be fools," I told him, lifting my chin in dismissal. He had already wasted enough of my day.

Catching my hand, Rían pressed a kiss to the pulse at my wrist. "Then I am a fool, Aveen. But I'd like to be your fool, if you'll have me."

Keelynn giggled. "Oh, ambassador, you are a delight. You simply must come to my birthday ball on Saturday night."

His eyes flicked to mine as his lips lifted into a smile. "A ball? How grand."

"Keelynn, I am sure the ambassador is quite busy with his own life. I doubt he has time to attend a ball."

"My dearest Aveen. I will make the time."

With another bow to Keelynn, Rían turned and strode toward the door, continuing into the garden before returning to wherever cursed princes went when they weren't plaguing innocent women.

Keelynn's hand flew to her forehead as she fainted dramatically onto the settee. "Bloody hell, Aveen. A pillock? That man could charm the knickers off an old maid. If he isn't perfect for you, I don't know who is."

Rían wasn't perfect for me.

He only wanted me to break his curse.

7

MOST DAYS, I ENJOYED BEING ALONE, ESPECIALLY IN THE GARDEN. Nothing but me and the dirt and plants with no opinions. No agenda. No judgement.

The same could not be said for the nights. Nights felt too close. Too restrictive. With the rest of the world slumbering, one was left with nothing but one's own thoughts.

And my thoughts were currently plagued by *him*.

Was it any wonder? I'd let him kiss me at the foot of this bed. He'd touched the back of that chair. Ran his finger over the mantle. *Laid on this pillow.*

Such silly little things that shouldn't be burned into my memory.

I toyed with the soft purple petals on the flowers the irritating fae had given me. Although the fuchsia weren't wilted, they drooped toward the tabletop, beautiful but also too heavy. Perhaps that was why I loved them so much.

They were like me.

Pretty on the outside but with a heart too heavy for happiness.

My heart was so full of worry over my sister and my father's demands that there wasn't room for anything more.

There wasn't room for love.

Perhaps that's what I should wish for: love.

What a foolish notion. I buried my head beneath my pillow. Love wasn't something you wished for. Love, if it existed, found you. And if love was meant to find me, surely it would be strong enough to wheedle its way into my heart the way that infernal fae had wheedled his way into my mind.

I loved my sister. That should have been enough.

It used to be.

I wasn't so sure anymore.

The moment the thought crossed my mind, I swore I could smell cinnamon. I threw my pillow aside and scanned the room, disappointed to find it empty.

No. Not disappointed.

Thrilled. Totally and utterly thrilled that the prince had found something else to entertain him for the night. When would he return? What would I tell him when he did?

Worry. Worry. Worry.

That's all I ever did.

What if I wished for freedom from worry? Was that possible?

Probably not.

The things he'd mentioned in the carriage had been tangible. Dresses and horses and diamonds. How about a small cottage by the sea? With a garden full of blooms where I could live out the rest of my life however I wished . . .

No, no. I could never be so selfish. If I was off living in some cottage, what was to stop my fate from becoming Keelynn's? And if our father forced her to marry anyone but Robert, she'd be miserable. I should save my wish and use it for her.

Still, when I closed my eyes, I pictured a tiny, white-washed cottage with yellow shutters built on a height, overlooking a stormy sea. Bright red poppies, blue cornflowers, and yellow forsythia growing on either side of a stone path shuddered in the salty breeze.

Dark clouds lurked off the coast, promising rain. I could see myself racing across the field, my heart singing with happiness even as my lungs burned from exertion, eventually reaching the door. Twisting the cold, damp brass handle. Throwing it open.

And finding Rían smirking on the other side.

I bolted upright.

Was that cinnamon? It was.

"Rían?"

Only silence answered.

I shoved my curls back from my sweaty forehead. I was slowly going mad. It was this room. That had to be it. I kicked the covers aside and dragged my dressing gown from the back of the chair.

The empty hallway felt like a cavern in the darkness. My father's snores echoed from his room at the end of the hall. I turned to my sister's chambers three doors down from my own and opened the door.

When we were smaller, we used to share this bedroom. Roughly the same size as my own, her bed had a whimsical white canopy and a quilt with lace edges—uniquely feminine and unblemished by memories of cursed princes.

And bloody freezing.

The coals in the hearth glowed a dull orange. Why was it so cold?

Lacy curtains on either side of her window fluttered. Was she mad? Leaving the window ajar so anyone could come in—

My eyes flew to the bed.

Empty.

Oh, Keelynn. What have you done? I didn't have to think too hard to know where she had gone—and with whom.

Robert.

I could have gone looking for her, but the truth was, I didn't want to know what they were doing. Instead, I sank onto the mattress, the weight of my burdens making me droop until my head hit her lavender-scented pillow.

Some time later, a soft curse lifted on the breeze. A hand appeared on the sill, followed by a head of dark hair. Keelynn threw herself into the room, collapsing onto the pink rug beneath the chaise, her hair falling in a heavy curtain over her face.

I sat up slowly to keep from startling her.

The moment she began to sob, I jumped out of bed and fell to my knees at her side.

When she saw me, she cried harder, hiding her face behind her hands.

"Are you all right?" I asked, trying to pry her fingers away from her eyes. "Are you hurt?"

The question made her wail.

No sense talking to her when she was like this. The best thing to do was let her get all the tears out first. So, I held her until her sobs turned to sniffles and her trembling stilled.

Pressing a palm to her sticky cheek, I brushed her dark strands aside and brought her face to mine.

"Robert begged me to meet him in the garden," she confessed, her eyes downcast. "He—*we* . . ." A sniffle.

Dammit. I should've been protecting her instead of wasting my time dreaming of something that would never be. I couldn't use that wish for myself. I couldn't.

I helped her out of the soggy gray cloak and handed her a new shift, taking the stained one she'd worn and throwing it into the fire along with her undergarments. If the maids found them, there'd be gossip. And the only thing more damning than the truth was a vicious rumor.

Once she was dry, I settled her into the bed next to me and patted my chest. "Head here."

She snuggled in close, her hair tickling my cheek.

"You are strong," I reminded her. "You will get through this."

"You don't understand. I am ruined. If Father finds out—"

"He won't find out. You can never tell anyone, do you hear? This is a secret you hold inside."

"Are you angry with me?" She sounded so small and meek, nothing like the vivacious young woman who had teased me about my suitors in the parlor.

"I'm angry at Robert, not at you." And I was angry at myself. "I don't understand what you see in that miserable oaf."

"He said he loved me."

Robert didn't know what love was, wielding the word like a weapon, using it to his advantage. "You are far too good for him."

"Why can't he see that?" she sniffled, wiping her nose with her sleeve, then tucking her cold hands beneath my back.

"He's obviously thinking with something a lot smaller than his brain."

Keelynn snorted. "It did seem rather unimpressive."

"And do you really want to be stuck with something so unimpressive for the rest of your life?" A book on her bedside table caught my eye. The same one she'd been reading in the library. I gathered her hair back from her eyes. "Would he be willing to save you from a wicked witch like the knight in your story?"

"He'd probably use me as a human shield," Keelynn grumbled, her hands beginning to warm.

"Exactly." Robert Trench only cared about a woman when he wanted something from her. He and Rían probably had that in common. Would the prince have sought me out a second time if he didn't believe I could break his curse?

Squeezing Keelynn tighter, I felt her relax into my embrace. "What's done is done. Let's get some sleep. Tomorrow, we'll figure out how to get you a happily-ever-after."

I had been so focused on my own misery that I had forgotten about my sister's struggles. That ended tonight. Tomorrow, I would tell my father that he could choose my husband. It didn't matter who he picked when all the prospects were awful. My fate was sealed, but that didn't mean hers needed to be.

"Why did you come to my room?" she asked after a drawn-out yawn.

I couldn't tell her the truth, not after all she'd been through. "I knew you needed me."

"I'll always need you."

It wasn't true.

She would have her own life. Make her own mistakes. Find her own happiness.

It didn't take long for Keelynn's breathing to even and slow into soft snores. When I was younger, the noise had annoyed me. Now I found it as comforting as the downy mattress beneath us. Craving a few hours of blissful nothingness, I slipped my arm from beneath her head and drew the covers to her chin.

She would be nineteen in a few days, but lying there, thick lashes dusting her cheeks and hair splayed across the white pillowcase like a dark wave, she looked impossibly young.

The reality of what had happened with Robert would hit her in the morning.

My mother had died before she had the chance to explain what happened between a husband and a wife, and my father had never broached the subject. I had learned the mechanics from books I wasn't supposed to read and one unfortunate incident when I stumbled upon a maid and stable boy in the woods.

But selfish men had taught me firsthand that they took what they wanted without so much as a backward glance or second thought as to how it would affect us.

That was the real reason I hated them. Not only did they lord themselves over us, they made all the rules in their own favor. If we didn't follow blindly, we were *ruined*.

Keelynn didn't look ruined to me.

She looked perfect.

Afraid my agitation would wake her, I returned to my own room. The moment the door clicked closed, my shoulders fell, and tears pricked the backs of my eyes. The weight of the past week came crashing down, smothering me until I couldn't breathe.

I deserved better than being forced into a loveless marriage.

I deserved better than being threatened to break a prince's curse.

I deserved better.

8

Rían hadn't shown his cursed face in four days. Instead of being happy about his absence, I was on edge, constantly wondering when he'd pop in on a whim. Any time a person stared too long in my direction, I found myself glaring back at them, studying their eyes to see if they were an overwhelming shade of blue.

Last night, my father had been acting strangely, smiling at dinner instead of glaring, and I was sure Rían had stolen his identity. But his eyes revealed him for what he was. When I asked about his change in mood, he told me it was nothing for me to concern myself with. Which concerned me even more.

With concerns mounting, it was all I could do to put one foot in front of the other.

Rían.

I heard his name on the wind. In the rain. In the utter silence in the dead of night.

Rían. Rían. Rían.

Friday brought sunshine and the first mild day since winter. Sunny days in Airren were so few and far between, we made the most of them. This morning, I'd asked Keelynn to go to the seaside. She'd refused. All week she'd been melancholy, preferring to stay inside despite the turn in weather.

So I spent the day in the gardens, pulling weeds that had sprouted over the winter, preparing the beds for planting. My forearms, cheeks, and nose bore the sore effects of a day in the sun. I'd have to slather on an extra layer of cream to cover my new freckles for Saturday night's ball.

A ball with one invited guest I hoped wouldn't show.

Although it killed me to do it, I asked Padraig to ready the carriage for town. My face couldn't take any more sun, and if my father caught me riding, he'd have my sunburned head.

The market should've been empty, with most of the townsfolk spending the day at the shore. Instead, it was more crowded than ever, with hordes of people gathering near the square. I hurried to the back of the crowd, struggling to see over heads and hats.

I squeezed between a woman clutching her brooch and a man in a tweed suit and matching flatcap. "Pardon me, but do you know what's happening?"

The woman nodded, her gaze darting to me before returning to whatever was going on up ahead. "They're executing two monsters from Tearmann."

Although executions were prevalent, I'd never been present for one. Why would anyone want to watch someone else die? More spectators filled in behind me, blocking my exit. I lifted to my toes, catching a glimpse of a woman with white hair dangling from the gallows.

Bloody hell . . .

They'd hanged the fortune teller.

A second noose waited, swaying slightly in the light breeze. The sun beat down on my head, leaving sweat collecting at the back of my neck. When I saw the next creature, my stomach lurched.

Red hair sprouted from holes in his threadbare breeches, covered his arms and hands. A heavy brow shadowed kind brown eyes. I'd never seen him without his cloak, but I knew it had to be the grogoch from the cathedral steps.

"What were their crimes?" My voice quivered.

"The old fortune teller was a witch caught practicing black magic," the woman whispered behind a gloved hand.

"I always knew she was a witch," the man to my right chimed in, stroking his bearded chin.

A witch who had been hiding in plain sight until I visited her. "And the grogoch?" What could he have done to deserve such a fate?

The man's hand fell to the dagger at his belt. "Convicted of theft. The bastard stole Lady Eithne O'Meara's purse."

The hooded executioner fitted the noose around the grogoch's head, tightening the knot at the base of his skull.

Lady Eithne's purse . . .

Oh god . . .

He hadn't stolen it.

I had.

This was my fault. He shouldn't be up there. It should be me.

"Stop!" I screeched. The people closest to me turned to stare. I gripped my skirts and shoved forward, squeezing between bodies to try and reach the wooden dais. "Stop!"

The grogoch's head turned to me.

And he smiled.

"Please! He didn't do it! He didn't—"

The executioner kicked a lever, and the grogoch dropped. The rope went taut. A sickening crack echoed through the square.

"No! Please! Please!" They needed to lift him up. Didn't they hear me? He didn't do it!

A hand clamped around my arm. A man I didn't recognize, with orange hair and a vicelike grip, dragged me back through the crowd, away from the grogoch, whose eyes had gone vacant.

"Let me go! They need to stop—"

"*Shut up.*"

Tears blurred the faces of the men and women who watched

me being taken away. Not one person offered to help. I opened my mouth to scream, but the sound caught in my throat. No matter how many times I tried, I couldn't cry out. The man's grip tightened, and he dragged me into an alley.

My spine slammed against the plaster wall.

"Have you lost your feckin' mind?" Piercing blue eyes cut me to my core. "Interfering with executions is treason."

I knew those eyes. "*Rían?*"

He clamped a hand over my mouth. "*Quiet.*" He peered around the corner of the building. "Do not use my name."

I managed a nod. He removed his hand with obvious reluctance.

"They killed him . . ." *Oh god.* "They killed an innocent man."

"Charlie was caught with a stolen purse. There were witnesses."

Charlie.

The Grogoch's name had been Charlie.

So simple. So common. So *human.*

I shook my head, hair sticking to the tears on my cheeks. "You don't get it. He didn't steal it. I did."

Rían's unfamiliar face paled. He flicked his wrist, and heaviness filled the air. "Tell me exactly what happened." His voice was followed by the slightest echo.

Tears rolled down my cheeks as I confessed to every awful thing I had done that day.

"I asked Eithne about you . . . And she said awful things and made me so bloody angry. So I-I . . . I blackmailed her." How stupid. How naïve, stealing another person's coins for something so petty. Why did I think there'd be no consequences?

"I took her purse and gave it to the grogoch—to Charlie. I thought he could use the coins and . . . *Oh god.* I'm going to be sick." My stomach clenched and heaved. I twisted, bracing my hands against the rough plaster wall. The acidic taste in my mouth was nothing compared to the bitterness growing in my heart. Why hadn't Eithne told the truth? Why had she blamed an innocent man?

Rían held a handkerchief toward me. "Take this and go home."

"I c-can't." My hand shook as I shoved my hair away from my sweaty forehead and used his handkerchief to wipe my lips. There was something I needed to do. Something important. "I have to collect Keelynn's dress."

Two people were dead because of me, and I was worried about my sister's bloody dress.

"Tell me where it is, and I will collect it for you."

I pressed my overwarm cheek against the cold plaster, praying the spinning world would stop moving for one blasted minute.

Rían brushed my hair back, his fingers gentle as they grazed my cheek. "Is it at Meranda's?"

"I don't want your help." I didn't deserve anyone's help.

"Don't make me threaten you." He flicked his wrist. The heaviness hanging in the air evaporated. With another flick, a hulking black horse appeared in the alley, saddled and ready to ride. "Get out of here before you get sick all over my boots."

I couldn't leave on his horse. "My coachman—"

"I'll handle it." He lifted me as though I weighed no more than a feather, plopping me unceremoniously on top of the horse. Swirling ancient symbols decorated the rich leather saddle. He barked what sounded like an order in a language I had never heard.

The horse's ears twitched. Handing me the reins, Rían smacked the beast's hindquarters, and it took off. The crowd parted as the horse worked its way past the shops and stalls and cathedral to a back alley that connected to the main road leading north. I didn't have to steer until we reached a fork. I urged it to the right, and it obeyed, picking up its pace.

It should've been me.

It should've been me.

It should've been me.

Only it hadn't been me. It had been Charlie.

Had he protested his innocence? Had he been afraid? Was he at peace?

The fields and trees turned into blurred streaks behind my tears. I scrubbed my eyes with my sleeve, trying to pull myself together.

I couldn't let my sister see me like this. Or my father.

When I arrived at the end of the long drive, the horse came to a skidding halt.

Padraig stood in the center, weathered hands braced at his hips, shoulders no longer stooped but straight.

I threw aside the reins.

The moment my slippers hit the soft earth, Padraig's arms came around me in a fierce hug. "Shhh . . . There, there, milady. There's nothin' to be done." He patted my head.

"You don't understand. I—"

"Not a word more. Not a word."

I managed to breathe a little easier when he let me go, patting my cheek with a rough hand. I'd be lost without him. He was so much more than a coachman—

Hold on.

Where was the carriage? How had he beaten me here?

Rían's horse nudged my back with his muzzle.

Padraig hobbled around me to catch the bridle.

"Padraig? How are you here?" He should've taken at least three times as long driving the carriage. There was only one road in and out of town. *How was he here?*

"Let's make a deal, shall we? I won't ask why the prince gave ye this beast," he grumbled, leading the horse toward the trees, "and ye won't ask how I made it home."

The prince.

Rían.

He'd said he'd handle it.

He must've gone to Padraig after I left. Why would he introduce himself instead of maintaining his disguise? And why wouldn't Padraig meet my gaze?

The horse trudged alongside him, its head bobbing as it walked.

I touched the coarse wool of his Padraig's dark overcoat. "You know who he is?"

Impossible. Padraig was a good man. He would never associate with someone like Rían.

He stilled, his flatcap slipping when his head fell. "I know wherever the devil goes, death and destruction follow." Padraig jerked the horse's head so they were nose-to-nose. "Ye will tell 'im that he'd do well to set his sights on someone else."

The horse's eyes shined a deep, golden yellow. There was knowledge there. Like he understood Padraig's warning. I could've sworn the horse *smiled*. And then it vanished.

Just like Rían.

Either the beast had magic . . . or Padraig did.

I'd known Padraig almost my entire life. If he had magic, I would've sensed it . . . Wouldn't I?

He was small and more wrinkled than not, with wisps of white hair sticking out from beneath his dark wool cap. The short white whiskers on his chin glistened in the evening light.

He looked as human as me.

Until the kind blue eyes I'd seen a thousand times began to glow.

"Padraig?"

It couldn't be. I knew him. I *knew* him.

As I stumbled back, my boot caught on a stone.

The world tilted.

There was a flash of pain.

And everything went dark.

Warm, soothing chamomile tickled my nose, reminding me of carefree days racing with Keelynn through the gardens. The long-forgotten memory left me smiling. When I opened my eyes, I found myself on a raggedy sofa beneath the lone window in Padraig's tiny cottage.

The place seemed smaller than the last time I'd been here. It must've been at least six years ago. A tatty quilt covered the small bed in the corner; two worn upholstered chairs had been parked in front of the fire.

Padraig's wife had died around the time our mother had passed. I could barely recall what she'd looked like, but I remembered her always serving chamomile tea.

Pots and pans clanged as he moved around the area that served as a kitchen. A set of cupboards hung unevenly above a dry sink. Steam rose from a pot over the fire, licking at the dry-stacked stones on the chimney.

Padraig glanced at me over his shoulder. In his gnarled hands, he clasped a chipped cup of fragrant herbal tea. "Here. Drink this."

His flatcap hung on the back of one of the two chairs at a tiny wooden table. His thinning white hair barely covered the tips of his ears.

Ears that came to a delicate point at the top.

And then I remembered his eyes.

"You're not human," I choked, my hands frozen at my sides.

He still smiled the same kind smile. Still had the same wheezing chuckle. He shoved the cup into my hands, forcing me to grasp it to keep from spilling the steaming liquid over my lap.

"My mam was a faerie who gave up her wings," he explained, taking a seat with a low groan, "and my Da a clurichan."

"What about your wife? Was she—?"

He shook his head, a small sad smile on his thin lips. "My Nellie was as human as ye, refused entry into Tearmann by the Queen."

The Phantom Queen ruled the Black Forest, a cursed stretch

of land between Airren and Tearmann. Legends spoke of her ruthlessness toward humans. Hearing her name left goosebumps on my arms.

"So, we made our life here," he said, scratching one pointed ear. "Usin' this damn glamour is illegal, but 'twas the only way to get honest work in this place. I'm trusting ye with my secret."

I would never tell a soul—not even Keelynn. My sister, as fascinated as she may be, was also terrified of the creatures. It would kill Padraig to have her look at him differently. To have her treat him differently. As much as he cared for me, he loved my sister like she was his own. "Your secret is safe with me."

"I know it is, milady." His mouth flattened. "Will ye trust me with yers?"

I clutched my teacup a little tighter. If Padraig already knew about Rían, I'd be a fool not to confide in him. Perhaps he knew of a way to get rid of the prince for good. I took a sip of my tea, steeling my nerves. "Rían—"

"Shhh! Shhh! Shhh!" He flicked his wrist, and the same heaviness that accompanied Rían permeated the air. "Sayin' the bastard's name will bring bad luck on yer head."

Too late for that. "What did you do just then?" I flicked my wrist the way he had.

He held out a fist and knocked against what sounded like a hollow wall . . . but there was nothing there. "Made us a tost," he said. "A soundproof barrier to keep yer secrets from unwanted ears. Vital when sayin' things ye dinna want others to overhear."

So that was it. Rían had been creating tosts.

"Go on. Ye can speak freely now."

I told him about meeting Rían at the market—leaving out the bits with the dagger and the kissing. The dagger because, after Rían had helped me today, I figured I owed him. And the kissing because it was irrelevant.

"Now he claims that I'm the only one who can break his curse," I finished, taking another sip of tea.

Padraig's eyebrows came together. Leaning an elbow on the

tabletop, he scratched at his chin. "Doesn't make a lick of sense. Far as I know, the lad isn't cursed."

The lessons from my youth came flooding back. We had been taught not to trust the creatures, that they were all liars bent on tricking humans, luring us down dark paths.

Only I was no longer a child listening to tales with a child's fear. I was a woman who had lived. Who'd had twenty years to make up my own mind. To learn that anyone could be evil just as anyone could be good.

Like Padraig. He was the best man I knew, and he wasn't human.

And that poor grogoch, Charlie.

Rían, though . . .

Rían was exactly the type of creature they had warned us about.

"If he's not cursed, then what does he really want from me?" He must want something if he kept coming around.

"I haven't the foggiest." Padraig scratched his whiskers. "That lad plays his cards close to the vest. Trusts no one. Torments humans and Danú alike. Makes no sense that he'd offer ye a lift back here."

Danú. That sounded better than calling them "creatures."

I explained about Rían threatening Keelynn and promising me the wish for helping him.

Padraig's hand stilled on his cheek. "Put 'im off fer as long as ye can. Whatever ye do, don't agree to a bargain. If ye accept the wish, yer in his debt. And in his debt is a place no one should be."

I set my cup aside and took his hands, his calluses like sandpaper beneath my fingertips. "Thank you, Padraig. For this and for all you've done for Keelynn and me. If there is any way I can repay you, all you have to do is ask."

"'Tis my pleasure, milady." He patted my knuckles with dry, cracked palms. "Best be off with ye now. Ye have a big weekend ahead."

Oh. I had completely forgotten about the ball.

How was I supposed to smile and laugh and dance and feign happiness knowing my stupidity had sent an innocent man to his death?

I thanked Padraig again and ran for the house, through the gardens and into the back parlor.

The servants readying the entry hall for tomorrow night's festivities watched me as I flew past, up the stairs and down the hallway to my door.

On the center of my bed sat a large box wrapped in silver paper with a beautiful blue bow.

Rían had come through for me.

But at what cost?

9

YOU CAN DO THIS.

You can *do this*.

Those words became my mantra as I sat at my dressing table, staring at my reflection. If Rían showed tonight, I wasn't going to let him walk all over me. I would speak my mind. It wasn't like he would try anything with so many witnesses. And if he threatened me or my sister again, Padraig said he'd report him straight to the Danú leader in Tearmann.

I wasn't sure what their leader could do to a prince. Hopefully it wouldn't come down to that and I'd never have to find out.

Our ladies' maid Sylvia gathered my golden curls at the top of my head, jamming in pin after pin after—*ow ow* ow—pin. Her own dark hair had been hidden beneath a white mop cap.

If I had my way, I'd leave my hair down. But like everything else in my life, it wasn't up to me. According to Father, respectable ladies who were on the verge of matrimony wore their hair *up*.

I pulled a few curls free to frame my face. A small act of defiance.

The door to my room flew open, cracking against the wall. My sister stalked through, headed straight for the closet. As if any of my dresses would fit her tall, willowy frame. My skirts wouldn't even reach her ankles.

"I have nothing to wear." Keelynn sifted through the garments hanging inside. "The red dress looks awful, the purple one makes me look like a bloody grape, and the green one is too tight. I should've skipped lunch."

The idea of skipping a meal to fit into a dress made about as much sense to me as Rían's lies.

"Sylvia? Would you mind giving us a moment alone, please?"

The maid bobbed a quick curtsy and slipped out the door.

"You're lucky you have such a brilliant sister," I told Keelynn, collecting the box hidden beneath my bed.

"You didn't . . ." She rushed over, found the corner of the bow, and tugged. The wrapping paper ended up in a ball in front of the fireplace. "You did!" she squealed, clutching the magenta gown against her chest. "Oh, Aveen! It's stunning." She smoothed a hand down the jeweled bodice to the silk ribbon at the waist. "Thank you, thank you, *thank you!*" Her arms came around my shoulders, knocking me into the chair. "You are the best sister. I mean that. I don't know what I'd do without you."

She smelled of lavender and sunshine. Youth and happiness. Love and loyalty.

"I could hardly let you attend your own party wearing one of your *old rags*." That's what she called all the dresses she'd worn once—*maybe* twice.

"You know me so well." Keelynn brought her dress to the full-length mirror in the corner. "Did you get one for yourself?" she asked, holding the garment in place and swaying from side to side, fluttering the dyed feathers along the skirt. No one would be able to take their eyes off of her tonight.

I glared toward my closet, stuffed with enough gowns and cloaks and random bits to last a lifetime. "Why do I need a new one when I have plenty of dresses?"

"Because new dresses are fabulous!" She spun in a circle, loose waves lifting from her slim shoulders. "Which one are you wearing tonight?"

"The blue one."

She snorted. "All your dresses are blue."

"Not true. There's a purple one in there somewhere."

Her laugh was like a balm to my soul. "I hope someday to be as content as you."

I wasn't content. I was resigned.

She kissed my cheek before dancing out of the room with her gift. Eventually, I settled on a silk gown the color of a clear sky, with capped sleeves and long white gloves to hide the dirt that refused to scrub clean from beneath my short nails.

Sylvia returned to help me into my stay, drawing the laces tight. Next came the dress. She fastened the buttons with expert fingers and added a ribbon across my waist, above the a-line skirts that shimmered like sunlight on freshly fallen snow.

I put the finishing touches on my makeup, covering my freckles and sunburn, highlighting my lips with rouge, and dusting my lashes with kohl. I didn't look like myself but rather a grand lady whose sole purpose in life was entertaining the gentry. Fitting, considering that was what I was to become.

With my mother's cameo choker tied around my neck, I hurried to the entrance to greet guests as they arrived. Graystones' gentry climbed our front steps in glittering gowns and coats with tails. Men and women resplendent in finery, wearing their wealth for everyone to see. When Eithne and her husband arrived, she lifted her chin as she swept past.

I wanted to haul her back by her hair and demand she explain why she'd lied about Charlie.

Keelynn beamed as guests wished her happy birthday. I committed her laughter to memory, something to hold close when I was alone.

Had I ever experienced that level of joy?

If I had, I couldn't remember.

Once the line of people had disappeared, my father escorted Keelynn into the ballroom. There was no sign of Rían posing as the ambassador. Had he sneaked past pretending to be another guest? Keeping close to my sister, I scanned the crowd for a pair of wicked blue eyes.

The high walls in the ballroom had been draped with pink gossamer fabric. Pink candles dripped wax onto shimmering white tablecloths. In the center of a long trestle table sat a three-tiered cake, iced in white cream and embellished with pink peonies.

My father led Keelynn straight to the dance floor, and the band in the corner struck up a lively tune. Instead of finding a partner and joining them, I went to the table overflowing with food and desserts to make sure the servants hadn't forgotten anything.

Robert's father stood beside the table, his hands clasped behind his back, watching the goings on with a stern expression.

"Good evening, Lord Trench." I offered him a low curtsy. He was handsome for an older man, with a distinguished amount of gray at his temples and a monocle over his left eye.

Although he looked down his nose at me, he bowed his head slightly in greeting. "Lady Aveen. You must've been hard at work planning such a grand event."

Party planning had been child's play compared to the other hardships I currently faced. "It's not work when it's for someone you love."

Speaking of my sister, where had she gone?

I spotted her taking a turn with Tomas Billington.

Thank heavens.

Lord Trench offered me the closest thing he had to a smile as I collected a plate and added a few slices of honeydew. What I really wanted were the chocolate covered strawberries, but my dress would make enjoying them impossible. "How is Lady Trench? I didn't see her arrive with you."

"Unwell, I'm afraid. Suffers from awful pains in her stomach."

Speaking of pains in the stomach . . . the boning jamming into my guts would be the death of me. "Fitzwilliam's recently received a shipment of herbs and tinctures from Vellana." The local apothecary was one of the best-stocked shops in Graystones. The owner, Mr. Fitzwilliam, spent a fortune importing from the larger islands and the continent. I'd seen the shipment arrive earlier in the week. "If you call in and explain her symptoms, he may know of something to soothe the pain."

"I will try that." He sounded genuinely appreciative. "Thank you."

I finished my melon and picked a glass of champagne from a passing tray. Before I could take a drink, the faux Vellanian Ambassador walked through the door.

Our eyes met from across the crowded ballroom. His lips curled into a smile that left my heart pummelling my rib cage. As if he could hear it, his smile grew.

I downed the champagne, abandoned the glass for a full one, and headed straight for the devil.

You can do this. You can do this. You can do this.

A few men called to me as I passed. I ignored them all.

Rían bowed low, a performance for those closest to us. When he straightened, his eyes reflected flickering candlelight from the chandeliers. Eyes that weren't clear but bloodshot and glassy. "Lady Aveen, it is a pleasure seeing you again."

You can do this. You. Can. Do. This.

"Unfortunately, I cannot say the same, *ambassador*."

Chuckling, Rían stepped closer. "Is that any way for the lady of the house to speak to a distinguished guest?"

Distinguished guest, my foot.

Good god. What was that awful smell? I held my gloved hand to my nose to keep the stench at bay. Rían may have looked pristine, but he reeked of booze and perfume. "It is when the *distinguished guest* smells like a bawdy house."

His eyes flashed. "And how do you know what a bawdy house smells like?"

The ridiculous question didn't deserve a response. "It's a wonder you decided to show at all. You were obviously enjoying yourself elsewhere."

"And have your sister think me rude?" He clicked his tongue. "I wouldn't want to ruin her high opinion of me."

She only had a high opinion because she didn't know the man. And if I had my way, she never would. I lowered my hand to take a sip of champagne, careful not to inhale. "Says the man who showed up to her party drunk."

"Drunk?" He pressed a hand to his chest. "Such a scathing accusation. I'm sober as a clam."

Lady Gore watched us from her chair with a bit too much interest, her gout-riddled leg propped on a tufted ottoman.

As thrilling as it was to speak my mind, I refused to be fodder for the biggest gossip in Graystones. "Right. I'd best be off. Enjoy the party."

I found Keelynn by the cake, chatting and laughing with a few girls her own age. If I wanted my reputation intact tomorrow, I couldn't stay next to the prince all night. No matter. I could stay beside Keelynn.

Rían fell into step next to me, snagging a glass of champagne from one of the servants carrying trays.

If he insisted on following me, I couldn't go to her. I needed to go somewhere else. Somewhere like the line of chairs beside the balcony doors. The moment I reached them, I whirled, nearly colliding with his chest. Although chilly, the air outside held warm notes of spring. "Did you need something else, or do you plan on following me all night?"

"That depends . . ." The golden bubbles in the glass floated toward his lips when he took a large gulp.

"On?"

"Whether or not you tell me your wish."

You can do this.

I propped my hands on my hips, wishing there were some way to make myself look more imposing for this conversation. Oh well.

He could look down at me all he wanted. It wasn't as if I would be seeing him after tonight. "I have decided that I do not want to bargain with you."

He drew in a deep breath, a smile playing on his lips. "Is that right?"

I nodded. "Yes. And I know you're not cursed."

"Am I not? Well, that's a relief."

If he wasn't careful, that sarcasm was going to earn him a glass of champagne turned upside down over his head. "While I appreciate what you did for me yesterday, I did not *ask* for your help, so I don't feel I owe you anything in return. The only reason I'm tolerating your presence tonight is because my sister invited you. So you can take yourself and your wish and find someone else to torment."

He nodded as he listened, eyes fixed on my mouth. Sipping champagne. Licking it off his perfect lips.

Where had I left off? Oh, right.

Torment.

"I think it's best if you go your way and I go mine so that people don't get the wrong idea."

Rían kept nodding even though I'd stopped speaking.

"Ambassador!"

He blinked, then grinned. "I like your dress."

What was it about that smarmy smile that made me want to wallop him? "Were you listening to me?"

"No one is paying us the least bit of attention."

Sure enough, those closest to us seemed to be minding their own business, and the dancers on the dancefloor appeared too focused on their partners to notice either of us were in the room.

His Adam's apple bobbed as he finished his champagne then set the flute on the windowsill. "They're too busy nattering about Lady Samantha's husband going off with Lord Ketter's wife, and Lady Julia's baby bump which is rather large for someone married only three months."

Lady Samantha's husband huddled in the corner near the

musicians with three more men my father's age. All of them swirled and sipped their brandy, no doubt very pleased with their male accomplishments.

Lady Samantha sat on a chair surrounded by a handful of women, dabbing her eyes with a handkerchief. Now that I was looking, Lady Julia's bump beneath her burgundy gown did look quite big.

"You can hear them from here?" All I could make out were coughs and murmurs and music.

"Fae hearing." Rían tapped his left ear. "Although this one's fecked," he muttered, tapping his other one.

"Why? What happened to your ear?"

He dragged a silver flask from his back pocket, taking his time unscrewing the lid. "You look positively delectable tonight."

Heat crept along my neck. My jaw. My cheeks. "Did you hear what I said?"

Squinting, he pointed at me with the top of his flask. "Did you hear what *I* said?" He eased forward, his breath tickling against my neck. "I wonder if you taste as good as you smell."

"You mustn't speak so improperly," I breathed, choking on the sour stench of alcohol. "Someone may hear you."

With a flick of his wrist, the sounds around us fell silent.

He'd created one of those tosts.

The couple eating cake to our right didn't seem to notice anything amiss. The tost must be working. Would they hear me if I screamed?

"There. Now I can say whatever I want and *noooo* one can hear us." He took a deep gulp from the flask. Using his sleeve to wipe the drink from his lips, he went back to smiling. "You're a viper tonight. Makes me want to do all sorts of *improper* things with you."

I didn't want to hear any of his undoubtedly lewd suggestions that would probably involve him and I alone. Touching and kissing and . . . My toes curled inside my slippers. "That's quite enough, Rían."

"It's Ambassador DeWarn, remember? Or Edward, if you're feeling *improper*." He flicked his wrist.

Sound exploded. Voices. Music. Laughter. Carefree and utterly oblivious.

"Seeing as you and I no longer have any business together, I'm off to have fun with these humans. If you're looking for a bit of devilment, you know where to find me." Rían's shoulder grazed mine as he sauntered past, plucked another glass of champagne from a tray, and inserted himself in the middle of a group of young women fluttering their fans and eyeing him like he was a slice of delicious cake.

I'd come prepared to fight, and he hadn't even batted an eye at my refusal to bargain.

Nothing about that man made sense.

I grabbed a glass of champagne, hyper-aware of Rían's every breath. Every movement. Every twitch of his fingers, blink of his dark lashes, flash of teeth when he smiled.

If only I had fae hearing and could listen in on the undoubtedly *improper* things he whispered in Tilly Dalton's ear.

He was like a flame, beautiful and enticing.

But flames scalded and burned.

And a woman in my position couldn't afford to be reduced to ash.

A few men asked to sign my dance card, which I'd left in my bedroom. I declined them all. I had more important things to do than dance the night away. Like watch Rían shamelessly flirt with anyone in a bloody skirt.

The only time he was out of my sight was when I'd danced with Keelynn. She was the only person in this ballroom I'd happily agreed to dance with. My sister giggled the whole time, the belle of the ball, with a full dance card and fuller smile.

"Is it just me or has James Wallace gotten prettier?" Keelynn said when we came together. When she retreated in a swirl of magenta skirts, I found the man she'd mentioned against the wall near the hallway.

We came back together to spin in a slow circle, hands an inch apart. "He's passably attractive."

"Perhaps you can marry him." She twirled away, her hair flying over her shoulders, then spun back and caught my hands. I felt her giggle in my soul.

"Pass." I'd greeted James when he'd arrived, and he'd choked on his response, blushing more than I had at Rían's suggestive comments. As much as I despised Rían's cockiness, at least he had a spine.

"Come now, sister. If you must marry someone, he may as well be pretty. And you've turned away every other man who has called. It's like you've given up."

I had given up, but now wasn't the time for that discussion.

Rían made his way toward Robert and his brothers, a glass of wine in his hand.

All of the Trench men had the same tall, broad frames, square shoulders, and dirty-blond hair. The eldest two had beards, and the next in line had a manicured goatee. But Robert, the youngest, always kept his face clean-shaven because his facial hair grew patchy and soft.

I hated that I knew that about him.

I hated that he knew things about me too.

Next to them, Rían looked like a dark devil, all wicked smiles and glinting eyes and danger. How many drinks had he had? Between flute after flute of champagne and the flask and the brandy and the wine, it had to be at least ten.

"Or . . ." Keelynn drew out the word. When I looked back, her eyes narrowed. "You already have someone in mind."

"Don't be daft."

"That's it, isn't it?" Her eyes sparkled when she grinned. "Could it be a mysterious man with dark hair and blue eyes so deep you could drown in them?"

She thought I was interested in Rían? In what world would I ever want to be with someone so conceited and condescending and rude and annoying and . . . The list of his shortcomings far outweighed any redeeming qualities he had, if any.

Keelynn wiggled her fingers at someone behind me. Rían grinned at her from where he stood. Then the bastard winked at me, sending my sister into a fit of giggles.

"I am *not* marrying Ambassador Flirt."

"Why not?" In my ear, she whispered, "Did you see his arse in those fitted breeches?"

"Keelynn!"

The infernal prince was full on laughing now. Stupid bloody fae with their stupid bloody super-sensitive hearing.

A man sidled up next to us. When I saw who it was, I stifled my groan.

"May I cut in?" Robert asked, nodding toward my sister.

Keelynn lifted her chin like a haughty princess, glaring up at the man who had broken her heart. "You can wait your turn."

Good woman. That was the first time I'd seen my sister do anything but jump at the chance to please him. Robert would walk all over her if she let him.

"Are you really going to make me look a fool in front of everyone?" he said under his breath.

"That depends." She planted her hands on her hips. "Are you finished being an ass?"

I stifled my laugh behind my glove.

A muscle in his jaw ticked. "I am sorry, all right?"

Were my ears deceiving me, or did Robert Trench just apologize?

Keelynn's lips lifted as she turned, her eyes giving away the extent of her happiness. "Do you mind if I dance with Robert?"

"Of course not." When I let her go, I shot Robert a warning glare.

He swept her into his arms, and they were off, waltzing as if they belonged together. Robert appeared to only have eyes for Keelynn—for the moment, anyway.

He had this uncanny ability to make a woman believe she was the only woman in the room. Keelynn would forgive him, although I wasn't convinced he deserved it.

A warm hand caught mine, and I found myself drawn toward a toned chest. I looked up into piercing cerulean eyes.

10

Rían held my hand in his, slipping the other onto his shoulder. A shoulder that felt incredibly toned beneath his fine black jacket.

"What do you think you're doing?" His vicelike grip kept me from pulling away.

"Ambassador Flirt and his fitted breeches are dancing with you," he drawled, leading me with feline grace between waltzing couples.

Dammit. I knew he'd been listening. "And if I don't want to dance with a drunken wastrel?"

Despite the amount of drink he'd consumed, his eyes were no longer bloodshot but clear. And trained on my mouth. "First, I'm far from drunk. Second . . . Actually, there is no second point. I am the worst of wastrels." There wasn't an ounce of remorse in his cocky smile. And why would there be? Rían was a prince who did as he pleased.

He adjusted his grip, pressing me closer with the hand on my lower back. "This party is boring."

"Then perhaps you should leave."

We reached the corner of the dance floor. He turned me, leading us back to the center.

"Ah, here now. You're going to hurt my feelings."

"I wasn't aware you had feelings."

He chuckled, but he was too close for me to see his smile. How had we gotten so close? One deep breath away from brushing chests.

"Speaking of feelings," he said, low against the shell of my ear, "your sister looks awfully cozy with your lover. I hope you're not too jealous."

My entire body went rigid. "Robert and I aren't . . ."

He'd caught Robert leaving my bedroom. What was he supposed to think?

"Keelynn loves him, not me," I amended.

Light from the glittering crystal chandeliers reflected in his rolling eyes. "Love is for fools and simpletons."

A fellow cynic. How refreshing. "Does that mean you've never been in love?"

He drew away, brows arching toward dark curls. "Have you?"

Always answering a question with another question. What was he trying to hide?

"No. I haven't." True love from the storybooks was patient and kind. It weathered storms. It wasn't hurtful or selfish. It didn't use you and cast you aside.

The song ended, then rose into another waltz. Instead of releasing me, Rían brought me closer. I hated the way he made me feel. Powerless. Weak. Not in control of my own body.

My erratic heartbeat. My flushed cheeks. My light head.

The parquet floor was barely visible for all the dancing couples, but it may as well have been just the two of us. All I could focus on were his hands, secretly wishing they'd move lower, hold tighter, press closer. His lips lifted into a cocky grin, as if he could read my thoughts.

He couldn't though . . . could he?

I hate you, I thought, just in case.

Sir Henry Withel slinked over and tried to cut in. Rían flicked his wrist. The man turned on his heel and left.

"What did you do to him?" I asked.

"Let him wait his turn. I do not share."

"You can't do that to people." I forced my feet to still. Couples around us swerved to avoid a collision. "You can't use them like pawns in some game."

He smirked. "I can do what I like."

Sir Henry came back carrying two glasses of champagne and wearing a glazed expression. Rían took them from him and offered me one. When I refused, he drank one straight after the other, gave them back to Sir Henry, and said, "She's all yours."

Sir Henry blinked. His eyebrows came together, looking at the two glasses as though he had no idea where they'd come from.

"Allow me." I took the empty flutes, bringing them to one of the high tables near an open window, hoping the cool breeze would snuff out the heat of desire building in my core.

Rían had acquired another glass of brandy. He kept his back to me as he spoke to someone near the balcony. When he shifted his weight, I glimpsed a familiar face.

Lady Eithne.

Giggling, she reached for his arm and squeezed. There was no mistaking the coy look she gave him from beneath her kohl-smudged lashes.

This was what happened when one was forced into a loveless union. One sought pleasure and happiness elsewhere.

Robert approached from the dancefloor, his hands fisted at his sides. I turned to escape only to find the way blocked by a line of chairs.

"I need to speak with you." Robert's gaze flicked to where Rían stood, chatting and laughing with Eithne. "In private," he added through his teeth.

I wanted to tell him to shove off. But this wasn't Rían. This was Robert. "I'm afraid I must decline. It wouldn't be proper for me to be alone with a man who is not my husband."

"You and your bloomin' rules." Puffing out his chest, he huffed a breath, settling a fist on his hip. "You want me to say this here? Fine. I want you to steer clear of the ambassador."

My stomach tightened when my eyes connected with Rían's, still talking to his lover.

"And why is that?" I asked.

A deep wrinkle formed between Robert's light eyebrows when he frowned. "You are a lady, so I'll put this delicately. He has made it quite clear that he has designs on you."

Designs on me? Poppycock. It was perfectly clear from the way Rían bent to whisper in Eithne's ear exactly who he had "designs" on.

Robert had some nerve, thinking he could come over here and tell me what to do and who to stay away from. All the warning did was make me want to stomp right over to the prince, shove Eithne aside, and kiss his irritating, beautiful mouth until the entire ballroom stopped to stare.

My fists clenched at my back until my hands ached. "I fail to see how that is any of your concern."

His hand slipped from his hip, falling open between us. "I only have your best interests at heart."

Best bloody interest, my foot. "And I appreciate it." I didn't. "Now, if you'll excuse me, I need to check the desserts."

"Why must you always be so stubborn?" Robert spun toward where his brothers waited in their circle by the mantle, laughing and drinking and toasting while their wives looked on from their chairs.

Eithne slipped onto the balcony and down the stairs toward the garden.

My garden.

I couldn't tear my eyes away from Rían as he finished his drink, discarded the empty glass on a windowsill, and melted into the dark night like a shadow.

My feet started for the open doors. Wisteria and sea salt danced on the refreshing breeze.

Rían could dally with whomever he wished. But not in my

home. And not in my bloody garden. Where had they gone? They couldn't be far. To the koi pond or the willow or the raised beds at the very back?

A feminine giggle blew in from the roses.

My roses.

The gravel along the path ground beneath my heels as I stalked toward that grating sound, not knowing what I'd do when I found them. I should have told her husband and let him catch them together. It wasn't too late to turn back, and yet I continued forward.

"Spying is terribly rude." *Rían.*

He appeared on the bench beneath a trellis of flowering vines, an ankle thrown over his knee, toying with the laurel leaves at his back. His hair was no longer curly and brown but rich mahogany, with the front swept back from his forehead and the sides cut close to his ears.

He'd gotten a haircut.

I hated that I noticed.

"These are *my* gardens. I suggest you take your tryst someplace else."

His eyes glowed faintly, glinting sapphires. "And I suggest you go back to the party."

I would go back inside when I was good and ready, and not a moment sooner. "Lady Eithne is married, you know. She has a husband right inside."

"That sounds like her problem, not mine."

"I should've known a . . . a man so lacking in morals wouldn't care about sacred vows."

Rían clicked his tongue. "Ah, here now. If you're jealous, I'd be more than happy to show you how lacking in morals I really am once I finish out here."

Damn it all if my face didn't ignite. "I'm not jealous."

He snorted. "Liar."

I wasn't jealous.

Well, perhaps I was a little jealous.

Mostly, I was disappointed. Which was madness. How could I expect someone like him to be anything but a monster? What had happened yesterday when he'd helped me in town must've been a fluke.

"You are the worst person I have ever—"

Rían vanished. A hand clamped over my mouth. An arm snaked across my chest, dragging me until my spine collided with a solid frame. Dark shadows leaked from beneath his shirt cuffs as he yanked me back and back, until we blended in with the hedges. Twigs scraped my cheeks. I would've cried out, except Rían had gone utterly still.

"Do not make a sound." Heat from his whispered command left my stomach clenching. If I didn't know better, I'd say he was frightened. Absurd. What could frighten someone like him?

And then I heard it.

Hooves thundering against the earth, growing louder and faster as they approached.

The fetid stench of carrion slithered on an icy breeze, coiling around my throat, striking my senses with its acidic bite. The thunder came to a halt impossibly close. On the other side of the hedge, there was a thud and a jingling of metal. Footsteps, slow and stunted, stalked around the bushes, each one more ominous than the last as they grew louder and louder and louder.

And stopped.

"*I smell your fear,*" a gravelly voice whispered, not from the direction of the lengthening shadow but from inside my mind.

Rían's hold on me tightened.

My heart thudded against my ribs.

Terror thickened in my throat.

What was it?

"*Nightmares made flesh, child,*" the voice responded, as if I had spoken my thought aloud. "*What is your name?*"

Rían drew me tighter against him.

A pair of muddy boots came into view, belonging to a man in a soiled, threadbare soldier's uniform. I'd seen illustrations of soldiers who fought the creatures in the war for Airren. Only, in the drawings, the men had heads.

These shoulders, concealed beneath a stained overcoat, ended at the stump of a neck.

The Dullahan.

I had convinced myself he wasn't real. That something as horrifying as a headless horseman couldn't possibly exist.

A white whip dragged in one of his hands, the fall glinting like links in a chain. Only the links weren't metal but bones from a human spine. In the other hand, he held an object aloft like a lantern, only it gave no light.

A head.

Bloody fingers clutched matted strands of inky black hair. Eyes rolled back into the sockets. Bugs crawled from the nostrils, over the brown teeth, and into the gaping mouth.

I whimpered, squeezing my eyes closed, but it was too late. The image had been seared into my memory. The monster turned toward where we hid. And stopped.

"You know my name, now give me yours," the Dullahan demanded. *"Give it to me, or I shall take it."*

Unforgiving pressure squeezed my skull, like my head was being crushed beneath the monster's muddy boots.

"Whatever you do," Rían whispered, his fingers contracting against my jaw, "do not tell him your name."

Had he heard the monster's request?

Every part of me screamed to give in, to tell the Dullahan my name. All I wanted was this pressure to end.

"I know you're there," said the voice, the stench of death and rotting flesh overpowering everything else. *"I can feel you."*

Feel. Not see. Rían must've used his magic to conceal us somehow.

"I can take away the pain. All I need is your name."

My name lived on the tip of my tongue. If I told him, the pain would subside.

"He's not here for you. Fight it." Rían sounded so far away, and yet I could still feel him holding me in the steel cage of his arms.

"Think of something else. Anything else. Distract yourself."

He moved his hand, uncovering my lips.

I couldn't do it. I couldn't think of anything else.

My name is—

Rían's heat at my back vanished. Something warm and soft pressed against my lips.

Tasting like alcohol and cherries.

My lashes flew open to find blue eyes staring at me from only a fraction of an inch away.

Bloody hell.

Rían was kissing me.

Why was he kissing me? Why did I like it so much? It had been one thing to kiss him in my room that first night. I knew better now. I should pull away. I shouldn't close my eyes and let the slick heat of his tongue sliding across the seam of my lips convince me to open my mouth so he could slip inside.

Someone called for Edward. A woman.

All at once, the pressure in my mind eased. The stench and footsteps retreated.

Rían's hands came around my ribs, skimming below my breast. I arched into his caress, loving the way it burned. His fingers constricted as they drifted higher. A low growl vibrated against my chest. I kissed him with every ounce of fear and terror, drinking in his magic, wishing I could feel it moving inside of me. Could feel *him* moving inside of me.

He tasted like the shadows. Overwhelmed like the sea. Consumed like an inferno. I didn't know what caused this fire blazing through my veins or why it only happened with him, but I craved it.

To my detriment, I craved it.

Rían tore his mouth from mine and shoved me away. My hip collided with the bench just as a woman's scream pierced the night.

"Get inside before I send you to the underworld myself," he spat, gesturing toward the house, eyes narrowed and lips swollen.

My knees unlocked. I fled for the manor. A crowd of men flooded down the stairs, shouting and pointing. Women waited on the balcony, hands pressed to their chests, covering their lips, fanning themselves as they stared into the darkness. If anyone saw me now, they'd start asking questions. I found a familiar head of dark curls leaning over the railing. Keelynn was safe. Nothing else mattered.

I turned right, racing to the evergreens edging our property, following the trail to the other side of the house, praying the Dullahan was gone. In all the commotion, I slipped back in through the main doors unnoticed and raced to find an eerily empty ballroom. Keelynn stood on the stairs, calling my name. When she saw me, she collected me in a hug so fierce it felt as if my bones would shatter.

"What is it?" I asked. "What's wrong?"

"It's Lady Eithne." The fire in my blood turned to ice when Keelynn took my gloved hands in hers and said, "She's dead."

11

AFTER WHAT HAD HAPPENED LAST NIGHT, I EXPECTED TO SEE RÍAN. But Rían never showed.

12

It had been a week since my sister's birthday ball, and I hadn't seen or heard from Rían once. Lady Eithne's funeral on Wednesday had been packed with false mourners more interested in gossiping about the deceased than shedding tears over her passing. There hadn't been a damp eye in sight. Even her husband had seemed oddly relieved.

I couldn't help thinking of Charlie as Keelynn and I huddled at the graveside beneath a shared umbrella, rain pummelling the mound of fresh earth next to the hole in the ground. Had there been a funeral for the grogoch? What about the witch? Did they have family back in Tearmann to mourn them? Or were their lives to be forgotten like smoke in the wind?

Eithne wouldn't be forgotten. Her headstone was twice the size of the ones next to it.

The doctor had claimed Eithne died of an aneurysm.

I knew the truth: The Dullahan had claimed her life.

He's not here for you, Rían had said only moments before he'd kissed me.

It had been his kiss, not the headless monster, that had plagued my dreams. The feel of him. The taste of him. The hunger and desperation. Our first kiss had been nothing more than a shocking brush. The way he'd kissed me in the garden . . .

There had been passion. But also despair.

So much despair.

Despair that now grew like a vicious weed inside my head and my heart. I shouldn't want to see him again. I shouldn't want anything to do with a man who would allow his lover to be murdered so viciously.

And yet, every time I came across a pair of blue eyes, my heart leapt.

As much as I wanted to stay hidden, there were things to be done. The ferns needed transplanted from the greenhouse to the raised bed near the pond, and the hazel needed to be thinned. Our gardeners could do it all, but they knew to wait for my permission before tackling any of the tasks in case I wanted to do them myself. And I did. Gardening had become the only distraction that kept my mind off of *him*.

I changed into one of my comfortable gardening dresses and stepped over the corner of the rug on my way to the door, not wanting to litter it with the dried mud crusting the soles of my gardening boots.

Muffled voices sounded from down the hall, in the direction of my father's study. Making idle conversation with his guests sounded like my personal version of hell, so I turned toward the servant's stairs leading down to the kitchens. The back door opened to the delivery entrance at the side of the house. I could slip out unnoticed and hide in the gardens until the visitors had gone.

"Ah, Aveen," my father called the moment my fingers clasped the cold knob. "Just the woman I needed to see."

Drats. I had been so close. When I turned, I found his eyes narrowed and expression grim.

"What in heaven's name are you wearing?"

"My gardening dress." The most comfortable garment, it was

utterly shapeless but loose around my hips and chest. The best part: it didn't require a corset or stay.

"You will change this instant. I'll not have my daughter looking like a bloody servant. When you're decent, I want you in my study. Be quick about it. I don't want our guests kept waiting."

With that, he and his loud boots retreated.

I felt myself wilt as I drifted back to my bedroom to cinch myself into a soul-crushing stay and a blue day gown embellished with golden thread. The tops of the stockings squeezed my thighs, and the matching blue slippers pinched my poor toes. Were men this uncomfortable in their finery? Probably not. No man I knew would endure discomfort like this.

Knowing better than to delay, I hurried down the hall as quickly as my aching feet would allow. Taking a moment to catch my breath, I rapped my knuckles against the wood.

My father's low baritone sounded on the other side. A moment later, the door opened. "Come inside and have a seat, Aveen," he said, ushering me into the room.

When I saw his guests, my feet stilled.

Robert sat ramrod straight on one of the leather chairs, staring grimly toward the shelves of leatherbound ledgers, arms crossed and jaw set. His father stood behind him, lips pinched and disapproving.

My father cleared his throat, reminding me of my manners. "It's a pleasure to see you again, Lord Trench," I said, dropping into a low curtsy and bowing my head.

"You as well, Lady Aveen." Lord Trench inclined his head. "You're looking as lovely as ever, isn't she, Robert?"

"What?" Robert's hazel gaze bounced to mine. "Oh. Um. Yes. I suppose she is."

My father gestured to the chair beside Robert's as he rounded the desk to settle into his. "I have some brilliant news to share with you, daughter," he began, clasping his hands together and setting them atop the desk next to the inkwell. "Lord Trench and I have been discussing the relationship between our families and how we wish to solidify an alliance. And we can think of no better way to do that than through marriage."

I couldn't believe it. Robert had always claimed he would never marry. What had changed his mind? Did he understand what this sort of commitment entailed? Would he remain faithful to Keelynn?

I'd threaten him, just in case.

I offered Robert a congratulatory smile. He kept his eyes on his shiny brown boots.

His father's face remained impassive.

What if Robert didn't want to marry Keelynn? What if he was being forced to wed her? Had Lord Trench found out about their tryst? There had to be a way to fix this. Keelynn deserved to marry someone who genuinely wanted to be with her. She deserved love.

"Once the two of you are wed . . ." My father's voice cut through the haze.

The two of you.

Robert finally raised his eyes to mine.

The dish of yogurt and berries I'd had for breakfast curdled in my stomach. Dread slid an icy finger down my spine. "I'm sorry. I believe I misheard. Who is getting married, exactly?"

My father's smile tightened. "You and Robert, of course." He waved a hand at us. "I know how fond you were of one another when you were younger. I'm confident you'll find a way to rekindle that once again."

Words came tumbling out of his mouth, but they didn't make a lick of sense.

"You expect me to marry him?" I couldn't think of anything worse—and I'd nearly met the Dullahan.

"I'm not exactly thrilled about it either," Robert grumbled, tugging on the bottom of his plaid waistcoat.

Lord Trench clamped a hand on Robert's shoulder, leaving his son wincing.

This couldn't be happening.

This was not happening.

My father looked as giddy as a child in a bloody sweet shop. "Why don't the two of you take a turn in the garden and leave us to iron out the details?"

I rose woodenly, ignoring Robert as he trudged beside me to the staircase and out the main doors. Sunlight peeped through cottony clouds as they blew past on a breeze. How could my father do this to me? To Keelynn?

When I told him to choose a husband, never in a million years did I believe he'd pick Robert Trench.

"How could you sit there and say nothing?" I asked, struggling to keep my voice level. He was a man. He held all the control in this cursed world, and he hadn't said one bloody word.

He stopped next to me, hands shoved in his pockets like a bold child. "Look, Aveen, no one is more upset about this than I am."

"Oh, really? No one is more upset? Not one person?"

Robert's shoulders lifted with his resigned sigh. A bloody sigh. These were our lives, and two old men were making our decisions. Everything about this was wrong.

"I get it. You're not thrilled. But perhaps we could find a way to make this work."

Not thrilled? I wasn't thrilled when there was no fresh cream for scones. This . . . This was a travesty. "We hate each other."

Wincing, he plucked a leaf from a potted boxwood, pruned to look like a swirl. "You didn't always hate me."

I inhaled a shaky breath. If only I could clear my head. There had to be a way to fix this.

"I know. I know I didn't. But that doesn't change the fact that we are not suited. You care for my sister." *Dammit.* We had to fix this before Keelynn found out.

Robert's frown deepened. "Keelynn and I have had a disagreement." He tore another leaf, crushing it in his fist. "I'm afraid she no longer cares for me."

No longer cared for him? My sister worshiped the ground he walked on. "She loves you."

"That will change once she learns of our betrothal."

Keelynn rounded the corner of the house, a basket of wildflowers on her arm. The breeze blew loose waves across her flushed cheeks. "What betrothal?"

Oh no. No no no.

My hands shook when I clenched my skirts. How could I tell Keelynn the truth? She would hate me forever. I couldn't do this to her. I just couldn't.

Cursing under his breath, Robert straightened his waistcoat and stepped toward my sister. "Aveen and I are to be wed next month."

The basket fell to the ground, spilling blooms across the golden gravel. "No . . ."

Say something, dammit. But what *could* I say?

Robert put his hands on her shoulders. "Keelynn, listen to me—"

"How could you do this to me?" Tears welled in her narrowed eyes. The accusation wasn't for Robert. It was for me.

"I'm sorry, Keelynn."

She tore from Robert's grasp and ran. I made to go after her, but Robert caught my hand. "I'll speak to her."

As much as I wanted to chase her down and insist she listen to reason, I was the last person she wanted to see now. Perhaps she would hear him out. It certainly couldn't hurt. I nodded and watched him take off around the house.

Surely Keelynn would forgive me.

The sacrificial lamb didn't get a choice.

I hadn't asked to be born first.

Even if she didn't forgive me, I vowed to spend the rest of my life making up for this.

I drifted to the potting shed, where fresh topsoil and compost permeated the air. I picked up a pot with the intention of filling it . . . then hurled the blasted thing against the wall.

The shattering ceramic didn't matter.

Nothing mattered.

And I screamed.

I screamed until my throat grew sore and I had nothing left to give.

I screamed, and not one person came to my aid.

Empty and alone, I picked up the shattered pieces of pottery, accidentally cutting my palm against its sharp edge.

It should've hurt. But I felt nothing as I stared at the blood spilling onto my skirts.

Felt nothing as I grabbed my trowel and stood.

Felt nothing as I went back outside.

Felt nothing as I knelt next to one of the barren flower beds, stabbing the ground over and over and over.

My tears watered the seeds.

My broken heart seeped into the soil.

My hope flew away with the breeze.

This wasn't my fault.

And yet I felt guilty.

Why? Because I'd been born a helpless woman whose only worth lay in her ability to make a good match? How was that my fault?

I wanted to do more. Wanted to be more. But any time I tried to stand on my own two feet, my father knocked my legs from beneath me.

Enough was enough. It was time for me to take control.

Consequences be damned. I would go straight to my father and refuse.

With my hands and skirts covered in dirt and blood, I raced toward the house to find my father still in his study, looking chuffed with himself, smiling down at the freshly signed betrothal contract on his desk.

"Father?" I closed the door and hurried to where he sat watching me through narrowing eyes. "I need to speak to you. It's urgent."

His clasped hands fell on top of the desk. "You need to change your dress before someone sees you."

My dress? My life was over and he was concerned with my bloody dress?

Although I had never denied him outright before, I knew I had it in me. This wasn't just about my own happiness, it was about Keelynn's as well. I would do anything for her.

Anything.

You can do this. You can do this. You can do this.

"I will not change my dress, just as I will not marry Robert Trench."

My father's dark eyebrows slammed down over slitted eyes. "You will marry him."

"You don't understand—"

His fist smacked against the tabletop. "It is you who does not understand." He picked up the contract to dangle it in my face. "This is a contract—a binding legal document. If broken, there could be serious consequences. Lord Trench has the power to ruin us."

I knew what a bloody betrothal contract was. And I also knew that it could be broken thanks to Lady Jane Fuller eloping with the butler instead of her fiancé, Lord Whitmore.

"How could he ruin us?"

By saying we'd broken a contract? It may cause a small scandal, but it certainly wasn't enough to *ruin* us.

His eyes shuttered, and he turned to stare out the window at the sea birds soaring through the clouds. "Some of my business ventures have not been as profitable as expected. Without an influx of cash from Lord Trench, I would have to dismiss the household staff and perhaps sell the estate." Sighing, he dropped his head into his hands. "Your dowries are gone, Aveen."

Suddenly, it all made sense.

The ultimatum.

The timeline.

Lady Eithne's remarks that day in town.

Here I was, spending money hand over fist on Keelynn's party and new dress like a dolt. Why hadn't my father reigned me in?

Why hadn't he shared this crisis with us instead of keeping us in the dark?

Before I could voice the question, the answer became clear: my father hadn't confided in us because we were nothing more than useless girls.

A nuisance. A burden. *Profitable.*

"Lord Trench understands our situation," he went on, "but believes you will make a fine wife for his son. Without him, we would have nothing."

I collapsed onto the chair, trying to make sense of the world falling apart around me.

"Robert cares for Keelynn."

"I am aware of their affinity for one another." His lips flattened. "However, Lord Trench does not feel Keelynn is mature enough. And I'm inclined to agree.

"So, you see why we cannot break the contract," my father finished, opening the top drawer in his desk and tucking away the piece of paper signifying the end of my freedom. "You have a duty to this family—to your sister. I expect you to remember that the next time you lose the run of yourself."

Break the contract, and we'd be left destitute.

Father could sell the estate for all I cared. After all, there were only three of us. What did we need this big old house for anyway?

Without money, we would no longer be welcome in the same social circles. Again, I didn't care. But Keelynn would. She'd be devastated to see an end to the parties and dresses and other comforts she'd grown accustomed to.

And she still wouldn't be able to marry the man she loved.

Unless I could find a way to fix this.

Rían had promised me a wish.

I could wish for gold. Lots of gold. Enough to pay our debts and keep the house and make the betrothal contract obsolete.

Except Lord Trench wanted Robert to marry me.

What if I ran away?

And leave my father with a broken contract and my sister penniless?

Dammit. I couldn't do that either.

I left the study without a word. What could I say? That it would be all right? It wouldn't. That I forgave him? I didn't.

The walk to the staircase felt like a death march. Each stair, a death knell. Every trudging step forward bringing me closer to the end.

Keelynn sat on the front steps, rubbing her red-rimmed eyes with a handkerchief. When she saw me approaching, she stood to straighten her skirts. I couldn't bring myself to look her in the eye as I came to stand next to her. The manicured lawns seemed to stretch on forever, reminding me there was no escape.

"Keelynn, I'm so very sorry."

She crushed the handkerchief in her clenched fist. "So, that's it then? I'm supposed to sit idly by and watch you steal my future?"

"Keelynn—"

"I hope you're happy together," she spat, skirts flying behind her as she hurtled past and shoved the door aside.

My life had turned into a disaster, and there was no end in sight to the misery.

Unless I could wish for Keelynn to take my place.

13

HOW DID I GO ABOUT CONTACTING A FAE PRINCE? THERE WAS only one person I could think of to help. I raced across the gravel toward the stables to find Padraig brushing Keelynn's horse and shouting orders at two stable hands. When he saw me, he straightened and started forward, meeting me by the first stall. My mare bobbed its brown head as if in greeting.

"What is it, milady? Are ye all right? Did something happen?" He reached for my dirt-crusted hand as his eyes swept me from head to toe. My father hadn't cared enough to ask me what had happened. He'd only given out about my appearance.

Not Padraig though.

"I need your help."

A nod. "Of course. Whatever it is. Tell me."

I had a feeling that if I told him I'd murdered someone, he'd grab the shovel leaning against the wall and help me bury the body, no questions asked. At least there was one person in this world besides my sister I could rely on.

The stable hands watched us, listening to every word. This scene would undoubtedly be described to the maids and footmen and sweep through the rest of the household staff by dinnertime.

"Not here. I need to speak with you in private."

Understanding crossed his weathered features, and he nodded. "Ger, finish here with Lady Keelynn's horse. Liam, when I get back, I expect the stalls to be mucked and cleaned." With that, he took my hand, laced it through his arm, and started for his cottage, waiting until the stables faded from view before speaking. "I assume this has to do with the bastard prince," he said.

"I need you to find him and bring him to me."

Padraig's uneven steps faltered. "Ye shouldn't seek him out, milady. Wherever the devil goes, death and destruction follow."

I hadn't forgotten the warning. With what had happened to Eithne, I knew it was true. And yet, I couldn't think of any other way to get out of this situation without letting someone down.

With the lawns stretching all around us, I explained to Padraig what had happened.

"Robert Trench isn't good enough for either of my girls," Padraig grumbled, giving the gravel a kick.

"Unfortunately, Keelynn's heart is set on him. And I'll not be the one to break it."

He ran a hand over his whiskers, mumbling to himself and casting furtive glances back toward the stables. "If I find yer man, what's yer plan?"

"I'm going to bargain with him."

Padraig caught my hand, blue eyes wild. "I'm beggin' ye. Find another way. Reason with yer father. Ye cannot be in Prince Rían's debt. Ye won't survive."

One wish. It was worth it. "Will you do this for me or should I find someone else to help?"

"I'm sorry, milady. I'd do just about anything fer ye, but this will only end in disaster."

What? No, no. He had to help.

There must be a way to get a message to Rían. He wasn't some nameless Danú, he was a Prince of Tearmann. Surely other people in his world would know him. If they didn't know him, they'd know *of* him.

Who else could help?

None of the lords or ladies in my acquaintance. On the off chance they did know Rían, admitting such a connection would be akin to social suicide. Prince or not, he was Danú.

I needed someone worldly.

Someone who knew all the gossip, heard all the whispers.

Someone like . . .

Dame Meranda.

I turned to Padraig, the barest vestiges of a plan forming in my mind. "Saddle my horse, please."

"Yer upset. Why don't I drive ye instead?"

"I'm fine, Padraig." At least I would be once I found Rían.

Padraig's wrinkled brow furrowed as he studied me. I was sure he'd protest again. Instead, he bobbed his head and hobbled back to the stable.

I should've changed my dress but didn't want to waste any time. I dashed inside to collect a cloak from the closet and met Padraig at the start of the drive.

In no time at all, I found myself passing Graystones's welcome sign, descending toward town. Most of the shops had closed for the evening, but the sign hanging in Meranda's window still said "Open."

When I tried the knob, I found it locked.

I knocked once. No answer.

Twice. A third time.

"Meranda? It's Lady Aveen. I need to speak with you. It's urgent."

The door flew open.

Meranda's fiery hair wasn't in its usual pile atop her head but tumbling free in a mess of frizz around her shoulders. Her eyes widened when her gaze fell to my skirts. "Heavens above, Lady Aveen. What happened?"

"I need your help. I need to get a message to someone but I'm not sure how to reach him. And I thought perhaps you would know or would've heard of someone who may know how to—"

"Aveen?" Meranda's hands came to rest on my arms. "Take a

breath. I don't know if I can help ye, but I will certainly try. Who is this person yer looking for?"

Right. Time for the tricky part. "He doesn't live in Graystones."

Her eyebrows lifted. "Where does he live?"

"Tearmann."

Meranda's hands dropped. "Why did you come to me then?"

"You seem to know everyone. And I met Rían in town, so I thought—"

"Rían, you say? As in, Prince-of-Tearmann Rían?"

"So you have heard of him." *Thank god she knows him.* Wait . . . why did she know him? Never mind. It didn't matter. All that mattered was that she could help me—if she *would.* "Do you know of anyone who could get an urgent message to him?"

Biting her lip, her eyes flashed toward the darkening windows. "I might know someone."

I threw myself into her arms. The first bit of good news I'd heard all day. "Thank you. Thank you. *Thank you.*"

She didn't return my smile as she pulled from my embrace, rounding the counter to collect an ink pen and a bit of paper. "Write the message here, and I will have someone deliver it to the castle."

Right. My message.

What did I say?

I didn't want to give too much detail in case he refused.

I must speak with you.

And to convey a sense of urgency, something like . . .

It's urgent.

That was all I had.

Hopefully, it would be enough.

Two days.

That was how long I waited before giving up hope.

Two long, drawn-out, depressing days full of rain and silence.

Robert and I were to be married next month, and preparations for our betrothal ball were well underway.

Keelynn hadn't spoken to me in all that time.

And all I could do was sit in my bedroom and stare out the window, wishing Rían hadn't let me down. Rain drops collected on the glass, rolling toward the white sill.

I'd gone to Meranda again yesterday, and she'd assured me that her messenger had delivered the note.

Meaning Rían had received my plea and ignored it.

What had I expected? That a prince would've dropped everything to rush to my aid?

What a fool I'd been. Tears welled in my eyes like those raindrops, spilling down my cheeks.

A bloody fool—

"I cannot stand weepy women."

I shot to my feet, whirling so fast I had to catch myself on the back of the chair.

"You're here . . ." Rían was *actually* here. Lying once again on my bed, legs crossed at the ankles, watching me through long, dark lashes.

"Did you miss me?"

I had, but only because I'd needed him. "Of course not."

My blood ignited when his lips lifted into a smile, all dimples and wickedness.

He looked taller. Leaner. Infinitely more handsome.

"Did you just want to stare at me or was there something *urgent* you wished to discuss?" he muttered, picking at his clean nails.

I'd read everything I could find about bargaining with the fae. All of the books warned against the perils of such agreements. Although there were a few useful lessons as well.

First, be specific. Fae were born tricksters, likely to twist your words to suit their own wicked desires. Look at the way Rían had gotten around his promise to leave Keelynn alone.

Second, be aware of loopholes. There always seemed to be some loophole to allow one side or the other to avoid keeping their promise. I needed an iron-clad agreement. One swayed in my favor, not his.

"I want to avail of that wish you promised," I told him.

His hand stilled. "I promised you a wish in exchange for breaking a curse. Seeing as you've refused to do your part, there shall be no wish."

"Please. I need that wish." I'd beg if I had to. I'd grovel. Pride was nothing compared to freedom.

Rían quirked an eyebrow. "Why? What has changed?"

"I am to be married to a man I cannot stand."

"Do you want me to kill him?" Rían said it as if he were asking for butter on his toast.

What sort of question was that? "Of course not."

His head tilted. "Then what do you expect me to do about it?"

I closed the distance between us, stopping when my knees met the bed. "I want you to convince Lord Trench to pair Robert with Keelynn." Then I would be free, my father would get his money, and all would be well.

"My magic doesn't work like that." Rían sniffed, brushing invisible specks from his dark waistcoat. "I can curse him, or I can kill him. If neither of those options suit, then I'm afraid this discussion is over." He rolled off the bed, standing to his full height next to me.

This discussion couldn't be over.

He had to help.

I caught him by the wrist to keep him from vanishing. A shock went through my fingers. "I am desperate." Willing to pay any price. For my life. For my sister's happiness. "I would rather die than marry Robert Trench."

Something flickered across Rían's features. "You would rather die," he repeated. Slowly. Testing the weight of the words. Turning them over on his tongue. Rían brought his fingers to rub idly at his bottom lip. "If I grant you this wish, what will you give me in return?"

"What do you want?"

His smile grew, eyes unfocused. "A favor of my choosing."

"I cannot give you a blanket favor." He could ask for *anything*, and I would be forced to comply. I would literally be selling myself to the devil, trading one form of servitude for another.

"That is your choice, and you are free to make it. Goodbye, Aveen."

And with that, Rían was gone.

The sinking in my chest became so unbearable, I collapsed to my knees.

One favor for a wish. Had I been a fool not to accept the bargain?

I was a fool either way.

"Rían!" I shouted, not knowing if he could hear me. "Come back! I accept your bargain."

A warm hand clasped mine, and I felt the power of the bargain take hold, like an invisible chain linking my life to his. Heavy and unyielding.

Rían's eyes glittered as he knelt in front of me, holding steady until the magic had bound us together. "I have a plan to give you what you desire, but for it to work, you will need to do exactly as I say. Do you understand?"

I didn't. I nodded anyway.

"Go about your life as though nothing is amiss. Once everything is in place, I will return to give you further instructions."

This time, when Rían vanished, I did not call him back.

As much as I did *not* want to make plans for a wedding I hoped would never happen, I didn't have much of a choice. If whatever mysterious plan Rían had come up with didn't work, I'd be forced to go through with it.

That afternoon, a designer visiting from Vellana and her assistants came by to fit me for my gown. I had asked my father how we could afford such luxuries, and he'd explained that Lord Trench had agreed to finance the wedding and my trousseau as part of the betrothal contract.

Meaning I got to stand still for hours while being poked and prodded by pins, holding my arms out or up, being told I should go on a diet of tea and brown bread until the wedding. Even the designer's assistant had nodded in agreement.

I wasn't going to starve myself to marry anyone, least of all Robert.

As they finished, the bakers arrived, toting baskets of cake samples. Every time the designer or one of her assistants gave me a judging look as they packed up their bits, I ate another bite of cake. By the time everyone left, my stomach was so bloated I looked as though I was with child, and I spent the next hour in the privy, sick from overindulging.

Wedding planning was torture, and it was only day one. How would I survive another four weeks of this?

"I am proud of you, Aveen," my father said, settling himself on one side of the tet-a-tet in the parlor. "Now that your wedding is on the horizon, it seems as though you have finally accepted your lot in life. Contentment suits you."

Contentment. I hated the bloody word. I was as far from content as a woman could be. Still, if he believed it to be true, then I must be playing my part perfectly. I wanted to pick up a cushion and launch it at his head. Instead, I smiled a *contented* smile and said, "Thank you, Father."

I excused myself, saying I had to change for dinner, already dreading more conversation. More pretending.

Would there ever be a time when I could be me?

Upstairs in the hallway, an arm snaked out of the bay window.

I opened my mouth to scream, but a hand stifled my cry.

"*Shhh*," Rían whispered in my ear.

What was he doing wandering around my house? What if someone saw him? What if someone saw *us*?

"Listen carefully, there isn't much time." He let me go to dig something out of his pocket. "Put this on."

He handed me a silver ring with a sapphire the size of my knuckle. Why in the world would he give me a ring? When I slipped it onto the index finger on my right hand, he groaned.

"Not that finger." He flicked his wrist, and it reappeared on the ring finger on my left hand. "Now pretend to be madly in love with me."

"W-what?"

"Pretend you love me," he repeated, slower this time, the words emerging in an exasperated huff. "Oh, and we're engaged."

"You cannot be serious."

"Deathly serious," he said with a chuckle, peering around us to scan the hallway. A moment later, he linked our arms and towed me toward my bedroom.

With my heart hammering, I couldn't find words to protest as he opened the door and thrust me inside. I found my back pinned against the closet, Rían staring at me with an intensity that made my knees weak.

"I'm going to kiss you now." He wet his lips, his gaze landing on my mouth. "Try your best to play along."

The warning barely registered before his mouth captured mine. This wasn't a kiss like the others. No hint of magic, only his tongue lashing and lips punishing. I clutched his collar, bringing him closer. This wasn't real. I was only playing along. I wasn't enjoying the feel of his hard body overwhelming my softness or his hands tangling in my hair.

"I do hope I'm not interrupting," a silken male voice drawled from the corner nearest the window. A voice that held the promise of darkness.

Rían dropped his forehead against mine for a split second before stepping aside and turning to face the intruder.

Stubbled jaw. Golden curls.

A body of lean muscle. A face of sharp angles.

Magic glowing in emerald-green eyes.

The man's ears came to a delicate point at the top, just like Padraig's.

"You must be Aveen." The man vanished only to reappear at my side, his accent lilting, rolling like the Airren hills. He smelled of almonds.

My heart constricted and stomach fluttered when he reached for my hand. Strangely cold lips grazed my knuckles. "It is truly an honor to meet the woman who has bewitched my brother."

My brother.

This man was Rían's *brother*?

"Although," the man said, tracing a solitary finger down the center of my palm toward the pulse at my wrist, "Rían has been quite stingy with details. Tell me, how did the two of you meet?"

How did we meet? Was I supposed to lie or tell the truth?

As if he could hear my bungled thoughts, Rían tugged me by the elbow, tucking me beneath his arm. "We're not here to discuss that."

The smile on his brother's face never wavered. "No matter. I'm sure the truth will come out eventually." He gave Rían a pointed look over my head. "It always does."

The air hummed with electricity as if lightning were about to strike.

"What's your name?" I forced through my dry throat.

The man grinned, revealing a set of straight, white teeth. "You can call me Tadhg."

Tadhg.

Rían's *brother*. Presumably a prince as well.

A prince with a wrinkled shirt that looked like it had been worn for days.

A prince with grass stains on his elbows.

A prince with dirty handprints smeared down the thighs of his wool trousers.

"Why are your clothes in such an awful state, Tadhg?"

Dropping onto the chair in front of the barren fireplace, Tadhg unfastened the two remaining buttons on his emerald-green waistcoat. "My brother bet me that I couldn't convince anyone to share my bed if I didn't look like a prince. And I've been proving him wrong for"—his eyes narrowed on Rían—"how long now? It must be at least a century."

"You're cursed to look like a woman's fantasy," Rían shot back, hands flexing into fists. "Of course you won."

Chuckling, Tadhg smiled at me. "Do I look like the man who visits your dreams, Aveen?"

I didn't dream of men often.

When I did, they all looked like Tadhg.

Although there was no way I could tell him that. "I find you repulsive."

Tadhg snorted. The way his smile tugged on his full lips left my chest tightening. "You're a terrible liar. Perhaps my brother can give you some lessons."

Rían kicked over the chair. Tadhg's laughter echoed around the room. He didn't bother moving from where he'd sprawled on the floor, just slipped his hands beneath his head and stared up at the ceiling. "Ah, ah, little Rían. Wouldn't want your dark side showing now, would you?"

As fascinating as it was to see Rían on edge, the long day had taken its toll. "I hate to interrupt, but I'm trying to figure out how Tadhg is supposed to help in my . . ."

Rían's brows rose.

"In *our* situation," I amended. It wasn't as if a handsome face would sway my father, or Robert's.

"You didn't tell her?" Tadhg's eyes widened. Clicking his tongue, he shook his head, then stood and righted the chair. "Dearest Aveen. My chivalrous brother wants me to kill you."

14

Tadhg didn't say he was going to kill me. I must've misheard. That's what this was. Some sort of misunderstanding. Even so, I stepped back. Away from Rían. Away from Tadhg. Until the backs of my legs collided with the bed. "I'm sorry, my brain is all muddled. I thought you said Rían wants you to kill me?"

"Why must you always be so feckin' awful?" Rían snapped. "Aveen, look at me." He took my shoulders, twisting me to face him. "It's not as bad as it sounds." His smile would've been more reassuring if it had reached his eyes. "If my brother kills you, you can come back."

Bloody hell.

He *did* want to kill me.

This was my punishment for bargaining with a fae.

I pulled free of his grasp. *You can come back.* "Humans cannot return from the dead. That's impossible."

"I assure you that it is quite possible. His lips are cursed, you see." From over Rían's shoulder, Tadhg winked and blew me a kiss. "All you need to do is kiss him, die, and then come back. Your father cannot expect you to marry Robert if you're dead, and your family can save face."

Cursed lips. Cursed to look like a woman's fantasy. A Prince of Tearmann.

Only one being on this island had the power to kill with a kiss. "You're the Gancanagh, aren't you?" I whispered.

"At your eternal service," Tadhg quipped, sweeping into a low bow. "Although I'd prefer if you called me Tadhg. Less formal." His emerald eyes flashed. "Less dreadful."

With me dead, Keelynn would be free to marry Robert. She'd get what she wanted.

And so would I. *If* I came back. What if Rían was lying? What if I kissed the Gancanagh—kissed *Tadhg*—died, and *didn't* come back? I glanced at where Tadhg lounged on the chair, batting my curtains like a lazy cat.

"I don't know if I can do it."

"It's the only way for us to be together." Rían brushed my hair from my face. "Is our love not worth the sacrifice?"

Tadhg snorted.

If I didn't know better, I would almost believe the tenderness in Rían's gaze. But it was a lie. Rían had no feelings for me, and he certainly had no intention of marrying me. This was all part of our bargain. If I didn't come back from the dead, Rían wouldn't get his favor. He seemed selfish enough to collect on such things.

I could live, marry Robert, and be miserable. Or I could die, come back, and be free. The thought of Keelynn's face when she'd found out about our betrothal played over and over in my head. I had spent my entire life looking after her. Why should I stop now?

Marrying Robert wouldn't just ruin my life. It would ruin hers as well.

"Love is worth the sacrifice," I said. Not my fictional love for Rían but my love for my sister. "I'll do it."

Rían's thumbs stroked my cheekbones as he peered down at me, searching my face. "You're sure? You'd really die to be with me?"

From the corner of my eye, I saw Tadhg turn to watch us with a thoughtful expression.

The only thing I knew for certain was that, if I had to choose between my own happiness and Keelynn's, I'd choose her every time. Even if it meant a visit to the underworld that could well be permanent.

"Yes," I said. "This is what I want."

Rían kissed me, hard and fast, then let me go to drag a hand through his hair. "Right. Yes. Right." He began pacing along the rug between the fireplace and the bed, the floorboards creaking underfoot. "We should do this straightaway. The quicker you die, the quicker you'll be back."

Tadhg stood, his shoulders tensed and chiseled features draped in shadows. "What's the matter? Afraid she'll change her mind if you don't rush her into it?"

Rían's eyes narrowed. Cinnamon magic hummed in the air.

"I'm not going to change my mind," I assured Rían, catching him by the sleeve. "But I would like a little time to say goodbye."

To Keelynn and Padraig.

"You cannot tell anyone of our plans," Rían insisted, lacing our fingers together. "Not one word. Promise me."

Keelynn would be devastated. I wouldn't tell anyone else, but I had to tell her. To let her know that I never wanted any of this but that dying was the only way to ensure she could live the life she wanted. Still, with Rían so adamant, I couldn't tell him any of that.

So I promised.

My hand tingled until Rían let me go.

Tadhg appeared beside me, bringing with him an almond-scented breeze as he flicked one of my curls over my shoulder. "Don't worry, Aveen. I'll make your death a pleasurable experience for the both of us."

Rían caught him by the collar. "Go find someone to seduce."

"Why find my own when you're letting me borrow one of yours?" Tadhg winked at me again.

Rían twisted his hand, tightening his hold on his brother's shirt. "Don't make me kill you."

"You know, for someone who wants my help, you really should be nicer to me," Tadhg choked, flicking Rían's knuckles until he let go. Straightening his wrinkled shirt, Tadhg smiled at me. "Aveen." He bowed, caught my hand, and pressed a kiss to the pulse at my wrist with those ice-cold lips. "Until we meet again."

And then Tadhg vanished.

It took a few moments for my heart rate to return to normal. Rían watched me through wide eyes, quietly assessing from beside the fireplace.

"So, your brother is interesting." What must it be like, to be the sibling of a heinous murderer? Part of me had believed the Gancanagh was an old wives' tale used to caution young women about the dangers of entertaining men without a chaperone.

"I'm surprised you didn't fall at his feet." Rían dropped onto the bed with a heavy sigh. "You did well. I think he was properly convinced."

I sank onto the mattress beside him, my legs no longer able to keep me upright. "Why the ruse? He seemed more than willing to help."

"Only because I told him we were desperately in love."

Pity the girl from Graystones who loved a heartless prince . . .

What a ludicrous idea. Me loving someone like Rían. My sister was the one with the foolish notions when it came to men, not me.

My sister.

"You didn't mention Keelynn, did you?" If Tadhg knew about her . . .

He glanced sidelong at me. "If you want to keep me from your sister, I assumed you'd want to keep the feckin' Gancanagh from her as well."

He'd considered my sister's wellbeing. I don't know why that made my heart swell. Perhaps there was a tiny speck of goodness in him after all.

We laid together, staring at the canopy above us in companionable silence. I kept expecting him to leave, but he didn't.

Was I really going to do this? Was I going to trust this man lying beside me?

He'd saved me twice.

He'd come to my aid when I sent the note.

But did I trust him enough to let myself die?

Marriage to Robert would be another type of death. The death of my happiness. The death of Keelynn's.

I hadn't given real death much thought, assuming it would be waiting for me at the end of a long life. That I'd be ready for it when it came.

"Do you think it will hurt?"

Rían was so still, I thought he'd fallen asleep. Then he shifted, rolling onto his side to face me, propping himself up with his elbow, and resting his chin on his hand. "Yes. But coming back will be worse."

"How much worse?"

His gaze dropped to the quilt. "It's not as bad as being hanged but considerably more painful than getting decapitated. Think being burned at the stake but without the godawful smell of singed hair and melting flesh."

The scones I'd had for tea threatened to make a second appearance. "Are you serious?"

A grin. "Any other questions?"

Only about a thousand. "How do you know? Have you died before?"

"I've been hanged, stabbed, pushed off a castle roof, drowned in a river, drowned in the sea, impaled by a lance . . ." He rattled them off as if making a list of items to purchase at the market. "My mother struck me with an iron bar once, and my brother's favorite way to kill me is to slit my throat." He untied his cravat, revealing a silver scar across his neck. My fingers ached to trace the mark at its thickest point in the middle. The ends went off in different directions. There must've been at least twenty.

With magic in their veins, most creatures could live forever, but if they were killed, they wouldn't come back from the dead. Only true immortals, those with the strongest magic, could die and return.

I should've known Rían would be one of the latter.

His father had been Midir, after all, a powerful fae known for slaughtering humans on the battlefield. His brother was the bloody Gancanagh. What about his mother? Was she as infamous and powerful?

"Who is your mother?"

Rían's entire body went rigid. "It doesn't matter."

For him to refuse the information, she must be terrible. Who could be worse than the Gancanagh? "Why won't you tell me?"

"Because it's none of your damned business." He shoved to his feet, anger rippling the air.

The ring on my finger felt like a dead weight as I sat up to face him. "You're asking me to trust you with my life. I think the least you could do is show me a little trust in return."

"You expect me to trust you?" he growled. "A feckin' human? Not a hope." He pointed to the ring I wore. "That's mine. As soon as you're dead, I'm taking it back."

Where was this coming from? All I'd done was ask a simple question.

I tried to breathe through my anger. To swallow it down, even though it burned like bile. "You can have it back now if you wish. Here. Take it and go away." As if I wanted to wear his hideous ring. I pulled the thing free and tossed it at him. The ring bounced off his chest and landed by his boot.

"Fine. I will." He snatched it up and shoved it into his pocket. "Fine."

"Fine." He flicked his wrist the way he did before he evanesced, except . . . nothing happened. His eyes widened. He tried it again. And again. And again. To no avail.

"Why isn't it working?"

"I don't feckin' know."

"Fix it."

"If I don't know what's wrong, I don't know how to fix it, now do I?" he ground out, trying and failing to leave the room.

Someone knocked on my door.

Rían's panicked expression mirrored my own. "You have to disappear," I hissed. "If anyone catches you in my bedroom, my life is over."

"At least then we wouldn't need my brother."

"Rían!" I kicked the bastard in the shin.

"Ow! All right, all right." He turned in a circle, presumably scanning the room for a place to hide.

"Just climb out the window."

"I'm not climbing out the feckin' window."

The person knocked again.

I didn't have time for his stubbornness.

"Fine. Get under the bed."

His nose wrinkled. "Is it clean? If there's dust, I'll sneeze."

The all-powerful fae prince with no power had *allergies*. Just my bloody luck. "Get in the closet and stay quiet."

"Aveen?" *Keelynn.* "Are you in there?"

"Just a moment. I'm . . . um . . . indisposed." I shoved Rían toward the closet doors. The space would be tight, but if he moved the dresses aside and hunkered down, he should fit. There wasn't time to make sure he was hidden before the door opened.

The dark shadows from the fading day were nothing compared to the dark smudges beneath my sister's eyes. "Can I come in?"

I wanted her to. Desperately. "I don't think you should."

"Oh," she startled. "I just wanted to apologize for the way I've been acting. I know none of this is your fault. That you wouldn't have chosen to marry Robert yourself. If there was any way around it, you'd find it. I just wanted to say that."

I had found a way around it. And if Rían weren't hiding in my closet, I would have told her everything. "It's going to be all right," I said, clasping her cold fingers. "I'll fix it."

"*Aaaachoo!*"

What in the world? That sounded like the daintiest sneeze I'd ever heard.

Keelynn's head snapped up, and her eyes narrowed. She glanced over my shoulder into the room. "Is there someone in there with you?"

"It's . . . um . . . Sylvia. She's helping me decide which dress to wear tomorrow." Lies. So many lies. When would they end?

"Really?" Keelynn folded her arms across her chest. "I just saw Sylvia on the stairs not five minutes ago, carrying a vase of flowers to the parlor."

Think, Aveen. Think.

"I . . . Um . . ." How did I explain a fae prince without explaining a fae prince?

"Aveen, dear? Do you mind helping me with these buttons? They are dreadfully hard to reach."

"Who is that?" Keelynn mouthed.

The woman's voice sounded unfamiliar. But it was definitely a woman.

A tall woman with black ringlets, wearing my dress.

A woman with cerulean blue eyes.

Bloody hell.

"This must be Keelynn," Rían said in a high, cheerful voice, bouncing over to my slack-jawed sister. "I have heard so much about you. Aveen talks of nothing else." He took her hand and gave it a vigorous shake.

Keelynn's eyebrows bunched over wide eyes. "That's right. Who are you?"

"Lady Marissa DeWarn, of course. Don't tell me Aveen has kept me a secret! You little minx." Rían smacked my shoulder, sending me back a step. "Aveen and I met a few weeks ago at the market. She has been such a dote, helping me settle into life here in Graystones. It's so different from Vellana. Dreadfully dreary and mundane. I could die of boredom."

"You're from Vellana?" Keelynn asked.

"Lady Marissa" nodded. "My brother is the ambassador, perhaps you remember him?"

What game was he playing? His lies kept piling up and up and up. It was only a matter of time before they came crashing down.

"Oh, Edward. Yes. I met him." A V formed between Keelynn's brows. "It's so strange I haven't met you though. He never mentioned a sister."

"That's because he's wretched," Rían said with a playful swat.

The first true thing he'd said.

"Thinks women should stay cooped up in the house, spending their time pushing needles and thread through bits of fabric and banging keys on the dreadful pianoforte."

Keelynn giggled. "If he believes that, then perhaps he is wretched. Are you staying for dinner, Lady Marissa?"

Rían said "yes" at the same time I said "no."

I glared at him. He was *not* coming to dinner.

"I'll, um, leave the two of you to sort that out. You should stay for dinner though. Aveen never has friends over. I was beginning to think I was her only friend." Keelynn's hesitant smile was as false as my own as she closed the door behind her.

Rían, still posing as a lady, waltzed over to look at himself in the mirror.

"What the hell do you think you're doing? *Lady Marissa?*"

"Have you seen the layer of dust at the back of your closet? You should fire your maid." He cupped his chest, lifting his breasts higher and turning from side to side as he admired his own figure.

"So, you have enough magic to turn yourself into a woman, and yet you cannot vanish?" How was that possible?

"It's a good thing too. Otherwise, that would've been dreadfully awkward." He twirled to check out his backside. "Does this dress make me look fat?"

"Rían!"

"All right. You don't need to yell. I'm standing right here." Rolling his eyes, he sauntered to my side. "I do not know why my magic is acting up. It has never done this. It's quite embarrassing. But you have to admit, I do make quite a stunning woman." He pulled out the front of his dress, smiling as he peered down.

I smacked his hand away. "Don't do that."

"Why not? They're mine, aren't they? Not as nice as yours, though," he mused, tapping his dainty chin. "Should I make them larger?"

Instead of swatting his hand, I caught it. "You can do whatever you want after you take one of my cloaks and leave out the front door."

"Leave?" Blue eyes widened. "My dear, why on earth would I leave when I've been invited to my fiancée's house for dinner?"

15

RÍAN, POSING AS LADY MARISSA, WORE MY FAVORITE NAVY-BLUE evening gown to dinner. Although I'd never admit it, the dress looked far better on him than it did on me. I had warned him within an inch of his life that if he was not on his best behavior, there'd be consequences. As to what those consequences would be, I hadn't the foggiest. After all, what could I do to him that would have any impact?

Keelynn must've informed our father that we'd be having a guest, because when we arrived there were four place settings at the mammoth dining table instead of three. My father had his usual spot at the head, with Keelynn to his right, and Rían and me to his left.

When our father met "Lady Marissa," he pressed a kiss to the back of her hand and welcomed her to our home. Instead of taking the farthest seat, Rían had the gall to sit in the one right next to him.

"So, Lady Marissa, how are you finding life in Graystones?" my father asked after the wine had been poured and our first dish, braised pork belly, had been served. He couldn't keep his eyes off the prince. And who could blame him? Symmetrical features, lashes like fans, rosy, red lips. I would've killed for "Lady Marissa's" cheekbones.

I had to keep reminding myself who he was.

That he wasn't real.

"It is quite dreadful, isn't it?" Rían sipped his wine daintily. "Life here is so tedious and backwards. Can you imagine, the menfolk are so archaic that they believe a woman's only worth is her ability to marry a wealthy man? Poppycock."

Keelynn choked on her wine. Muttering an apology, she attempted to hide her smile behind a gloved hand.

"But I can tell you are different, Lord Bannon," Rían went on. "You are a modern man. Very forward thinking."

My father's chest puffed out like a strutting cockerel. "It is kind of you to notice."

Heavens above. Rían needed to stop filling his head with nonsense.

And I needed more wine. I tilted the bottle into my glass, filling it a bit more than I should since no one seemed to be paying me any attention. And why would they, with someone as *fascinating* and *enthralling* as a shapeshifting fae prince at the table?

"Keelynn was telling me you moved here from Vellana. It must be taxing for someone who is used to the splendor of a fine city to relocate to such a humble town. Nevertheless, we have our hidden gems."

"Speaking of gems, your home is quite lovely." Rían nodded in approval as he scanned the room, from the glowing sconces to the tall windows and back again. "Is it an ancestral seat for the Bannons?"

Houses and ancestry. Next would be the weather. My father loved talking about the weather. It rained a lot. What more was there to say? Thankfully, one of the servants set out a fresh bottle of wine. I mixed it with what little remained in my glass, watching my father shake his head.

"This house was a gift from the king himself for service," he said proudly. "The previous tenant met an untimely demise. His Majesty needed a man with strong ties to Vellana to live here, lest the property fall into the hands of those who sympathized with the monsters."

The drink in my mouth went down wrong, leaving me choking and spluttering.

Rían's eyes flashed. A slow smile curled on his lips. He wouldn't hurt my father. He wouldn't.

Except, he would. He'd let the Dullahan kill his former lover. He had no affinity for me or my family.

"Is that right?" Rían drawled, spinning the stem of his wine glass between slender, feminine fingers. The wine began to bubble as if it were champagne.

"I'm afraid Lord Middleton was caught communicating with one of the things claiming to be their leader and hanged for treason."

Keelynn's face turned green.

I had to intercede before it was too late. "How about this wine?" I lifted my glass aloft with an unsteady hand. "It tastes wonderful. It might be my new favorite."

"Treason you say?" Rían pressed a hand to his throat. "How scandalous."

"If you ask me, the lot of them should be exterminated like the rats they are. *Magic*," my father spat. "Unnatural. An abomination. A blight on this once-great island."

"How about this weather?" I blurted. "It rained today. Probably going to rain again tomorrow."

Keelynn patted my father's hand, nodding in agreement.

Steam rose from the bubbling wine in Rían's glass.

When my father opened his mouth to speak again, I slammed my hand on the table, sending the saltshaker onto my empty plate.

"Father!"

Three pairs of eyes landed on me.

"I believe a lighter topic would be more appropriate dinner

conversation. We wouldn't want such dark stories to make our guest uncomfortable, now would we?"

"There's no need to change topics on my behalf," Rían said with a shrug. The wine had stopped bubbling. "I've always been fascinated by the macabre. The bloodier, the better."

In my haste to reach for more wine, I knocked the bottle onto its side. One of the servants rushed from the alcove to right it and throw a serviette on top of the stained tablecloth. It was only a matter of time before my father started giving out about my lack of manners.

"No, no. Aveen is right," my father said with a long-suffering sigh, like being surrounded by women had become incredibly tedious. "I wouldn't want to offend your delicate sensibilities, Lady Marissa."

Delicate sensibilities. Ha.

If I didn't fill the silence, my father was bound to say something else offensive.

I started blathering about the gardens and my plans for a new raised bed along the southern wall. By the time I finished, the dishes had been cleared, and everyone's eyes had gone glazed.

Everyone's except Rían's.

He sat there, watching me with such an unnatural intensity that I had to look away. Even with my attention focused on what little wine I had left, I could still feel the heat of his stare boring into the side of my head.

"I didn't realize you were so invested in bringing life to the world," Rían said once I'd finished.

"I wouldn't call throwing a few bulbs in the ground 'bringing life.'"

"What would you call it?"

"A hobby."

"Hobby? More like an obsession. Aveen loves gardening," Keelynn chimed in. "I think it's the only place she is truly happy."

Rían's eyes lit up like two blue flames. "We have gardens that bloom year round."

It was the first time he'd divulged information about his life without me having to pry. Not that it was much. Gardens blooming year round. Were their flowers the same as ours? I imagined they'd be more stunning. Bigger, brighter, and better than anything that grew in Airren. If I had magic, I'd make flowers grow from everywhere. The windows. The ceiling. The floor.

"At the townhouse?" Keelynn asked, drawing me from my useless fantasy.

Townhouse? What townhouse? Rían didn't live in a townhouse.

Rían shook his head, as if snapping out of a trance. "Not in the townhouse. Back in . . . in Vellana."

"Lady Marissa and her brother are renting a townhouse near the modiste," Keelynn explained to our father. He nodded as though he'd known all along.

"Just until something larger and more permanent becomes available," Rían added smoothly.

How did he keep track of all the lies?

The grandfather clock in the corner chimed. I'd been so focused on Rían's performance that I hadn't realized it was so late.

"Would you look at the time?" My father threw his serviette onto the table. His chair scraped the tiles when he pushed back. "Lady Marissa, your company has been a delight. I do hope to see more of you in the future."

Rían stood, smoothing a hand down his wrinkled skirts. "I'm sure you will. Your daughter and I have grown quite close over the last few weeks. I cannot imagine life here without her."

More lies to add to the list.

"You're not leaving, are you?" my sister asked, brow creased with worry as her eyes darted to the dark windows. She'd been afraid of the dark since childhood. "You should stay. There's plenty of space."

Stay? Oh no . . . She did not just invite Rían to stay the night.

I shot to my feet and grabbed his hand, squeezing as hard as I could. The bastard didn't so much as flinch. "He—I mean *she* cannot stay." I propped my hip against the edge of the table to keep from falling over. Why was I so dizzy? "There's that thing you have to do in the morning. Remember?"

Keelynn rounded the table to take Rían's other hand. "Oh, but she must. It is far too late to bring her back into Graystones. You know the roads aren't safe at night."

Rían batted those lashes at me, eyes glinting. "Your lovely sister has a point. I hear wicked creatures prowl these forests from dusk until dawn."

Rían was the wickedest creature of the whole bloody lot.

"It isn't as dangerous as all that," my father countered, rolling his eyes, "but I must agree with Keelynn. You should stay here tonight. Stay as long as you'd like."

"Why, thank you, Lord Bannon." Rían curtsied. "You are most kind."

"Come, Marissa." Keelynn tugged him past my father, out of the dining room, and toward the staircase. "I'll show you up to the spare room."

No . . . Not the spare room.

The spare bedroom was beside Keelynn's. There was no way I would let a mischievous fae prince stay in a room next to my sister. No bloody way.

I raced toward the hallway, colliding with the doorframe on my way to get to them before they reached the top of the stairs. My stupid bloody skirt caught on my stupid bloody slipper, and I nearly toppled headfirst into stupid bloody Rían.

I caught Rían's hand, tugging him away from Keelynn. "Marissa will need something to sleep in, and your night dresses will be far too slim."

Keelynn shrugged, said goodnight with a little wave, and drifted off toward her chambers.

Instead of bringing him to the spare bedroom, I led him into mine. The moment the door closed, I whirled. "This has gone on long enough. You need to go away. Now."

He flicked his wrist but didn't evanesce. "Looks like you're stuck with me a little while longer. Could you imagine what would happen if it never came back and I had to stay here forever?" His grating chuckle made me want to slap him.

"I can't think of anything worse."

He tugged one of my curls, letting it spring back against my cheek. "She's feisty when she's drunk. I like it."

When I tried to prop my fists on my hips, they slipped. "I'm not drunk."

"I've known my fair share of drunk women, and you, my dear, are sozzled." He flicked me on the nose. "Now, if the drunk lady would kindly show me to the spare room, I would like to get out of this feckin' corset." Wincing, he dragged a hand across the boning at his waist.

"You're not staying in the spare room. You can stay here." I grabbed my favorite pillow from beneath the quilt. "I'll take the spare room. But you must promise not to leave this chamber."

His grin widened. "I promise."

"I mean it, Rían. You must swear on your own life that you will not set one foot out of this room."

"I swear."

He was lying. *Dammit.* How was I going to ensure he didn't go near my sister? The moment I left the room, he'd probably evanesce right into her chamber and use his fae "charms" to woo her into heaven knows what.

I threw the pillow at his smirking face and stomped to my armoire to drag out two sleeping gowns. If I'd owned a pair of iron chains, I'd have chained him up in the closet. "Change into this. You can sleep on my floor."

"I'm not sleeping on a floor when there's a perfectly good bed right there."

"You're not sleeping with me."

"*Not drunk, my arse,*" he muttered, rolling his eyes. "You're sleeping in the spare bedroom, remember?"

"It is clear that I cannot trust you to stay on your own. I will stay here all night and guard you." I held the night dress toward him. When he didn't take it, I tossed it at him.

He caught it, balled it up, and threw it back. "I don't need a guard. Show me to the spare room, and I will be gone by morning."

"I don't trust you!"

My furniture rattled as if in the tremors of an earthquake. He was no longer Lady Marissa but Rían, eyes glowing with barely contained rage. "Then let's call this whole thing off."

"Fine." He wouldn't hold me hostage any longer. "What do I need you for, anyway? I will simply ask Meranda to get a message to your brother and bargain with him instead." Perhaps I'd ask him to do it tonight, so I didn't have to go through with any more of the wedding planning.

Rían's lips twisted into a vicious smile. "I'm sure Tadhg would be more than happy to oblige. Although I can't help but wonder what poor Padraig would say if he learned you were off bargaining with the Gancanagh." Folding his arms over his chest, he tapped his pointed chin. "Speaking of Padraig, wouldn't it be a pity if someone were to tell the Airren authorities that your beloved coachman has been using an illegal glamour for the last three decades?"

No . . . Padraig . . . "You wouldn't."

"Would I not?" he sneered.

How could I have believed for one second that I held the upper hand? That I had any bargaining power? I had come to him empty handed and desperate, and he was using that desperation to keep me beneath his thumb. What a fool I'd been, inviting the monster back into my life when he'd turned his sights elsewhere.

Rían stepped so close, I could see his pupils dilate. "Now, where is that spare room?"

"You're not sleeping there. You're sleeping here." I snatched up the fallen night dress and brought it behind the changing screen. Once I'd changed and layered on my dressing gown, I avoided looking at Rían as he settled himself beneath my covers.

He'd draped his waistcoat and cravat over the edge of my chair. His boots waited by the fireplace. He was still in his shirt, and since I couldn't see them, I assumed he still wore his breeches as well.

I dragged a crocheted blanket from the top of my closet, collected my pillow from the floor, and curled onto the chaise, keeping my back to my unwanted guest.

"Are you seriously going to stay there all night?" he clipped.

Somewhere between agreeing to die and his threat to kill Padraig, I'd lost the will to fight.

A draft came from beneath the window as the winds outside raged. Nights like tonight were the only nights I didn't enjoy living near the sea. In a book of old Airren myths I'd read as a girl, it was said that when the winds and waves ravaged the shore on a moonless night, the banshee culled the sea of its dead.

"Aveen, you are being ridiculous."

The floorboards creaked alarmingly close to where I huddled. Rían scooped me up and threw me unceremoniously onto the bed.

"I cannot share a bed with you!"

The bastard chuckled. "Don't worry. You're about as appealing as a raw turnip when you squeal like that."

The mattress dipped next to me, and I pulled the covers to my chin. This wasn't happening. This was *not* happening. I'd pretend to sleep until he actually fell asleep and then I would go back to the chaise. I was *not* going to sleep with Rían.

"If you touch me, I'll kill you."

Weighted silence stretched between us. When I turned, I found him staring at me, a wrinkle between his drawn eyebrows. "What have I done to make you believe I would force myself on you?"

"In the shed, you—"

"Stopped the moment I realized you weren't Eithne." He rolled his eyes.

"In the garden, you—"

"Saved you from being the Dullahan's next meal? I'm not a good man by any means, but there are lines even I will not cross." Taking a deep breath, he placed a hand over his heart. "Tonight, I swear on pain of death that I will not lay a hand on you. Unless you beg me to," he added with a wicked glint in his eyes.

"Like that would ever happen. I'm not even attracted to you."

His chest rose and fell as he inhaled a deep breath through his nose, a smile playing on his lips. "I love it when you lie."

"It's not a lie. You're a disgusting troll."

"A troll?" His grating chuckle vibrated all the way to my toes. "So you're not the least bit tempted to kiss me?"

"Not the least." I couldn't think of anything more revolting than having his perfect lips caress mine again. *Disgusting.*

Rían's long fingers drummed against the quilt, close to my thigh but never touching. "Then it's safe for me to assume that you have no desire for me to slip you out of that shift and taste every inch of you."

My toes curled against the sheet.

That sounded . . . *awful.*

"You shouldn't say things like that to me." I couldn't imagine how terrible and . . . and . . . *revolting* it would be to have his mouth exploring the most intimate parts of my body. It'd probably be the worst experience in the history of worst experiences.

He arched an eyebrow. "Does it make you uncomfortable?"

"Yes." Terribly, deliciously uncomfortable.

He inhaled again. "Do you like it?"

"N-no."

His dimples deepened when he laughed, a carefree, almost happy sound. "Oh, my dear. You have no idea how bad a liar you are. It's quite endearing."

No one had ever seen through my lies. Why him? Why now? "I'm not lying," I insisted, grinding my teeth.

Sighing, he tucked a hand behind his head and rolled onto his back to stare up at the canopy. "I can taste the lies when they fall from your lips. They're sweet, like honeysuckle."

Another lie. It had to be. People couldn't taste lies . . . could they?

Bloody hell.

If that was true, then he knew every word I'd said to him since he threw me into this bed had been a lie.

"A good liar sticks as close to the truth as possible," he went on. "A great liar mixes the two. You don't bother. You say what you believe you're supposed to say in order to make others happy or save face. It's fascinating."

I felt exposed, stripped bare. Every time I had lied to him, he'd known. He'd bloody known. How was that fair? Did humans have any advantage at all? Why did he get to be powerful and free while I got to be weak and controlled?

"Ah, here now. There's no need to get cross."

"I'm not cross."

His brows arched toward the hair falling across his forehead.

Dammit.

Arrogance oozed from his smarmy smile.

I punched his shoulder, wishing I had magic so I could put a bloody curse on him.

Rían laughed as if the blow hadn't even registered. "Careful now, human. Striking a prince has dire consequences."

Prince. Prince of what? Darkness and deceit? I hit him again for good measure.

He hissed, and his eyes began to glow as he rubbed his bicep. "Do it again and see what happens."

Do it again.

Technically, he'd given me permission.

See what happens.

I'd consumed enough alcohol to make foolish decisions.

I balled my hand into a fist and gave him a good wallop on the shoulder. He flew upright, sending me tumbling back onto the mattress in a useless attempt to escape. Something snaked around my wrists. When I checked, I found only air and shadows. The invisible bonds tightened, drawing my arms over my head until my fingers brushed the headboard. Not painful, but unyielding and undeniably there. Another force pressed across my hips, pinning me in place.

Rían planted his hands on either side of my head, his glowing eyes glazed and unfocused as he lowered his face to mine. Our breaths mingled, his exhale becoming my inhale, a heady winter cocktail of wine and cinnamon.

"You said you wouldn't touch me," I choked, my voice not the only part of me trembling as panic seized my chest. "You swore on pain of death."

Fool. I'd forgotten myself and pushed him too far.

His hair tickled my cheek as his nose grazed the column of my throat. "Ah, but I like pain and enjoy death." He inhaled deep, his chest brushing mine. In my ear, he said, "And I swore not to lay a *hand* on you." His fingers tapped the pillow beneath my head. His voice dropped to a whisper. "What you fail to realize, *human*, is that I do not need my hands to make you come undone. I could use my mouth." He pressed a kiss to my pulse. "My teeth." He nipped my jaw. "My tongue." Flames swirled over the spot where he'd bitten me. "My cock." His hips rocked once. There was no mistaking what nudged against my thigh. "My magic." The bonds around my wrists and hips squeezed.

"I'd let you choose, Aveen. Choose how I unravel you."

The truth was, he hadn't needed any of those things.

All it took were his whispers to unravel me like a spool of thread and leave me in a tangled mess.

"I hate you," I breathed. His arrogance. His cocky smile. His dimples.

Most of all, I hated the way he made me yearn for dark, forbidden things.

Men controlled my world.

I refused to let one control my body. Or my heart.

"First honest thing you've said all night," he chuckled, rolling back to his side of the bed and settling himself deeper into the pillow. With a flick of his wrist, the bonds holding me evaporated.

I dragged the covers from where they'd slipped to my waist back to my chin. "You are the worst person I've ever met."

"Another truth. Very good." He gave me a sidelong glance. "Does violent Aveen have any more confessions?"

I yanked the covers off him, tugging them around myself before rolling onto my side. The arrogant prince could freeze to death for all I cared.

"Ah, here now, sullen Aveen is no fun. Bring back the violent one."

I kicked him.

The bastard chuckled.

16

THIS MORNING, I CRAVED THE FEELING OF MY HANDS SINKING INTO the earth. Mud beneath my fingernails, settling in the lines of my skin. Anything and everything to burn away the memories of Rían.

Rían.

Rude, condescending, manipulative Rían.

Rían, who made me burn with every look. Every touch. Every inappropriate suggestion.

Rían, who'd left my bed at some point in the middle of the night.

Rían, who still remained a mystery.

Footsteps on gravel sounded from the direction of the rose garden. Before I could stand and dust the dirt from my skirts, Robert rounded the corner.

Brilliant.

Just what I didn't need this morning. My head pounded like a blacksmith's hammer. I hadn't had nearly enough sleep to deal with him.

When he saw me, he had the gall to smile. Then his gaze fell to my dirt-smeared skirt, and his nose wrinkled.

"Good morning, Robert." He wasn't worth getting up for, so I grabbed a bulb from the canvas sack and set to burying it in the raised bed beside a stone cherub.

"From this day forward, I expect you to greet me with a kiss. I am your fiancé, after all."

This time, when my trowel sank into the dirt, I imagined I was digging his grave. "I'd rather kiss a goat." My hand flew to my mouth. What was wrong with me? I never spoke to him like that. Never.

Robert snorted. "Kiss a goat?"

I shot to my feet, sending the trowel clattering to the ground. "I'm sorry. I don't know what came over me."

Robert's smarmy smile lifted, leaving dread churning my stomach.

And then he turned into a goat.

A goat with blue eyes.

I grabbed my trowel and aimed it at the bloody fae. "Change back. Now."

The goat became an irritating prince. "*Ohhhh* look who's back. Violent Aveen. If you're going to stab me with your tiny shovel, would you mind cleaning it first? This is a new shirt." He patted his pristine white sleeve.

I pulled a clump of dirt from my skirts. The cold, wet mud oozed between my fingers when I squished it into a ball . . . and launched it at his head.

He vanished at the last second, leaving the ball to fall into the grass.

"I could turn you into ash, you know," he snarled into my ear.

The wind picked up, fluttering the waxy leaves on the laurels. If Rían truly planned on turning me to ash, he'd hardly warn me first.

Having him this near made me feel things that I shouldn't want to feel. Dark, dangerous things. Reminding me of his confessions last night.

Choose how I unravel you.

I needed him far, *far* away.

"If you turned me to ash," I whispered, trying not to inhale, "then the breeze could blow me against your precious, clean shirt." I whirled and dragged my hands down his sleeves, leaving a trail of brown streaks in their wake.

Rían let out an indignant yelp. The look of sheer horror contorting his features left me doubling over in a fit of laughter until a wet palm slid across my cheek. Cold muck slipped down my face, plopping onto my chest.

"There." Rían smiled, even as he kept his dirty hand well away from his clothes. "Now, we're even." With a flick of his wrist, his shirt and hand were clean.

I scrubbed my cheek and slapped mud onto his black waistcoat. "*Now* we're even."

Rían kicked a mound of mud toward me, splattering my skirts.

I stomped in a puddle, soaking us both.

Rían magically appeared in a clean outfit.

If I'd had his magic, I would have picked up the entire wheelbarrow of topsoil and dumped it over his head. I supposed I'd have to make do with a handful. Black soil spilled down his ears, over his collar, and onto shoulders.

Loosing a string of vicious profanity, Rían unfastened the buttons at his throat, continuing until his shirt gaped open over his tanned, toned chest. A thick silver scar shaped like a crude **X** marred the skin over his heart. I told myself to turn away. My feet didn't budge. I commanded my eyes to close. If anything, they widened as Rían untucked his shirt from the bottom of his breeches and shook the fabric, sprinkling the grass with black earth.

Another curse. Another flick. Another clean shirt.

This one I covered in compost.

"That's it. You're finished." Rían stalked forward, sending me back and back until the branches from the laurels stabbed my spine. Trapped. Paralyzed. A mouse staring into the narrowed eyes of a hungry cat. The pounding in my chest filled my ears.

I expected another flick of his wrist. Instead, Rían lunged, caught me by the thighs, and threw me over his shoulder. This was worse. Far worse.

Budding flowers and discarded gardening tools witnessed my humiliation as Rían started toward the trees at the edge of my father's property. If I had any strength at all, I would've beaten him until he released me.

"Put me down this instant!" The sea sang in the distance, rhythmic and violent as the darkness gathering in my core. A forbidden song forming deep in my marrow.

"If you wanted to get me undressed, all you had to do was say 'please.' You didn't have to ruin my feckin' clothes."

Unbidden heat collected in my stomach when I thought of the ridges of his abdomen. The cut of his chest. That strange scar. I scrubbed my grimy hands down his back, painting his black waistcoat mucky brown.

Rían cursed again. "Stop that! I don't have any more clean shirts." His fingers tightened where they gripped my thighs. If I weren't so angry and he weren't so irritating, I may have liked the way his hands felt. Strong. Possessive.

"The fancy prince doesn't own more than four shirts?" *Don't think about his hands. Don't think about his hands.* "Poor fancy prince. You really are cursed. The curse of four shirts. Lucky for you, I know how to break it. See, there's a place in town where you can buy such things."

"I have more than four feckin' shirts, you wretched human. But the others aren't pressed." The pine needles beneath his boots left his footsteps completely silent. A misty breeze blew in off the coast, smelling of fish and seaweed. Waves slammed against the shore, then retreated to the sea only to come crashing back again.

I thumped him on the back. "Heaven forbid someone sees you in a wrinkled shirt."

"Do it again and see what happens."

The same warning he'd given me last night.

Choose how I unravel you.

He kept trekking down the pebbled beach toward the waves, his feet never faltering despite the shifting stones. He wasn't going to throw me into the sea. He was bluffing. I would freeze to death.

"Put me down." Wiggling only had him tightening his hold. "I mean it. This isn't funny anymore. Put me down. I'll not go in the sea. I won't."

"Next time you'll think twice about covering me in shite, now won't you?"

As if there would be a next time. "If you put me in that water, I'll—" A wall of icy liquid stole the words from my mouth. The thoughts from my head. The air from my lungs. Salt water burned my eyes. All I could see were bubbles rising from endless darkness.

When I finally managed to get my legs beneath me, Rían was gone. My scream of frustration was cut short when a dark head emerged an arm's length away.

A smile tugged at Rían's lips. Not a sneer or a smirk. A full-on, impish grin. Drops of seawater rolled down his forehead. His straight nose. His dimples. His chin. *His mouth.*

"There. Don't you feel better now that you're clean?" he taunted, splashing me in the face.

I launched myself at him before he could disappear. For some reason that I could only put down to as hypothermia-induced madness, instead of strangling him, I crushed my lips against his.

He tasted like saltwater and hysteria. Bad decisions and destiny. And magic. Sweet, intoxicating magic. Every nerve in my body came alive, buzzing with the heat of anticipation and desire. My sole focus was his mouth moving on mine. Hungry. Devouring. Devastating.

Rían's hands slipped around my back, cupping my bottom, lifting and fitting my legs around his trim hips, pressing himself against where I ached. I gripped him as tightly as I could, so that not even a drop separated us. He lost his fingers in my tangled mass of hair, tasting and taking until my chin began to quiver and my muscles seized.

"Why is it like this with you?" I breathed.

"Stop talking," he begged against my lips, lifting and rocking me against him, fanning the flames.

"Rían—" Was this the way humans felt when they kissed one of the creatures? The nature of magic and forbidden desire? The hysteria. The madness.

"For the love of all that is holy, shut your beautiful mouth and —" Rían dropped me so suddenly, I didn't have time to catch my breath before slipping beneath the waves.

I came up sputtering and cursing.

"*Quiet*." He caught my arm, shoving my body behind his.

My chest heaved as I gasped in unsteady breaths. His shirt clung to his lean frame the same way I had only moments ago. The way I still wanted to. Rían went as still as stone, staring toward the darkened water rising and falling along the horizon.

"What is it?" The swirling current tugged and twisted my skirts.

He didn't spare me so much as a glance. "Merrow."

"Merrow don't live in our sea." The half-human creatures with fish-like tails rumored to lure humans to their deaths lived on the pages of books, in fishermen's lore, and off Tearmann's coast.

Rían threw out a hand above the waves and clenched his fist. "Then what is this?" Water droplets rolled down his bare forearm to the sleeve bunched at his elbow. A haunting screech echoed toward the gray clouds as a writhing form lifted from the waves.

The thing, which was the size of a human, turned vicious, setting her bulging eyes on me, clawing at her throat with webbed fingers. Her skin was the blue of a drowned corpse, her breasts small and bare. Shimmering blue and green scales covered the tail where her legs should have been. She hissed, revealing a row of jagged black teeth.

"I'm in no mood to play today," Rían drawled, offering the creature a sardonic smile. "Tell your friends to return to the depths, or I'll boil the feckin' ocean and feed you to my mother for dinner."

He opened his hand, and the merrow fell into the waves with a splash. A moment later, at least twenty tails shimmered in the gray light, darting toward deeper water.

I began to shake, and not just from the cold. What would have happened if Rían hadn't been here with me? Would they have tried to lure me into the depths? Would I have been able to resist their siren's call?

The muscles in my arms and legs ached like I'd been swimming for hours. If I didn't get out now, mythical sea monsters wouldn't be my only problem. I twisted toward the shore, my heavy skirts making it feel like I was wading through a bog. Rían's splashing movements sounded like they were right behind me.

"Get out of that dress before you die from the cold," he ordered, like the idea of me dying was more of an inconvenience than a tragedy. All signs of the teasing, dimpled man I'd kissed had been washed away.

Probably for the best. Rían was hard enough to resist when he was being awful. What chance did I have if he decided to be charming?

"And wear what?" I shot back.

A dress magically appeared, stretched across the stones. I didn't thank him; my disastrous state was his fault.

Rían conjured a massive fire of tented driftwood, instantly bringing warmth back to my bones. "Hurry it on. I have places to be."

"T-then go. I d-d-don't want your h-help." With my chin trembling so badly, I sounded pathetic and weak when I wanted to sound angry.

"Will I take back the dress and leave you in that then?" His stormy blue gaze drifted down my body, lingering on my breasts. My hips. My thighs.

I didn't want him looking at me like that. I didn't want him looking at me at all. "T-turn around."

With a long-suffering sigh, he twisted so his back was to me. I took a moment to study his outline, silhouetted against gray clouds. So perfect on the outside. What a shame his soul was rotten.

I tried to work the ties free on my dress. Removing clothing was hard enough when the garments were dry. Wet? Impossible. Everything stuck together, and my frozen fingers couldn't open one damned button. My arms felt like they weighed ten stone. Eventually, the shivering got so bad, I was afraid it'd start a bloody earthquake.

Then came the sound of ripping fabric, and the top of my dress fell away. I clutched my hand over a torn seam to keep my breasts from spilling free. When I whirled around, Rían was still staring at the sea.

I peeled myself out of the heavy garment and let it slop onto the stones.

Sea birds circled overhead, their lonely caws echoing against the vast expanse of nothing. The breeze kicked up, and I changed as quickly as I could into the dry gown made of the softest navy-blue cotton and long blue cloak lined with fur that appeared a moment later.

"I'll have you know that was my favorite gardening dress."

"And I'll have you know this was my favorite shirt." Rían had changed back into the shirt with two dirty handprints on the sleeves.

"All you have to do is wash it."

"Are you asking me to go for another swim?" he threw over his shoulder, wiggling his eyebrows.

I told him to shove off.

I would rather take my chances with the murderous merrow than swim with him.

"I spoke to my brother this morning," he said, drawing his knees to his chest. "He'll meet you in the garden on the night of your betrothal ball."

That meant I had one week left.

One week to pretend. One week to live.

"Why then?"

"The more witnesses, the better. Wouldn't want anyone to think you're faking your own death."

I wouldn't be faking it though. I'd actually be dying, no longer in this world but part of whatever lay beyond. "How long will it take for me to come back?"

He picked up a skinny piece of driftwood, snapped it in half, and tossed it into the fire. "It'll feel like you just closed your eyes."

"That's not an answer."

Rían winced.

"Tell me," I demanded.

"I can't."

"Yes, you can."

"No, I mean I physically can't. It's part of my brother's curse. But I can tell you this." He held up a finger.

"What's that?"

Rolling his eyes, he gestured to the digit.

"One?" I said slowly.

He nodded.

"One day?" I guessed.

He shook his head.

"One week?" Another shake. "One month?" I started to panic when he winced and shook his head again. "One *year*?"

Rían gave me a sardonic clap.

I shot to my feet. "I'm going to be dead for a bloody year? Are you mad?"

"A lifetime of misery, a year of death, or destitution for your family. Those are your choices, are they not?"

"How do you know about my family's . . . financial difficulties?"

"I make it a point to learn all I can about those who wish to bargain with me."

With the options listed so clinically, it felt like I'd chosen the best of the lot.

Still . . . a *year*?

That may not have seemed like a long time to a powerful

immortal like Rían, but it was three hundred and sixty-five days of my life I would never get back.

Keelynn was the only person who would truly miss me. "Who will you torment while I'm gone?" I asked, dropping back to the rocks.

"Probably some orphan. Or a heartbroken widow. Or a crippled old man."

I picked up a stone and tossed it at his back. "You are awful."

He chuckled, not bothering to dodge it the way he had the mud. "I know."

"Will you be there when I wake?"

His shoulders stiffened. "No."

For some reason, I had expected him to say yes.

"But I will ensure you are kept somewhere safe," he went on, collecting another sliver of wood to twirl between his fingers. "And then you can put all this nastiness behind you, and live out the rest of your short human life playing in dirt."

"Until you come to collect your favor."

His smile faltered before he turned back toward the flames. "Right. Until then."

A year. That was all.

And when I came back, I could go . . . *anywhere.*

Anywhere I wanted any time I pleased. I could stay in Airren or travel to Vellana. Or Iodale. Or the continent. It would be up to me.

My choice.

Only mine.

I'd want a base though. Somewhere to call home. A place for Keelynn to visit. And Padraig.

I closed my eyes, envisioning the whitewashed cottage from my dream. "A cottage by the sea." I inhaled the salty air. "With a garden."

Preferably with two bedrooms, one for my sister when she visited and one for me.

One would work as well, I supposed. We'd shared a bed plenty of times before. It might be nice to huddle up and pretend we were still young and carefree.

When I opened my eyes, I found Rían staring at me, his head tilted.

"That's what I would've wished for," I explained, tugging the hem of the dress to cover my bare feet, gritty from the sand beneath the stones. "A place of my own where I could live as I chose without anyone telling me what to do. What to wear. Who to marry." I could sell flowers in the market and grow my own vegetables. It would be a simple life but one that belonged to me.

"If you could have anything in the world, you'd want a shack and some flowers?" Snorting, Rían added more bits of wood to the fire. "Humans are so disappointing."

I snagged another stone and threw it at his back. "All right, almighty prince. What would you wish for?"

The ghost of a dimple appeared as he peered down at his clenched hands. "Someone took something precious from me long ago. If I could have anything in the world, I would make her pay for it with her life."

I understood wanting someone to suffer. I thought of Lady Eithne. I'd hated the woman for years. But now that she was gone, I realized her death hadn't fixed anything.

It hadn't taken away my guilt.

It hadn't brought Charlie back.

Her suffering was just that. *Her* suffering.

It hadn't eased mine.

"You'd honestly rather punish the person than have the item returned?" I asked.

Rían's penetrating gaze met mine.

"Sounds like a waste of a wish to me," I said, standing and brushing off my skirts.

Rían could keep his vengeance.

All I wanted was a shack and some flowers.

17

THE WOOLLY GRAY CLOUDS HOVERING OVERHEAD LOOKED AS IF one poke would flood the entire town.

"You're awfully chipper for a woman claiming she doesn't want to get married," Keelynn grumbled, trudging by my side toward the first of three stops.

"I'm trying to make the best of things," I told her.

Our father had met me on the back patio with a to-do list of useless tasks for a wedding that wouldn't happen.

When I finished them, I wanted to swing by Dame Meranda's. Padraig had delivered her a trunk of my dresses, along with a note explaining my desire to sell the lot. She was the only one I trusted to give me a fair price. I would need funds to start my new life. I had a little in savings, along with the few pieces of my mother's jewelry that she'd left to me. I didn't want to sell those but would if it came down to it.

Somewhere between my father's house and town, it struck me: Keelynn may be the one marrying Robert in the end. If that was the case, I was planning her wedding, not mine.

Tarnett's dressmakers was empty at this hour, with most people enjoying lunch in the pubs and tea houses around town. Dresses and bolts of fabric had been organized into neat rows along the walls, nothing like the mayhem inside Meranda's cluttered shop.

I collected a deep burgundy day gown from one of the racks, holding it against my chest. The color didn't suit, and I'd never have a chance of fitting into the thing.

On Keelynn, though, it would be a vision. "What do you think of this one?" I asked.

Keelynn traced the lace along a daring evening gown with no back. "Why does it matter what I think?"

"Come on? Please?" A pang of guilt struck my heart. Would she forgive me for what I was about to do? She'd be upset at first, but Robert would be there to comfort her.

A sigh. "It's beautiful."

Anything she smiled at or seemed to linger over I added to the growing stack of items for Lord Trench's tab. The dressmaker skipped behind me, pulling dresses from hangers and dress forms and bolts of cloth, piling them on the main counter. With the tower ready to topple, I figured we'd bought enough.

I pulled a folded piece of paper from my purse and slipped it into the woman's hand. "I would like all of the dresses made to these measurements."

Her thin brows pulled together. "I have your measurements on file, Lady Aveen."

"Not the ones on file," I said, too low for Keelynn to overhear from where she loitered next to the entrance. "Use the ones I've written down."

Our second stop was to the designer making my wedding gown. I told her that I had started the tea-and-brown-bread diet she'd suggested and needed my gown altered to the same measurements I'd given the first woman.

The next shop—and my favorite of the lot—was the florist.

The heady scent of roses filled the air in the converted chapel. I touched the feather-soft petals on a hydrangea bloom. My sister's favorite flowers. "For the church and my bouquet, I'm thinking of going with these." When I turned around with a cluster in my hands, Keelynn's face fell.

"Shouldn't you choose your favorite flower?" she sighed.

"I think having white flowers at a wedding is more timeless."

Tears brimmed in her eyes. Bless Keelynn: her heart was breaking, and yet she forced a smile. "They're perfect."

I ordered the bouquet and decorations for the church, knowing full well I wouldn't be there. Once we finished, we stepped out of the florist's shop into the market.

The fish monger called from his stall, waving people toward what was left of his catch. Next to him, Farmer Warren tied bunches of blooms with twine, settling them in clumps next to a basket of dirt-crusted potatoes.

Keelynn started up the street toward the carriage.

When I didn't immediately follow, she stopped to give me a questioning look.

"I need to go to Dame Meranda's," I told her.

"For what? You've already bought an entire year's worth of dresses."

"For something special."

Rolling her eyes, Keelynn drew her cloak closed over her stunning emerald-green dress. "My feet hurt. I'm going back to the carriage with Padraig. I'll wait for you there."

I could taste her disappointment, bitter and sour as the smells wafting from the pub across the street.

It's all for you, I wanted to scream.

"Keelynn." I caught my sister's wrist. "You know I do not love Robert, right? I'm not going to marry him," I vowed, to my sister, to myself, to the folks not paying us one bit of attention as they ventured from one stall to the next. "I'm going to fix this. All of it."

She gestured toward the dress shop. "But you just paid for your trousseau."

"Father insists I do all of these things, and I am complying so he doesn't get suspicious. I have a plan. I'm going to—" Pain shot through my head, and the confession died in a strangled choke.

Keelynn's eyebrows lifted as I struggled with the truth.

"There's something I must tell you," I tried again, gasping and gripping her shoulders. "I'm not—" The pain was too excruciating. I couldn't get it out without collapsing.

Bloody Rían.

What had he done to me?

"I will make this right," I managed, my gaze landing on the brick townhouse next to Dame Meranda's that the wicked prince had claimed to be renting.

Keelynn sighed. "Your hands are as tied as mine. Just get your last few bits and meet me in the carriage." Her posture remained rigid as she swept past the fortune teller's empty booth and disappeared around the corner.

Shoppers carried boxes from the bakery past a group of sailors pouring from the pub, singing a bawdy tune. The air buzzed with the sounds of spring—bees and birds and bustling servants.

The townhouse stood out like a beacon. I hadn't a clue if Rían was actually renting it or if he would be home. But if I found the bastard, I would give him a piece of my mind.

When I reached the blue door, I pounded it with my fist, pretending it was his face. A moment later, it opened, and Rían—posing as Lady Marissa—dragged me inside by the elbow.

Ornate patchwork tiles in the hallway gleamed beneath my boots. The place smelled of fresh plaster and paint. Above our heads, a small chandelier cast glittering rainbows against the white walls.

"You're here." With a flick of his wrist, he was back to his evil self, in a black shirt and fitted trousers. "Why are you here?" His eyes narrowed. "And you're angry. Why are you angry? Did something happen?"

He could take his false concern and choke on it. "You happened you . . . you . . . you cad."

His brows flicked up. "I'm a cad, am I?"

"You are worse than a cad. You're a fiend—and a villain."

The corner of his lips lifted ever so slightly. "Thank you."

"It wasn't a compliment!"

"Maybe not to you." He threw an arm around the mahogany newel post. "Out of curiosity, what have I done to earn such scathing insults?"

Damn it all, the smile playing on his lips made me want to smack him. And he'd probably like it. "I tried to tell my sister about our bargain, and it felt like nails were being driven into my skull."

"Ah. That." His shiny black boots tapped against the tiles as he rocked back and forth on his heels. "A simple binding spell to ensure you kept your promise."

I had promised not to tell her, but I hadn't meant it. "I was lying."

Gasping in mock horror, his hand flew to his chest. "You were *lying*? I am shocked and offended."

"Oh, shove off."

"I must admit, I like angry Aveen. She's quite entertaining."

I'd show him entertaining. My hands clenched into fists. "Remove the spell."

"Ah . . . No." He turned and started for the first room off the hallway. A small parlor with blue striped wallpaper, a fireplace, and damask curtains.

That was it.

No furniture, no rugs, no knickknacks.

Then Rían flicked his wrist.

Two chairs appeared, separated by a low coffee table. "Would you like some tea?" he threw over his shoulder.

"I'm not staying for tea. I just want you to get rid of the bloody spell."

He eased himself onto the blue velvet chair. "I hate to disappoint, but I'm afraid the spell remains."

A silver tea set appeared. He poured one cup, then another, setting the first in front of the empty chair.

A chair that looked very familiar. "Is that . . ." *Bloody Rían.* "That's my chair from my bedroom."

"Is it?"

I stomped over to check the back. Sure enough, I found a small burn mark at the bottom from the time I'd moved it too close to the fire. "You can't do that. You can't just take whatever you want."

"It's a gray area." He lifted the lid from one of the small silver cups on the tray. "Sugar?"

"Two please—I mean, no. I don't want sugar because I don't want tea." Even so, I plopped onto my chair. Who stole a person's chair? Who did that?

A villain, that's who.

Two lumps of sugar splashed into my cup. I only picked it up to give my hands something to do besides strangle him.

He held the cream toward me. "No cream?"

"No cream."

By the time he finished preparing his cup, it was more cream than tea.

"What do you mean 'it's a gray area'?"

Settling himself against the blue cushion at his back, he took a long, slow sip. "The law says that I cannot shift items from a ship or a shop or a bank, but it does not explicitly state that I cannot shift personal items that have already been purchased if the owner leaves his or her door unlocked."

Well then. I'd just have to remember to lock my bloody door next time, wouldn't I?

I took a sip of tea. "And what does the law say about binding spells?"

"It says that if a human is foolish enough to bargain with the fae, she accepts the consequences." His smile peeked from over his cup. "So, while I appreciate you calling for tea, I must decline your request to remove the spell."

I wanted to stamp my foot or pull my hair or—or pull his hair. Instead, I set my tea back on the tray. "Why?"

His finger tapped against the chair like the ticking of a clock. "Because using magic to avoid marriage is another gray area. And the fewer people who know of my involvement, the better."

"My sister would never tell anyone."

"Forgive me for not taking the word of a liar."

"I'm not a—" The words melted on my tongue. I had just admitted to lying to him about not telling my sister. What a bloody disaster.

Rían hid his grin in his teacup.

What was the point in staying here if he wasn't going to give in? I shot to my feet and started toward the door.

I didn't expect Rían to turn himself back into Lady Marissa and follow me.

"Don't you have anything better to do?" I hissed, catching the latch and throwing the door aside. Town had gone quiet, with only a few servants darting between shops, carrying canvas bags of fruit and veg.

He skipped behind me, dancing out of the house, not bothering to lock the door. "*Ohhhh*, angry Aveen is my favorite."

I hurried to Meranda's and quickly climbed the three stairs to her door. The bell over the door gave a welcoming jingle.

"Lady Aveen," Dame Meranda greeted with a broad smile. "I hear congratulations are in order—"

The bell jingled a second time. Rían stood in the entryway, swishing his skirts from side to side.

Meranda's face paled when Rían wiggled his fingers in a flirtatious wave.

"Would you excuse me for a moment?" I caught Rían by the arm, forcing him behind a tall dress form holding a violet gown with a sequined bodice. "You can't be here."

Rolling his eyes, Rían flicked his wrist. "What kind of fiancé would I be if I didn't accompany my wife to pick out her trousseau?"

I'd already picked out my trousseau but didn't bother correcting him. "You're not really my fiancé."

"It's best to keep up appearances. You never know who's watching. And thanks to my brilliant disguise"—he fluffed his skirts—"the humans won't mind." In my ear, he whispered, "Unless someone catches us kissing in a dark shed."

Memories of yesterday at the beach came flooding back, bringing with them the forbidden heat of desire deep in my belly. I could taste his magic. Feel his lips. His body.

Choose how I unravel you.

Clearly unaffected, Rían flicked his wrist and drew away, his skirts swooshing as he bounced around the cluttered space, touching everything like a toddler on his first trip to town. Shuffled through hanging dresses, leaving them askew on their hangers. Sifted through folded garments on tables.

Dame Meranda's smile tightened as she watched her shop being turned upside down.

Rían stopped at a basket filled with loose fabric. It wasn't until he lifted a piece of black lace between his fingers and twisted to grin at me that I realized what he'd picked up.

Lacy undergarments, barely enough fabric to cover a woman's backside.

He wiggled his arched eyebrows. "Your husband would love these."

I ripped them out of his hands. "I'm not buying those." My face lit on fire as I shoved them to the bottom of the basket.

Rían reached back in, withdrawing another pair. "Why not? They'd look fabulous on you. Wouldn't you agree, Meranda?"

Meranda nodded from where she stood behind the counter. "Lady Aveen could wear whatever she wishes and look like a goddess."

"See." Rían shoved them back at me. If I didn't know better, I would've said his voice had thickened. "Buy them."

"Absolutely not." I stuffed the blasted things beneath a box of stockings.

Shrugging, he went back to creating havoc in the shop. The sooner I got this over with, the better—for everyone.

"Did you get my note?" I asked Meranda, trying my best to ignore Rían when he picked up a brassiere and held it over his chest.

Meranda nodded. "I've had a glance at the garments. Some of them look as if they've never been worn."

"They haven't. And they're doing no good sitting in my closet." I needed money more than I needed dresses.

Rían tossed the brassiere aside in favor of a set of garters, dragging and pulling on the stretchy bits.

"Do you think we could make a deal?" I asked.

Meranda's eyes darkened when Rían let the garters fly across the room and into the window. "Take care of your friend, and I'll work up an offer."

By the time I meandered around the tables and dress forms, Rían had plucked a dress from a rack and brought it to the long oval mirror propped against the wall. The color matched his eyes.

Babysitting a mad prince had not been on the agenda for today.

I ripped the hanger from him.

"Rude. I was thinking of buying that." He swiped for the hanger.

"No you weren't."

"You try it on then. It'd suit you."

"I own plenty of dresses." So many, I was getting rid of them. What did I need a new one for anyway? It wasn't as if I'd have any place to wear it once I came back from the dead.

"Meranda?" Rían called, thick lashes fluttering. "I think Aveen should try on this dress, don't you?"

Meranda glanced up from the trunk of garments. "It is a beautiful dress. The boning can be removed if need be, but you'll have to try it on."

"Brilliant." Rían grabbed my hand. "We'll be right back."

Before I could protest, he dragged me behind the curtain to the fitting area.

The air grew heavy. Another tost. I tried to push through the curtain. An invisible barrier kept my hand from connecting with the material.

Rían sank onto one of the chairs around the perimeter of the dressing room.

If he thought he could keep me prisoner, he had another thing coming. Meranda would come to my aid, see what was happening, and raise the alarm. "What game are you playing?" I asked.

"Perhaps I simply wish to treat my fianceé to a new dress."

Nothing with Rían was that simple. I may not have known him for very long, but it didn't take a genius to realize he always had an agenda.

He nodded his chin toward the forgotten garment draped over my arm. "Are you going to try that on?"

I threw it at him. "*You* try it on."

"If you insist." With a flick of his wrist, he was no longer Lady Marissa. I watched in rapt horror as he unbuttoned his shirt and folded it over a free stool.

I pressed my back against the invisible wall, desperate to escape the heat from his bare skin. "What are you doing?"

"The dress will look silly if I put it on over my clothes."

He wasn't going to strip bare. This was another game.

He slid his leather belt free from the buckle. Unfastened the button on his trousers.

"*Please stop.*" My words were a breathless plea.

He glanced up with a knowing grin. "Do you want me to try on the dress or not?"

I clutched it to my chest. My hands ached to run down the ridges of his abdomen. To trace the thin trail of dark hair from his belly button to where his trousers slipped low on his hips. "I . . . I . . . I will try it on," I rasped.

His clothes were back on a *flick* later. "Would you like help? Undressing women is one of my favorite pastimes."

I knew he expected me to say no. To snap and tell him to go away. I was sick of being on the receiving end of his teasing and taunting. Of biting my tongue instead of biting back.

I leaned over him, bracing my hands on the arms of the chair, and said with remarkable steadiness, "Since you're here, you may as well be useful."

Blue eyes darted to mine. "I take it back. *This* Aveen is my favorite. What should I call her?"

"Call me whatever you want," I said with a coy smile, feeling more powerful than I ever had in my entire life.

Rían's throat bobbed as he swallowed. "Hello, 'whatever you want.'" He traced a solitary finger along the swell of my breast. "Shall I undress you?"

"You are ridiculous."

"No, I'm Rían." That finger moved to the hollow at my throat. "And you didn't answer my question."

How far was I willing to push him?

How far was I willing to push myself?

I *wanted* to say yes.

No I didn't.

Rían was the worst.

He didn't care about me. Not really. He was a man. Men only cared about themselves. He wouldn't even be here if it weren't for our bargain.

I couldn't give in.

I wouldn't.

"No." I jerked upright, clutching my hands over my breast, feeling my heart thundering under my skin.

Uncertainty flickered in his eyes. "What happened?"

I turned away.

"Just then," he said. "Something made the fire in your eyes go out."

"I just . . ." I huffed a defeated sigh. "I just want you to go so I can try this on."

He stood stiffly. The air cleared, and by the time he pushed through the curtains, he was back to being Lady Marissa.

The dress fit like it had been made for me. I'd never found one that fit so well without adding or removing stitches.

But I didn't need a new dress.

I needed funds for a new life.

I found Rían with an elbow propped against the counter, chatting with Meranda. "It fits perfectly, doesn't it?" he said with a smirk.

"It doesn't matter. I'm not looking to purchase anything today."

"Lucky for you, I am." He took the dress and tossed it onto the counter next to a pair of lace undergarments. I shot him a glare.

"What?" He was all false innocence and smiles. "They're for me." He winked, handing over a purse of coins from heaven knows where.

Meranda looked between us, brow furrowing. Instead of saying whatever was on her mind, she took the money, slipped it beneath the counter, and began packaging the dress. I knew better than to protest. What good would it do? He was clearly used to getting his way.

"You didn't have to buy me a dress," I said under my breath.

He knocked his hip against mine. "Consider it a replacement for the one I ruined yesterday."

When she finished, Meranda handed me a large box along with an envelope. "This is what we were discussing earlier."

"Thank you, Meranda." I set the box on the counter to stuff the envelope into my purse. "I truly appreciate it."

"Don't you want to check what's inside?"

"There's no need. I trust you." Most of the shops in Graystones wouldn't even consider taking used dresses. "And I appreciate it more than you will ever know."

This money would set me on the path to independence.

Now to find someone to purchase the random bits I'd

collected from around the house. Three candlesticks, a clock from the spare room I was sure no one would miss, some mismatched cutlery, and a silver flagon from a box I'd found in the attic.

The bell over the door rang. Rían glanced over my shoulder, then stiffened. Robert watched us from between two dress forms.

"Ah, Aveen, my love. I heard you were in town," Robert said, navigating around a table of ribbons and buttons.

My love? Where had that come from?

My fiancé turned toward Rían, and his lips lifted. "Aren't you going to introduce me to your friend?"

Instead of waiting for me, Rían offered his hand. "Lady Marissa DeWarn. And you are?"

"Robert Trench." Robert planted a kiss on Rían's knuckles. "Aveen's betrothed."

If only Robert knew whose hand he had actually kissed.

"Oh, Aveen," Rían gasped, pulling free of Robert's grasp to press a hand to his chest. "You never told me he was so dashingly handsome."

Robert preened.

Rían's smile vanished. "Although he is quite short, isn't he? Is his father overweight, by chance? Men that short often go quite"—he puffed out his cheeks—"*round* once they hit forty."

Meranda concealed her giggle behind a more mannerly cough.

"And that tragic hairline." Rían clicked his tongue. "His feet are small as well. You know what they say about men with small feet. They have small—"

I slammed my hand across Rían's mouth, pasting on a smile to conceal the laugh swelling in my throat. "You must excuse Lady Marissa. She was raised in Vellana. You know their manners leave something to be desired."

Before he could say anything else, I grabbed my box and hauled him out of the store. Afraid Robert would insist on following us, I tugged Rían into the alley behind the dress shop.

I fell back against the brick wall, clutching the box to my chest.

The horror in Robert's eyes had been worth it. *So* worth it. "I cannot believe you said that to his face."

Rían propped his elbow against the wall next to my shoulder. "Lady Marissa is a very outspoken young woman."

Lady Marissa might be my new hero. To say such things aloud. What freedom.

"*Lady Marissa* is a terrible influence and needs to return to Vellana."

Cupping his chest, Rían sighed and whispered, "Until we meet again," to his breasts. A split second later, he was back to being a fae prince.

Part of me wished I could stay in this alley forever, hiding away from my life and my duty. "What has gotten into you?"

"I'm in a good mood."

Rían in a good mood seemed infinitely more dangerous than Rían in a bad one. "And why is that?"

"Why didn't you let me undress you?" he countered with a smirk.

I wasn't answering that. It was none of his bloody business. Besides, I'd tarried long enough. My sister was probably going mad in the carriage. "I need to go. Getting caught alone with you would ruin my reputation."

He flicked his wrist and turned into the ambassador. "Better?"

"Not really, no."

"Too bad." He took the box, laced my arm through his, and tugged me toward the street. "I cannot help that we happened to both be in the market on the same day and ran into one another."

People strolled arm-in-arm past us, not bothering to offer so much as a sideways glance. Perhaps I was overthinking this. There wasn't a law against meeting a casual acquaintance. The only person who would be upset was Robert, and I didn't give a toss what he thought.

"I am such a gentleman that I offered to see you safely to your carriage. There are terribly wicked creatures lurking about, you know," Rían went on, nodding to folks as they passed. "And you'll be so grateful that you'll forget you're engaged to that short, destined-to-be bald and rotund human that you give me another kiss. And you'll enjoy it so much that you won't want to stop. We may end up back in the shed yet."

"You think far too highly of your kisses. I've had better."

"I have a weakness for women who lie to me, you know. If you're not careful, I may not let you go." His eyes flicked to something behind me, and his smile faltered.

Robert's flushed face and sweaty brow stepped into my line of sight, and I could feel my mood deflate.

"Ambassador, it is good to see you again," he wheezed, out of breath. "While I appreciate you and your sister taking such good care of my fianceé, I'm afraid I must speak with her in private. I'm sure you don't mind."

"I do mind, actually."

"Please don't make a scene," I begged, keeping my voice low.

Rían's expression went blank. He handed me the box and walked away.

I should have been happy to see him go. Instead, I felt empty. As irritating as he was, he'd distracted me from the heaviness of what this weekend would bring.

"Have you lost your damn mind?" Robert took my shoulders, turning me away from Rían. "I will not settle for my fianceé traipsing around town on the arm of another man as though she has no regard for our relationship."

Did men hear themselves when they said such foolish things? "We have no relationship. I feel nothing for you."

He planted his hands on his hips, glaring down at me. "You weren't my first choice either, Aveen. But if I do not marry you, my father will cut me off."

It was easy to forget that I wasn't the only one being forced into this. That Robert's hands were as tied as mine. Not that it mattered since I had found a way out.

Sighing, he raked a hand through his blond hair. "If we are to be stuck together, can we at least try and make the best out of it? Please?"

I didn't bother telling him I'd rather eat raw fish guts. Still, Rían had said I was to continue as if nothing was amiss. And if our plans fell through, I would end up marrying this man. Making an enemy of him now would be foolish.

So I smiled and said, "All right."

The words had barely slipped free when he eased forward and pressed his mouth to mine.

I'd felt more passion in the single touch of Rían's little finger than in the entirety of this kiss. Engaged couples were permitted some displays of public affection, so I endured the way he lingered, telling myself this was another way of playing along. The entire time, I wished his lips belonged to someone else.

18

Tomorrow *I* am going to die.

And tonight . . .

Apparently, tonight I was to be plagued by a wicked fae prince.

Rían lounged on my chaise, hands tucked behind his head, feet crossed at the ankles—the picture of nonchalance. "I refuse to let you spend your last night alive moping about, boring me to tears. What do you want to do? And make it good."

Whoever authored those fairy tales had gotten their facts dreadfully wrong. Handsome princes were unruly and as irritating as a splinter in your foot. The princesses had probably begged the witches for a curse to escape the spoiled man's incessant whining.

What do you want to do?

Rían had asked me that question three times now. And each time, I'd given him the same answer. "I want to tell Keelynn the truth."

"And since you can't do that, you'd rather . . ." Rolling his eyes heavenward, he gestured toward me. "Go on, now. Don't be shy. Surely there is something you want to do before my brother kills you."

Did he have to be so crass? Tadhg may have been killing me,

but I was dying of my own free will. "I just want to get this over with." Rían had been right the other day. The sooner I died, the sooner I would return. And the sooner the ache in my chest would subside. I wasn't betraying my sister, *dammit*. I was giving her everything she'd ever wanted. And yet, not being allowed to share the joyous news, letting her believe I would take this ultimatum lying down, was destroying me.

Rían jolted upright, his boots slamming onto the floor, rattling the pots of cream on my dressing table. If he didn't keep it down, he was going to wake the whole house.

"Do you like tarts?" he asked.

How had he gone from discussing death to dessert? "What are you on about?"

He popped up, cupping one hand in front of him. "You know, fruity little pastries sprinkled with sugar." He pretended to sprinkle something over his hand. "Do you like them?" he asked, holding the invisible dessert toward me.

"If this is an attempt to distract me from my misery, can you not? I want to wallow." I meandered past him to fall onto the bed. Had my mattress always been this comfortable?

"Just answer the feckin' question, miserable Aveen."

"I don't know. I suppose they're all right."

He began to pace at the foot of the bed, brushing against my skirts each time he passed. "Our kitchen witch Eava makes the best cherry tarts, and I happen to know she baked a fresh batch this morning." He flopped onto the bed, bouncing me in the air. His eyes glittered as he leaned close. "What do you say I steal the lot, and we feast on tarts until sunrise?"

"Someone like you would surely prefer widow fingers or orphan ears."

Rían deadpanned. "I save those delicacies for special occasions. I could always ask Eava to whip some up if you like?"

I couldn't hold my laughter in any longer. "I'll eat the bloody tarts, you loon."

Rían's dimples deepened when he grinned. "Brilliant." He rolled off the bed.

"You're leaving?" I raised to my elbows. I had assumed he'd flick his wrist and they'd appear out of thin air.

"There's no need to worry your pretty little head." He patted my hair like I was a dog. "I'll be back."

I'd have his *pretty little head* on a platter if he didn't watch his tongue.

"When I return, I want you wearing your best dress and a smile. Do you hear me, miserable Aveen?" He flicked my shoulder.

"I hear you, oh magnanimous prince."

With a chuckle, he vanished.

Eventually, I rolled off the bed to drag one of the few remaining gowns from my closet. It seemed a silly thing, dressing up to celebrate my impending death. But I had a feeling sleep would elude me and didn't want to be left alone with my thoughts.

Once I'd dressed, I sank onto the chair in front of my dressing table, going through the motions of applying layer upon layer of creams and makeup, creating a perfect mask for the world to see.

I felt Rían's presence before I saw him, like an electric charge, lifting the fine hairs at the back of my neck.

I caught a glimpse of him in my mirror's reflection. His dark blue waistcoat matched the dress I'd chosen.

"Lovely," I muttered. "You're back."

"Uh oh. Melancholy Aveen," he said with a frown. "How can we get rid of her?"

I almost smiled. "You can't." When I reached for my tin of kohl, I knocked one of the glass pots onto the floor, sending it rolling toward Rían's gleaming boots.

"We'll see about that," he muttered, bending to pick up the pot. Instead of setting it on the table, he popped open the lid and gave it a sniff. His nose wrinkled, and he coughed into his fist. "No wonder you're melancholy, smearing this shite on your face every day."

He was so dramatic. It didn't smell that bad. "You are ridiculous."

He shoved the lid back on and set the pot of cream by the others. "It's better than being melancholy."

"I'm not melancholy. I'm nervous."

"What's there to be nervous about? All you have to do is go like this"—he closed his eyes and pursed his lips, smacking them together and making a slurping sound—"and my brother will take care of the rest. We can practice if it'll make you feel better."

I didn't know why my stomach fluttered. It wasn't as if I wanted to kiss him again and again and again. And again. "What if something goes wrong and I don't come back?"

He took my hands, dragging me to my feet. "I swear on pain of death that you will come back."

I turned the words over in my head. There didn't seem to be any way around it but, he'd tripped me up so many times before ,I didn't trust my own ears. "You lie."

His hair fell across his forehead when she shook his head. "About most things, yes. But not this."

What choice did I have but to trust him when the alternative was to marry Robert Trench? After what had happened in town, I didn't want Keelynn to marry him either. But that was a decision she deserved to make for herself.

Rían put his thumbs on either side of my lips, forcing them upright while making a sound like a creaking hinge. "Give me a different Aveen. This one's broken."

I forced a smile.

He snorted. "Fake Aveen? Pass. Next."

I kicked him in the shin.

"*Ohhh*, violent Aveen. Welcome back, my dear. I've missed you. Grab your cloak, my little viper. We're leaving."

I rolled my eyes, fighting a laugh as I went to grab the blue cloak he'd given me from the closet. I draped the heavy wool around my shoulders and drew the hood over my hair. "Where are we going?"

Rían swept me into his arms and the world went dark.

Then we were falling.

Through darkness.

Through space.

Through nothing at all.

The darkness eased like morning approaching, replaced by light from a sparkling chandelier and a hallway filled with patchwork tile. We were back in the townhouse. He set me on my feet, allowing me a moment to get my bearings before leading me to the parlor.

My feet stilled at the entrance.

Deep magenta and purple fuchsia spilled from the windows, bloomed from the curtains, filled vases on the mantle, overflowed from jars and jugs and all manner of fancy containers lining the baseboards.

A small table waited in the center of the room, beneath a chandelier of crystals and flowers.

Never in my life had I seen anything as beautiful. I turned in a circle, wishing there were some way to take it all in at once.

"There she is," Rían whispered.

I blinked at him. "Who?"

"Happy Aveen."

A ferocious blush crept up my neck. How could I not be happy? The room was positively magical. But why? Why would he waste his magic on this? On me?

"Well, if you aimed to impress, you have succeeded."

More than succeeded. Awful Rían had done something I never thought possible.

He'd touched my heart.

"This?" He flicked one of the drooping blooms in a vase. "Oh, you think I did this to impress you?" He started shaking his head even as his smile grew. "I hate to disappoint, but this is what

I do every other Friday. You should not feel special. Because you aren't."

Damn it all, his grin was infectious.

"Don't lie to me. Not tonight." Even if it hurt, I needed the truth from him.

"All right. I don't do this every other Friday. It's usually on Tuesdays." He winked, and I may have melted. But only a little.

With a flick of his wrist, golden plates appeared on the table, along with golden goblets and a golden tiered stand laden with mini cherry tarts. I removed my cloak, draping it over the back of my chair.

Who owned gold plates? They must be worth a fortune. "A bit garish, don't you think?" I teased, tapping a gilded edge. Even for someone who never had a hair out of place.

"As tonight is a celebration, I thought a lowly human such as yourself should dine on gold." He pulled out my chair, and I settled onto the cushion. Instead of sitting on the other side of the table, he dragged his chair right next to mine.

He placed a tart on my plate with a flourish.

The first bite: utter bliss. Flaky crust. Halved cherries covered in goo that burst when I bit into them. *Soooo good.*

"These have to be the best things I have ever tasted." When I opened my eyes, I found him sitting back in his chair, clutching his goblet of wine to his chest. His own plate remained empty. "Aren't you having one?"

"I'd rather watch you enjoy yourself."

If he didn't want any, then I may as well eat two. Wouldn't want them going to waste.

I finished, washing it down with enough wine to make me feel warm and fuzzy inside.

Rían nudged the stand closer. "Have another."

"I couldn't possibly."

"Do you want it?"

Did I want it? More than my next breath. "I do."

He plucked one from the top and set it on my plate. "Then take it."

"That's your motto, isn't it? If you want it, take it." With a *flickety-flick* of his wrist, Rían got whatever he wanted.

He sipped his wine. "If it was, we wouldn't be sitting here eating tarts."

"No?"

He shook his head.

I wasn't sure if it was the wine or the magic of the night or my impending death or the terrible fae prince—perhaps a combination of all four—but the cautiousness that had lived within me for twenty years just . . . snapped.

"What would we be doing instead?" I whispered, tracing the rim of my wine glass with my fingertips.

"It would involve fewer clothes and more screaming. Unfortunately for me—and for you," he added with a wink, "I don't bed maidens."

My innocence hadn't seemed like an issue for him the night we'd shared a bed. "What makes you think I'm still a maiden?"

He adjusted his position in the chair, throwing one arm over the back and his ankle over his knee. "'*It's not appropriate for a man to enter a lady's private quarters,*'" he mimicked in a high voice. "'*You mustn't speak so improperly. It wouldn't be proper for me to be alone with a man who is not my husband. Getting caught with you would ruin my reputation.*'"

Hearing the things I'd said thrown back at me left my face ablaze with embarrassment. So many rules I'd been given. All of them broken for the man sitting next to me.

"Shall I go on, or would it be *improper*?"

We'd passed improper the day he'd saved me from the Dullahan.

I guzzled what was left of my wine, drowning my nerves with notes of oak and alcohol. "Let's say, for argument's sake, that I wasn't a maiden."

His eyes widened as he inhaled, easing forward to hover by my lips. "Have you given yourself to another?"

Caden had been the captain of a ship docked in port visiting from Iodale. Four years my senior and so ruggedly handsome, he'd brought me up short when I first saw him in the market. Since fuchsia weren't in season, I'd been collecting daffodils to decorate for my nineteenth birthday.

Caden had sun-kissed blond hair tied back in a leather queue. Eyes rich and brown like fertile soil.

He had acted nothing like the gentlemen I'd known my entire life.

I had believed every one of his lies.

I love you, Aveen.

Lie.

I'll sail back for you come summer.

Lie.

I'd give up the sea, give up my life for you.

Lie after bloody lie.

I'd gone to the market every day that June, searching the port for those black sails. June melted into July. July slipped into August.

As August faded into September, my hope faded as well.

Robert Trench had been the first man to break my heart.

Caden Merriweather became the reason I'd given up on them all.

And he was the reason I could look Rían in his searching blue eyes and say with all honesty, "I have."

The way his gaze drifted to my heaving chest then slowly slid back to my mouth left heat pooling low in my stomach. And then he smiled and said, "Will I unravel now or wait until you finish that tart?"

19

His darkness sang to my own, calling it forth. Urging me to give in.

I wanted him.

All I had to do was move the words from my mind to my tongue.

The cherry tart could wait.

"Now, please."

Like a wild beast released from its tether, he caught me by the back of the head, and slammed his lips to mine. The intoxicating taste of wine and magic left my head reeling. My body clung to his, forming and molding. I clutched his collar with the last bit of strength I possessed. Too much space separated us, and I closed the distance, climbing onto his lap, straddling his hips.

With one kiss he stole every reason I shouldn't want him, leaving only the darkness and an unbiddable yearning growing deep in my soul.

He pulled away, his curved knife appearing in his hand. My stuttering heart thundered when he brought the blade to my throat.

"Do you fear me?" he asked.

"No." I wasn't afraid. Not of him. Not of anything. Not tonight.

Icy steel flattened against my neck, sliding it until it reached the swell of my breast.

And nicked me.

"You should," he whispered, transfixed by the blood welling from my broken skin. Searing heat burned through his fingertip as he drew it along the length of the wound, smearing deep red onto the neck of my dress. He brought his finger to his mouth and licked it off.

"What are you doing?" The fae didn't drink blood.

Rían's eyes were no longer blue, but black. "I'm only half fae," he confessed, red still on his lips as he adjusted his grip on the dagger, sliding the sharp point down my breastbone, not hard enough to draw blood but enough to leave a white line on my skin. Against the shell of my ear, he said, "My mother is a witch."

He dragged the blade down the bodice of my gown, slicing the fabric like it had been made of spiderwebs.

"Tell me where he touched you so that I may burn his memory from your skin." Rían drew down the sleeves of my shift. "Here?" he whispered against my bare shoulder.

My breathing caught. "Yes."

Lips of flame dragged along my collarbone. His tongue traced the neckline, dipping between my breasts.

When he moved away, I whimpered.

His hands cupped my chest. "Did he touch you here?"

Magic slipped up my shift like a thousand phantom fingers, dancing along my legs, my thighs. His head dipped to sample the peak of my breast through the fabric.

My back arched, thrusting my chest deeper into his grasp.

Every glance felt like an intimate caress. Every brush of his heated breath an experience in and of itself. Every touch igniting, driving me to the point of insanity.

I opened my mouth to cry out, felt a whimper leave my throat, but there was no sound.

The way his tongue swirled and teeth scraped were my undoing.

He caught the hem of my shift, dragging the garment up and off. Embarrassment warmed my cheeks. Seeing the way his black eyes drank in the sight of me tore it all away.

When he returned to my breast, the spark burned a thousand times stronger. His fingers trailed the skin at my waist, my hips, and my inner thighs, before drawing my undergarments to the side and sinking in. "Here?"

I nodded, burying my head in his neck.

"Don't hide from me. I want you to watch."

With his free hand, he fisted my hair, drawing my head back with a strong tug. "Do you feel this?" His hand began to glow. I melted at his touch. "I can make you burn for me the way I burn for you."

Rían became fire and flame.

Making me burn.

I slid my own hand into his breeches, finding his length hard as marble and just as smooth. I felt clumsy and inept, but the way he cursed and twitched in my grasp emboldened me.

Rían's fingers worked into a steady rhythm as I tightened my grip, matching his pace.

"How many times did he have you?" he rasped, the pad of his thumb finding the bundle of nerves. His two fingers curled deeper, drawing a whimper from my chest. "How many times must I take you before you feel me and only me?"

"Only once," I confessed. My first and only time had been awkward but sweet, painful but beautiful.

Rían let go of my hair and withdrew his hand, leaning back to look me in the eyes. "Once?"

I nodded.

His hands trailed down my sides to catch my hips, rocking me against his hard length. I propped my feet onto the chair's rungs to gain purchase. Grinding harder. Deeper. Desperate to feel every inch of him.

"Will I stop at one?" he muttered between kisses to my lips, my throat, my breasts.

My hair, damp from sweat, fell over my bare shoulder when I shook my head. When I reached for the buttons on his waistcoat, he flicked his wrist. His shirt and waistcoat disappeared.

"How shall I unravel you, human?" He drew out the words as he hooked his fingers into the waistband at the side of my knickers, ripping the seams until they fell away. "Tell me what you want."

I found him again, drawing a curse from his lips. "This. This is what I want."

He unfastened the belt at his waist with devastating slowness. The sound of the leather strap slipping through the buckle was a melody. "Shall I take my time?"

"Make it last," I told him. The moment this ended, I knew what would come.

Bracing my weight on the chair, I lifted so he could ease his breeches down and down until they pooled around his ankles.

Feral possessiveness took my chest in its iron grip as I drank in the sight of him.

Mine.

I wanted this deceitful prince to be mine.

Life. Death. Nothing mattered but the way his fingers returned to me, making way for what I really wanted. His free hand gripped my backside. "Lift those lovely hips."

I did as I was told, raising myself so he could position his thickness against my entrance. I sank slowly, holding my breath as I clutched the back of the chair. Beads of perspiration collected on his brow.

The stinging pain stole my breath as his body invaded mine. "There you go . . ." His fingers dug into the flesh at the backs of my thighs. "How does that feel?" His free hand found its way to my neck, stroking down my throat.

"It hurts."

He brushed my hair back from my cheeks, the look on his face almost reverent as he eased forward to dot kisses down my neck to the hollow at my throat, quickly turning his attention to the hard peaks of my breasts. Nipping, then soothing the pain with his tongue.

My muscles began to loosen,

There was still pain when I shifted, but also delicious fullness and searing heat.

He lifted his hips, pressing mine down at the same time. "I knew you'd be perfect. I feckin' knew it."

Gripping his shoulders, I rose slightly, reveling in the way he slipped out then back in and out and in and out. Rhythmic waves of give and take. Delicious heat. Sweet anticipation. Heady abandon.

The muscles in my thighs began to tremble. "Help me."

Black eyes bore into mine. Rían adjusted his grip, lifting and lowering in a steady rhythm. "Not too fast. I won't last if you go fast."

Every time I tried to pick up the pace, he'd slow me back down.

I changed my mind.

I didn't want to go slow anymore.

I wanted to go fast.

To steal away the memories of the women he had been with so that only I remained. This moment. The two of us coming together. A meeting of flesh and desire.

Heat flooded between my thighs, a rushing river swelling behind a damn.

"Rían . . . Please . . ."

He caught my chin, forcing my eyes back to his. "Say it again."

"Please?"

He shook his head. "My name."

So I said his name. Over and over. A cry. A whisper. A moan.

His eyes squeezed closed as his head fell back, hips bucking with violent abandon. "Don't stop."

I cried his name as the threads holding me together unspooled, unraveling us both. Rían shuddered, whispering in a mysterious language against my throat.

"What does that mean?" I breathed, pushing my damp hair back from my forehead.

Palming my breast, he nuzzled my collarbone. "It means you are beautiful." His lips swept over my heart. "You are perfect. You are all that is right and good in this world."

"I think you're lying." That was too many meanings for three small words.

His chuckle vibrated against my breast. "You'll never know, now will you?"

I pinched his arm.

His stomach flexed. He twitched inside me. "Easy now, human."

Laughing, I dragged my nails down his chest, fascinated by the red streaks and goosebumps they left behind everywhere except that strange scar. "What's this?" The moment I went to trace the X he caught my wrist.

"A reminder to take control while you can."

His hold loosened. Leaning forward, he caught my lower lip between his teeth, biting down hard enough to leave me gasping. I could feel him begin to harden again.

I rocked forward, dragging a vicious curse from his lips.

"Are you sure you want to die tomorrow?" he groaned.

In this moment, with him holding me, I wasn't sure about anything but how perfect this felt. How right.

"What if you don't go through with it?" he whispered.

I froze. "You mean, marry Robert?"

He swept my hair back from my face, running his thumbs along my cheekbones. My jaw. My lips. "I mean . . ." He raised his hips in an aching thrust. "Tell them all to fuck off."

I closed my eyes, imagining how freeing it would be to waltz into my betrothal ball tomorrow night and give the whole bloody lot of them two fingers.

"You can live here." He moved again, harder, deeper. "And I could . . . come to you . . . whenever . . . you want."

Live here? In his townhouse?

I wouldn't have to die.

My father and Keelynn could come as well.

The sale of the estate would surely provide enough funds to pay my father's debts and save us from destitution.

My mind spun with possibilities. I couldn't think straight with him moving . . . like . . . *that*.

Dammit.

None of those things addressed the real reason I had bargained with him in the first place.

Keelynn loved Robert.

One year.

That's all it would cost me to fix every single problem in one fell swoop.

I pressed a hand against the tensed muscles of his abdomen, and he stilled. "I can't."

Brow furrowing, he stared up at me through clear blue eyes. "You can. But you're choosing not to."

He wanted to argue over *semantics* right now? "That's right. I'm *choosing* not to." I was making a choice for myself—and for Keelynn. I wouldn't let some man swoop in and tell me what I should do. "This isn't about me—or about you, for that matter. This is about my sister."

His eyes shuttered before he looked away. "Right. My apologies for misreading the situation." He gestured toward our connected bodies. "I thought perhaps it may be a *little* about me."

Why did men have to be so bloody selfish?

"So, what? You just want me to live in this townhouse for as long as you're interested? What sort of life would that be for me?"

"Forget I said anything."

How the hell did he expect me to do that when it was all I could think about?

I shoved him back and climbed off his lap, needing to get

away, to clear my head. My damp thighs shook as I searched for something to wear that hadn't been shredded. Brilliant. My undergarments were ruined. Where the hell was my shift?

"You're overreacting," he said.

"Am I? Because I'm fairly certain you just asked me to be your whore." He hadn't professed his undying love or offered me marriage.

He had offered me a house and sex.

By the time I'd situated myself, Rían was fully dressed. He handed me a beautiful blue dressing gown he'd shifted from heaven knows where.

I tore the gown from his grasp and threw it in the fire where it belonged.

Rían's expression turned as dark as the black smoke twisting up the chimney. "Aveen, I'm sorry I said—"

"No. No more talking." I couldn't handle him saying something else and making me feel worse than I already did. I collected my cloak and threw it around my shoulders. "Take me home."

Rían reached for my arm. "It was a foolish suggestion made in desperation. You don't have to leave."

"Yes, I do."

His fingers grazed mine. "Stay with me."

"I'm choosing not to."

His expression hardened. He held my hand while we evanesced back to my bedroom. The moment my feet met the carpet, I threw his hand aside and stomped to my bed.

"I was only trying to help," he confessed, still standing next to the window.

The only person Rían had been trying to help was himself.

I turned down the covers to the cold sheets beneath. "Thank you for tonight." For the first part of it, anyway.

"That's it? That's all you have to say to me?"

The things I wanted to say would fill the ocean. But saying them when I was going to die tomorrow was pointless. "You got your ride. What more do you want?"

Like a candle being blown out, the fire in his eyes vanished, leaving only vacant blue.

Turning my back so he couldn't see me wince, I climbed onto the bed and drew the covers to hide my trembling and let my tears melt into the pillowcase.

The air felt lighter. Colder. I didn't have to check to know he had gone.

20

THE ENTIRE TOWN OF GRAYSTONES HAD SQUEEZED INTO OUR ballroom, filling the space with useless chatter and false laughter. And yet it felt like no one could see me. They spoke to me, sure. But none of them saw the misery beneath my smile. I'd been forced to stand between Robert and my father while guests arrived, each one more resplendent than the last. I'd never felt so alone.

The moment the doors fell closed, I excused myself, escaping to one of the curtained alcoves in the ballroom to gather myself before my final performance.

Two more hours. Just two more hours.

And then all of this would be over.

My father must've spent a fortune of Lord Trench's money on this soiree, extending invitations to every person he'd ever met. He should've been ashamed that his poor investments and bad business ventures had ruined us. Instead, he stood in the corner gloating with his friends over the fine match he'd made for his eldest daughter.

And he expected me to sit back and smile about being sold to the highest bidder like a pawn.

"Aveen?" My sister's voice went through me like a dagger as

she squeezed herself into my alcove. The frilly pink dress she wore had been a birthday gift from our father last year.

"What do you need?" I asked. Tears welled behind my eyes as I committed the scent of her lavender perfume to memory.

"You said you weren't going to marry him." Keelynn's voice broke on the final word. Silver tears gathered along her thick lashes. "You swore you'd fix this."

"Keelynn, please keep your voice down." These could be the last few minutes I spent with her alone. If someone found us, it'd be over. I closed my eyes so I didn't have to face her pain, saying a silent prayer for strength. "I will fix it, but you have to be patient." I couldn't say more than that without giving myself a splitting headache.

"Father announced your betrothal two weeks ago, and you've done *nothing*."

If only I could tell her all that I had done to ensure her happiness. Trunks full of beautiful dresses waited for her in the spare room, an ivory gown made to her measurements hung in my closet, and cartloads of hydrangeas were ready for the church. She and Robert would be off to Iodale on their romantic honeymoon getaway the day after they wed. "Delicate matters take time to resolve."

She continued as if I hadn't spoken. "I'm the one who loves Robert. I've always loved him," she sobbed. "Why didn't you tell Father to pair him with me?"

I wanted to be the one to wipe away her tears. To tell her the truth.

To tell her that I *had* tried.

I had done everything within my power to avoid this fate. And it had been all for nought.

So instead, I gripped her shoulders, waited until her eyes locked with mine, and said, "You have to trust me. Have I ever let you down?"

Her lip jutted out, but she shook her head. "Not yet."

Not ever.

"Lady Aveen? I believe I have the next dance," a voice announced from behind.

Dammit. I knew we'd been too loud.

According to the full dance card dangling from my wrist, Sir Henry Withel was next. I wanted to throw the thing into the fire but needed to play along. For a little while longer at least. "I love you, Keelynn. No matter what happens, please remember that."

Keelynn's expression hardened.

Sir Henry called my name again.

I didn't want to dance with him. I didn't want to dance with anyone. I wanted to spend my last few hours with my sister.

She clamped her mouth closed, looking through me as though I were a ghost.

Soon, I would be.

Icy dread slithered beneath my skin as I started for the gangly man and offered a false smile along with my hand. "My apologies. I was speaking to my sister."

With a nod, he led me to the floor, where I danced with partner after partner until my feet ached and my smile felt like it would shatter my face.

The hairs on the back of my neck suddenly lifted. My eyes collided with Rían's from over my partner's head before he quickly looked away. Instead of coming over to me, he sauntered toward my sister, who was guzzling champagne by herself in one of the chairs set along the wall. If she didn't slow down, she'd have a terrible headache tomorrow.

Tomorrow.

I wouldn't be around to help her or giggle about the events of the night.

Tomorrow, I'd be no more.

Lord Stilt, a man whose stomach stretched the seams of his waistcoat, spun me in a reel, making it difficult to watch Rían snag two glasses of champagne and take the seat next to Keelynn.

Pain shot through my foot. Lord Stilt mumbled an apology, sweat dripping down his brow, his face an unhealthy shade of red.

I couldn't do this anymore.

Letting go of his hand, I fanned my overwarm cheeks, my foot throbbing. "Would you mind terribly if I took a short break? It's quite warm in here."

"Not at all, milady," he wheezed. "Delicate flowers . . . need to rest . . . lest they wither."

I'd show him a bloody delicate flower.

With a growing pang in my chest, I watched Rían lead Keelynn to the dance floor. There should've been more space between them. Why did he hold her so close? What game was he playing now? He was supposed to keep her occupied, not make her fall for him.

Robert glared at Keelynn from his usual spot by the fireplace, surrounded by his brothers. He was some fool. What did he think would happen if we actually got married? Keelynn would fall in love with someone else, leaving him well behind.

I collected some champagne, finished it in three gulps, then discarded the empty glass on one of the high tables only to grab another. Would a hangover follow me to the underworld? There was only one way to find out.

Rían whispered something to Keelynn that left her lips quirking into a smile. His eyes found mine over her head before making his way toward the dark hallway just as the clock in the corner struck the hour. I said a silent goodbye to Keelynn, and good riddance to this house and to these people.

Before I could make my exit, Robert caught Keelynn by the elbow and dragged her onto the balcony.

"I wanted to say goodbye," a familiar feminine voice said from behind me. I turned to find Lady Marissa in a scandalously low-cut blue gown, glossy black ringlets tumbling down her shoulders.

I hated that Rían had seen me undressed. That he knew me so intimately.

Most of all, I hated how much his suggestion had hurt me.

I knew he had meant it as a solution. But it had highlighted that, deep down, a half-fae half-witch prince was still a man.

I said, "Goodbye." I meant *good riddance*.

Keelynn blew through the door, her dark hair disheveled as she started for the hallway.

Rían's feminine lips flattened. "Aveen, last night I said something I—"

"You think I want to discuss last night?" I barked a laugh. That wasn't happening. "I never want to speak of it again. As far as I'm concerned, nothing happened."

"I understand better than anyone that intent does not matter," he said, shoulders sagging. "But I want you to know that it was not my intention to use you in any way. I just got caught up in the lie. It will not happen again."

I didn't want to hear his beautiful apology or my weak heart to break at the despair in his tone. I wanted to put Rían and this world—this life—behind me.

"Go take care of my sister."

"Lady Aveen!" Lady Samantha swept toward me, red skirts swaying and arms open wide. Why was she coming over? She and I never spoke. "Congratulations! I hadn't heard you and Robert were courting, and now you're engaged?"

"It was a last-minute arrangement," I said, somehow managing not to choke on the perfumed cloud that accompanied her.

The space where Lady Marissa had been standing only a moment ago was empty.

Lady Samantha moved on from my betrothal to her own husbandly woes, barely pausing long enough to breathe. When she started whispering about her husband's penchant for bawdy houses, I took it as my cue to leave.

"Excuse me for a moment," I said, patting her gloved hand. "I'm feeling unwell and could do with some fresh air."

A symphony of starlight greeted me the moment I stepped outside. I touched buds as I passed, committing to memory their softness against my fingertips. Nippy spring air kissed my cheeks, enveloping me in its lilac-scented caress. My footsteps slowed as I approached the final hedge and rounded the corner to find a cloaked figure sitting on a bench. "I thought perhaps you'd changed your mind," Tadhg said.

Sinking onto the cold, damp bench, I tucked my trembling hands beneath my thighs. "I'm not changing my mind." His white teeth flashed when he smiled, making my stomach flutter. Even in the dark, he was beautiful.

"You seem troubled. Are you having second thoughts?" Tadhg's low, soothing voice felt like sun-kissed honey slipping down my throat. "Not that I blame you. Rían doesn't deserve someone willing to sacrifice herself for a—" He winced and hissed in a breath.

"A what?"

Biting his lip, he shook his head. "Nothing. He just doesn't deserve you."

I didn't want to talk about Rían.

I licked my dry lips, my gaze dropping to Tadhg's mouth. His breath was sweet, almost decadent as it mixed with mine, smelling faintly of glazed almonds.

"Are you going to kiss me?" I asked.

"I prefer a woman to make the choice. It makes it easier to believe you're sacrificing yourself rather than that I'm about to steal your last breath."

I glanced toward the house, rising like a skeleton in the distance, and said one final silent goodbye to the only person in this world I would be willing to die for.

"He's not coming."

I twisted back around to find Tadgh staring. "Who's not coming?"

"My brother." A golden curl fell across his brow when his head tilted. "He said that if he had to watch me put my 'vile mouth' on yours, he'd 'lose his feckin' mind.'"

"Why does he care?"

Tadhg's brows knitted, and I realized my foolish error. Rían and I were pretending to be engaged. Of course he would care if

I kissed his brother. "I mean, I don't know why he cares since this was his plan. It is the only way we can be together, after all."

Tadhg gave my knee a gentle pat. "He cares more for you than I have seen him care for anyone in a long, long time."

Tears clouded my vision. Why was I crying? All of this was a ruse.

I just got caught up in the lie.

Perhaps I'd gotten caught up a little as well.

"What makes you say that?" I asked.

Tadhg shifted closer, his eyes widening. "Hasn't he told you?"

I shook my head.

"Rían is convinced you're his soulmate."

Turns out, I didn't need to kiss Tadhg to stop my heart.

Rían's *soulmate?*

Of all the insane, ludicrous notions.

Rían and I.

Soulmates.

Tadhg chuckled to himself, scrubbing a hand down his stubbled jaw. "The lad has harped on about soulmates for as long as I can remember. Used to love the old stories of two people made for each other by the fates, a perfect match in every way. I never believed in the shite myself. What are the odds that there really is one person in this world made just for you? And if there were such a person," he said almost to himself, deep in thought, his teeth scraping his bottom lip, "what are the odds you'd meet?"

The odds were impossible.

Sighing, Tadhg shook his head and shrugged, bringing his gaze back to mine. "Anyway, Rían said you were his, and here we are. If anyone can love Rían as much as Rían loves Rían, it must be fate."

My heart started beating again. Harder. Faster. "He actually said that? About me?" It must've been a lie—a part of the ruse.

Tadhg wrapped one of my curls around his finger, smoothing his thumb along the golden strands. "Mind you, it was after a considerable amount of liquor. Said kissing you was like being on fire. He talked of nothing else for hours. Wouldn't shut up." A chuckle. "He's a terrible drunk."

That made no sense.

"But Rían—" I caught myself before I could confess that he didn't care for me.

He couldn't.

Could he?

Tadhg's finger slid along my lower lip. "He'd kill me if he found out I told you," he said with a grin that turned my insides to mush.

I couldn't handle this right now. Not with everything that had happened.

Not with the end so near.

Not when I had finally found my escape.

So, I screwed my eyes shut and kissed the Gancanagh.

Aching frostbite seeped into my bones. Froze my lungs. My heartbeat slowed. I could feel myself slipping away, heaviness settling into my limbs. Dizziness overwhelmed. Muscles seized. Easing me onto the bench, Tadhg pressed a kiss to my temple and whispered, "He doesn't deserve you."

His almond scent drifted away, replaced by the cloying stench of rotting roses.

Part Two

21

BLOODCURDLING SCREAMS PIERCED THE SILENCE. A FLASH OF light tore through my cocoon of darkness. Everything hurt but nothing would move and there was nothing and then there was everything.

Screaming.

Crying.

A horrible cackle.

The pungent sweetness of surging magic invading my nostrils. A gasp that left my lungs and throat ablaze like someone had stuffed my mouth with hot coals. But that was nothing compared to the tourniquet of invisible barbed wire twisting my torso, shredding my skin and muscles.

Darkness collected at the edge of my vision, transforming into a pair of soulless eyes, peering down against a backdrop of gray sky.

A scream caught in my chest.

The eyes disappeared over the edge of the gold box I'd been left in.

The air smelled strange. Like magic and decay. Life and death.

Death.

Suddenly, I remembered.

I'd died.

This wasn't a box. It was a coffin.

Rían sprinted past as though he hadn't noticed me lying there, helpless and hurting. I tried to sit up, but all I managed to do was turn my head.

Black smoke leaked from a shrieking black-haired woman kneeling in the grass. A second woman with brown hair collapsed, clutching her chest. The blood-drenched dagger in her hand fell next to another body. A man with dark hair, staring at the clouds through sightless black eyes.

The smoke twisted toward the dagger, now bursting with unnatural green light. The dark-haired woman reached a shaking hand toward the blade. Rían snagged the dagger, glanced at the struggling woman, then drew the tip along the dead man's palm.

My eyes darted to my own blood-smeared hand and the silver scar stretching from my middle finger to my wrist. Had someone done the same to me?

The man Rían had cut jerked upright, his face changing into another face. *Tadhg.*

His hair wasn't brown but gold. He saw the brown-haired woman and let out a gut-wrenching wail. Crawling to her body, he rolled her over and—

Keelynn?

The world stopped.

She wasn't moving. Why wasn't she moving? I shouted for my sister. My limbs came back to life with a burst of heat and excruciating pain, like all my bones had been broken, set wrong, and had to be broken again to reset.

I writhed in the gilded coffin, struggling to see past the pain.

Blood trickled from Keelynn's nose.

Her mouth.

She choked and twitched.

"Keelynn!" She shouldn't be here. She should be married to Robert. She should be happy.

WHY WAS SHE HERE?

Why was Tadhg bending his head? WHY WAS HE KISSING HER?

Why was a strange black stain spreading from her mouth, down her chin, to the base of her throat?

Rían finally looked at me from where he knelt, clinical coldness in his eyes. I managed to catch the sides of the box and roll myself onto the grass. On legs shakier than a newborn foal's, I stumbled for my sister's body.

This made no sense. None of it.

The tears rolling down his cheeks. The way Tadhg held her in his arms, crying, "It wasn't supposed to be her. It was never supposed to be her. I was the one meant to die. Why didn't you save her?"

Rían's eyes lit up like two blue matches. "As weak and pathetic as you are, you serve a purpose," he spat, standing and brushing dirt from his breeches.

I tore my sister from Tadhg's grasp, clutching her against me. He didn't get to touch her. He shouldn't know she existed.

Unblinking gray eyes stared past me.

"Keelynn?" *Please wake up. Please, please wake up.* "I'm here. I'm back. Please wake up."

Tadhg growled, black shadows invading his green eyes. His cold, blood-soaked fingers wrapped around my wrist. "Give me back my wife."

My wife.

My wife.

My wife.

The Gancanagh had not just called my little sister his wife.

Tadhg ripped Keelynn's lifeless hand from my grasp, lifted her body into his arms, and stalked toward the crowd of people waiting by a castle's gate.

Creatures of all shapes and sizes stared at us with a mixture of fury and panic on their faces. In Airren you never saw so many gathered in one place. Unless we weren't in Airren . . .

Were we in *Tearmann*?

The creatures' haven on the west coast of the island. A lawless territory where no human could hope to survive.

"Where's he taking her?" The words rasped from my throat as I rolled unsteadily to my feet. "Tell me what's happening!"

Something flickered across Rían's impassive expression. He clasped my elbow, towing me through the crowd of whispering, glaring Danú toward a hulking stone castle with four turrets invading the sky. A strange sensation tickled my skin when we passed beneath the barbican, almost like walking through a cobweb, only there was nothing there.

An empty courtyard waited inside the walls. Crude wooden carts of fruit and veg had been abandoned next to a donkey and a wide, trickling fountain.

Rían didn't stop until we were inside the entrance of the keep.

Tapestries depicting gruesome battle scenes hung across the stones. Everything in the long, barren hallway echoed. Our footsteps. My ragged breaths. My pounding heart.

"Say something," I demanded.

He stopped before reaching a round table with a vase of blue roses. "Don't snap at me. This isn't my fault."

"I don't care whose fault it is! Tell me why your brother murdered my sister."

"Because murdering her was the only way to save her life."

Did he even hear himself? That made no sense.

His head tilted as he watched me, bloodstained hands clenched at his sides. "Now instead of being dead forever, she's only dead for a year and a day. After all the shite I've had to deal with over the last six months, I'm counting it as a win."

Six months. Not a year.

I'd been brought back sooner.

Perhaps I could bring back Keelynn as well.

Dammit. I shouldn't have to bring her back at all.

"Why is she here in the first place?" Why wasn't she off with Robert, making happy memories?

Rían flicked his wrist, summoning a tost. "She caught you and my brother in the feckin' garden and got it in her meddlesome head that she needed to save you."

Keelynn had seen me kissing a cloaked man. Dying right before her eyes. She knew the myths and legends better than anyone. She would've known I'd met with the Gancanagh.

What must she think of me?

"Why didn't you just tell her the truth?"

The bastard rolled his eyes. "Should I have done that before or after your father caught her on top of me?"

"No," I choked. He'd seduced my bloody sister? I'd kill him. I'd . . . I'd . . . I'd stab him right in his black heart.

Rían kept on as if he didn't notice me plotting his demise. As if he didn't see me drowning in rage. "And your father thought himself so feckin' clever, saddling an ambassador with his youngest daughter as a wife. All he cared about was my yearly income."

"You married my *sister*?" *Oh god. Oh no.* I braced my back against the wall, trying to catch my breath. "But Tadhg said . . ."

"Ah, Tadhg." Shaking his head, Rían huffed a humorless chuckle. "There's a good story. Shall I tell it to you?" He paused but didn't give me time to respond. "I married your sister, left her in the townhouse, faked my own death so she could marry her precious *Robert*, and do you know what 'innocent young Keelynn' did? She found this island's second most vindictive witch, bargained for a cursed dagger, and set off on a hair-brained revenge mission to kill a true immortal and bring you back to life."

Words.

So many bloody words, and none of them made a lick of sense. Witches? Bargains? Cursed daggers?

Keelynn?

"You'll never guess who she wanted to kill," he said, folding his arms over his chest, scowling at me as if I had an answer in my whirling brain.

Kill a true immortal.

Revenge mission.

"She wanted to kill Tadhg."

"Now you have it." His sardonic clap echoed off the stone walls. "She believed she could slay the monster who murdered you. Fate, being the cruel bitch she is, thought it'd be a feckin' brilliant idea for the two of them to cross paths. So he's all doe-eyed, believing that wasp is the sun, moon, and feckin' stars, marries her because they're 'soulmates,' and guess who shows up?" He gestured toward the closed door. "The witch she bargained with, holding your precious sister to her promise to slay the Gancanagh. That just about catches you up to today. Any questions?"

Only one. The same one he'd refused to answer at the beginning of all this.

"Why didn't you tell her the truth?"

His eyes shuttered. "I have my reasons."

"Do you now?" I took a halting step forward, struggling to channel my rage into coherent thoughts when all I wanted to do was scream. "You have your 'reasons.' Well, that's bloody brilliant, because I was afraid all of this happened because you *lied*."

"I'm too feckin' wrecked to deal with you right now." He flicked his wrist, and the air grew lighter. Turning on his heel, he started for the stairs.

"Don't you dare walk away from me." I rushed forward, shoving him square in the back, sending him into the table.

The vase toppled. Rolled. Exploded on the stones. Shards of glass skittered across the floor. I wanted to strangle him by the cravat. I wanted to hit him over and over and over until he begged me to stop. All men ever did was use me and let me down.

Rían's eyes lit up like twin flames. "Shove me again and see what happens."

I flattened my palms against his chest and pushed.

He flicked his wrist. My hands snapped to my sides. No matter how I struggled, I couldn't break the invisible bonds.

"Let me go this instant, or so help me—"

He circled, a predator toying with its prey. "So help you, what?" he snarled, eyes flaring. "What are you going to do to me, human?"

"I hate you." I hated his power. His presences. His lies.

He stilled. Inhaled. And smiled. "Good." He stepped over the fallen roses and what remained of the vase. "Come on."

"I'm not going anywhere with you."

His boots clicked as he climbed the first two stairs. "We both need sleep, and I refuse to deal with cranky Aveen."

Cranky Aveen? I wasn't a bloody child throwing a bloody tantrum. "I'm not sleeping here."

Rían stopped mid-stride, drumming his fingers against the banister. "Would you prefer to sleep in the dungeon?"

"I would *prefer* getting my sister and bringing her back to Graystones."

I'd have to come up with a way to explain my resurrection and find someplace to hide her body. Perhaps Padraig would have some ideas. Of course, that was assuming my father still lived at the estate. If Keelynn hadn't married Robert, he may have been forced to sell.

And if he'd been forced to sell, there'd be no estate to return to.

Meaning I had no home. No money. No clothes. No sister.

I had nothing and no one.

"And how do you plan on doing that?" Rían drawled. "The penalty for crossing the Black Forest without the Queen's permission is death, and our sea is swarming with hungry merrow. Go on." He rolled a hand toward me. "Tell me your grand escape plan."

Was he saying I was trapped in Tearmann?

Oh god.

No. It must be another lie. Rían didn't know how to tell the truth.

I would find a way out.

And when I did, Keelynn and I would leave this cursed land and go somewhere he and his brother would never find us. Bargain be damned.

"That's what I thought." The arrogant bastard pointed toward the next floor. "Now, you can either walk up these stairs on your own, or I can carry you. What's it going to be?"

Again, I tried to move my hands. Again, I failed.

Despite knowing there was no hope of escape, I retreated toward the door on principle.

Rían caught me, spun me around, and hefted me over his shoulder like a sack of flour. My indignant screams reverberated off the stone walls. No matter how hard I struggled, his bonds were stronger. Sweat trickled down my forehead into my eyes as he climbed higher and higher. When it became clear no one was coming to my aid, I stopped shouting.

Where were all the servants? Did no one care that I'd been taken hostage?

On the third floor, Rían left the stairs, plopping me onto my feet next to an arched wooden door. I glared toward the staircase. How far would I make it before he caught up?

"Don't even think about it," he growled, twisting the knob and throwing the door aside.

A white sleigh bed sat in the center of a modest bedroom. The thick rug beneath the bed stretched all the way to a stone fireplace.

Rían flicked his wrist, and the bonds fell away. A second flick and the fire in the hearth roared to life. "If you need me, my room is down the—"

"I won't need you."

Not now. Not ever again. Dead to me. That's what he was. Dead as my sister.

"Dammit, Aveen. Why can't you just believe I did what I had

to do and leave it at that?" He banged a clenched fist against his thigh. "You are the one who sought me out. The one who begged me to help you. This"—he gestured to the room—"wasn't part of the plan."

His plan? He wanted to talk about his bloody *plan?* "You promised to keep her from your brother. You promised to keep her safe. To keep *me* safe." Look at me now. Stranded in Tearmann. Empty. Hopeless.

Rían stalked forward, stopping when his boots met mine. I stood my ground, refusing to cower. His rage may have glowed in his eyes, but mine burned in my heart.

He leaned so close the heat of his breath slammed into my face. "Your sister threw herself at *me*," he said. "She kissed *me*, and when I tried to remove myself from the situation, your father showed up like a feckin' bull. Every bone in my body screamed to evanesce, to escape and leave her to her fate, and yet I stayed. I stayed because I knew, as angry as you'd be about me marrying Keelynn, you'd never forgive me if I abandoned her."

I wrapped my arms around myself, desperate to ward off the truth ringing in his voice.

If he hadn't married Keelynn, her life would've been over, all hopes of making a good match out the bloody window.

Men didn't want "soiled goods."

My father would've given her to the first man to make an offer and washed his hands of us both.

"As for the rest of it," Rían said, drawing back and tugging on the ends of his waistcoat, "I cannot control my brother or your sister. They found each other through no fault of mine. And you . . ." He let out a ragged breath. "You were never meant to wake up in this cursed place."

Turning on his heel, he stalked toward the doorway, pausing with a hand on the knob. "And for the record, I never touched her."

I didn't want to think about the two of them together. I didn't want to think about anything. "Get out."

Instead of arguing, he nodded. "Do not leave this room. Lock the door and—"

I stomped over, slammed the door in his face, and threw the bolt into place.

My wobbly legs gave out, and I collapsed into a heap on the wooden floor. The tears I'd managed to keep at bay finally broke free.

What a disaster.

What a bloody mess.

"Oh, Keelynn," I cried, burying my face in my hands. "What have you done?"

22

I AWOKE IN A COLD SWEAT BENEATH A MOUND OF BLANKETS, unable to remember getting into the bed. Someone had left a silver jug of water and a glass on one of the bedside tables.

I drank the whole lot.

The logs in the fire appeared fresh, but the sky outside was dark. Now that I'd slept, my mind felt clearer.

Rían had married my sister to save her from ruination. A heroic act *if* he was to be believed.

That was the problem, though. How could I believe him?

He'd claimed to have a reason for keeping her in the dark.

How could he expect me to blindly trust him? I'd done that before and look at me now.

I couldn't place all the blame at his feet. If I'd accepted my fate and married Robert, none of this would've happened.

I needed to find a way to fix this.

He'd mentioned a cursed dagger . . .

I opened my palm in my lap, running a finger along the silver scar. I'd wager he meant the one with the emerald in the hilt that I'd seen yesterday.

Slay a true immortal, resurrect someone from the dead.

That seemed simple enough.

First, I needed to find where Tadhg had hidden my sister.

Second, I needed to figure out how to escape Tearmann.

Third, get the dagger.

Finally, I'd toss a coin to decide which prince to kill.

Since I couldn't do the first in this bedroom, I peeled back the covers, rolled out of the bed, and pondered the second.

There had to be some way in and out of this place besides the Black Forest. No humans were permitted to set foot in the Queen's territory without her permission.

That's it.

The Queen was there to deter humans from entering Tearmann, right? But I was trying to get out. Surely she wouldn't refuse me if I explained the situation.

I just needed to find a way to meet with her.

It felt good to have a plan. Someplace to start.

I caught a glimpse of myself in the full-length mirror when I passed. Pale, grayish skin. Dark circles beneath my eyes. Blood smearing my cheek.

I looked like death.

New plan: Make myself look less like a corpse, *then* Keelynn, and *then* the Queen.

I opened the armoire beside the mirror, not caring what I had to wear as long as it wasn't covered in blood.

At least a dozen dresses hung inside. All of them stunning. And all of them blue.

They probably belonged to one of Rían or Tadhg's former— or current—paramours. I silently thanked the unnamed woman as I traded my soiled gown for one of chiffon that miraculously fit like it had been made just for me.

I scrubbed my face as best I could with what little water remained in the jug.

In the bottom of the armoire, I found a small gold hand mirror and comb. Once I had my tangled curls tamed and pulled back from my ghostly white face with a spare bit of ribbon, I went to the door.

The moment my fingers connected with the wood, Rían's warning growled in the back of my mind. *Do not leave this room.*

Rían may be a prince, but he wasn't *my* prince. And he sure as hell wouldn't dictate my comings and goings.

Sliding the bolt aside, I eased the door open, half expecting to see a guard at my door. Instead, I found only candles in sconces letting off a steady orange glow. The borrowed slippers kept my footsteps silent as I tiptoed toward the staircase.

Up or down?

Anyone upstairs would probably be asleep.

Down it was.

After descending three flights, I reached the main entrance. Someone had cleaned up the glass and flowers but hadn't bothered replacing the vase on the table.

The tapestries became terrifying nightmares in the dim light. Three banshees, with black eyes and white hair, hovered above a body-strewn battlefield. On the second tapestry, a woman wearing all black stood amidst the carnage, eyes closed and face raised toward the clouds, cradling two severed heads.

And I thought the decorations in my father's house had been hideous.

I stepped back, ramming into something hard. I would've thought it was a wall if it hadn't been warm. And *breathing*.

Whirling, I found myself staring up at a pair of narrowed golden eyes. The owner of those eyes was the size of a tree, with hair as black as coal and a white linen shirt unbuttoned at the throat.

He grinned, revealing elongated canines that could easily tear me apart. "I heard we had company."

I opened my mouth to scream but couldn't make a sound.

The man leaned forward . . . and sniffed me. Like a bloody dog.

His strange eyes widened. "Ye smell like dirt." Another sniff. "And rose petals. I like it."

His head tilted as he paused, waiting and watching.

What did he expect me to say to that? "Thank you?"

He gave a nod. "Yer welcome. Have ye come down to join us?" He shook something at me.

A bottle of wine.

Was he asking if I wanted a drink? That had to be a good sign, right? That he wasn't planning on ripping me limb from limb—at least not before he had his wine. "Who is 'us'?"

"Me and prince lonely heart. We're drowning his sorrows." He hooked a heavy arm around my shoulders, the liquid in the corked bottle sloshing as he corralled me into a mammoth parlor at least three times the size of my father's.

Tadhg lounged on one of two settees with his head against one arm and worn boots falling over the other.

Prince lonely heart.

More like prince no heart.

Pity the girl from Graystones, who loved a heartless prince . . .

Perhaps the fortune teller hadn't been talking about me. Perhaps she'd been referring to Keelynn all along.

For the only way to save him was at her own expense.

I wasn't sure how Keelynn had saved Tadhg, but the final phrase certainly applied.

"Look who I found wanderin' the halls." The black-haired man slammed the bottle onto the coffee table between the settees and a wingback. Floral curtains had been drawn tight over what I assumed were windows along the far wall.

When Tadhg saw me, his full mouth pulled into a frown. "Paws off, Ruairi. She's Rían's."

I didn't belong to anyone—least of all his wretched brother.

Ruairi's grin widened. "Even better."

Snorting, Tadhg tossed something toward the crystal glasses. It clinked against the rim, then fell to the floor. A coin. A *gold* coin.

Ruairi bit the top of the cork, worked it free, and spat it into the fire crackling in the fireplace. "Take a seat and tell me yer name, human," he said, pouring three glasses. His accent was thicker than Tadhg's and Rían's, still lilting but not as smooth.

I sank onto the settee closest to the fire, spreading my skirts to keep the draft from my ankles. "My name is Lady Aveen Bannon."

Tadhg launched another coin that bounced off the edge of a glass. "She's Keelyn's sister."

Instead of taking the open chair, Ruairi sat right next to me, his muscular thigh and shoulder pressing against mine. He smelled like crisp autumn leaves and worn leather. As much as I wanted to know what kind of creature he was, asking felt rude.

"What has the bastard prince done to deserve someone like ye?" he asked, handing me a glass.

What had Rían done to deserve me? Simple. "Not one bloody thing."

"Careful. If Ruairi thinks he has a chance, he'll follow you around like a pup until you turn him away." Tadhg tossed another coin. This one landed in a half-filled cup with a *plop*.

Ruairi wiggled his thick black eyebrows. Although he wasn't handsome in a conventional sense, there was something wildly masculine about him. Almost barbaric.

If he was as strong as he looked, perhaps he was powerful as well. Would he be willing to help me escape Tearmann?

Either way, with those fangs, I wanted to stay on his good side. "Is he housetrained?"

Tadhg snorted. "Mostly. Just don't let him near your wardrobes."

"Piss in a closet once and they'll never let ye live it down," Ruairi grumbled, clinking his glass against mine before drinking the whole lot in one gulp.

I lifted the glass for a sniff, and my stomach lurched. *Good god.* It smelled like rotting compost.

Another coin fell to the ground. Tadhg groaned as he reached for his glass, cursed when he sniffed it, then choked it down, spilling a good portion on his shirt, which was stained black with dirt and blood.

Ruairi topped up their glasses, then held the bottle toward me, eyebrows arched in silent question.

"No, thank you."

Tadhg launched a coin, hitting Ruairi square in the forehead. "You're the only one who likes that shite."

Ruairi cursed, found the coin where it had landed by his worn boots, and threw it back.

"I see the children are making a mess again," a familiar voice drawled from the doorway.

Rían.

When he saw Ruairi next to me, he evanesced, reappearing at the corner of the settee. "You will back off, mutt, or I will end you."

"Spoilt little prince was never taught to share," Ruairi whispered with a wink before rising and crossing to the wingback.

The spoiled prince was never taught a lot of things.

Rían glared down at me. "Did you not hear me when I said to stay in your room?"

"I heard you perfectly well," I said turning away from his pulsing jaw to offer Ruairi a brilliant smile. "So, Ruairi. I know Tadhg murders women and Rían torments humans, what is it you do? Dine on children?"

"Whatever it is the lads need done," Ruairi said with a gruff laugh, saluting Tadhg with his drink.

"Ruairi is excellent at burying bodies," Tadhg chimed in, pouring himself more. "But shite at kidnapping."

Bodies? Kidnapping?

I needed to get out of here. The sooner the better.

"Do either of you know the Phantom Queen?"

Tadhg spilled alcohol all over his breeches. Ruairi's glass stilled halfway to his mouth.

Rían stole my untouched drink, slammed it onto the table, and grabbed my hand. We evanesced into a candlelit room with bookshelves lining two of the walls.

Spread wide on top of a massive mahogany desk was a map

of Tearmann. A shadow of black marred the eastern border. *The Black Forest.*

Rían flicked his wrist, and the map vanished. Another flick, and the air changed. A tost.

"What do you think you're doing?" he ground out.

I gave him my most innocent smile. "I don't know what you're talking about."

"Aveen . . ."

"*Rían.*"

"In Airren, I played by your ridiculous human rules. You're in my world now. It's time to play by mine."

I shrugged. "If it suits."

"Not if it feckin' suits." He raked his hands through his hair. "I know you're young, but I did not think you were this childish. This world has bigger problems than your little sister taking a feckin' nap in the underworld."

The harsh words were like a slap in the face. He thought I was being childish? He thought I was the problem? "One truth, Rían. That's all it would have taken."

"I can count the number of people I trust on one feckin' hand. And your sister is not one of them. Did you ever consider how this bargain could affect me? How it could affect Tadhg?"

I . . . I hadn't.

Not at all.

"I could've said no. I could've turned you down. I should have," he muttered, huffing a breath. "Instead, I chose to help you."

In keeping this secret, he'd been protecting himself. He'd been protecting his brother. From what? I wasn't sure. But how could I fault him for doing the same thing I would have done if our roles had been reversed?

"So, what? You expect me to sit around here for the next year and trust that you'll help me find a way out of this mess when it's all over?"

"Yes."

"Sorry, *Your Highness*. I have my own *plans*." I would organize a meeting with the Queen, secure safe passage through the Forest, and say good riddance to Tearmann and cursed princes once and for all.

I tried to walk away, but my feet stuck to the carpet. Heat twisted in my chest like a burning wire ensnaring my heart.

"Aveen Bannon." Rían's voice rang with quiet authority. "To pay the favor you owe, you will remain in Tearmann until your sister returns from the underworld."

No. No. *No no no* . . .

"Until then, you are to live in this castle with me."

He held out a hand. I tried to hide my own behind my back, but magic took me in its steely grip, forcing my palm into his.

Was this my destiny? To forever be imprisoned by men?

At what point did I give up and stop fighting?

Tears scalded my cheeks. "I will never forgive you for this. Never."

He flicked his wrist, dismissing the tost. "I can live with that." When he offered me a handkerchief from his pocket, I turned away, dashing at my tears with my sleeve. I didn't want his help. I didn't want anything from him.

A hulking figure appeared from the hall, propping a shoulder against the doorframe. "Everything all right, human?"

Rían's expression hardened. "Everything is fine, Ruairi. Go back to the parlor."

Ruairi tilted the glass in his hand from side to side, watching me through wide eyes. "I wasn't askin' ye."

Rían flicked his wrist, and Ruairi disappeared.

If only I could do the same to Rían.

The wretched prince gave me a wide berth as he started for the door. "Now that we have that nasty business out of the way, would you like to see your sister?"

I nodded, not having it in me to summon a response. I drifted behind my captor, out into the hallway and back to the parlor.

Tadhg was still on the settee, elbows propped on his knees and his head in his hands, not bothering to glance our way.

Rían kicked his brother's boot. "Where are you hiding her?"

Tadgh lifted his head, glaring at Rían through red-rimmed eyes.

Could it be true? Had the Gancanagh, a being known for his insatiable appetite for women, truly fallen in love with my sister?

"Why does it matter to you?" Tadhg asked, scratching at a stain on his knee.

"I'm sure Aveen would like proof that you don't have her locked in some cage to rot."

Tadgh shoved to his feet, catching himself on the edge of the settee. When he straightened, his shin collided with the coffee table, rattling the glasses. "She is safe. I swear it."

One prince was holding me hostage and the other was a legendary monster. "You'll forgive me if I don't take your word for it." I'd learned Rían's definition of "safe" the hard way.

Tadgh mumbled something under his breath but didn't budge.

Rían shoved his shoulder, urging him toward the door. "If you hurry it on, I will ward the room in case any of your other 'friends' decide to make an appearance."

Although Tadhg appeared skeptical, he nodded and started for the hallway. Why would Tadhg need Rían to create wards? Didn't he have power of his own? When I asked, all I got from Rían was that his brother was pathetic and weak.

No surprise there. Rían thought everyone was pathetic and weak.

Tadhg had placed my sister's body in a gold coffin in an otherwise empty room at the top of the castle's tallest tower. Sunlight filtering through the window kissed her pale cheeks.

Rían remained by the entrance, arms crossed and boot braced against the wall. Tadhg sidled next to me, his almond scent almost nonexistent beneath the reek of booze.

"I know you won't believe me, but I love your sister," he

confessed with a sigh, brushing a finger down the length of her pale hand.

He was right. I didn't believe him. "Lust and love are two different things."

His mouth flattened. "I am acutely aware of the difference."

Tadhg's false love didn't matter—and it didn't change the fact that he was wrong for her. I needed to save Keelynn before she ended up trapped in Tearmann like me. So, I would stay and bide my time.

In a year, this nightmare would be over.

I'd lasted almost twenty-one years under a man's thumb. What was one more?

I brushed a glossy strand of dark hair back from Keelynn's pale face, wishing I could talk to her. Wishing there was some way to bring her back . . .

Wait . . .

That was it.

Rían had said I couldn't leave until Keelynn *returned from the underworld*, not that I had to stay for the year.

Had he done that on purpose, or had he slipped up?

"Is the cursed dagger the only way to bring her back before the year is up?" I asked, needing to be sure there wasn't an easier way.

Rían pushed off the wall, bracing his hands on his hips. "I'm afraid so."

"And all I have to do is kill one of you with it?"

"You can kill me," Tadhg said with a resolute nod.

Rían rolled his eyes. "If I have to listen to this martyr shite for the next year, I'm going to stab myself with the feckin' thing."

"Where's the dagger now?" I asked.

Rían gave me a pat on the head. "That, murderous Aveen, is none of your business."

My hands fisted at my sides. "What's the matter? Afraid I'll trade your life for Keelynn's?" After all he'd done, I would. In a heartbeat.

Sneering, he took a menacing step forward. "You don't have it in you."

Men had been underestimating me my whole life.

Never again.

I stepped toward the invisible line he'd drawn on the wooden planks. "Give me the dagger and we'll see."

Tadgh gave a startled laugh. "I like this one. She's vicious."

Rían flicked his wrist. A dagger appeared in his palm—not the emerald one from yesterday but the one he'd used on me the night before I died. A night I wanted to forget. He flipped it into the air, catching the blade between his thumb and forefinger, and held it toward me. "Go on, then. Stab me with it."

I caught the hilt, cold yet surprisingly light as my fingers wrapped around it.

I thought of my sister.

I thought of how much Rían had let me down.

"Like I said. You don't have it in—"

I plunged the thing into his bicep, all the way to the bone. My stomach lurched when I saw his shirtsleeve blooming red, but somehow, I managed to smirk. "You were saying?"

Rían's eyes went black as he dragged the knife from his flesh, blood dripping down the blade. "You ruined my feckin' shirt."

Rían and his blasted shirts. Perhaps I'd find his room later and take a dagger to the whole bloody lot.

The thought made me smile.

"You." Rían shoved Tadgh's shoulder, pushing him toward the door. "Out."

"And miss this? Not a feckin' hope. I must say, until this exact moment, my day has been shite. Ruairi's going to keel over when he hears—"

Rían flicked his wrist, and Tadgh disappeared. The dagger gleamed at his side, drops of deep red collecting on the wicked tip. Drip. Drip. Dripping onto the floor.

His head tilted, the gash on his arm already beginning to heal as his lips quirked into an uneven smile. "Feel better now?"

A little, actually. Who would've thought stabbing someone would be so cathartic? "I'd feel better if I'd stabbed you in the heart."

Brushing a curl from my cheek, Rían eased forward to whisper, "Get in line, my little viper. You'll have to wait your turn."

23

WHEN RÍAN PULLED AWAY, I WASN'T DISAPPOINTED.

Not at all.

Not in the slightest.

Relieved. That's what I was.

Especially when he turned and started for the door. "Are you hungry? Because I am famished."

Hunger. That's what the clawing ache in my belly must be. After all, I hadn't eaten in six months. "I suppose even hostages need to eat."

With a flick of his wrist, a clean blue shirt replaced his soiled one. "Would you prefer widow fingers or orphan ears?"

You are a hostage, Aveen. *Do. Not. Smile.*

"Surprise me."

The kitchen was on the lowest level, down the hall from the parlor and study. The sounds of pots and pans clanging, and the savoury smell of bacon grew stronger as we approached.

A portly woman with gray hair escaping a white mop cap bustled from the fireplace to the ovens and back again, stirring bubbling pots and humming away.

When she saw us, she threw the dish towel in her hand across her shoulder and hurried over.

From the black in her eyes, I assumed she was a witch. Her nose wasn't hooked, and her features weren't grotesque, as witches in the storybooks were often portrayed. If it weren't for her eyes, she would've looked like someone's old granny.

"There's my boy!" The woman gave Rían a pat on the cheek. When she saw me standing awkwardly in the doorway, her smile grew. "Is this who I think it is?" Her hands clapped under her double chin. "Oh, she is a dote! Come closer, girl, give us a look at ye."

I stepped forward, not sure what to make of the woman or her warm greeting.

Rían waved toward me like he was shooing away a fly. "This is Aveen. Aveen, this stunning young woman is Eava."

"Oh, you!" Eava whapped his shoulder with the back of her hand. "Deceitful wretch. Young woman, my arse."

Eava.

I remembered the name from the night before I'd died. I offered a tentative smile. "It's a pleasure to meet the woman responsible for the world's best cherry tarts."

She took my hands, squeezing them both. "I'm surprised this selfish bastard shared. He must be smitten with ye."

Smitten? I'd hardly call holding someone against her will "smitten."

Rían groaned as he passed. "Eava's mind is going. We only keep her around out of pity."

"Careful, boy. Or the next time I make ye tarts, they'll be poisoned." She dragged out one of the high stools at a butcher block table and patted the top. "Hop up there, and we'll see what we have fer brekkie."

Bowls and jars lined the center of the table, none of them labeled.

If I wasn't so set on hating it here, I could see myself liking Eava.

The witch went to a press in the corner to withdraw three plates. "Where's yer brother?"

Rían lifted lids off pots and pans, sniffing everything. "Busy drinking himself into a stupor, no doubt."

"Right so. He'll be needing soakage when he's through." She set the plates in front of me, then went to a different cupboard to drag out a tin of flour, sugar, and two eggs.

Some man my sister had married. A lousy, no-good drunk.

Throwing himself onto another stool, Rían leaned his chin on his hand and twisted to watch me.

If he didn't stop staring, I was going to shove him off.

A wrinkle formed between his bunched eyebrows. "Besides widows and orphans, what do you like for breakfast?"

Eava chuckled.

"I'll eat just about anything," I said. Keelynn had always been the picky one.

"I didn't ask what you'd eat. I asked what you like."

What did I like?

I'd never given it much thought. My father usually left the meals to the staff. I knew how to work out a menu with the cook, but it had never been necessary. Cook took care of everything on her own.

"I like . . . um . . . poached eggs and toast."

Rían nodded, turning to Eava. "Did you hear that, you old bat?"

She launched a wooden spoon at him, narrowly missing his head. "Next time I'll hit ye square between those pretty blue eyes."

His answering grin left my stomach in knots.

Hostage. Hostage. Hostage.

A hollow bang echoed through the wooden floor. No one else seemed to notice.

Eava dropped off four slices of toast, two for Rían and two for me, then went back to the hob to sprinkle a handful of herbs into one of the pots.

I reached for the dish of butter Rían had conjured from somewhere, halting when something banged again.

"What's that noise?" And where was it coming from?

It happened again, rattling the dishes.

Rían sighed. "That's Ruairi."

"It sounds like he's under the floor." I checked beneath the table for some access point but found only a brush and pan.

The toast crunched between Rían's teeth when he took a massive bite. "He is."

"Where?"

"Where he belongs."

Eava slammed a tray with two egg cups and two glasses of fresh orange juice onto the table. "What'd I tell ye about sendin' that poor boy to the dungeon?"

Ruairi was in the dungeon? Had he been there since this morning?

Rían took another crunching bite of toast. "To be fair, I did warn him."

Warned him? Hardly. "How can you punish him for coming to my aid?" Ruairi had been the only one to check on me, and I wouldn't soon forget it.

"You didn't need his aid," Rían countered, tapping a spoon against his egg, cracking the shell.

My hand tightened on the butter knife. "Do I not? My apologies. I thought you were keeping me hostage."

"Little Rían . . ." Eava clicked her tongue. "What'd I tell ye about keepin' hostages?"

His pointed his spoon at her. "The same thing I told you about calling me 'Little Rían.' I am not a child."

"Then ye should stop actin' like one."

I couldn't help my startled laugh. "Eava, I think you might be my hero."

She gave me a saucy wink and said, "If ye don't stand up fer yerself around here, these pretty boys will wreck yer head—and yer heart."

A cook who talked back to a prince.

And a prince who took it on the chin.

What sort of place was this?

The occasional scrape of cutlery and Eava's good-natured insults kept me company as I ate my breakfast, trying to make sense of this strange country.

Eava dipped her hand into a tin of flour and sprinkled the counter with the white dust. I'd never had an interest in baking, but if I was to be stuck here for the next year, perhaps I'd develop one.

"Eava?"

"Yes, child?"

"Will you teach me to cook?"

Her black eyes sparkled like obsidian chips. "It'd be my pleasure. Come down any day ye like."

When I thanked her, Rían threw his serviette onto his empty plate. "I don't know why you'd want to learn from Eava. Her cooking is revolting."

"Clearly."

Snorting, Rían brought his dishes and mine to a sink overflowing with bubbles.

"Pay him no mind. That's the lad's way of saying he loves something," Eava laughed.

"No, it's not." He dropped the dishes into the bubbles and grabbed a rag.

A powerful prince who despised dirt, was allergic to dust, and washed dishes.

Did anything about Rían make sense?

I slipped off the stool to collect the dish towel Eava had left down. Rían didn't bother acknowledging me when I took the clean dish from the drying rack and ran the towel over it. "How do you know when he hates it?"

Rían handed me the next dish. "Simple. I hate everything."

"He's a tricky one, our Rían. With him, ye need to listen with yer eyes and yer heart." She tapped her left breast, dusting flour over her dress.

Listen with my eyes and heart?

Did all witches speak in riddles?

When I looked back, I found Rían returning the dishes to the press. "Time to go, human."

I didn't want to go with him. I wanted to stay with Eava and ask the thousands of questions on the tip of my tongue.

"If that one pushes ye, give him a good push back," Eava chuckled, nudging me toward the door. "And remember," she said, giving my cheek a pat, "yer only a hostage if ye let him treat ye like one."

I followed Rían back through the hallway to a large dining room. Dark exposed beams held up the double-height ceiling. The click of Rían's boots echoed as we passed a table big enough for twenty to a set of double doors.

Compared to the drafty castle, the air outside felt warm and close, like the inside of a greenhouse. Had it been this way yesterday as well? If it had, I'd been too preoccupied to notice.

And I could hear the sea. It sounded close. What I wouldn't give to feel its salty spray against my cheeks.

Beyond a sandstone patio spread a maze of high laurels that made our own hedges back in Graystones look like twigs.

I nodded toward the opening. "The gardens?"

Rían rolled his eyes. "No. The dungeon."

If I was to spend the next year with him, I really needed to get my own dagger. Perhaps I'd ask Eava for one.

With each step I took, I pretended to grind his smarmy smile beneath my heels. Bees buzzed through the air, darting this way and that. If I had been dead for six months, it should be autumn. Yet when I rounded the corner, flowers bloomed in raised beds along the hedges. In stone-lined gardens around marble fountains. Between cracks in the high stone walls. Some I recognized, most I didn't; a vibrant kaleidoscope of color. The mix of floral scents felt like a balm to my shredded soul.

"Do you like them?" Rían asked from a few paces behind, without a hint of sarcasm.

I didn't want to like anything about this place, but how could I not like this? "They are more beautiful than I imagined."

"Humans. So easy to impress." He'd said it with a smile. "This way."

I may as well get my bearings. Later, I would come back to explore the gardens properly—without an audience.

Rían started for the courtyard. Two men with chestnut-colored skin and lashless eyes appeared deep in discussion next to a black horse. A white-haired woman with translucent skin floated near the entrance, her hair lifting around her slender shoulders. It was rude to stare, but I couldn't help it. What type of creatures were they?

They stared back at me as if I were the oddity.

I supposed here, I was.

When we passed the fountain, which looked more like a small pool up close, a dark head rose from the turquoise water. Black eyes set in a blue face focused on me. I knew what she was without seeing her tail.

A merrow. Just like the ones Rían and I had seen that day on the beach.

At the back of the castle, two grogochs in short breeches and brown tunics knelt in the vegetable gardens, pulling carrots from the ground. Beyond a patch of pumpkins grew a small orchard of various fruit trees.

Rían came to a stop next to a patch of grass and a small wooden shed.

"Here," he said.

"What is it?"

"It's a shed."

I ground my teeth together until my jaw ached. I could bloody well see it was a shed. "Why are you showing me a shed?"

"It's your shed."

"You expect me to live in a shed?"

Cursing, Rían stomped to the door, slid the bolt, and threw it aside, sending a blast of cedar-scented air over me. "Just look inside."

Shelves lined the wooden walls, filled with every gardening tool imaginable. A skinny table sat in the center, topped with pots of all shapes and sizes, packets of seeds and bulbs.

He was giving me a gardening shed?

Rían watched with an unreadable expression on his face.

"Why?"

He shrugged.

"Thank you." When he rolled his eyes, I bit back my retort.

"Don't bother me if you need anything else. Bother Oscar." Rían waved toward one of the grogochs in the garden. The stooped man returned the wave with a hairy hand.

"Why are you being so nice?"

His face paled as he glanced over his shoulder. "I'm not being nice. I'm showing pity to a powerless human hostage who serves absolutely no purpose whatsoever."

Heat bloomed in my chest, my anger flaring into fiery rage.

And then Rían did something so unexpected that it made me wonder what in the world was going on.

He winked at me.

Before I could demand an explanation for his mercurial mood, a roar erupted from inside the castle.

Rían clapped his hands, his eyes sparkling with mischief. "Brilliant. Tadhg is back."

We found Tadhg in the study, thrown across the chair behind the desk, covered head-to-toe in dirt. The only clean part of him was the bottle of amber alcohol cradled in the crook of his arm and the full glass in his hand.

"The feckin' oubliette?" he snarled. "Really? What are we, nine?"

Rían flicked his wrist. The bottle and glass disappeared. "Don't let your magic get so low and you won't have to spend your time drinking in a dark, dank hole."

Tadhg flicked his wrist, and they both reappeared. "Go to hell and I won't have to look at your dark, dank face."

"That's your comeback?" Rían snorted. "Put aside the drink, get some food in your gut, and come up with something better."

"I'm not hungry," Tadhg muttered into his glass.

Rían plucked the glass from him and dumped it on Tadhg's head.

Spluttering and cursing, Tadhg stumbled to his feet.

Its drawers rattled when Rían slammed the glass onto the desk. "Stop moping about. You need to be in Gaul by half eleven."

"You go to Gaul."

His eyes darted to me. "I have things to take care of here."

I wasn't sure why my stomach tightened. I didn't care whether Rían was here or not. He could jump off a bloody cliff and it wouldn't bother me in the slightest.

Tadhg dragged the stopper from the snifter, muttered, "So do I," and drank straight from the bottle.

I withdrew one of the books from the shelf and opened to a random page, pretending to be engrossed in Tearmann law instead of enthralled by two quarreling princes. Did they fight like this all the time? Keelynn and I rarely argued.

"So, what? You're going to spend the next twelve months in a drunken stupor?"

Tadhg's eyes darted to me. "It's what you did, isn't it?"

Rían's shoulders stiffened. "Unless you want me to kill you, I suggest you get down to Eava and put some food in your belly. Once you've sobered up and washed yourself, I will bring you to Gaul."

"If I leave the castle, you know what will happen. She'll never forgive me if I go off with anyone else."

Tadhg couldn't be serious. If he cared for my sister, he

wouldn't *want* to go off with anyone else. How were men so bloody obtuse?

Rían sneered, leaning over his brother. "We both know you won't last the year. You pretend that you are different, that you are better than me. But we're both villains."

I'd known Rían was a villain from the very first day, yet hearing him confirm it himself struck differently. He sounded almost resigned.

"How about we skip to the end where you accept it and rule your pitiful kingdom?" he finished, patting Tadhg's cheek.

Shadows writhed from Tadhg's shirtsleeves, curling in on themselves as he shoved Rían's hand, stood, and collected the bottle. "You will oversee the executions. I am locking myself in my room with this."

"I will give you one day!" Rían shouted at his back when Tadhg stalked past me.

Rían dragged open a drawer and rooted around, withdrawing a black leatherbound ledger. The door slammed closed. "I need to go to Gaul."

"Why?"

"We're expected to send a representative when Airren authorities execute our citizens."

A representative.

That's what he'd been doing that day in Graystones when Charlie and the fortune teller had been killed. He'd been there to watch them die.

He flicked his wrist.

Footsteps pounded from down the hall, growing louder until Ruairi appeared in the doorway. "You bastard! I ought to rip out yer throat."

"Not now, pooka. I'm dealing with something important." A dark overcoat appeared folded over Rían's forearm.

Ruairi was a pooka—a shapeshifting fae who could become any animal at will. Dangerous, wily, and powerful. According to the books I'd read, I should be terrified. Only, Ruairi seemed like the most congenial—and stable—of the lot.

"Where's Tadhg?" Ruairi demanded.

"Holed up with drink. Where else?" Rían shoved his arms into the coat. "This is what happens when you fall in love. You turn into a weak, miserable shell of who you once were." He straightened his cravat and collar. "And since my brother is a useless piece of shite, I have to go to Gaul."

Rían looked past me to Ruairi. "You are responsible for making sure no one kills my hostage and that she does not leave the castle grounds. If anything happens to her, you'll wish for the dungeons."

With that, Rían sauntered out the door, leaving me alone with a pooka.

24

WHAT WAS I SUPPOSED TO DO NOW? RÍAN WAS GONE, TADHG was drunk, and Ruairi was looking at me as though I had five heads. Locking myself in the bedroom would only remind me that I was trapped here, so I didn't want to do that either.

Perhaps a few hours in the garden would help clear my head. It wasn't as if there was anything useful for me to do.

I returned the book and squeezed past Ruairi, escaping to the hallway. Although his footsteps were almost silent, I felt his presence behind me like a dark, heavy raincloud. Before I could reach for the door, he lunged and caught the handle, drawing it open and holding it until I was down the stairs.

I thanked him.

He smiled, revealing those fangs. "Yer welcome."

The area had cleared out since this morning, although there were still two women chatting beside the gates. One had riotous orange hair falling to her waist and a baby on her hip. The other had short black hair and gold piercings snaking up her pointed ears.

The merrow from the fountain lounged on the wide ledge, green and blue scales glistening and pale blue skin shimmering. When we passed, she opened one black eye.

"Rotten fish," Ruairi greeted with a nod.

She smiled, revealing a mouth full of sharpened black teeth. "Smelly mutt."

Ruairi's answering chuckle vibrated deep in his chest. A chest that peeked from between the gap as he unbuttoned more of his grimy white shirt.

I forced my eyes ahead, focusing on the shed of gardening tools.

Again, Ruairi opened the door. Again, I thanked him. Again, he said I was welcome.

Pooka may have been big and burly, but at least they had manners.

I grabbed the first things I saw: a beautiful trowel with a gleaming blade and a bowl of bulbs.

Now I needed a place to plant them.

Where? Not with the vegetables or in the orchard, and the main gardens already had enough flowers. Digging them up would be like fingerpainting over a masterpiece.

"Ye look confused," Ruairi said.

"I don't know what these are or where to plant them," I confessed, showing him what was in the bucket in case he knew whether they needed sunlight or shade.

His broad shoulders lifted in a shrug. "Doesn't matter where ye bury the things. The magic inside the wards will make them grow."

Where was the joy in that? I wanted to do it myself.

"What about outside the wards?"

Ruairi frowned toward the open gates. "Rían won't like it."

"I don't care."

A chuckle. "Brilliant. Neither do I."

At the gate, Ruairi breached the wards without issue. When I tried, it was like I had hit an invisible wall.

Bloody Rían.

I gave the invisible barrier a kick but swallowed my scream. He would not break me.

"That man is infuriating." If he were here, I'd dump the bowl of dirt-crusted plants over his head and stab him with my trowel.

Ruairi came back, studying the shafts of sunlight bursting through the murder holes. "Yer only figuring that out now?"

The pathetic thing was, I had figured it out on day one and still hadn't stayed away.

I longed to feel the breeze swaying the long grass in the fields beyond the gates. Since I couldn't, I stomped back to the shed and threw the bowl onto the ground.

"Are ye all right?" Ruairi asked in his deep, gruff voice.

If Ruairi hadn't been standing there, I probably would've burst into tears. I had woken up in a strange land, surrounded by strangers, not knowing the day or the month or anything beyond the fact that my sister was dead.

Still, he didn't need to know any of that, so I said, "I am fine."

"Ye don't smell fine." His eyebrows lifted toward his disheveled raven hair as he sniffed the air. "Ye smell like bonfire smoke and . . . oud."

I collected my tangled mass of curls, lifting the ends to my nose. Although it could do with a wash, it didn't smell any different to me. "What are you on about?"

"Yer scent. It changes when yer angry. Which is odd. Fer a human, anyway." He sank onto the grass, laced his fingers behind his head, and laid down.

Surely he wasn't going to stay. I couldn't clear my head with him watching me the whole time.

I nudged his brown leather boot with my toe. "Don't you have anything better to do?"

"So many things." His eyes remained closed. "But seeing as the bastard prince told me to guard his hostage, that's what I'm doing."

I didn't want a bloody guard. I wanted to be left alone. "What's the point if I cannot get past the wards?"

"I'm not making sure ye don't leave. I'm making sure no one in here kills ye."

Besides the grogochs who had moved from the carrots to potatoes, the courtyard was clear. Nothing but us, the fountain, the line of empty stables, and the stone walls. "There's no one here."

"Doesn't mean it's safe. If an abhartach shows up, yer fecked. They don't feed on humans as often as they used to, but that's not to say they'd pass up an easy meal if it presented itself."

The abartach were a race of ancient witches who sustained themselves on blood. So much for the rumor that they were extinct.

Ruairi gestured to me with a giant hand. "Ned could swing by, and ye do *not* want to meet him."

"Who is Ned?" With a name like that, how scary could he be?

"Looks like a man, about so high." Ruairi held a hand above his head. "Actually, he's this high since his head isn't attached." He drew a finger across his own throat. "Rides a black horse named Lightning or Wind or someshite like that. Stinks of rotten flesh. If ye see him, he's hard to miss."

The Dullahan's name was *Ned?*

"Ned's job is collecting the souls too wicked for the banshee," he went on. "And the Phantom Queen doesn't leave the forest often, but news of a human in Tearmann is the sort of thing she'd be interested in." He shuddered. "It's a good thing yer a hostage."

The Phantom Queen.

Hearing her name left me shuddering as well.

"It's only a matter of time before Muireann will want to gut ye."

Heavens above. Another one? Perhaps I should've asked for a list of people who didn't want me dead. It'd be a lot shorter. "And Muireann is . . . ?"

"She's Rían's—" Ruairi's mouth snapped shut. Color climbed his flexing jaw. Suddenly, he found the grass next to him very interesting, and he began pulling it out blade by blade.

"Rían's *what?*"

"His merrow *friend* who resides in the fountain," he muttered under his breath.

The word "friend" had a bit too much emphasis. No wonder the merrow had glared at me. She ought to get over herself. If she wanted Rían, she could have him.

"The sprites watching us from the trees probably wouldn't kill ye directly, but they could make ye hallucinate so ye end up walking off the cliffs."

Something moved in the higher branches of the closest tree, behind one of the lushest, ripest pears I had ever seen.

Brilliant.

"So basically, everyone wants me dead." As if I needed another reason to not want to be here. I sank to my knees to gather the spilled bulbs back into the bowl.

"Basically. Yer human. And in these parts, humans are the enemy until they prove otherwise."

The Danú were hated in my world. It made sense they would feel the same about me in theirs.

I gave over my useless worry to the earth. Each time the blade cut into the ground, turning aside the grass to the dark, rich soil beneath, I could feel the tension in my shoulders loosening. If I closed my eyes, I could almost imagine being back at my father's house, doing what I loved without a care in the world. With the heat pricking my skin, I pretended it was a summer day.

My sister would be reading in the library. We'd share lunch when I finished, laughing and giggling over some silly nonsense that used to matter to her. Gossip. Scandals. Cake.

The moment I opened my eyes, the illusion shattered.

Ruairi watched, as if digging in the dirt was the most fascinating of pastimes.

I shoved my hair back where it had fallen over my sweaty brow. Why was it so warm and close in this infernal land? "Staring is rude."

"Sorry. It's just . . . ye seem remarkably well adjusted fer a hostage. Ye barely screamed at all."

So he had heard me screaming last night and hadn't come to my aid. I stabbed the ground. So much for finding an ally. "Have you met many hostages?"

I didn't like the look of his answering smile.

Brilliant. I was just another captive added to the long list. Bloody brilliant.

Ruairi picked up a lump of dirt to break it apart with his fingers, removing the small stones and setting them aside. "Why's he keepin' ye?"

The trench I'd dug was large enough for three bulbs. Not knowing how much room they needed, I left plenty of space between them. "I made a fool's bargain."

"Don't they teach humans not to bargain with the fae?"

"I was desperate and foolish."

And I silently vowed to never be that desperate or foolish again.

The next morning, I awoke to a tray of food in my room. After eating my fill of fresh peaches, yogurt, and toast, I dressed and made my way to the entry hall.

Expecting to see Ruairi, I froze in my tracks when I found Rían waiting for me at the bottom of the stairs.

"Hurry it on," he grumbled, twisting toward the door, a leatherbound book tucked beneath his arm.

Hurry it on?

What sort of greeting was that?

And then I remembered.

Hostage.

Today, Rían seemed as thrilled about this arrangement as I was.

Fate certainly had a cruel sense of humor.

He'd helped me to avoid marriage only to be forced into marriage himself. Some sort of poetic justice for his lies.

It was a wonder he was forcing me to stay instead of parking me on the edge of the Black Forest and saying, "Good luck."

Another balmy day greeted us outside.

Part of me wished it were rainy and miserable so I could add it to the growing list of reasons I hated this place.

The prince stalking toward my shed won a spot at the top of said list, followed closely by his lecherous brother.

Rían shifted a blanket and sat with his back against the wall.

Content to go about my day pretending he wasn't there, I dragged out my rake, spade, and trowel, and the rest of the bulbs from yesterday.

He didn't so much as look at me when I sank to my knees and started digging.

I wasn't sure how much time had passed, but my stomach began to grumble. I glanced at the sun, still low in the sky. "Is it almost lunchtime?" I asked the terrible prince.

Rolling his eyes, he set aside the book he'd been reading and shifted a silver pocket watch. "It's half ten."

Only half ten? Was he saying we'd only been out here for thirty bloody minutes?

He sent the watch away and collected his book.

A ripe, red apple appeared in my lap.

When I thanked him, he rolled his eyes again. If I weren't so hungry, I would've thrown it at his head.

I took a bite of the apple, the perfect blend of tart and sweet. Yesterday, my time in the garden had flown by. Today it crawled like the snail climbing the wall at Rían's back.

Would it be so bad to talk to him?

It certainly would help pass the time. It wasn't like I was punishing anyone but myself by sulking in silence.

I bent my head, trying to catch a peek at the title. "What are you reading?"

"Do not speak to me, human," he snapped.

I took another bite of my apple. Perhaps I would throw it at him.

He shifted his position and tapped his finger against the gold-embossed title on the front of his book. *Tearmann Law Vol. 20.*

Strange. Not the book—a prince would obviously need to be well versed in his country's laws. But his reaction.

I took another bite, chewing slowly as I tried to figure out the puzzle that was Rían. He looked especially handsome today, the sleeves of his light blue shirt rolled to his elbows. Dark trousers fastened with black braces. It felt strange seeing him without a waistcoat or cravat.

Casual Rían.

Sunlight played with the reddish tones of his dark hair. He would be much easier to despise if he were atrocious.

"How was Gaul?" I asked.

"That's none of your damned business, now, is it?"

My nails dug into my apple. If he didn't stop speaking to me as if I was a nuisance, I was going to—

Rían flicked his wrist. "Gaul was shite. Three leprechauns had been caught 'stealing' a farmer's old cow," he said in a much calmer voice, keeping the lower half of his face concealed behind the yellowed pages.

What in the world was going on? Why did he need a tost to say that?

I glanced over my shoulder. The merrow was there, sunning herself as she had been the day before. And Oscar was in the vegetable garden.

For some reason, he mustn't want them hearing about his day in Gaul.

"You don't think they did it?" I asked.

"What would a leprechaun need with a feckin' cow? Drink, sure. Gold, most certainly. But a cow?" He shook his head slightly.

"Did they have proof?"

"Proof?" He huffed a humorless chuckle. "Humans do not need proof. All they need are 'witnesses.' And the two half-drunk slobs lied through their feckin' teeth."

He'd said in Charlie's case there had been witnesses as well.

Witnesses who must've been lying, because Charlie hadn't done anything wrong. "Did you tell the magistrate?"

With a slight shake of his head, he said, "Do you think a human would listen to someone like me?"

He flicked his wrist. "This garden is shite," he clipped. "Get back to work before I change my mind about the dungeon." Another flick and the tost returned.

Right.

So not only did he want to keep his trip to Gaul a secret, he wanted his people to think he was treating me like dirt.

I positioned my body to face the wall instead of Rían so no one could see me speaking to him.

"We're not brought to defend the Danú," he said, flipping to the next page in his book and raising it higher so that only his eyes were visible. "We're only there so humans can remind us of how powerless we really are."

Rían? Powerless? That couldn't be further from the truth. He could literally flick his wrist and have anything he wanted.

I took another bite of apple, cleaning the juice spilling down my lip with the back of my hand. "So, what? You sat back and did nothing?" Were there no consequences for the people who had lied?

"I never said I did nothing." There was a smile in his voice.

"Tell me."

His eyes sparkled when they met mine. "I may or may not have introduced them to my mate Ned."

Ned.

The Dullahan.

Eithne.

Had her death and Rían's presence been more than a terrible coincidence? Had Rían orchestrated it all?

I tossed the apple aside, unable to stomach another bite. "Did you kill Eithne?"

"If I remember correctly, I was with you the entire time."

Rían and his fae non-answers. "You would send your lover to her death?"

His narrowed gaze lifted, slamming into mine. "That's what she did to Charlie, isn't it?"

"Charlie was my fault, not hers." My poor attempt at black-mail had put the series of events leading to his death into motion.

His wrist flicked, eliminating the tost. "Stop staring at me, pathetic human." As quickly as the barrier had vanished, it returned. "You blackmailed Eithne. According to Airren Law, you could be subject to up to fifteen years in prison depending on how much money was involved. She could have turned you in. Instead, she blamed an innocent man, resulting in the man's death."

He said it so cooly, without a hint of emotion. That woman, as awful as she was, had been his lover. Did he feel no remorse over her death?

I glanced over my shoulder to find the merrow watching us.

Ruairi had mentioned Rían and the merrow were "friends." He was probably trying to avoid making her jealous. Had they been "friends" when he was sleeping with Eithne? When he'd been with me?

"If you cared for Eithne, you could have turned a blind eye." What if he had considered Charlie's death my fault? Would he have sent Ned after me?

"I cared for that horrible woman about as much as I care for dirt on my feckin' waistcoat." He rolled his eyes. "Eithne's husband —who happens to be Graystones' magistrate—has strong ties to the Vellanian King. His terrible wife had a knack for learning secrets. And I had a knack for convincing her to share them with me."

A small part of me was relieved he hadn't actually cared for someone like Eithne. But mostly, I was horrified that he would use someone like that for information. "Rían, that's . . . That's appalling."

His eyes dropped to the book still in his hands. "Not nearly as appalling as fucking Eithne."

25

My heart was a traitor.

It had been four days since I'd seen Rían.

Four days of digging in the dirt, chatting with a pooka about everything and nothing.

Four days of searching the faces as they came and went—never in the castle, only in the courtyard—hoping to catch a glimpse of a blue-eyed prince.

My head knew what he was. What he'd done.

And yet my heart justified it all.

Keelynn had thrown herself *at him.*

Rían had married Keelynn *to save her from ruin.*

I'd woken up in Tearmann *because my sister brought me back.*

Rían was keeping me hostage *because I was stubborn enough to disregard everything he'd said and end up getting myself killed.*

I stretched my hands toward the ceiling, rolling my shoulders and neck to try and ease out the kinks. The white coverlet slipped down to my waist as I pushed myself upright against the headboard.

I liked Rían.

There. I admitted it. I wanted to hear about his shite trips to Airren. To have him tease me. To have him do more. But I couldn't do any of that if he didn't come back to the bloody castle.

Like every day before, a silver tray waited for me on top of the desk beneath the window. I caught a glimpse of myself in the window's reflection. A bit of color had returned to my skin, but my freckles had yet to appear. A few more days in the sun and heat, and they should be back. I desperately missed them.

Sinking onto the rigid chair, I removed the lid on the silver platter to find a plate of eggs, bacon, toast, and a small pastry box.

A cherry tart waited inside.

The subtle reminder of my last night alive left my stomach fluttering.

Was Rían back from wherever he'd gone? I'd asked Ruairi yesterday, but the pooka had said that he'd been charged with keeping tabs on a hostage, not a bastard prince.

The tart's crust flaked off on my fingers.

Heavenly. That's what it was. Absolutely heavenly. Crispy crust and gooey cherries still warm from the oven. The only way it could have been better was if there were ten more.

I ate the whole thing and considered licking the box it had been served in. It wasn't as if anyone would know.

After breakfast, I threw on yet another blue dress as quickly I could.

Being held captive in a house full of men meant no lady's maid to help me get into these garments. Yesterday, I'd had to ask Tadhg to help button the back of my dress. You'd swear I'd asked the man to eat a raw chicken.

What I needed were a few plain ones like my gardening dress. Next time I saw Rían, I'd ask. As much as I loathed the idea of living off his charity, as long as he insisted on keeping me locked up, he could deal with my needs.

After an altercation between my wild curls and a hairbrush, I made my way to where my sister was being kept. A ticklish sensation brushed my fingers when I reached for the golden handle.

Rían had made good on his promise to ward the room. But instead of blocking me as they did at the gates, the wards let me through without issue.

Next to her casket sat a pillow, blanket, and a half-drunk glass of amber liquor. Tadhg spent most of his days up here—and I suspected the nights as well. He'd added a fresh bouquet of purple hydrangeas since yesterday.

I still didn't think he was good enough for Keelynn, but seeing his utter devotion made me feel a little guilty for dismissing his feelings as pure lust.

I'd known plenty of lustful men. And if any of them had been in the same situation, they would've been lost in a woman, not a bottle.

My sister looked exactly as she had every other time I'd visited. Dark lashes dusting pale cheeks. Rich brown waves falling over slim shoulders. Black stain from her lips to her throat.

"I miss you," I confessed.

I would have given anything to hear her return the sentiment.

"And I miss *him* too. Silly, isn't it?" I laughed. "You wouldn't think it was silly, though, would you? You'd think it was romantic. You'd tell me I should let him sweep me off my feet."

Heaviness settled over the room, and a voice from the doorway said, "I do not sweep women off their feet. I drag them down with me."

Rían had a shoulder propped against the door, swirling a glass of amber liquid in his hand. His white shirtsleeves bunched at his elbows, revealing tanned, toned forearms.

"How much of that did you hear?"

He lifted the drink to his lips, hiding his smile. "Did you just miss me today, or have you been pining over my absence all week?"

Brilliant. He'd heard everything. "Don't be ridiculous." With my face burning, I shoved past him—and rammed headfirst into an invisible wall.

"I missed you too, my little viper," he breathed against my ear. "Will I show you how much?"

"That sounds like torture."

His dark chuckle teased against the fine hairs at the back of my neck. "It would be." Cinnamon and whiskey swirled around me. His teeth grazed my throat.

My eyes fluttered closed. This was what I'd wanted. Why was I fighting when I could allow myself to revel in dark desire? He wanted me, and I wanted him, and it wouldn't change who he was or who I was. If I kept my expectations low, gave him my body, perhaps I would emerge unscathed.

I leaned into him, my breath catching when his free hand slipped around my hip bone, kneading ever so slightly.

Then he was cursing and jerking away. The heat writhing my belly screamed. My eyes flew open to find Ruairi scowling at us from the other side of the tost.

A different kind of heat bloomed up my neck and over my cheeks.

Rían flicked his wrist.

"I've been shouting fer ye," Ruairi growled.

"We're a little busy," Rían muttered into his drink before taking a deep gulp.

"He's in an awful state."

I didn't need to ask who he meant. I hadn't seen Tadgh sober since I woke up.

"Does he not realize what day it is?"

"Oh, he knows. He's waitin' in the great room now."

The glass in Rían's hand vanished, replaced by a black waistcoat. "Get rid of him. Tell Oscar I'll be down in a moment."

"What's today?" I asked, watching Ruairi take off down the stairs.

"It's Friday," Rían said with a long sigh, slipping into the waistcoat. "And on Fridays, St. Tadhg hears the quibbles and complaints of the masses. Since he has become a worthless drunk, the responsibility has once again fallen on my shoulders." It took him three tries to get the first button on his waistcoat buttoned. "Ruling over the Danú is like minding a bunch of unruly children."

For some reason, I found myself reaching for the second button. His throat bobbed as his hands fell away, letting me fasten the rest. "And you don't like children?"

His lips twitched. "Only for breakfast."

When I finished, I found him studying me with a thoughtful expression.

"Thank you."

"Careful, now. If you keep this up, I may start thinking you have a heart."

"A trip to the dungeon would remedy that," he said with a wink, shifting a black coat.

He slipped his arms into the sleeves and straightened the hem, giving the staircase a wary glance. "Would you . . . Never mind."

I stopped him with a hand on his elbow. "Would I what?"

"Would you like to come?"

"Am I allowed? Wouldn't want to blur the lines between hostage and captor."

His dimples appeared when he smiled. "You blurred those lines the moment you said you missed me."

In the great hall, two wooden chairs sat on a dais, one large and ornately carved, the other shorter and plain, as if it had been taken from an old dining set and added as an afterthought.

Whispering Danú formed an orderly line from the foot of the dais, along the windowed wall, around to the entrance, and out into the hallway.

There had to be at least fifty of them.

I wasn't sure if the wary looks were directed at me or at Rían as he sank onto the larger chair and called the first person forward. I stayed behind, content to fade into the background in case any of them were looking for an afternoon snack.

The first person, with the body of a man and the face of a wolf, said he was there to pay taxes on his land. He set a heavy purse on the dais at Rían's feet, then left via the main door without another word.

Two short men with bulbous red noses wearing red tweed caps came up next, glaring at one another and grumbling under their breath. One tried to pass the other only to get hauled back by the shirtsleeve.

"See what I mean?" Rían muttered under his breath so that only I could hear. "Children."

When the men reached the top step, they both bowed their heads.

I bit my lip to keep from smiling.

Tenting his fingers beneath his chin, Rían looked down his nose at them and asked, "What is your issue?"

The taller of the two pointed an accusatory finger at the other man. "He's been takin' fruit from my tree again."

The shorter man smacked his counterpart's hand away. "As I've said time and again, 'tisn't yer tree at all. 'Tis mine."

"It's on my land."

"Growing over my feckin' fence."

They glared at one another, nostrils flared, fists tight at their sides.

Rían pinched the bridge of his nose. "So this is about a tree, then, is it?"

"*My* tree," the tallest confirmed with a bob of his head.

"The tree is—"

Rían's fist cracked against the throne's arm, sending vibrations through the floor. "Enough!"

The hall fell silent.

A book appeared in Rían's lap. He opened it to the middle, flipping to find whatever he was looking for. As his eyes scanned, he huffed a curse. "It would seem there is no law regarding a tree growing on the border between two properties." Another flick, and the book disappeared. "And as there is no previous ruling, I shall make my own."

Glares shifted to worried glances as the people at the front of the room began to whisper.

"The fruit tree belongs to neither of you," Rían announced. "It will be harvested, all fruit brought to the castle's store house, chopped down, and burned to the root."

"Prince Rían, ye cannot—"

"'Tis the best tree we got—"

Rían held up a hand and the hall went silent as a catacomb. "Did you or did you not come to me to solve this dispute?"

Neither responded.

"You could have worked it out amongst yourselves, but you didn't. And now neither of you get the tree. Now, get out of my sight before I decide to take your homes for wasting my time and everyone else's."

Their shoulders slumped as they turned and made their way through the crowd and out of the hall.

The next handful of disputes were resolved quickly and without issue. Each time, Rían called a rule book, found a previous ruling or law, and gave a clear verdict, outlining what was to happen.

It was fascinating.

How did he know which book he needed and exactly where to look?

He was absolutely brilliant. For all his eye-rolling and drawled responses, he was clearly enjoying himself. And the people, though wary, never argued with him.

They took his ruling as law.

More people paid their taxes with coins or food or bolts of hand-woven cloth. And then a red-faced man with a sloping jaw stomped forward, yanking a woman with orange hair toward the dais.

A woman I recognized from the courtyard on my first day.

She stumbled forward, her muddy slippers catching on the torn hem of her dirty skirts. Her knees cracked off the stones. Without thinking, I ran to where she'd landed, offering her a hand. Red, swollen eyes met mine. The tears streaking the woman's grimy cheeks tugged at my heartstrings.

With my help, she righted herself and smoothed a shaking hand down her skirts. "Thank ye, milady."

I nodded and returned to the dais.

"What's the issue, Madden?" Rían asked.

The man smirked. "I caught this deceitful witch shiftin' goods from Airren, bolts of cloth and the like."

Rían's eyebrows arched toward his perfect hairline. "Anwen, you have been charged with theft. How do you plead?"

The woman's gaze dropped to the stone floor. "Guilty, Prince Rían. But Maisie was sick, and little Sean needed new shoes, and with the new baby . . ."

That's when I saw them, two orange-haired children weeping at the door, the eldest clutching a baby to her chest.

The few remaining spectators exchanged worried looks. Like he had every other time, Rían called a book forth. I glanced over his shoulder as his finger slid down the entries, and my stomach filled with dread when I read the words.

The book disappeared.

Before he could speak, I caught Rían by the sleeve. "I need to talk to you." I tugged him toward the study door. Rían jerked free of my grasp but came along.

The door closed with a quiet click.

"How dare you order me around in front of an entire room of people. I should send you to the feckin' dungeon, human," he growled, narrowed eyes swirling with black. He flicked his wrist, and the tost descended. In a softer voice, still tight and clipped he said, "You cannot do that here, Aveen. Do you understand?"

For some reason, my head nodded, even though I was as confused as ever.

"Good. Now say you're sorry. And cry, if you can."

He flicked his wrist, and the barrier lifted.

I stared at him until he mouthed, "Go on," waving a hand toward me.

"I-I'm sorry?"

Rolling his eyes, he tugged his ear. "Louder," he whispered.

"I'm so, so sorry," I practically shouted. "Please forgive me. It won't happen again."

Nodding, he flicked his wrist. "That was shocking, but it'll have to do. Now, say your piece and hurry it on."

"You cannot kill that woman."

His eyes shuttered. "Theft of this sort is a capital offense." His voice held no emotion. No warmth.

"It's just cloth," I insisted, my heart thudding against my ribs. "Surely the law allows for extenuating circumstances."

"There is no gray area in this, Aveen. I'm sorry."

I caught his hand, determined to make him see reason. "Rían, please."

"Allowing emotions to cloud my judgement will only end in disaster. And if I do not follow the rules, then no one else will either." He unhooked my fingers. "You should remain here until I return."

I watched him flick his wrist and walk toward the door, wanting nothing more than to stay in this warm study and pretend that everything was all right.

But I couldn't.

I hurried after him, catching the door before it fell closed. Rían shot me a hard look, but instead of reprimanding me, he walked stiffly to the throne and sank onto the edge. "The law is quite clear in this matter."

No no no . . .

The woman's eyes glittered with tears.

"Anwen, you will be executed at sundown. Take this time to get your affairs in order."

I had to catch myself on the edge of the empty chair to keep from collapsing. How could he be so heartless? Did he have no compassion? The woman had children, and he had sentenced her to death.

The woman fell to her knees, sobbing, while the man who had accused her sneered and twisted toward the exit. Her children rushed to clutch her skirts. She wiped their tears with her thumbs, hugging them tight. "Mammy has to go away. But ye need to be brave." The eldest wept, burying her face in her mother's chest. "There, there. Yer gonna have to look after the smallies. Think ye can do that for Mammy?"

Sniffling, the girl nodded.

I couldn't bite my tongue and watch a woman be killed for trying to support her family. What could I do? I was nothing and no one. *Helpless. Useless.*

My gaze landed on the door leading to the hallway.

But I know someone who isn't.

I left via the study, running through the hall and up the stairs beyond. By the time I made it back to the fourth floor, the muscles in my legs ached and burned. I found Tadhg sitting on the stones beside Keelynn's casket, eyes closed and face raised to the ceiling. A silver scar across his throat stood out against his tanned skin.

"Do you know what I love most about your sister?" he slurred, not bothering to open his eyes as he stretched his legs in front of him. Muck covered the soles of his scuffed boots, and his buckles had been left unfastened. "She forgave me for everything I'd done even though I didn't deserve it."

Still drunk. Brilliant. Perhaps he'd be easily swayed.

The closer I got to him, the heavier the air smelled of drink. "Do you share her views on forgiveness?"

Glassy green eyes found mine. "Why? What has my brother done now?"

"He sentenced a woman to death."

Tadhg cursed. "Who?"

"I think her name was Anwen."

Groaning, his head fell back.

"She stole things to take care of her family, but Rían . . ."

Saying his name made me want to stab something. "He didn't even listen to her explanation. Didn't care."

"Rían's world is black and white. But the world isn't black and white, is it? It's a million shades of gray." A smile ghosted across Tadhg's cursed lips. His gaze fell to the golden coffin. "Your sister's eyes are the most beautiful shade of gray. Like storm clouds rolling in from the sea." Sighing, he pushed to his feet and brushed his hands down his dark breeches covered in stains. "I will fix it."

For the first time since he'd killed Keelynn, I saw a glimmer of a man worthy of forgiveness. "Thank you."

Tadhg nodded. "He doesn't deserve you. The sooner you realize it, the better."

The door flew open, making both of us jump.

Rían stood on the other side, clicking his tongue and shaking his head. "Now, now, brother. You know better than to meddle in my affairs."

Rían's eyes tracked me as I stepped closer to Tadhg. "And *you*. Was it not enough for you to question my authority and make me look like a fool? Now you run off to my feckin' brother and beg him to undermine me?"

Sneering, Tadhg settled his arm around my shoulder. "You may have played leader today, but Aveen knows who's really in charge."

Rían's eyes went black. With a flick of his wrist, Tadhg disappeared—along with the only hope of saving that poor woman.

I positioned myself between Keelynn and Rían, never taking my eyes from the prince's menacing stance, waiting for his breathing to calm. "I'm sorry, but you gave me no choice."

His head cocked to the side. His black eyes narrowed. "Do not say you had no choice when you did. You had a choice, Aveen." His fist banged against his thigh. Once. Twice. "And so did that witch. She knew what she was doing was illegal. She knew and did it anyway."

It sounded to me like the crime had been born of desperation. A last resort. "She deserves another chance."

"Does she now? And how many chances should I give her?" Holding up his fingers, he counted as he spoke. "Two? Three? No, wait. Four. Or should I give her five? I know! Six. Six strikes and then she's beheaded." He wagged a finger at me. "No exceptions though, I mean it."

Did he think this was funny? He had sentenced someone to death. And not death that lasted a year and a day. Real death. Final, eternal death.

"This isn't a joke, Rían."

"I'm not feckin' joking! That is what I hear when you say I should make exceptions. Who do I make these exceptions for? Just certain people? The ones with the most tragic backstories? Only the mothers? What about the fathers? Or should I make an exception for everyone? Should the law be eradicated and everyone be allowed to do whatever they please?"

Although I didn't want to admit it, there was no denying the validity of his argument. Where was the line between good and evil—wrong and right—if the law didn't make one?

It took a moment, but Rían's ragged breathing eventually steadied. In a calmer voice, he said, "Months ago, my brother offered Anwen some of the castle's rations if she could not afford to sustain her family. And yet her pride kept her from asking for help. She deserves to suffer the consequences of her actions."

Deserves to suffer?

What good did that do?

"You're wrong," I said. My words would fall on deaf ears the way they always did, but I couldn't give up yet. Not without saying one last thing. "Anwen doesn't deserve consequences. That woman deserves mercy."

26

My first scream was tentative, weak, and buried in my pillow.

For once in my life, why couldn't things be simple?

My second scream was a release, venting twenty-one years of anger and frustration.

I don't know why I bothered with the pillow. I was a hostage, after all. Hostages probably screamed all the time.

After my argument with Rían, I'd escaped to my room, hiding away from everything and everyone. I could shout and rail about the unfairness of what had happened all bloody day, but when it came down to it, I was a human living in a world where I didn't belong.

More than that, I was a woman, and Rían was a man.

And men did as they pleased.

My third scream was cut short when the door burst open.

Rían appeared in an untucked white shirt and loose black trousers. His hair stuck up at the back like he'd been snoozing away without a care in the world.

"It's the middle of the feckin' night. If you don't stop roaring, you'll be sleeping in the oubliette."

Was that supposed to scare me? Rían's threats were as empty

as his soul. "And if you don't get out of my room, I'm going to stab you again."

Instead of leaving, he dropped onto the foot of my bed. The curved dagger appeared in his outstretched palm. "Go on then. Stab me if it'll make you feel better."

I should stab him. It was the least he deserved for making me feel so torn up inside. How could I care for someone like him? A man without mercy. A villain. A liar. What was wrong with me? "I don't want your blood soiling my sheets."

He chuckled, sending the dagger back to wherever such things were kept. "Why were you screaming? Not that I care."

"That's what hostages do, isn't it? They scream."

"Hostages only scream for a short while." The mattress dipped when he fell onto his back. Heat from his body warmed my cold toes where they hid beneath the covers. I pushed myself against the headboard to get away.

"Then they cry and beg," he said, glancing sidelong at me, his eyes sparkling. "Will I make you cry and beg, human?"

Dark heat pooled in my stomach. How could I still be attracted to him at his worst?

I pulled my knees into my chest, holding them close. Another barrier between us.

As if he knew the way my body reacted to his threats, his lips lifted.

"I was screaming because I hate you," I told him.

He inhaled deeply through his nose, his smile growing. "No, you weren't."

Stupid man with his stupid ability to smell lies. "I was screaming because I am sick and tired of being held hostage by someone as evil and merciless as you."

He flicked his wrist. The tost's air thickened in my throat. Raising to his elbows, he fixed me with a withering look. "Am I holding you hostage? Most of my hostages do not live in my home, eat my food, or stroll through my gardens. I haven't even gotten around to torturing you—and that's my favorite part."

Listen with your eyes and your heart.

What if I chose to put all rational thought aside and believe him?

"In Graystones, you are dead," he went on. "You have no place to go and no means to support yourself. I'm not holding you hostage, Aveen. I'm giving you sanctuary."

It was true. All of it.

How would I begin to explain my resurrection to my father? To the other close-minded people back in my hometown?

"Why would you bother?"

He sat up, twisting to face me, his knee pressing against my shin. "You'll think I'm mad if I tell you."

"I already do."

He chuckled. "You and I . . . We are meant for each other."

My conversation with Tadhg in the garden came flooding back. "This is that soulmate nonsense, isn't it?"

His head dropped. "I'm going to kill Tadhg," he muttered, shaking his head.

This probably wasn't the best time for me to suggest he use the cursed dagger so I could get Keelynn back.

"It's not nonsense," he insisted.

In what world would fate pair the two of us together? We were attracted to each other, sure. But attraction wasn't the same as some cosmic force binding us to one another.

Rían caught my hand, bringing it to his face. The spark was there, only it felt stronger than before. "Do you feel that?"

I shook my head, not wanting him to see through my lie.

His eyes started to glow. "Don't lie to me. I know you do. I am cold and dead inside, but when you touch me, something ignites, and I burn," he confessed in a desperate whisper. "I burn for you just as you burn for me."

His tongue nipped out, leaving his lips glistening. "I know I'm not good—that I don't deserve you. I tried to let you go. Then you sought me out, and I thought maybe fate wasn't playing some twisted game. Maybe something in my cursed life was finally going right. Maybe I wasn't meant to give you up."

I pulled my hand from his cheek, rubbing it against the blanket to rid my skin of the incessant burning.

Rían's empty hands fell into his lap. "I should've known better."

I knew the look flickering in his eyes—felt it to my core.

Regret.

He stood, taking the fire with him as he retreated toward the door.

"Why did you come to my room?" I whispered.

His hand stilled on the knob. "Because you screamed."

I'd screamed, and the only person to come to my aid was my villain.

"Hostages are no good to me dead," he added with a wry smile before leaving me to burn alone.

Tiny shoots sprouted from the rich soil, but it would be at least a month before my garden looked like anything more than a plot of dirt.

Last night, sleep had come in waves, crashing over me. I was pulled into darkness only to be dragged back the surface by a blue-eyed prince.

I am cold and dead inside . . .

I burn for you just as you burn for me . . .

Why?

Why must I burn for someone like Rían? Why couldn't I burn for someone good and compassionate and merciful? What had I done wrong to deserve this fate?

Clearing his throat, Ruairí nudged a basket of almond fingers toward me. The pooka had met me in the entry hall this morning, the basket of goodies hanging from his arm. "Would ye like another one?"

Why couldn't I burn for someone like Ruairi? He seemed kind. Definitely polite. And funny as well.

I plucked an oval biscuit from the basket and took a bite. Crumbly on the outside, dense and moist on the inside. Tiny slices of heaven. "Eava must be the best cook on this island."

Ruairi nodded his agreement, crumbs tumbling down his chin. "She is. But she didn't make these." More crumbs landed in the dirt. "I did."

I held up what was left of the biscuit. "*You* made *these*?"

"I'm more than just a pretty face and charm." He laughed, grabbing another and eating the entire thing in one bite.

Now I really wished I burned for Ruairi. A pooka who could cook. Who knew?

"Your talents are obviously wasted on guard duty." It seemed such a pointless task considering I'd been here a week and not one person had made an attempt on my life.

He snorted. "Obviously."

His massive hand rested atop a discarded pile of stones we'd picked out of my garden.

I wonder . . .

"Can I see your hand?"

His brow furrowed, black eyebrows drawing together. "Why?"

"Just give me your bloody hand."

With narrowed golden eyes, he lifted his hand. Holding my breath, I placed my fingers in his and . . .

Nothing.

Not even a bloody spark. Just warmth and calluses and comfort.

"Are you all right?" he asked, head tilting, reminding me of a curious puppy.

"I'm fine," I lied, removing my hand and grabbing another biscuit. It was time to bury the disappointment settling in my stomach beneath a layer of butter, flour, sugar, and almonds. Some small part of me had hoped that perhaps the whole burning sensation had been a fluke, a common reaction for any human who touched one of the Danú.

So much for that.

I needed something to distract me from the growing realization that perhaps there was some truth to Rían's madness.

"Where do you live?" I asked, breaking another almond finger in half and savoring each delicious bite.

Ruairi folded his arms across his chest, studying me through narrowed yellow eyes. "Not far from here."

Lovely. Another person not willing to give me a straight answer. "Do you have a large house?"

"I'm comfortable."

"Tell me something personal."

"Why?"

Because I need you to take my mind off of HIM!

"You're one of the only people who talks to me all day and the only friend I have in this bloody place." I snatched the last almond finger before he could get it. "I am trying to get to know you."

His brow furrowed. "Ye think we're friends?"

"Sure." He could be my friend. It wasn't like anyone else showed any interest in me. Half the time it felt like the Danú no longer noticed I was here. After a week, I'd become as boring as the stone wall surrounding this castle.

"All right, friend. Let's see." Dragging a fang across his lower lip, he lifted his face toward the cloudless sky. "My favorite color is red."

I dropped my head into my hands. Why were men so dreadful at opening up? "That's not personal." When I looked up and found him laughing, I punched him in the thigh. He didn't even have the decency to wince. "Give me something else. Are you married?"

"No."

"Are you seeing anyone?"

"I see lots of people." He gestured to the merrow sunning

herself. "I see Muireann. And Finola and Anwen. And I can see ye."

Did he just say—

Across the courtyard, two women lugged baskets toward the castle. One of them had orange hair.

Anwen.

I scrambled to my feet, ignoring Ruairi when he shouted my name, sprinting across the grass and gravel to the women now staring at me with horrified expressions.

"You're alive." It wasn't eloquent or polite, but it was all I could think to say.

Anwen's wide eyes darted to the castle and back. The woman who'd been walking with her paused for a moment before continuing on to the main entrance.

"I am," she said with a bob of her head.

"How?"

She adjusted the basket on her hip, filled to the brim with ripe red apples. "Royal pardon, milady."

Tadhg had promised to fix it. I'd assumed Rían had sent him away so he couldn't. The next time I saw him, he was getting a hug, whether he smelled of booze or not.

"What did Tadhg say?" I asked, my voice catching. Perhaps my little sister's husband wasn't so bad after all.

Her light eyebrows lifted. "I didn't see Prince Tadgh. 'Twas Prince Rían who issued the pardon."

I opened my mouth, but no words emerged.

Rían had pardoned her.

Rían had shown mercy.

Rían had *listened* to me.

Anwen gave me one final frown before hurrying to where the second woman waited on the castle steps.

Hold on.

If Anwen was to have been executed at sundown yesterday, that meant Rían had pardoned her before he'd come to my room last night.

And the bastard hadn't told me.

As if I'd called his name aloud, Rían emerged from the castle, apple in hand, taking a bite as he strolled down the stairs and past the fountain.

My feet took off of their own volition, bringing me closer and closer and—

Rían turned in time for me to throw my arms around him.

He'd listened to me.

Actually listened.

And he'd done the right thing.

I squeezed him harder. Perhaps there was hope for him after all.

"What the hell do you think you're doing?" He shoved my shoulder, knocking me back a step.

When I saw the dark look on his face, my stomach dropped. "Giving you a hug?"

"A *hug?*" he scoffed. "You think just because I don't keep you locked up, that means you're allowed to touch me?"

Oh no . . .

"I'm . . . I'm sorry."

"I don't think you are." His pupils blew out, flooding his eyes with black. "But you will be." Rían caught my arm. Yanked me toward the back of the castle.

I tried to drag my feet in a useless attempt to deter him. He only pulled harder. Muireann sneered. Ruairi called my name.

Rían wouldn't throw me in the dungeon. He wouldn't. He was bluffing.

An ominous black door marked the entrance to the castle dungeons.

With a flick of his wrist, it flew open.

Oh god.

He wasn't bluffing.

The torches on the wall sparked to life. His blunt nails bit into my skin as he towed me down a spiral staircase, deep into the bowels of the cliff. Damp, dank air held an unmistakable coppery tang. At the bottom, the stairs opened to a narrow hallway with doors made of metal bars on either side as far as the eye could see.

He shoved me into one, stepping in behind, then slammed the door so loudly, the rattling bars echoed.

"I'm sorry," I cried, tears streaming down my cheeks. "I'm sorry. I'm sorry—"

He flicked his wrist.

With the tost, no one would come to my aid. No one would find me. Would he leave me down here for the year, just because of a foolish hug?

His black eyes narrowed as he stalked forward, forcing me into the corner. My spine collided with the gritty stones. My head hit the manacles dangling from the ceiling.

Rían braced his forearms on either side of my head, his eyes feral as they bore into mine. "I will tell you this once," he said, his voice smooth and lethal, the edge of a sharpened blade. "You cannot touch me or speak to me as if I am anything but the vile bastard I am. I have no friends in this castle, in this kingdom, or in this world. If anyone learns what you mean to me, I will be forced to kill them." He kissed me. The sweetest, softest brush of his lips against mine. "You are my only weakness. And if the world found out, it would take you away."

Like a key in a lock, everything clicked.

The soundproof barriers. The mood swings.

You are my only weakness.

Listen with your eyes.

I'd glimpsed the goodness in him, and then he'd hidden it away beneath snide remarks and scowls.

Listen with your heart.

My heart. The traitorous thing pummelling my chest. The only constant in this madness.

I'd wanted Rían from the moment he pinned me against that wall in the shed.

When he was sweet. When he was ridiculous.

I'd even wanted him when I hated him.

I used to believe all whispers were lies.

But Rían didn't whisper his lies. He whispered his truths.

There were two Ríans. One he showed the world and one he kept a secret.

One vile and heartless.

The other irreverent and ridiculous.

One belonged to the world. The other . . .

Could he belong to me?

"If I could, I would hold you close and never let you go," he confessed, his forehead dropping to mine. "I would kiss you for the entire island to see. I would take you in the middle of the feckin' courtyard. But this place is more dangerous than you could ever imagine. The only way to keep you safe is to leave you be," he said, resignation ringing in each syllable. "But I'm not strong enough to let you go."

With my head whirling and heart hammering, and heat building like an inferno in my belly, the last thing I wanted was for him to let me go.

"Then don't."

He captured my mouth the way he'd captured my heart. Wholly. Without mercy.

Rían would always be a mistake, but he was *my* mistake. A mistake made of my own free will.

He wasn't strong enough to let me go. And I wasn't strong enough to make him. He'd break my heart, and I'd come back for more.

Long fingers slipped around my wrists, raising my arms over my head. Cold metal brushed my fingertips. Rían clamped the cold steel around my wrists, tracing the length of my stretched arms back down to my heaving chest.

His grin held the promise of pleasure and pain as he caught my thighs and lifted me against the wall. Settling my legs around his lean waist, his hips started to rock, slow and menacing. "Will I torture you, human?"

He hit just the right spot, making me gasp.

There would be consequences for this. There always were.

How could I think about consequences with every hard inch of him grinding in a steady rhythm against my center? Consequences be damned. We were wrong for each other—so very wrong. And yet, I didn't want him to stop. I never wanted him to stop. "Do your worst, *Your Highness.*"

His kiss punished and tongue conquered, dominating with each perfectly timed thrust. He was a vicious spark, and I became a writhing flame as he shifted his dagger and cut me free of my clothes, baring my burning skin for his tongue's wicked ministrations.

Glinting obsidian eyes combed down my body. "You are magnificent."

For the first time in my life, I felt magnificent.

He kissed his way down my breasts, past my navel, to the curve of my hip bone, peeling away the barriers as he went. Kneeling on the stones, he lifted my legs over his shoulders.

I expected his hands.

He gave me his tongue.

I wanted to tug him closer, to make him go faster and harder, but all I could do was whimper as the chains holding me rattled. I wouldn't survive if he kept going. I'd die if he stopped.

"Rían—" His name was my plea.

"That's it," he murmured. "Cry for me. Beg for me."

"Please . . ."

He didn't let up when my legs began to tremble or when I begged for mercy. His unrelenting torment didn't cease until I burst into flames, leaving me ravaged. Gasping. Crying out.

The bonds fell away.

I ended up flat on the cold floor littered with hay.

I didn't care that the stones scraped my back.

Didn't care about anything as I worked the buttons free on his shirt, raking my nails down the broad expanse of his chest to his abdomen.

He freed himself, and I pulled him closer, so ready and yet so unprepared for him to sheath himself in one thrust so devastatingly slow I thought it would never end.

The tense muscles in his arms trembled, holding his weight.

I raised my hips, urging him to move.

"I thought I was the one torturing you," he groaned against my neck.

"And I thought I told you to do your worst."

Those black eyes blazed as he withdrew only to return again. Harder. Deeper.

Filling, rocking.

Making it impossible to catch my breath.

To find my thoughts.

To do anything but be consumed.

"Scream for me," he pleaded, eyes growing heavy and unfocused. Hips losing rhythm yet picking up speed.

His name wrenched from my throat, he buried his head in the crook of my neck, coming unraveled with a curse. Sweat-slick skin slipped against mine. My arms fell around him, holding tight as he shuddered.

Who would've thought, all those months ago, that this beautiful, wicked man would be my undoing? That I would be held captive in his dungeon, begging for torture.

Rían collapsed onto the floor, chest heaving. "I've never felt so alive," he whispered, between ragged gasps.

With my racing heart and a delicious ache between my thighs, my lips tugged into a smile. I knew exactly what he meant.

What if we stayed down here forever, hiding away from the world? What if he was this person all the time instead of the other one?

He glanced toward the door, and his smile faded.

Just like that, the rose-tinted haze evaporated.

I sat up to collect my dress from the floor. Bits of hay stuck to the ripped bodice. Dirt stained the skirt. "You need to stop ruining my dresses."

"You need to stop wearing dresses with so many feckin' buttons," he shot back. He flicked his wrist, and a new dress appeared.

Once I'd changed and he'd shifted himself some clean clothes, he used magic to unlock the door. Before I reached the steps, he caught my elbow, pulling me into him.

"Don't you dare walk out of here with a smile on those lovely lips. Between Anwen and this, the whole feckin' country will think I've gone soft."

I gave him a peck on the cheek. "Now that I understand your game, I'm ready to play."

27

THE MOUNTAIN OF BLUE DRESSES ON MY BED REACHED NEARLY TO the canopy, and there wasn't a garment left in the empty armoire. I'd never cared much for fashion, choosing modesty over flash. But tonight, I wasn't happy with anything.

I wanted to look well. I wanted to be beautiful. To be *magnificent*.

Eventually I settled on a dress the color of Rían's eyes, embellished with gold thread along the sweetheart neckline.

I couldn't wait for him to see me in it—and out of it. The frilly lace undergarments I wore beneath looked suspiciously like the ones he had bought that day in Graystones.

I didn't want the prince thinking of anything or anyone else tonight.

Tonight, I wanted all of his attention on me.

After what had happened in the dungeon, I wasn't sure how he'd act when he saw me again. Then he'd shown up at my door an hour ago, inviting me to dinner. It was the first time he'd asked me to dine with the rest of them. The idea of not having to eat alone in my room was nearly as thrilling as imagining what tonight would bring after dinner ended.

Ruairi was the only one in the parlor, standing with a glass of green liquid in his hand, watching the flames in the fireplace dance. His waistcoat wasn't buttoned, but he looked as if he'd bathed and combed his hair.

When I walked in, he saluted me with his glass before taking a deep gulp. "It's about time he let ye out of that room at night."

I poured myself a glass of green wine from the bottle on the mantle. "I can be very convincing."

He took the bottle from me to top up his own drink. "Lots of convincing goin' on down in the dungeons these days."

I choked when I sipped but managed to keep from spewing the disgusting drink into the fire. So much for keeping us a secret from Ruairi.

Returning the bottle to the mantle, he grinned as he raised his own glass in a toast. "Think yer man will run me through fer sayin' yer lookin' well?"

"Probably." I laughed, tapping my glass against his. "But I won't tell him if you don't."

Ruairi pretended to lock his lips and throw the "key" into the fire.

"Where are the others?" According to the clock beside the drinks cart, it was half past. Rían should've been here thirty minutes ago.

"A lady showed up not an hour ago askin' fer Tadhg. Because of his . . . em . . . *situation*, Rían is meeting with her instead."

"What situation?" Why couldn't Tadhg deal with it himself?

"It's his curse."

"What about his curse?"

The moment the question left my lips, Tadhg strolled into the room in what appeared to be a clean pair of breeches and black braces. His dark green shirt, although wrinkled, had no visible stains.

"I am a whore, Aveen," he said, selecting a glass from the drinks cart by the window and withdrawing the stopper from a decanter of clear liquid. "Cursed to be used and cast aside for all of eternity," he explained, pouring himself a glass. His nail *tap tap tapped* against the crystal. "While I do not always have a choice about whom I am forced to sleep with, this castle is the one place I am safe from unwanted advances." He downed the drink in one go and slammed the glass back onto the cart. "And *that* is why my brother meets with women in my stead."

With that, Tadhg turned on his heel and sauntered back out of the room.

No wonder Tadhg had locked himself away when Keelynn first died.

Nothing in this blasted land was what it seemed.

I dropped onto the settee, splattering wine onto my skirts. Ruairi settled himself beside me, stretching a long arm across the back of the cushions.

"Any other curses I should know about?" I glared sidelong at him. "Are you cursed too?"

"We're all cursed," he drawled, cradling his glass against his chest. "I love those I cannot have, and you love a heartless, bastard prince."

I did *not* love Rían.

I loved having sex with him. And I loved it when he was ridiculous. But I wasn't foolish enough to give my heart away to a villain.

Speaking of villains, Rían had finally appeared, shoulder propped against the doorframe, dressed head to toe in black. His piercing eyes slid from my head to my slippers, leaving fire in their wake. "You look hideous."

"And you look villainous."

He bowed his head slightly. "Thank you."

I washed away my giddy smile with a gulp of disgusting wine.

Rían crossed the room in a few strides to kneel in front of the settee. "I hate this dress," he whispered, taking my face in his hands and pressing his lips to mine, banishing the world to shadows.

All our other kisses had been stolen in secret. But this. This felt different. Possessive.

Ruairi's weight on the cushion next to me disappeared.

"I hate it so much, I want to cut you out of it," Rían confessed against my lips.

"You'll hate what's beneath even more."

"Shall we find out?" His eyes sparkled as his hands slipped beneath my skirts. Along my shins. Over my knees.

"Rían—" I threw a frantic glance over my shoulder. There was no one there. But with everyone's ability to evanesce, there could be at any second.

Those fingers danced along my inner thigh, higher . . . *higher* . . . "Yes, Aveen?"

"Someone may come—" *Bloody hell.* His lazy strokes against the bundle of nerves at my center were driving me mad.

He clicked his tongue. "That, my dear, is the point."

"Come *in*," I finished breathlessly.

He hooked a finger beneath my undergarments and slid them to the side. "They know better."

My head fell back against the cushion, and I gave in to the delectable feeling of his thorough exploration, drank in the scent of his magic, not caring if we had a whole bloody audience so long as he didn't stop.

Heaviness collected deep in my stomach, building and growing. Blossoming. Blooming. Bursting in an explosion of light and color. Leaving me panting, and Rían grinning like the cocky bastard he was.

He withdrew his hand and brought his fingers to his mouth. "I've finally found something that tastes better than cherry tarts." The way he licked his fingers one by one nearly brought me back to the edge.

I reached for his belt buckle, ready to devour him.

He nudged my hand aside, rose to his feet, and adjusted himself in his breeches. "Later, greedy Aveen. We've kept the others waiting long enough."

The others.

Being with him made me forget everything else.

"I thought no one could know about us," I rasped, pressing a hand to my forehead, trying desperately to catch my breath.

He held a hand toward me. I laced my fingers with his and a jolt of lightning shot through my arm. "My brother and his pet don't count. Besides, that dog was sitting far too close to you. He knows better than to go near what's mine."

"I'm a person, not a pair of slippers. I don't belong to anyone."

He gave my nose a flick. "Doesn't mean you're not mine."

Rían kept my hand through the hallway and into the dining room, where Tadhg lounged at the head of the table. Ruairi sat to his right, his spine and shoulders as rigid as the chair beneath him.

My face burned when Rían pulled out my chair and sat down next to me. Neither Tadhg nor Ruairi looked at us, instead focusing on the silver serving platters of roast duck, carrots and parsnips, and buttery mashed potatoes that had just appeared.

I took a small portion of meat and veg, passing the dishes to Rían when I finished. All three men watched me with raised eyebrows.

"Aren't ye hungry?" Ruairi took an extra-large portion of veg but no meat.

"Starving, actually."

He pointed at my plate with a dripping spoon. "And that'll fill yer belly?"

Tadhg scooped out enough mash to cover most of his plate.

After too many years of judgemental glares and snide remarks from my father, I'd learned it was easier to keep my portions small.

My own meager helping would barely fill my mouth, let alone my belly. I'd be hungry again before bedtime.

Rían handed me back the plate of duck. "Eat what you want. Or don't. It's up to you."

It was up to me.

My choice.

I did like duck . . .

And my father wasn't here to make a comment about how a lady shouldn't appear gluttonous.

Perhaps I could have a bit more.

All three men smiled and nodded when I took two extra slices.

Conversation remained light, centering around castle maintenance and the strength of the wards. Tadhg's misery only surfaced when things went quiet. His eyes, growing glassier with each sip of wine, took on a faraway look every time he glanced at the empty chair beside Ruairi.

The only thing that flowed better than the conversation was the wine. Rían warned me not to drink too much, though there was little chance of that happening. Faerie wine tasted awful. But it also made me feel warm and giddy and weightless. Like I could float away on a cloud. A tingly, warm cloud.

Who would've thought when I first met Rían that I'd be sitting in his brother's castle, sharing a meal with a pooka and the Gancanagh himself?

Rían flicked his wrist and eased back in his chair, cradling his glass against his chest. "You know what I think we should do?"

"The last time ye said that, Tadhg ended up killing"— Ruairi's head swung toward the head of the table—"how many people?"

Tadhg's eyes darted to me. He offered a sheepish smile. "Only two. But one wasn't my fault."

"I don't know how I feel about my sister being married to a murderer," I confessed. The man was starting to grow on me, but I still wasn't sure if he was a flower or a weed.

Tadhg pointed an accusatory finger at Rían. "He killed seven."

"Eight, actually," Rían said with a smirk, not a hint of remorse. "And they were all my fault."

"You have to stop killing people, Rían. It's wrong." How could I object to Keelynn being with Tadhg when I'd fallen for a monster as well? Rían needed to do better. To *be* better. And that started with not killing people.

The men exchanged wide-eyed looks. Then burst out laughing.

"I'm sorry. But have you met my brother?" Tadhg asked between laughs, wiping tears from his eyes.

Rían's dimples deepened. "For some reason, she insists on seeing the good in me."

"What good?" Tadhg snorted, smacking his brother's shoulder. "You're not happy unless you're murdering someone."

Rían leaned against the table with a heavy sigh. "I do love a good murder."

"What's your favorite part?" Tadhg asked. "Is it the way the light fades from their eyes? Or the way they always look so surprised?"

"For me, it's the coppery tang of blood." Rían's chest rose and fell when he inhaled an exaggerated breath. "Positively delectable. The bloodier the murder the better. Although the shite stains something awful. Just last week I ruined my favorite waistcoat."

They were insane.

Absolute psychopaths.

How could they sit there and laugh about killing another living person? "Murder isn't a joke."

Tadhg hid his smile behind his hand, nodding as if in agreement.

"Would it make you feel better to know the people I kill deserve it?" Rían whispered against my ear, spreading delicious heat all the way to my curled toes.

"Mostly," Tadhg murmured.

Rían gave him a kick beneath the table.

"Careful now, lads." Ruairi reached for the terrible wine. Instead of pouring himself a glass, he drank straight from the bottle. "She's getting proper cross," he finished, wiping his mouth on his shirtsleeve.

"I like her when she's angry," Rían said with a wink.

He was ridiculous. "What were you about to suggest before all of you went off on a murder tangent?"

Rían gave me a sheepish grin.

"It had to do with murder, didn't it?" I groaned.

His smile widened.

Tadhg and Ruairi sniggered.

I was about to lay into them when the clock hanging in the corner struck the hour. All three men cursed.

Ruairi slammed the wine bottle onto the table. "Shite. We almost forgot."

"Eava!" Tadhg's shout echoed off the high ceiling. "Eava!"

Rían cupped his hands around his mouth, shouting for Eava as well. Then Ruairi joined in, all of them chanting and banging cutlery and fists against the table.

The portly witch appeared, her eyes narrowed on Tadhg as she stomped over and smacked him in the back of the head. "What'd I tell ye about roarin' down the feckin' castle walls like a bunch of heathens?"

Tadhg caught her by the wrist and pulled her into his embrace, nestling his head against her considerable bosom. "Never leave me, Eava. You know I cannot live without you. Marry me."

She swatted at his arms, a delighted blush blooming over her round cheeks. "Get off it, ye wastrel. I'd no sooner marry ye than the man in the moon."

Rían stood and took her free hand, executing a courtly bow and kissing her knuckles as if she were a queen. "Marry me, Eava. I'd never love another."

"I've always had a weakness fer the wicked ones," she cackled, cupping Rían's jaw before shoving his head away. "But seeing as I've changed both yer nappies, there's only so much shite a woman can take. Isn't that right, Aveen?"

I stifled a laugh behind my hand, watching Rían collapse onto the floor and pretend to die a dramatic death on the stones.

"Let's hear yer proposal, ya animal," she threw over her shoulder at Ruairi, giving him a saucy wink.

Ruairi stood and sauntered over to the witch, hefted her into his arms, and pressed a smacking kiss to her thin lips. "Ye will get neither jewels nor power from me, but I can promise plenty of sleepless nights."

Eava's head fell back. Her delighted cackle reverberated off the windows. "There's a good lad." She patted his cheek with a withered hand. "If yer ever lookin' to settle down, ye know where to find me."

"Right so." He gave a resolute nod and carried her cackling right out the door.

"On Saturdays, we propose to Eava," Rían explained, sliding back into his chair.

"She chooses a different suitor every week. Although she picks Ruairi more often than not," Tadhg slurred, throwing back the rest of his drink.

"She must be a saint if she deals with the lot of you day in and day out."

Ruairi came back with a basket and threw himself into the chair. "God love that witch. She'll have me fat as a fool."

"What'd she give you this time?" Tadhg asked, rubbing his hands together.

Ruairi set the basket between us and removed the cloth, revealing heart-shaped pear tartlets. He tilted the basket toward me. I selected the smallest one, setting it on the tablecloth beside my empty plate.

"Saturdays are my favorite days," Ruairi said, his mouth full of tartlet.

Rían and Tadhg grabbed one each, mumbling their agreement as they settled back in their seats.

With dessert this good, I was going to ask Eava to marry *me* next Saturday. "Any other traditions I should know about?" Fridays were for the Danú and Saturdays were for proposing. What about the rest of the week?

Rían dabbed his lips with the serviette before trading it for his wine glass. "After dinner, we retire to the parlor to take bets."

My father used to do the same, closeting himself away with

any male guests to drink and smoke cigars and trade tales of their brilliance.

"What do you bet on?" I'd always been curious. When I'd asked him, my father had said it was not a lady's concern.

Rían pushed away from the table and took my hand. "Anything and everything. Death. Life. Rain. Snails."

I caught a shared glance between Tadhg and Ruairi, but neither one said a word as they stood and started for the parlor.

"Snails?" How did one take bets on snails?

A draft blew in from the main door, fluttering the tapestries. I could've sworn the woman holding two heads watched us as we passed. Why anyone would want to commemorate something so brutal and grotesque was beyond me. Battles were something to be avoided and mourned, not celebrated.

"We've raced them," Rían said. "And frogs. And squirrels. And one time, worms, but we all ended up passing out before we saw who won."

"I won," Ruairi announced, holding open the door to the parlor, "but these two eejits were too mean to pay up."

"Ruairi never wins," Rían whispered, shaking his head.

Three of the most handsome men I'd ever known—and certainly the most powerful—raced snails like children. If the people of Airren knew the truth about the Danú and magic, they wouldn't be nearly as afraid.

Ruairi collected another bottle of faerie wine from the drinks cart and brought it to the short coffee table where five glasses appeared. "Will ye join us tonight? I'm sick of lookin' at these two bollocks. And ye might keep the deceitful prince honest fer once."

Warm, fluttery hope swelled in my chest. "You want me to join you?"

"Only if you want," Tadhg said over his fresh drink.

"I do. I really do. But I don't have any money." I was having such a lovely night, I didn't want it to end.

"Oh, we don't bet money." Rían flicked his wrist, and a silver cufflink appeared. Yanking a button off his waistcoat, Tadhg added it to the empty glass. Ruairi dragged a black medallion from his pocket and threw it in as well.

What did I have? I untied the blue ribbon holding my hair back from my face and dropped it into the glass with the other trinkets. "What's the challenge?"

Rían rubbed his hands together as if plotting our demise. "Snapdragon."

Tadhg and Ruairi groaned.

A curved porcelain plate appeared, filled with raisins and almonds. Tadhg shifted a bottle of what smelled like brandy to douse the nuts and fruit. Then Rían conjured a ball of fire in his palm and lit the alcohol ablaze.

"The lads never miss a chance to show off," Ruairi muttered.

All the candles in the sconces and the fire in the fireplace went out, leaving nothing but blue flames from the burning plate flickering over our faces.

The men began undoing the cuffs at their wrists and rolling their sleeves over their forearms.

"Ladies first." Rían scooted the plate toward me.

"What do I do?"

"You get one."

"One what?"

Rían gestured toward the plate.

He couldn't be serious. And yet he *looked* serious. "I'm not sticking my hand in fire."

Rían's eyes never left mine as he stuck his hand straight in, grabbed a flaming raisin, and popped it into his mouth.

"Last time we played this, it took a feckin' month for the hair on my arm to grow back," Ruairi grumbled, thrusting his hand into the fire and coming out with an almond.

Tadhg went next, moving quicker than anyone should have been able to move.

"This isn't fair. I'm not as fast as you are." Even so, I thrust my hand into the flames. It stung for a split second, but the pain quickly faded as I pulled out a flaming raisin. The bloomin' thing burnt the roof of my mouth, but I'd done it. I grabbed my glass of wine to ease the sting.

Around and around we went, until the plate was nearly empty.

"I fail to see the point in this." Unless it was to make my head spin. Because it was also going around and around and around.

"What's the point in anything?" Tadhg slurred, grabbing the last almond, dropping it into his wine with a *plop*, and throwing it back.

What *was* the point in anything? Especially when you couldn't die and had the power to get everything you ever wanted. What was there to fear when you were the most fearsome? What was there to be joyful about when everyone feared you? What was the point in existing without either?

I reached for my wine glass . . . and missed. Someone must've moved the bloody thing. I tried again, this time catching the stem before it escaped. "How do you pick a winner?"

Rían's teeth flashed. "Oh, we're not finished yet."

With the plate clear, Rían extinguished the flames with a wave of his hand, casting all of us in darkness. All I could see were three pairs of glowing eyes: golden, green, and cerulean blue.

"Now we play blind man's buff," he announced.

"In the dark?" My sister and I had used to play the game at Yule when we were children, but we'd always done it by candlelight.

"Everything's more fun in the dark," Rían said, his voice thickening.

Tadhg chuckled. "Ruari's it."

Ruairi cursed. "Dammit. I'm always first."

"Stop whinging and blindfold yourself."

My eyes began to adjust to the darkness. I could make out vague shadows of the chairs and the settee from the faint light filtering in through the window.

"Ten . . . Nine . . ." Ruairi began counting down. "Eight . . . Seven . . . Six . . ."

Furniture scraped across the floor. If I wanted any chance of winning, my best bet was to find a place to hide and hope everyone else got caught before me. I made my way toward the window to duck behind the curtain.

A warm hand snaked around my waist. Cinnamon-scented air tingled against my lips, and it felt as though the floor vanished beneath me. A split second later, the sensation subsided, and I heard Ruairi finishing his count from down the hall. The smell of leather and ink replaced the magic.

"Three . . . two . . . one. Here I come. Ready or not." There was a clatter and a curse.

"Who moved the feckin' chair?" Ruairi yelped. Someone—I assumed it was Tadhg—sniggered.

Rían lifted me onto the desk, knocking over an unlit candlestick.

"I'm pretty sure leaving the room is cheating," I mumbled against his smiling lips as he nudged my knees apart with his hips.

"They play their games while I play mine," he whispered, dotting hot, open-mouth kisses down my throat to the swell of my breast. "Stay with me tonight."

More cursing and glass shattering erupted from the other room.

I bit my lip to keep from moaning. "Why would I want to do that?"

"Because if you don't, I'll fill your bedroom with mice so they can nibble your toes. Or burn the entire castle to the ground except the dungeon." His idle threats hummed against my skin.

I threaded my fingers through his hair, clutching him against me. "I suppose I don't have much of a choice, then, do I?"

A chuckle. "Hostages rarely do."

28

A FEW DAYS LATER, I MADE PLANS WITH EAVA FOR MY FIRST cooking lesson. Rían had shifted some new dresses for me, similar to the one I used to wear in my garden. The soft gray and brown cotton was a nice change from all the blue.

I found Eava doing what she always seemed to be doing: flitting from one pot to the next, chopping this and that. Mixing and stirring and filling the kitchens with delicious aromas that left my mouth watering.

"Good morning, Eava."

She gave me a hurried wave before taking the steaming pot off the hob and setting it on a folded dish rag next to a second. "Morning, child. Good to see such fine color in yer cheeks. Tearmann suits ye."

I felt my face flush.

The sun in this place may have tanned my skin, but the color in my cheeks had come from waking up next to an amorous prince.

"I think you may be right." I wanted to smile all the bloody time when I thought about him.

Which wasn't ideal, considering the moment we set foot outside the castle, we had to pretend to be enemies.

I used to be good at pretending. I'd convinced my father and sister that I was content. Everyone in Graystones had believed me to be the perfect lady.

But Rían made it so damn hard.

Eava grabbed an apron from a hook on the back of the door and tossed it at me. "Put this on so ye don't ruin yer dress."

I slipped the loop over my head, and she helped me tie it at the waist.

"Now fer the blindfold," she said, giving my shoulder a pat.

"Blindfold?"

A scrap of cloth came over my eyes, wrapped around my head, and was tied tight.

"Ye need to feel the ingredients. Smell them. Taste them. 'Tis the best way to know if ye've added too little or too much."

That sounded a bit silly, but she was the expert. I gripped the edge of the table in front of me to keep my bearings. "You don't follow a recipe book then?"

"My recipes live up here." She tapped my temple.

She cooked by memory? How did she keep all of the recipes straight? Perhaps I didn't want Eava to teach me how to cook after all.

Dishes rattled and clanged around me. I could feel her skirts brush against mine as she went from what sounded like the corner press to the table and back again.

"I can take this off and help you," I offered.

"No need. I'm almost done. Now." She came to a stop to my left. "Give us yer hand there."

I held out my left hand. Eava thrust it into something cool and soft.

"Know what this is?" she asked.

I let the dust settle between my fingers. Smooth. Soft. Almost odorless. "Flour?"

"Very good." She moved my hand to the next mystery ingredient. "And this?"

Gritty and fine. Easy. "Sugar."

"And this one?"

My fingers sank into something warm and sticky. I immediately pulled back. "That feels disgusting."

"But what is it?"

"Rían Joseph O'Cleriegh!" Eava snapped. Not close by. From far away. "What'd I tell ye about messin' in my feckin' kitchens?"

I ripped off the blindfold with my clean hand to find two Eavas—one with laughing blue eyes and the other with stern black ones. Then I looked down to see my hand covered in lard.

With a flick of a wrist, the laughing Eava vanished.

"Forget everything that nutter said," Eava grumbled with a shake of her head, hefting a thick book down from a shelf in the corner. The pages were brown and worn and scribbled all over. "I always follow the feckin' recipe."

That afternoon, I met Ruairi outside the castle's main doors, bringing the mini vanilla cakes, one for each of us, that Eava and I had baked.

"Hostage," he said with a nod.

I smiled. "Guard."

Instead of taking me to the garden, he said he had a surprise and started for the gates.

The courtyard was quiet today, with only Oscar and Fillion changing the hay in the empty stables. The moment we crossed beneath the barbican, I felt the wards prickling my skin. Only this time, instead of blocking me, I stepped right through and out into the bright sunlight of Tearmann.

The sweetest breeze, smelling of salt and sand, lifted my hair from around my face. "He let me out . . ."

"Good hostages are rewarded," Ruairi said with a fanged smile, starting up an emerald hill toward the sound of crashing waves. Within minutes, I found myself on the crest of a cliff, staring out at the tumultuous sea.

The east coast where I'd lived eased into the water. But this . . . This wild land didn't ease. It came to a violent end.

It was the most beautiful thing I had ever seen.

Ruairi's hands slipped around my waist. I squealed. Whirled. And found a smirking prince where my guard had been only a moment ago.

"Disappointed?" he laughed.

"So disappointed," I countered, catching his collar and giving him a quick peck on the lips. "Why are you here?" He hadn't joined me since that day in the garden.

"To torture you. Why else?" With a flick of his wrist, he was no longer Rían but Ruairi, from the broad shoulders and raven hair to the sharp incisors, all mimicked to perfection. Everything but his blue eyes.

"Why can't you be you?" Besides the circling black and white birds, the waves, and the hills, there was no one to see us together.

He gestured toward the sea far below, to flecks of vibrant color I hadn't noticed flashing beneath the water. Merrow danced with the waves, beautiful and ethereal.

A small part of me wondered if all this secrecy had to do with his relationship with a different merrow. With Muireann.

A wool blanket appeared, stretched across the undulating grass at the cliff's edge, pulling me back from my darkening thoughts.

Rían tugged at the basket on my elbow. "What'd you bring me to eat?"

I let him slip it free and look for himself. "Something far nicer than you would have made." According to Eava, Rían had shown an interest in cooking once upon a time. And had nearly burned the castle to the ground.

"Ah, here now. I can't be good at everything." Rían handed me a cake and took the other for himself.

I sat, clutching my knees to my chest and watching the chaos below. The cake was almost perfect. A little dry, perhaps. I'd have to ask Eava what I did wrong.

Rían ate the whole thing in four bites. "Revolting," he said, dabbing at his lips with one of the serviettes from the basket.

That's what he says when he loves something.

Blue peeked from under his sleeve. I caught his hand, drawing his cuff back from his wrist, to find a blue silk ribbon tied beneath. "What's this?" It looked like . . . "Is that mine?" It *was* mine. I remembered betting it the other night.

"I was hardly going to let Ruairi or Tadhg have it."

"Sentimental Rían." Fanning my face, I pretended to swoon. Although the fluttering in my stomach wasn't pretend. It was as real as the heat building in my core. He'd stolen my ribbon. And was wearing it. "Be still my heart."

He chuckled Ruairi's chuckle. Smiled Ruairi's smile.

Would this powerful prince, hiding behind someone else's skin, ever stop surprising me?

For the longest time, I had been hiding too. Beneath lies of contentment and complacency. Beneath makeup and dresses and nods and smiles.

I may not look any different than I had back in Graystones. But I felt different.

All it took was being held hostage by a fae prince to make me feel free.

"Do you always stare at Ruairi this much?" Rían asked in Ruairi's voice, blue eyes crinkling at the corners.

"I stare at him all the time. Barely get anything done when Ruairi's around."

Gleaming white fangs flashed.

I missed his obnoxious dimples.

"Sounds like I need to find you a new guard," he said, nudging my shoulder with his—and nearly toppling me over. "A female one."

"What's the matter?" I nudged him back. "Afraid I'll fall in love with him?"

I thought his smile faltered, but it was probably my imagination.

"Love him all you want. The dog's a waffling eunuch."

I laughed. "Stop lying."

"It's not a lie." He reached for his belt, dragging the strap through the buckle. "I can show you, if you want."

"Rian!" I whapped him on the shoulder as hard as I could.

He captured me in his massive arms, hugging me to his chest. "Violent Aveen. My favorite."

I leaned into him, committing this perfect moment to memory. This sort of happiness never lasted. It wasn't like I wanted live in Tearmann forever. That would be madness . . . wouldn't it?

If the Queen gave me permission to cross the Forest, could I leave this behind? What about when Keelynn returned? If she cared for Tadhg half as much as the man seemed to care for her, she wouldn't want to leave him.

The obvious choice would be for both of us to stay.

Only, I wasn't sure how I felt about being in a secret relationship with someone in the long term. It may be exciting and exhilarating now, but we couldn't keep this up forever.

At least, I couldn't.

But what if Keelynn stayed? What if I never saw her again?

Suddenly, things didn't feel so simple.

They felt impossibly complicated.

I turned away from the sea, peering beyond the distant hills.

"Is that the Forest over there?" I asked, nodding toward the trees lining the far horizon.

"A forest, yes. But not *The* Forest. There's a river separating the two." His chest brushed against my back when he inhaled a deep breath. "Why? Are you planning on running away from me?"

I shook my head.

"Good. Because I'm not beyond actually holding you hostage."

I thought of Padraig and his human wife, living outside Tearmann because the Queen had refused her entry. He could have evanesced back and forth, no problem. Instead, he'd chosen to stay with her, build a life with her, in a land where he had to remain hidden.

"Has the Queen ever agreed to let a human cross?"

The sound of the sea and the breeze all died the moment Rían flicked his wrist. "Why?" he snapped, scooting back to look in my eyes.

"Calm down, it's just a question."

"Dammit, Aveen." He raked his hands through his hair, leaving it standing on end. "I thought we were past this."

"I'm only asking out of curiosity." There was no reason for him to get worked up about it. It wasn't like I was planning on leaving today.

"You're curious, are you? Well then, allow me to appease your *curiosity*. Yes, the Queen has let humans in to Tearmann. As a matter of fact, she let your sister through, accepting Tadhg's life as payment for her 'death tax.' There have been humans who want to get into Tearmann so badly that they bring another human to offer as a sacrifice. Do you know what else she's done? She's let people cross back and forth, then changed her feckin' mind so that those people could never cross the Forest again."

My stomach dropped. "Rían—"

He continued as if I hadn't spoken, eyes hazy and unfocused. No longer here but somewhere else. "And then those people were foolish and thought they could break the feckin' rules, and they ended up getting killed for it." His glowing eyes found mine "So, no, Aveen, it's not just a 'question.' Not to me."

Not to me.

Another piece of his puzzle clicked into place. The Queen had killed someone he cared about.

Perhaps even someone he loved.

"Who was she?" I asked, dread swelling in my chest.

His heavy sigh seemed to leave him deflated. "Her name was Leesha."

Leesha.

My heart shattered.

Rían had loved a human named Leesha.

"And the Queen . . . She killed her?" I don't know why I asked. The answer was obvious.

"Wanted me to do it, actually," he whispered, his hands flexing into fists. "To put my duty to my people over my useless emotions. 'Your human broke the rules and must suffer the consequences,'" he mimicked with a sneer.

I couldn't imagine. Couldn't even begin to fathom what I'd do if faced with such an impossible dilemma.

"When I refused," he said, "she did it for me."

She took something precious from me.

I remembered another day when we'd sat by another sea, speaking of wishes and dreams. How different Rían's had been from my own. Even for all my despair, I had been able to find some peace and solace in my fantasy.

Rían had wished for murder and death because someone had taken something from him.

Not something. *Someone.*

"Your vengeance," I whispered.

A nod.

And I'd dismissed his heartache as a waste of a wish. I was a fool. A bloody foolish fool.

Rían deserved his vengeance.

Rían deserved retribution for what the Queen had taken from him.

I reached for a hand that didn't belong to him. "You have the dagger now. Why don't you just kill her?"

His fingers tightened around mine. "If a true immortal cuts another using that cursed blade, the curse will claim them both."

Stupid fae rules. What good was an invincible weapon no one could wield?

Except, Keelynn had used it to kill Tadhg and the witch who'd cursed him.

If a true immortal cuts another . . .

Keelynn wasn't an immortal.

Keelynn was human.

"A human can use it."

Rían nodded. "All it takes is a single cut for the curse to steal our life force. But since no human can enter the Forest without her permission . . ."

If no human could reach the Queen, then she could never be killed.

"You see the problem," he finished, slipping a hand around my shoulder and drawing me into his embrace.

"What if the Queen leaves the Forest?"

"She doesn't."

"But what if you convinced her to? I'm human. And we both know I have it in me to stab someone."

"You're not human."

What was he on about? Of course, I was a bloody human.

He pressed a tender kiss to my hair. "You're mine."

On my way to the dining room that evening, I caught Tadhg drinking alone in the parlor.

Again.

Curtains drawn, no fire in the hearth, drowning himself in drink and darkness.

I could've kept going, left him to his misery. But then I remembered how miserable I'd been the night before I died.

And how Rían had refused to leave my side.

How good it felt to have someone around to take my mind off things.

So instead of going to the dining room for dinner, I went into the mammoth parlor, sank onto the settee beside my sister's husband, and stole the glass right out of his hand.

He scowled at me.

"Do you love my sister?" I asked.

His teeth scraped his bottom lip as his scowl became a pitiful frown. "More than life itself."

It was one thing to say pretty words and another thing entirely to mean them. I lifted the glass for a drink. The clear liquid scorched my throat on its way down to my empty stomach. "How do I know you're not lying?"

A furrowed brow replaced the frown. "Because I can't lie."

"You *can't* lie?"

Tadhg shook his head, ruffling his golden curls. "It's another one of my curses."

Not the response I had expected. The fire in my throat had eased, so I took another sip. "How do I know *that* isn't a lie?"

He plucked the glass from my fingers and took a drink himself. "You don't."

I settled back against the cushion, studying the Gancanagh through new eyes.

A handsome prince, to be sure. But also a man cursed to be used. A man cursed with death's kiss. A man cursed to tell the truth.

A man heartbroken over the loss of the woman he loved.

With a flick of his wrist, a bottle and a second glass appeared on the coffee table. He poured me a drink before topping up his own.

How would Tadhg handle losing her to the underworld for all of eternity when she succumbed to age or disease? He was immortal, and she wasn't.

Their story could only ever end in tragedy.

The same as mine and Rían's.

After our walk to the cliffs, Rían had brought me back to the gate and mumbled something about having business to attend to. I spent the next two hours in the garden trying to process what I'd learned. All it did was make me sad. And angry. And then sad again.

"Why do you love Keelynn?" I asked.

Tadhg didn't respond right away. Just sat there, arm thrown over the back of the settee, sipping his drink.

I expected him to remark on her beauty. Because Keelynn was beautiful. But she was so much more. Wild. Loyal. Silly and smart. She listened. She cared.

"She is the most forgiving person I've ever known," he said. "And when you're as cursed as I am, you need a lot of forgiveness."

I raised my glass in agreement. "I certainly can't argue with that."

29

"HE SAID WHAT?" RUAIRI GROWLED. HE SOUNDED BEASTLY WHEN he did that. Like a bear. A big, fluffy bear.

I giggled into my hand. Wasn't sure when Ruairi had arrived. Must've been a while ago since there were *sooooo* many glasses on the floor in front of him.

I also couldn't remember who had suggested sitting on the floor, the cross-legged pooka to my right or the Gancanagh lying on his back staring up at the ceiling. Whoever it was, I was glad he had suggested it.

When was the last time I sat on the floor for no reason at all?

"He said you were a eunuch. No! A *waffling* eunuch," I laughed, stretching my legs toward the crackling fire and wiggling my bare toes. How had I never noticed how fascinating fires were? White and yellow and orange and red. Or blue like the night we'd played snapdragon. Good thing we weren't playing now. I'd probably end up burning my hand off.

"That bastard," Ruairi muttered into his glass. "I can say with complete honesty that I am *not* a eunuch. Waffling or otherwise."

"Prove it," Tadgh slurred with a sloppy smile, an empty glass resting on his chest.

"And have yer brother castrate me when he finds out? Not a feckin' hope in hell, lad."

Rían probably would castrate him. The thought made me laugh for some reason, even though it wasn't the least bit funny. Poor Ruairi looked appalled.

"I'm sorry." The more I tried to stop, the harder I laughed. The harder I laughed, the harder it was to stay upright. I fell back, landing next to a pair of shiny black boots. Boots attached to a very angry looking prince.

"Which one of you pricks got my hostage sozzled?" Rían grumbled.

The glass on Tadhg's chest fell off when he raised an unsteady hand. "That would be me."

Rían gave Tadhg's worn boot a kick. Tadgh just smiled.

"You truly are worthless," Rían said.

I smacked his shin. "Be nice to your brother. He's heartbroken."

"Then perhaps he should be doing something about it instead of drowning himself in drink."

"You want me to do something about it? Give me the dagger and hold still."

"Another day." Rían scooped me up, one arm beneath my knees and the other behind my shoulders, cradling me against his chest. "This one needs her sleep, or she'll be cranky come morning."

Sleep? I didn't want to sleep. I felt brilliant. I didn't think I'd ever need to sleep again.

Ruairi chuckled.

Poor Tadhg looked like he was about to burst into tears.

"Way-way-way-way-wait! Tadhg?"

He smiled a sad smile. "Yes, Aveen?"

"Keelynn would hate it if she knew you were drinking every day of the week."

The smile vanished. "Goodnight, Aveen."

"Good night, Tadhg. Night, Ruairi!"

A chuckle. "Night, human."

I pressed my nose into Rían's chest as we evanesced, inhaling the sweet scent clinging to his shirt. "You smell like cinnamon biscuits."

His startled laugh vibrated against my nose. "Is that meant to be a compliment?"

I nodded. "I love cinnamon biscuits. Not as nice as chocolate though. *Mmmm . . .*" When was the last time I had chocolate? That sounded scrummy right about now. "Think Eava would make me a chocolate cake?"

"She'll make you whatever you want. Eava loves you. I'm not sure why though. You're an obnoxious drunk."

"Ugh. Grumpy Rían." I planted my index fingers on either corner of his mouth, forcing his lips into a smile the way he'd done to me once before. "I want a different one."

He dumped me onto a four-poster bed with no canopy. "Grumpy Rían is the only one who can deal with drunk Aveen."

I'd been staying in his chambers since the day I'd visited the dungeon. I had expected the space to be lush and opulent, befitting a prince.

Rían's bedroom was the opposite: Stark. Barren. Utilitarian.

I rolled off the mattress, catching myself on the corner post to keep from landing headfirst on the floor. "Why is your room so empty?"

"What do you call this?" He bounced on the end of the mattress, then reached for the buckle on his boots. When he finished, he'd return them to his closet next to at least four other identical pairs. "And that." He gestured to the small leather-topped desk. "And those."

Those. Meaning his three armoires.

I'd had a snoop the other morning. One for breeches. One for shirts and waistcoats. And one for boots. All his clothes had been pressed and hung. Most were black or white, but some were varying shades of blue.

"I mean decorations. Frilly bits. You don't even have a canopy. Or a rug."

"For what? Collecting dust?"

Right. The allergies.

Rían slipped out of his waistcoat and added it to the laundry basket dedicated to waistcoats. He had one of each of those for breeches, shirts, and miscellaneous bits as well.

He was so organized. So disciplined.

Then again, he didn't have maids around to clean up after him. He had to do it himself.

I fumbled with my buttons until I got enough undone to get the blasted dress over my head. I left it on the floor, waiting to see how long it took him to shift it into my own laundry basket.

Ten seconds.

Now for the stay . . .

Eight seconds.

And my shift.

Only five.

Rían remained seated on the bed, the muscles in his arms flexing as he braced his hands on the edge of the mattress. So strong. So handsome. His eyes flashed. So *hungry*.

I sauntered over to him, reveling in the way those glowing blue eyes tracked every movement. Every breath. Every pounding beat of my heart.

When I reached for him, he moved away. A fresh white shift appeared in his hands. "Cover your bits, drunk Aveen."

"Drunk Aveen wants grumpy Rian to put her bits in his mouth."

"What did you just say?" he choked, fingers digging into my hip bone.

"You. Heard. Me."

His fingers contracted. "Feckin' hell, woman. How much did you drink?"

"Just enough to feel invincible." After four glasses, I'd lost count.

"You may be invincible, but I can assure you that I am not." He draped the shift over my bare breasts. "Put something on. Please." His voice broke on the last word.

He wanted me to put something on? All right. I collected his waistcoat from the basket and slipped my arms into the sleeves. "Better?"

His eyes burned bright as the snapdragon fire. "Worse."

I made a show of drawing down the plain white quilt and slipping beneath. He joined me, staying as far on the other side of the bed as he could without falling off.

"I'm cold."

"Then put on some feckin' clothes."

I patted the space beside me. "Come over here and warm me up."

"I won't touch you when you're this drunk."

When I scooted closer, he gave an exasperated sigh.

"You don't have to touch me." That didn't mean I couldn't touch him. I slid a hand beneath the covers, finding him hard and waiting. His harsh intake of breath when I gripped his rigid length left me grinning.

"Aveen," he groaned, screwing his eyes shut.

I started slow, thinking of the way his hips moved when he was inside me. "Hmmm?"

Rían's fingers slipped around my wrist, stilling my hand, drawing me away despite my whimpered protest. "I am going to make your life hell in the morning."

Something tickled my cheek. A draft? An annoying fly? A rustling leaf?

It happened again, and I brushed it away. I'd been having the most fantastic dream. Rían and I were about to make love on the beach and—

Something flicked my nose. Hard.

A handsome prince grinned at me from the next pillow over. "Good morning."

Soft sunlight trickled through the curtainless window, highlighting his toned chest and that mysterious scar.

"Leave me alone." I stole the covers falling around his midriff, wrapping myself into a warm, snuggly, cinnamon cocoon, content to stay right here all day.

He flicked my nose again. "Not a feckin' hope. Wake up."

"I don't want to." Rubbing my sore nose, I turned my back to him, the movement making the room tilt and spin.

"And I don't care." Warm hands slipped around my bare waist, pulling me so our bodies aligned. Soft, warm kisses danced along my neck. "The sun is shining, and we are going out for a long, strenuous hike. At least ten miles."

A ten-mile hike? That sounded like hell.

I had a better idea.

A smile crept over my lips as I rolled my hips. Rían's soft curse left me giggling until the bastard flicked my nose a third time.

"Ouch! That hurts."

"Fair's fair. You torture me, I torture you."

Arching my back in a slow, languid stretch, I reached my arms toward the headboard, making sure the covers slipped to my navel.

Groaning, Rían palmed my breast, then whispered, "Out of bed, hungover Aveen. There's walking to be done."

I couldn't tell if we did ten miles or not, but it certainly felt like it. It was more of a coastline stroll than the hike he'd threatened, with my irritating prince showing not a bit of sympathy for my sore head and sick stomach.

By the time we returned to the castle, I could barely lift my legs. Rían had pretended to be Ruairi the entire time, and with the extra-long legs, I had to work double time to keep up with his mile-long strides.

At dinner, I ate an entire plate of braised pork and roast potatoes, while a green-faced Tadhg moaned and groaned at the head of the table. Ruairi looked no worse for wear, laughing and teasing the sick prince. I had a feeling I would've been the same if Rían hadn't forced me out of bed that morning.

That evening, Rían shifted me a hot bath, left a jug of water on the bedside table, and told me to get some rest.

When I closed my eyes that night, an unfamiliar, warm feeling settled into my chest, like someone had wrapped my heart in a fuzzy quilt. I realized there was nowhere else in the world I'd rather be. Drifting off with a smile on my lips, I finally knew what it meant to be content.

30

WHEN YOU FINALLY FIND YOUR PLACE IN THE WORLD, YOU WILL never want to leave.

That was the first thought to filter through the warm sunlight and into my mind when I woke in the arms of my prince. My second thought was that my prince slept like the dead. His tanned chest barely rose and fell. His breaths made no noise whatsoever. So unlike my sister—the only other person with whom I had shared a bed.

I eased off the arm he'd tucked beneath me, careful not to disturb him.

The man was usually up with the sun. Always had somewhere to go. Something to do. His existence made my own seem so aimless. Playing in my "patch of dirt" as he called it, and cooking with Eava was fun and distracting, but I wanted to do more. To help in any way I could.

I had found my place. Now I needed to find my purpose.

Without prying blue eyes to watch, I took my time studying Rían. Mahogany hair sticking up where it met the pillow. Forearm thrown over his eyes. Blue ribbon still tied around his wrist. Full lips that had kissed every inch of my body. The silver scar across his nose. Across his throat. Above his heart.

All of them were part of Rían's story.

And I wanted to read every page.

"Is this what you do every morning?" The throaty question emerged through smirking lips. "Wake and bask in my naked glory?" He didn't bother moving his hand from his eyes.

"This is the first time you've slept in past sunrise. I'm taking full advantage of it."

The dimple in his right cheek deepened. "I'd rather you take full advantage of me."

While the suggestion stirred desire deep in my belly, there would be plenty of time for that later. In this moment, I just wanted to exist with him. "Where did this come from?" I asked, tracing the sliver line across the bridge of his nose.

"A prick with an iron blade."

"Iron burns you, doesn't it?" That's what the old myths said about the Danú. According to the books, during the great war between the humans and the Danú, iron had been worth more than gold. Which made sense. You couldn't protect yourself with gold.

"It does," he confirmed with a frown.

The thick scars across his throat felt silky smooth beneath my fingertip. "And these. Are they all from your brother?"

"Mostly."

And just when I was starting to like Tadhg. "Why did he kill you?"

"Because I deserved it."

Of all the responses I thought he'd give, I hadn't expected that. What had he done to deserve being killed so brutally? I didn't ask because I didn't want to know.

Perhaps I didn't need to read all the pages of Rían's story.

Perhaps I could skip to the bits that included me.

Rían finally lifted his arm from his eyes, pinning me to the bed with his cerulean stare. "I have done terrible, horrific things. I'll not apologize because I'm not sorry. But for every law I've broken, I have suffered the consequences."

The confession didn't surprise me. Rían seemed to thrive on order. Look at his room: Always tidy. Uncluttered. Without frills or decorations. Everything neat and organized and in its proper place. The man folded his bloody socks. Who did that? Who folded their socks?

As someone who thrived on order, he expected people to follow the law to the letter.

And if they didn't, they suffered as he had suffered.

Except with Anwen. He'd shown her mercy.

"Why did you spare Anwen?" I had never asked, and he had never said.

His heavy exhale fluttered the golden curls splayed across my own pillow. "I'd hardly win over someone like you if I didn't at least to pretend to have a heart."

"Someone like me?"

Rían's fingertip found my collarbone, following the line to the hollow of my throat. "Good. Kind. Selfless."

Good? I wasn't good. Not really. I had blackmailed a woman for information. I had lied to my family, to my sister, to the world. I had taken part in an elaborate ruse to escape my familial duty.

Kind? I was kind to some but not to everyone. I clung to grudges and found it difficult to forgive.

Selfless? I may have died so that Keelynn could be with the man she loved, but that wasn't the only reason. I had also died for me. To free myself from my responsibilities. I had given up everything to get what I wanted.

"I am none of those things," I told him.

He dragged his finger up my throat, lifting my chin until I met his gaze. "You are all those things and more," he whispered. "I do not deserve you." His lips tugged into a smile. "But I am wicked, ruthless, and selfish enough to keep you anyway."

Rían left shortly after breakfast, saying he had to attend executions up north, near Mistlaline. How heartbreaking it must be, watching so many of his people put to death based on false accusations. If only there was some way to make the Airren authorities understand most of their witnesses were liars. If only there were some way to give these people a fair trial.

If I were a man, perhaps I could speak out against the injustice. Not that it would do any good when, according to Rían, the magistrates conducting the trials "had their fingers in their ears."

I came down the castle stairs to find a bouquet of fuchsias in a crystal vase on the hall table. Hopefully Rían would be back home soon. He'd only been gone an hour, and I missed him already. Pushing my useless pining aside, I started for the door. Outside, the sun shined as bright as ever.

Ruairi waved at me from the edge of the fountain, Muireann perched at his side. Before I reached him, he lumbered to his feet and gestured toward the gates.

Right. It was to be another walk this morning.

Although my legs ached from yesterday, I didn't protest when he brought me out into the fresh breeze.

Instead of heading for the cliffs, the path we took cut through the hills. If it weren't for the warm air, I could almost have imagined myself back in Airren, strolling to the market.

"Are we going far?" I asked, lengthening my strides in a poor attempt to keep up. Did these men not realize my short legs could only go so fast?

Ruairi shook his head. Strange. He usually had more to say.

"Are you feeling all right, Ruairi?"

He grumbled, "Headache," but didn't slow.

I understood his pain. Yesterday, it had taken almost two hours for my headache to subside. Rían had talked nonstop about absolutely nothing, laughing and patting my back every time I groaned. Delighting in my hungover misery. I wouldn't be drinking like that for a long, long time.

Since I wasn't evil, I spared Ruairi the conversation, entertaining myself by seeing how long I could kick a round stone down the path.

We passed rows of cottages, each with a small garden and a fruit tree of some sort growing within low stone fences. Some had laundry flapping in the breeze, others had sheds and tills.

Eventually, we reached the bordering forest teaming with life. Squirrels scurried along the uneven ground and birds flitted above. It would've been winter in Airren, but the trees here were greener than any I'd ever seen. If there were any doubt that this land was fueled by magic, these trees, this forest, was all the proof anyone would need.

I could practically hear the ferns growing, the ivy vines climbing, and the butterflies fluttering from one wildflower to the next.

Rúairi went to pass the first tree. My footsteps faltered. "Ye comin' or not?" he threw over his shoulder, barely glancing my way.

"Rían said I wasn't to go into the forest." And I'd promised him. After hearing what had happened to his first love, how could I not? The last thing I needed was to break our tentative bond of trust.

"He's the one who told us to meet him here."

That couldn't be right. Rían was in Mistlaline.

"Come on." Ruairi's hand dwarfed mine when he took it. "Don't worry. I'll keep ye safe."

I tried to pull free. Ruairi squeezed my fingers so hard I felt my bones crunch. "Ruairi, you're hurting me."

He grinned, his fangs dangerously close to my throat. "Foolish human. My name's not Ruairi."

Oh god . . .

His eyes. They weren't gold.

They were black.

I yanked and twisted in a useless attempt to escape. The man's eyes landed on something behind me. Before I could turn, a balled-up rag smothered my nose and mouth, stifling my cry for help.

Then the world descended into darkness.

Something scratchy and rough rubbed against my sore cheek. I opened my eyes but saw nothing. Opened or closed, my eyes saw only black.

The breeze kissed my face, meaning there wasn't anything over my head.

My eyes were open.

They were open, dammit! Why couldn't I see?

Oh god.

I was blind.

Whatever they'd put on that rag had rendered me sightless. How could I hope to escape if I couldn't see where I'd been or where I needed to go?

My hands flopped lifelessly in front of me, bound with coarse rope that bit into my skin. Twisting only made the ropes tighter.

"Hurry it on," a woman hissed, her voice harsh and grating.

"Do ye want to carry her?" a man ground out.

My body bobbed and swayed. From the way the man's body shifted beneath my abdomen, I knew he was carrying me over his shoulder.

"If he finds us, we'll wish for death."

The man snorted. "He won't give a shite."

"You don't see the way he watches her."

Rían.

They were talking about Rían.

The woman must've seen through our ruse. If Rían found these people, he'd tear them apart. But he wasn't in Tearmann. Even if he returned in time, how would he know I was missing? What if he came too late?

I couldn't rely on him to save me this time. I needed to find a way to save myself.

Maybe I couldn't see, but I could listen. Two sets of footsteps. One heavy and lumbering. One swift and light.

And breathing. The man, slow and steady. The woman, wheezy and ragged.

Twigs breaking. And water. Not close, far away.

Maybe I couldn't see, but I could smell.

I inhaled slowly, praying neither of my assailants would notice.

Decaying leaves and dirt, the perfume of fall. And something else. Something familiar.

I inhaled again.

What *was* that?

"Almost there," the woman said in her strange voice. It wasn't a voice I'd heard around the castle. At least, I didn't think so.

The man grumbled. "I hate this feckin' place."

His voice though. There was definitely something I recognized about it.

The air grew heavy like a cold, dense fog had descended, spreading through my lungs with each unsteady inhale and leaving a hollow ache in my chest. Carrion and death replaced the scents of fall.

The rushing sound of water drew ever closer. Too strong to be a stream. Too steady to be the sea.

A river.

The river separating a forest from *The* Forest.

The man adjusted his grip, sliding his hands to the backs of my thighs. My stomach lurched. He shifted, rolling me from his shoulder onto the unforgiving ground. I bit my lip to keep from grunting when my back collided with what felt like a sharp stone.

"Not there, you fool. Across the river."

"I'm not settin' foot in that feckin' place. Ye can bring her across."

The woman cursed. Long, spindly fingers wrapped around my forearm, dragging me closer and closer to the river.

My hands may have been bound, but my feet were still free. I dug in my heels, slowing her a fraction. Was the man still here, or had he gone? It didn't matter. I had to try something.

Think, Aveen.

Think.

If I had any hope of escape, it was in the element of surprise. As far as she knew, I was still unconscious.

The water grew louder, but so did the woman's wheezing. She stopped for a moment, letting me go.

My fingers met silty sand. I scraped as much as I could into my hands. The woman's jagged breaths came and went to my right. I sent up a quick prayer to whatever deity would listen.

I rolled left.

Stumbled to my feet.

Ran as fast I could.

Away from the river. Away from the woman's vicious cursing.

Quick footsteps gave chase. The sand beneath my boots became hard ground, littered with rocks, turning my ankles. It was only a matter of time before I ran into something.

I slowed, but only a fraction, lifting my bound hands in front of me to soften the blow.

Something caught my hair. I whirled, throwing the sand in what I hoped was the right direction and lunging. My nails scraped cold, clammy skin.

The woman shrieked. I tore free.

"Help!" I screamed.

Running.

Stumbling.

Too slow. Too slow. Too bloody slow.

My toe caught. I pitched forward. Falling and falling. My body slammed into the earth.

I'd failed. And now I would die.

A hand touched my back. A screech wrenched from my throat.

I wouldn't go silently. I wouldn't let her take me without a fight. I rolled and kicked and clawed.

Until I heard Rían's voice. "Aveen, stop."

Tears spilled from my sightless eyes.

Warm hands caressed my cheeks. "I'm here."

"I can't see. I can't see." My confession became a desperate plea. "Help me. I can't see you."

His thumbs came over my eyes, wiping my tears. "I'm right here."

His hands warmed. Soothed. Healed.

"Open your eyes."

I blinked. Light and color, blurry at first, slowly resolved into the most beautiful face I'd ever seen. Rían brushed the hair back from my sticky cheeks, brow furrowed and eyes black as midnight.

Behind him, an onyx river flowed like a vicious gash in the land. Dark stones and silty sand littered the opposite shore, marking the start of a forest of wicked black trees. The only movement beyond the wall of soulless black came from stacks of stark white bones floating along the slithering, onyx earth.

The Black Forest lurked in the background, a shadowy beast, waiting. Watching. Ready to devour.

And I had almost been its next victim.

31

Rían shifted his dagger, using it on the thick ropes around my hands until they fell away. Raw red welts and cuts marred the tender skin. Rían lifted me as if I weighed no more than a child. I curled into his embrace, replacing the dead air in my lungs with his spicy cinnamon scent. We evanesced to the castle gates. Burying my head in his chest, I wished I could hide from the whispering Danú in the courtyard.

When I opened my eyes again, we were in the parlor. Tadhg and Ruairi launched from the settee, surrounding me in a protective immortal circle.

Tadhg's green eyes narrowed. "What happened?"

"I found her tied up in the forest, shrieking like a feckin' banshee."

"They took me." It was all I could think. All I could say. "They took me to the Forest." They wanted to bring me across that cursed river and leave me for dead. They wanted me dead. I'd never hurt anyone, and those people had wanted me *dead*.

Ruairi's mammoth hand came to rest on my shoulder. "Who took ye?"

I flinched. I couldn't help it. Ruairi's brow furrowed. "He

looked like you. I thought he was you. I wouldn't have gone if I'd known. If I'd seen his eyes."

"What color?" Tadhg asked, gripping the back of his neck.

"Black." As soulless as those trees growing in the Forest.

Tadhg's gaze flicked to a stone-faced Rían before returning to me. "You said 'they.' How many were there?"

"Two. A man and a woman."

Rían blinked wide blue eyes, his jaw pulsing.

"Did you cross the river?" Tadhg pressed.

I shook my head.

Ruairi took a step toward me. My chest tightened. "Aveen? Is it all right if I come closer?"

Holding my breath, I nodded. He sniffed the air, my hair, my face, my dress, my hands. And then his wide yellow eyes flew to Rían.

Tadhg clapped the pooka on the shoulder. "We will handle it," he vowed, voice low. Lethal.

All Rían did was nod and evanesce to his room. He set me down, keeping me steady with a gentle hand until I could hold my own weight.

With a flick of his wrist, a tub appeared, filled with steaming water.

I gripped the edge, staring down at my rippling reflection. The dirt on my face. The terror still in my wide eyes. The bits of leaves and twigs sticking out of my wild hair.

"I'm sorry," I said

I'd been a fool. I should've checked the eyes. I knew the tricks Rían played. That he could impersonate anyone he wished. I should've known other Danú could have the same abilities.

He opened his mouth, then shook his head and motioned me forward. I stared down at the raw, red marks on my wrists as he unfastened the buttons on my dress and dragged it off, adding it to the fire along with my shift.

He didn't turn around when I climbed into the hot bath and let the water close around me.

My wrists hit the water, burning like the fire Rían stared into. "Are you going to speak to me?"

He didn't respond.

"I'm sorry that I—"

"Stop apologizing for something that is not your fault."

It may not have been my fault, but, "I should've known better."

His shoulders rose and fell. "No, *I* should've known better. This is my world, not yours. I never should've lifted those feckin' wards." He cursed.

"Where was Ruairi?" He should've been waiting for me instead of whoever had glamoured himself to look like my friend.

Rían's head fell. "He said you left him a note to meet him in the kitchens."

Someone had gone through the trouble of distracting Ruairi and impersonating him the a day Rían was out of town. They had planned this. And I'd fallen into their trap, all because I had forgotten to look at the man's bloody eyes.

I scrubbed my skin and scalp until both were sore. Icy dread gathered like frost in my chest. How did we move past this?

Unsteadily, I rose to my feet. Water droplets rolled down my skin, making me shiver.

What if they didn't catch the people responsible? What if they came back for me? What if they turned their sights on my sister?

Rían wrapped me in a towel, his movements warm and gentle, so at odds with the cold distance in his faraway eyes. A shift appeared on the end of the mattress. I didn't have it in me to change. Instead, I went straight to the bed and curled up beneath the covers. The moment my head hit the pillow, my heavy eyelids closed. And I was back in the Forest, blind, running for my life.

The mattress dipped. Rían's body molded to mine.

I never wanted to leave this castle. Never wanted to leave this room. This beautiful, wild land that had been my sanctuary had swiftly become my nightmare.

"I got a cat for my fifth birthday," Rían said, his chin rubbing my temple when he spoke. "I named him Sir Fluffy Paws."

I curled my cold hands into the collar of his shirt, needing his heat to warm my frigid fingers. "That's a good name," I whispered, tears pricking the backs of my eyes.

"It's a feckin' brilliant name. Think of the fluffiest thing you've ever seen, then multiply it by ten. That's how fluffy his paws were."

My tears spilled free, soaking into the soft cotton of his shirt. I tried to imagine a little dark-haired boy running around Tearmann with a ball of fluff bounding behind him, chasing butterflies and swatting at bits of long, swaying grass.

"One time, I glamoured myself to look like my father. Nearly got me into a very awkward situation with Tadgh's mam."

"*Tadgh's* mother?" I sniffled. Not his. That seemed like a strange distinction to make.

Rían gathered my wet hair from my neck, spreading it across the pillow. "He's only my half-brother. Same philandering father. Different mothers."

My father, for all his failings, had been faithful to our mother. As far as I knew, he hadn't so much as looked at another woman since my mother had passed.

"Could you make yourself look like me?" I asked, feeling some of the frost begin to melt.

Rían's chuckle vibrated against my cheek. "If I did that, I'd want to touch myself all the time. I'd never get anything done."

A little more frost disappeared. "You are ridiculous."

"Only for you."

I knew he was trying to distract me. It may be working now, but he couldn't keep talking all night. At some point, the dark memories lurking in the recesses of my mind would drag me back to that cursed Forest.

Today, I was lucky Rían had found me.

What about tomorrow? Or the next day?

He couldn't be with me all the time. If anyone ever attacked me again, I needed to be able to protect myself.

"Rían? I want a—"

A heavy knock interrupted my request for a dagger.

Rían extricated himself, stalking to the door.

I didn't need to see him to recognize the deep cadence of Tadhg's lilting voice.

A moment later, the door clicked closed. Rían turned, a somber expression on his face. "You need to get dressed. Quickly." Before I could ask why, he said, "We're having a trial."

They caught them already.

That was all I could think as I changed into the dress Rían had shifted.

It hadn't even taken them an hour.

With my hand in his, Rían brought me downstairs, keeping his thoughts locked away behind steely blue eyes. He'd refused to tell me their names. Refused to tell me anything other than, "It'll be all right."

We ended up in the study, surrounded by volumes of Tearmann Law. Would he call one forth today or did he already know the punishment for kidnapping? The door built into the paneling between the bookshelves had been left ajar.

I heard Tadhg speaking in a congenial tone, discussing the weather with someone. Then I heard a second voice. A voice I recognized.

Rían studied me, an unreadable expression on his face. "You know who she is."

It wasn't a question.

He held out a hand. "I need you to come with me."

"I can't." I retreated toward the desk. If I saw this person, my mind would end up right back in that forest. I wanted to hide in Rían's room and pretend that none of this had happened. Let them deal with the perpetrators how they saw fit. Leave me out of it.

"You are the only witness, Aveen. I need you to come with me," he repeated, taking my trembling hand. "We will be with you the entire time."

We will be with you.

Somehow, two princes and a pooka had become my family. As frightened as I was, I didn't have to go on my own.

I nodded, and he eased the door aside.

Unlike the other times I'd seen it, the great hall was empty save two people: Tadhg and someone I couldn't see from behind his broad shoulders.

He didn't step aside until I reached the top of the dais.

And I saw the merrow from the fountain.

Her tail had been replaced by two long, narrow legs of skin and bone. She stared at me through bulbous black eyes. Blinked. And smiled a sharp, black-toothed smile.

Shadows leaked from beneath Tadhg's shirt cuffs, twisting around her torso. She didn't struggle or fight, just kept staring at me and smiling.

Rumbling laughter erupted from the hallway.

A man strolled in, tall and broad. Mousy brown hair and a sloping jaw. I knew him. He'd been the one to accuse Anwen.

When he saw the merrow, he stilled.

And then his eyes flew to me.

The color leached from his face, leaving him as white as his shirt. He whirled, but Ruairi blocked his exit, a twisted smile on his lips. The man flicked his wrist. Nothing happened.

"Ah, Madden. Muireann." Rían clapped his hands beneath his chin, jogging down the dais steps. "Nice of you to join us."

Madden jabbed a thick finger toward the merrow. "The bitch made me do it. She made me."

Rían's head tilted. I could hear the smile in his voice when he said, "Made you do what, Madden?"

"Take the human to the Forest."

"Liar!" Muireann hissed, wriggling inside the bonds.

"And which human is that?" Rían asked.

Madden's hand shook when he pointed to me. Tadhg gave me a reassuring smile. Ruairi winked at me from the door.

For some reason, I had assumed the man would try to deny his involvement. That he'd protest his innocence.

Then I remembered: Rían could *smell* lies.

So instead, Madden was blaming the merrow.

Rían folded his arms over his chest, looking and sounding like a stern father giving out to his son for being bold. "And how did she 'make' you, Madden?"

Madden's mouth opened and closed, the skin around his loose jaw jiggling with the movement. "She . . . I . . . You see—"

Rían shook his head. "I don't see." He flicked his wrist, and a dagger appeared. Madden stumbled back, colliding with Ruairi. Rían raised his free hand. Madden's right hand jerked into the air and slammed against the wall with a *smack*.

"I can *make* you cut off your own fingers." Rían forced the dagger into the giant's left hand and flicked his wrist. Madden's face turned a deep shade of red. A vein in his forehead bulged. He struggled and cursed, bringing the dagger to his smallest digit.

Then he sawed it clean off.

Madden's broken cry reverberated off the high ceiling. The finger fell onto the floor next to Rían's boot. I clutched my churning stomach. Bile forced its way up my throat.

The merrow's smile returned. As if all of this was some sort of twisted game.

"See there?" Rían drawled. "That's me *making* you do something. Do you know what else I could do?"

"P-please . . ." Madden whimpered, tears streaming down his cheeks. He wouldn't have spared me if I'd cried. If I'd begged.

Rían's teeth flashed. "I could do it myself."

Rían yanked the knife free and hacked off the man's three remaining fingers.

Madden wailed, gripping his bloody stump at the wrist, trying to pull free from the blood-soaked wall.

"Now, Madden." Rían caught the man's chin, forcing him to look forward. Blood dripped down the blade in his other hand, splattering on his boots. "Did Muireann *make* you take my hostage? Because I find it hard to believe a strapping lad such as yourself could be so easily coerced by a rotting fish."

"No, no, Prince Rían. She—she told me if I helped her . . . I'd be gettin' back at ye fer lettin' that bitch off without so much as a feckin' day in the dungeon."

Chuckling, Tadhg muttered something under his breath. Beside him, Muireann's smile faltered.

Rían brought the dagger to his own chest, pointing at himself with the bloody tip. Drops of red bloomed on his pristine white shirt. "So, this is about *me* then. You thought it'd be a good idea to take something from *me*?" Clicking his tongue, he shook his head. "That was a silly thing to do, wasn't it?"

A choked sob broke from Madden's chest. "I'm sorry—"

"Are you now? Brilliant. I suppose I should let you go then."

The man sniveled and sniffed, scrubbing his nose on his shirt-sleeve. His blood oozed down the wall. Pooled by his scuffed boots.

"Or I could bring you downstairs."

"No. No." Madden wailed. "P-please—"

Rían collected Madden's bloody digits from the floor, tucking them into the man's waistcoat pocket. He gave them a pat and said, "I'll see you soon."

With a flick of his wrist, Madden vanished.

And then Rían turned.

Lifting her chin, the merrow glared down her straight nose at the prince. "We both know it's only a matter of time before she comes to take your plaything away," she sneered. "Do you really think—"

Rían evanesced, raised his dagger, and sliced the merrow from ear to ear.

Blood sprayed. She collapsed with a choked gurgle.

My stomach lurched and twisted, but I didn't have it in me to feel sorry for them.

I had done *nothing*. And yet they'd been willing to sacrifice me to get to Rían.

You are my only weakness . . .

The world had found out. And it had come for me.

Rían dropped to his knee next to Muireann, pressed a hand to her still chest, and inhaled a deep, slow breath. The merrow's face wrinkled as the skin around her cheeks and eyes sank into her skull, aging the woman a hundred years.

Ruairi and Tadhg surrounded me, asking if I was all right, blocking my view of the body. Although I told them I was fine, I wasn't sure how I felt.

Rían squeezed between them, bringing a hand to my cheek. Although he'd changed his clothes, I could still smell the blood. "Aveen, I'm so—"

"I do hope I'm not interrupting," a woman's pleasant voice called from the doorway.

Rían jerked back.

Tadhg and Ruairi twisted toward a shapely figure waiting at the entrance, flanked by two guards in black uniforms and black masks.

An obsidian crown rested atop her dark mahogany hair.

I had seen her before, woven in the terrifying tapestry hanging in the hallway.

The Phantom Queen.

Long black nails curled from her slender fingers. The candles flickering on the walls illuminated veins of black flowing beneath her almost translucent skin.

The Queen's black eyes landed on the merrow's emaciated body swimming in a pool of blood. Her red lips lifted.

The blue in Rían's eyes melted to black. "Hello, Mother."

32

The Phantom Queen was Rían's mother.

The bloody *Phantom Queen*.

If the world knew what you meant to me, it would take you away . . .

Rían hadn't been talking about the world.

He'd been talking about his mother.

She stole something precious from me.

The Queen had murdered her son's love. And now her soulless black eyes were fixed on me.

Rían strolled down the dais to press a kiss to her pale hand. "Lovely as always to see you."

"You always were a deceitful boy," she drawled, tearing her hand away and giving him a disapproving once-over. Tadhg received the same look. When the Queen's black eyes returned to me, they widened. "What's this? Another human in Tearmann?"

Ruairi draped an arm around my shoulders. "We liked her so much, we decided to keep her."

Not a lie. A careful truth. Had Rían inherited his ability to smell lies from his mother? I needed to remain vigilant, just in case. Guard the truth as if my life depended on it.

Because it did.

The Queen's chin lifted. "When you tire of it, send it across the border."

Rían's gaze darted to me.

"I've already fed you once this year," Tadhg said with a smirk, gesturing toward the hallway.

"I'm always hungry," she crooned. Feathers sewn into her cape fluttered as she followed Tadhg to the dining room and settled herself on the chair at the head of the table. Rían sat to her right and Tadhg took the seat to her left.

If the world found out about you . . .

If I sat next to Rían, she may grow suspicious. Instead, I sat by Tadhg. Ruairi took the free chair at my other side. The Queen had her guards, and I had mine.

Tadhg shifted two bottles of wine—one green and one black —and five glasses. "What brings you our way on such short notice, my Queen?" He poured the Queen's drink from the black bottle, then set it aside. For himself, Ruairi, and me, he poured from the green one. Rían's glass remained empty.

The Queen's thin eyebrows arched toward her crown. "Do I need a reason to visit my son?"

Rían stared at his empty glass in stony silence. I knew him too well to believe for a moment that his brain wasn't weaving webs of plans and lies and secrets.

"Of course not," Tadhg said with an easy smile.

"I wasn't aware you let your pets sit at the table." The Queen sniffed, glaring down her nose at Ruairi and me.

Ruairi grinned, sharp fangs gleaming in the candlelight. "Seeing you is always such a delight, my Queen."

"Careful now, *boy*. I'm in need of a new steed."

"I'd give just about anyone a ride"—Ruairi winked at me —"but I'm afraid the Black Forest wouldn't suit my sunny disposition. And I prefer the living over the dead."

What was he doing? Why was he trying to antagonize her?

The Queen swirled the deep red wine in her glass. A coppery tang struck my nose. My stomach twisted.

Not wine. *Blood.*

As if she could sense my horror, her black eyes met mine, and she took a slow, deep drink. When she smiled, blood dripped down her straight white teeth.

She set her glass aside in favor of the bottle, filling Rían's glass with blood before topping up her own. "Speaking of the dead, I heard a pack of pooka were executed near Mistlaline."

Mistlaline.

Was that the execution Rían had attended earlier?

Ruairi leaned forward in his chair, looking past me to Tadhg. "Is that true?"

Grimacing, Tadhg grabbed his own glass. "Anyone who chooses to live outside of Tearmann understands there is risk involved."

"Tearmann is a pittance of what it once was," the Queen countered, going back to swirling her glass. "When your father ruled, he commanded respect, controlling this island and everyone in it. The human uprising only succeeded because he showed them mercy."

Tadhg rolled his eyes. Ruairi yawned. Rían glared at them both.

"You. Human." The Queen pointed a black-tipped finger at me. "What is your name?"

Swallowing past the sudden lump in my throat, I said, "Lady Aveen Bannon, Your Majesty."

The corners of her lips quirked into the barest hint of a smile. "What brings you to Tearmann?"

Be like Rían. Use the truth to tell a lie. "A kiss."

Her chest lifted as she inhaled slowly the way Rían's did when he searched for a lie. A flicker of surprise ghosted across her features. "So you're one of Tadhg's then?"

"I am." One of the Gancanagh's victims, anyway. I took a sip from my glass, praying for fortitude.

You can do this. You can do this. You can do this.

"Funny. He usually puts them back," she mused, drinking some more. "Why do you linger?"

"Tadhg kissed my sister as well."

The candles on the table shuddered with the Queen's startled laugh. "Men. Human or Danú, they're all the same, aren't they?"

I could only nod because I couldn't agree aloud. The men at this table were better than any of the men I'd met in my world.

"Why did you kiss him?"

"To escape a fate worse than death." I smiled my most brilliant false smile, the one no one had ever seen through. "Marriage."

"I'd forgotten how delightfully entertaining humans can be." The Queen took another sip of her drink. "Is this true, Tadhg?"

His green eyes crinkled at the corners when he grinned. Raising his glass, he saluted me and said, "Every feckin' word."

Pressing her lips into a flat line, the skin around the Queen's mouth tightened. "What is your relationship with my son?"

Rían's bored expression never wavered as he listened to our exchange.

Answer a question with a question.

"What do you mean?" I asked.

Dark, elegant eyebrows arched toward her pointed crown. "I heard the two of you were engaged."

"We told Tadhg we were to convince him to kiss me. But no, we're not actually engaged. It was all a ruse." What would she have done if I had said yes? Would she have ripped my heart out here and now?

Her nail *clinked* against her glass in the same slow, steady rhythm as my heartbeat. "Well then. It appears as though this trip has been for naught. You see, I was told my useless son had smuggled his human fiancée into Tearmann and was hiding her inside this castle. Clearly, my source was mistaken."

"Clearly," Rían grumbled.

My heartbeat quickened.

So did the Queen's *clinking.*

Tadhg cleared his throat, setting his glass on the table with a loud *thunk*. "Now that we have that all cleared up, it's getting quite late. I'm sure everyone is tired."

Something slithered around my ankles, cold and scaly. I looked down but saw only shadows. The thing tightened, pinning my legs to the chair. The same sensation curled around my core, squeezing the air from my lungs, dragging my chair away from the table toward the Queen.

Ruairi cursed, trying to catch me as I passed. He vanished.

Tadhg shot to his feet. He vanished as well.

The Queen's infernal *clinking* sounded like a bloody woodpecker, fast and furious as my thundering heart.

Pounding sounded against the door. Muffled shouts. *Tadhg and Ruairi*. She'd locked them out. The Queen's brow furrowed as her black gaze raked down my face, landing on my chest.

My heart. My breathing. The *clinking*.

All of it stopped as she stretched a black-tipped finger toward my shoulder to trace along my neckline. Then her finger dipped lower, tugging down the front of my dress.

Her lips curled into a slow, victorious smile.

"Do you care to explain this, Rían?" She tapped the scar on my breast that he'd given me the night before I'd died.

I'd forgotten all about it.

Rían rolled his eyes. "If you're asking if I fucked her, the answer is yes."

I flinched.

The vulgar words were for her benefit, not mine. I tried my best not to let their sting settle.

The Queen withdrew a dagger with a glittering hilt, almost identical to Rían's. "Are you truly so weak that you'd lift your skirts for a pretty face and a few whispered lies?" she asked me, tracing the tip of the blade along my collarbone. "You'd abandon your family and your people to live amongst us, where you are despised, all for a man who has more interest in his collection of waistcoats than he has in you."

"I tell her all the time how pathetic she is." Rían reached for his wine glass. I prayed the Queen didn't notice how badly his hand trembled.

The Queen sneered, her blade coming to a halt above my heart. "Pathetic enough to fall in love with you."

Rían's eyes met mine from across the table.

"I am not in love with him."

Rían's eyes widened.

So did the Queen's.

"There's no need to lie to me, *girl*." She pressed just hard enough to bring tears to my eyes. A bead of blood welled from the tiny wound.

I refused to let the tears building behind my eyes fall.

"You wouldn't be the first human he's played with, and you certainly won't be the last." She pressed harder. "He insists on these childish rebellions, rutting with chattel and the like. I've come to remind my son that he cannot afford such distractions from his duties."

Rían's knuckles turned white where he gripped the glass. "Get out."

The guards stepped away from the wall, hands falling to the pommels of their swords. They'd been so still and silent, blending with the shadows, that I'd forgotten about them entirely.

"You think you can throw me out?" she scoffed. "You have no authority here."

Relief flooded my veins when she pulled away, until she gestured toward Rían with the dagger. "This isn't your castle. You're a lodger—a leech aligning himself with true power because you have *none*."

"You've made your point."

"Oh, I don't think I have." Laughing, the Queen adjusted her grip on the hilt . . .

And buried the blade in Rían's thigh.

Blackness exploded in his eyes. Not a speck of white or blue remained. Rían withdrew the dagger only to plunge it back into the gushing wound. Perspiration beaded on his brow. His teeth ground together as he pulled it out and stabbed himself again and again and again—

"You forget, *son*, that I have owned you since the day I tore the heart from your chest."

The room began to spin.

That vicious scar . . .

Was she saying Rían had no bloody heart?

How was that possible? How was he alive?

I'm cold and dead inside . . .

Rían directed a vacant smile toward me, his face ghostly white.

Was he alive at all?

The slurping, grating sound of blade sinking into flesh and across bone echoed through the room.

"*This* is what you *love.*" The Queen slapped his face, leaving a red handprint across his cheek. "An empty husk spelled to do my bidding whenever I choose to take control. If I wished him dead, he would cease to draw breath."

The blood-drenched dagger clattered to the stones. Rian's chest stopped rising and falling. His lips turned blue.

I lost the useless battle with my tears. "Why?" Why would she do that to her own son?

Rían's body slumped in his chair, vacant black eyes staring toward the ceiling.

Oh god. He was dead. She'd killed him. She'd taken him from me.

He was dead. He was dead. He was dead.

"Have you not seen his pathetic brother? A slave to foolish emotions and carnal desires. The humans do not *fear* him." The Queen huffed a laugh, gesturing toward Tadhg's empty chair. The pounding at the door grew louder. "It's only a matter of time before the Danú tire of being slaughtered and rise up against his reign. Our people need a ruler who will protect them at all costs. Someone who will never let emotion rule him."

A man like Rían.

The Queen rose to her feet, feathered skirts fluttering on a phantom breeze. "You have not broken the treaty, so your life is not yet mine to claim. But this life"—she caressed Rían's pale cheek—"belongs to me." Her hand fell. "You have my permission to cross the Forest once. Should you choose to remain in our land, I will have my son take care of you in my stead. Perhaps while you're enjoying breakfast in bed. Or while you're soaking in a nice, hot bath. Next week. A month from now. I'll make it a fun game to keep you guessing."

I didn't doubt her for a moment. Rían's lifeless body was the only proof I needed. The dagger at his feet. The blood leaking from his mangled leg. If she wanted me dead, there'd be no escape.

"Return to your world tonight, *human*," she spat, "for my mercy will not extend to daylight."

The doors burst open. Tadhg and Ruairi fell into the room. The Phantom Queen and her guards vanished.

Rían gasped, bolting upright in his chair, his face ashen. He scanned the empty room through black eyes as if he'd never seen the place before.

"Rían?" His name wobbled on my lips.

His head swung toward me and tilted at a sickening angle. His smile didn't reach his hollow eyes. He shot to his feet, knocking the chair to the ground.

Tadhg raced to his brother, catching him by the shoulders. "Look at me. *Look at me.* You have to fight her."

Ruairi positioned himself between us. I peered around him to glimpse Rían shaking his head, black eyes melting to blue.

"I release you from our bargain," he rasped.

And then the black returned.

Something in my chest loosened, like someone had pulled an invisible cord.

Our bargain.

Stay in this castle until your sister returns from the underworld.

Rían was letting me go.

He threw out a hand. Tadhg and Ruairi flew across the room. Wood cracked. Curses echoed. But all I could focus on were Rían's black eyes as he slowly stalked toward me, sending me back and back and back until my heels collided with the wall.

Nowhere to run.

Nowhere to hide.

"Rían . . . No . . . Please."

Rían traced a finger down my throat, ever so gently. "*Run.*"

Tadhg evanesced, dagger in hand, and drew a blade across his brother's throat. Blood spurted from the deep red gash, spraying my face and dress.

My knees gave out, and I landed in tandem with Rían's body. I heaved and heaved, swallowing back the bile scalding my throat.

"Eava!" Tadhg bellowed. "Oscar!"

The witch and grogoch appeared.

"He's spinning out," Tadhg rushed. "Get him to the dungeons before he kills us all."

Eava took one of Rían's hands, Oscar took the other, and they all disappeared.

Tadhg flicked his wrist, conjuring his own tost. To Ruairi he said, "Bring her straight through the Forest to the portal. Get her to Gaul. None of the usual haunts. They won't be safe."

Ruairi nodded.

Before I could protest, Tadhg had me in a clean dress, and I was being dragged into the courtyard, blinded by a flashing white light, and thrown on top of a mammoth black horse. Tadhg said he was sorry, refusing to meet my gaze. Then he gave Ruairi's hindquarters a smack, and the pooka shot toward the gates.

The night blurred into tears and darkness.

Ruairi ran faster than I'd ever seen anything move, like a demon escaped from the underworld. He slowed when he hit the forest, but only a fraction. I screwed my eyes shut when we reached the river. Held my breath, desperate to keep the rot of death from entering my lungs. The relentless thundering of Ruairi's hooves numbed the sounds of my breaking heart and the hollow howls of whatever beasts prowled the Black Forest.

If I didn't see them, they wouldn't be real.

If I kept my eyes closed, I could pretend none of this was happening.

Cold, fresh air slammed into my face. My eyes flashed open. Snow blanketed the ground and clung to the barren branches the way I clung to Ruairi's reins.

The portal Tadhg had mentioned was located inside a two-story cottage with a moldy thatched roof.

Ruairi knocked on the door. A woman with frazzled red hair answered, a small baby asleep in her arms. She didn't say a word, just stepped aside, allowing us into her home. A man sat on a plaid armchair, reading. On a matching sofa, two red-headed children slept.

We crept past, up the stairs and into the family's linen closet.

Traveling through the portal felt almost the same as evanescing.

Disorientation. Darkness. And falling.

Dampness and mildew replaced the comforting scents of linen and fresh laundry. We opened the door on the other side and climbed another set of stairs, emerging into a cavernous cathedral.

Morning light streamed through stained glass windows, painting the floors.

"Where are we going?" I finally managed to ask. Tadhg had mentioned Gaul, a seaside city on the west coast of Airren.

"Ye can stay at one of the inns fer now," Ruairi said, helping me down the cathedral steps and out into the brightening day.

For now.

What then?

That couldn't be the last time I saw Rían. It couldn't.

Row after row of townhouses wound around skinny cobbled streets. Sunlight glittered off their frosty slate roofs. We stopped at the first inn we saw, painted a sunny yellow, next to a blue and white tea house on the river leading to the sea.

"I'll meet ye back here tonight," he said, handing me a purse full of coin.

"You're not staying?"

"My kind aren't welcome at this inn," Ruairi said. His gaze flicked to the door at my back. And then I saw the sign.

No dogs. No creatures.

"We can stay somewhere else," I suggested.

Ruairi shook his head. "They'll be the first place he checks."

The dull ache in my chest turned sharp, as if the Queen still held the dagger against my heart. "Will he be all right?" Would she leave him be now that I was gone?

Ruairi glanced at a short, squatty man waddling toward the bakery across the street behind him. "I'll not lie to ye. That's as bad as I've seen him."

Although I appreciated his honesty, I wished his answer had been different. "I feel like a coward for leaving." Rían never would have abandoned me. Never. And there I was, running as far away as fast as I could the minute things became dangerous.

Ruairi gave my shoulder a light pat. "Remember, yer not like the lads. If Rían has one of his episodes and accidentally kills ye, the underworld isn't gonna spit ye back. And if something happened to ye, he'd never forgive himself." His hand fell, and his massive shoulders sagged with his heavy sigh. "Unless he gets back his heart, this is the way it has to be. He knew it from the beginning. And now ye know it too."

Unless he got back his heart?

Was that even possible?

"Head up, human." Ruairi nudged my chin with his finger. "Yer going to be all right."

I gave him my bravest smile. "I'll see you tonight."

Ruairi nodded. "I'll see ye tonight."

The innkeeper took my coins, handed me a key, and said he'd send up a tub as soon as he was able. My room at the top of the stairs wasn't luxurious, but it was clean and comfortable. The bed squeaked when I sank onto the end of the mattress.

Rían had no heart.

The Queen had called him an empty husk. He didn't seem empty to me. Not until last night.

How many times had I complained about being a "hostage" in Tearmann?

Rían was the hostage. Being controlled by his mother. A slave to his duty. Forced to hide his truth behind glamours and lies.

I had been controlled by my father. I had been a slave to my duty as the first-born daughter. I had been forced to hide my truth behind smiles and nods.

Until Rían had saved me from my fate.

And I had abandoned him to his.

Rían had a weapon that could end his mother and her hold over him. A weapon only a human could yield.

Pity the girl from Graystones . . .

I was that girl.

Who loved a heartless prince . . .

I loved him. Beyond reason, I loved him.

I pushed aside the rest of the fortune, prepared to create my own fate.

I was going to save my prince.

33

HURRYING THROUGH GAUL'S DARK STREETS, I'D FORGOTTEN HOW black the night could be when clouds smothered the moon and stars. I tucked the leather journal I'd bought beneath my new cloak, then drew the hood over my hair to ward off the chill. I missed Tearmann's heat.

I was late.

So late.

Ruairi was going to kill me.

Music reeled from pubs lining either side of the empty street, uneven notes twisting on the breeze. I missed Tearmann's peacefulness as well.

I'd spent the entire day at the library in Gaul, reading all the books I could find on the Forest. Each one said the same thing: no one could enter the Black Forest without permission. Those who entered without permission had to pay the "tax."

One life.

For each crossing, the Queen was allowed to take one life.

That was how Tadhg had gotten Keelynn through. She had accepted Tadhg's life in exchange for my sister's. What if she had refused his sacrifice and taken my sister instead? He had been a fool to take such a risk.

Once the "death tax" had been paid, the Queen could not take another life for the same crossing. Meaning if two people crossed, and one was killed, the second person was permitted entry into Tearmann.

Light from the flickering lanterns danced on the puddles left on the cobblestones. I skirted around a larger one. The heavy, damp hem of my skirts slapped against my ankles. If I weren't so late, I'd have gone back to the inn and change into one of the other dresses I'd purchased before going to the library.

The door to one of the pubs burst open. A man stumbled out, ramming into me and sending my journal tumbling into the blasted puddle.

"Dreadfully sorry," the man slurred, kneeling and fumbling for the journal.

"Think nothing of it." I took the dripping book from him, giving it a good wipe against my cloak before hiding it again.

"Aveen?"

I found a pair of bloodshot hazel eyes blinking at me. My stomach dropped to my toes.

Robert Trench.

Reeking of booze. Chin covered in patchy stubble. Clothes wrinkled and stained.

Robert bloody Trench.

His lips curved into an uneven smile as he stood. "Isn't this a pleasant surprise?"

A pleasant surprise? Was this fate's idea of a twisted joke? Robert had a townhouse somewhere in Gaul, where he'd attended university. Of the thousands of people in this city, how did I run into *him*?

Two young men fell out of the pub, each with an arm thrown around the other. When they saw me, their glassy eyes brightened. "Who do we have here, Rob?"

Robert's hand slipped across the small of my back to rest on my hip. "Looks as if my wayward fiancée has returned from the dead, lads."

The shorter of the two strangers bit his lip. His leering made me feel like I'd been doused in bog water. "Isn't she a looker?"

"Always was." Robert's finger grazed my jaw. "Right bitch though." He pinched my chin, bringing tears to my eyes. "Just like her sister."

I knocked his hand away. "I need to go." I didn't have time for Robert and his slimy friends. My prince needed me.

"I'd rather you stay," he countered. "Give us a chance to get reacquainted." Robert's glazed eyes narrowed when he grinned. "Lads?" He stole my journal, handing it to his friend. "Hold this for a moment."

With a smirk, the two separated, bowing at the waist and waving us past.

Robert's blunt nails dug into my side. He dragged me away from the flickering lamplight toward an alley. Shards of glass crunched underfoot. Something scurried toward the stack of wood leaning against the far wall. A broken barrel leaked black liquid onto the grimy street.

I waited until we were out of view of his friends and crushed his toes beneath my heel. He gave an indignant yelp, letting me go.

I was fast.

He was faster.

Catching my hair, dragging me back. Slamming my face into the plaster wall.

"Don't touch me!" I screamed past the pain.

He turned me around, pinning me between the wall and the heavy weight of his forearm across my chest.

"Aveen, do you take Robert to be your husband?" His breath reeked of liquor. His hands tugged at my skirts. His eyes blazed with rage.

I stomped again. I missed. "Stop it."

"The answer is, 'I do.'"

"Never."

The flat of his palm collided with my cheek. Pain exploded behind my eyes. Coppery blood filled my mouth.

"Try again," he spat.

"I-I do."

"Robert, do you take Aveen to be your wife?" A pause. "I do."

"Robert, please "

"Ah-ah, wife. No tears on our wedding night." His belt jingled as he yanked the strap through the buckle.

"Stop it. Stop it this instant."

He didn't stop. He fisted and lifted my skirts.

I shoved my dress back down; he smacked my hand aside.

I screeched, bucking and writhing. But he was stronger, parting my thighs with his knee, struggling with the buttons on his breeches.

Every part of me became ice, panic seizing my chest. Robert forced his mouth onto mine, tasting of liquor and hate. I sank into the dark recesses of my mind, where I couldn't feel him putting his hands where they didn't belong.

A dagger.

I *needed* a dagger.

I had it in me to kill him.

I hadn't escaped the Dullahan, the Phantom Queen, and Tearmann to become a victim to this weak, pathetic excuse of a man.

Robert bloody Trench would not be my downfall.

Fire collected in my belly, swelled through my core, my chest, my limbs.

I need a bloody dagger.

Something cold pressed against my palm. My fingers instinctively tightened, then jerked forward. Robert stilled, his eyes blown out. Warm wetness dribbled onto my hand.

When I let go, something clattered to the ground.

A dagger with a curved blade.

I shoved against Robert's heavy shoulders.

He didn't speak. Didn't stumble. Didn't cry out.

He slumped onto the heavy stones and did not rise again.

I searched the darkness for some sign of Tadhg or Rían—any Danú who could've shifted me the dagger. No eyes glowed from the darkness. No shadows shifted. Whoever had come to my aid must already be long gone.

I didn't stop to see if Robert was dead. All that mattered was that he didn't follow me when I ran out of the alley . . . straight into one of his friends.

I shrieked. The tall one caught my cloak.

The shorter one disappeared back into the alley. "She killed him, mate! The bitch killed him!"

Shit.

Think, Aveen. Think.

I reached for the clasp on my cloak, letting it fall away, and ran as fast as I could. Footsteps thundered at my back. Two men in red uniforms rounded the corner. Airren soldiers. My saving grace.

"Help me! Help me!" I cried.

Their heads swung toward us. When they saw me, they drew their swords in unison. "Stop at once!"

The footsteps came to a halt. Robert's friends lifted their hands. One of the soldiers, with gold pins in his lapels, asked me what had happened.

Robert's short friend railed and cursed. "The whore lured my best mate into the alley and stabbed him in the bloody heart."

"Liar!" I tore away my hood. The soldiers balked when they saw my face. My cheek ached and burned. I could only imagine what it must look like. "That man tried to force himself on me. He tried to—" I couldn't bring myself to say it aloud. The bastard was gone. Dead. He couldn't hurt me anymore. He couldn't hurt anyone else.

The one with the golden pins kept his weapon trained on the two lying bastards glaring at me. He nodded his chin toward the alley. "Check it out, Clive."

The other soldier jogged into the darkness.

"What's your name?" he asked in a softer tone.

"Lady Aveen Bannon."

His eyes widened as he took in the state of my clothes and hair.

"My father is Lord Michael Bannon of Graystones," I added, hoping the detail would make him believe me.

The soldier emerged from the alley, giving his partner a grim nod before pulling the two men aside for a chat.

"They're insisting she attacked him," the other soldier shouted.

"It's not true." He'd believe me. He would. He had to. It was the truth.

The soldier who had saved me grimaced, withdrawing a pair of shiny manacles from his thick black belt.

"I'm afraid I'll have to put the bonds on you, milady," he said reluctantly.

He was only doing his job. Following procedure. The truth would come out in the end.

"Once we have everyone's statement, we'll sort this right out," he assured me.

I held out my hands. The metal cuffs clamped over my wrists, scalding as if they'd come straight from the blacksmith's forge. A scream wrenched from my chest. I twisted and scraped, desperate to remove them. They were too bloody tight, and if I didn't get them off right this second, whatever poison they'd laced them with would eat through skin and bone, cutting my hands clean off.

"Take them off! Please! I'm begging you. Please. I'll come with you. I swear. Just take them off." Try as I might, I couldn't get my hands through the holes.

The soldier tugged me closer to get a look at my hands, then let me go just as quickly. His face paled. "This woman's a bloody witch!"

"I'm not a witch," I cried, my body trembling. I rubbed the manacles against my skirts in a useless attempt to scrub off the poison. "Take them off. Please, please. There's something wrong. They're burning me."

The soldier who'd been so kind before now gripped my elbow hard enough to make me cry out. He dragged me down the street, not bothering to stop or slow until we reached a towering fortress on the river's edge. He brought me through a barred door at its base and down a set of musty stairs.

We passed a guard's station across from a second door. Through a hallway to a line of empty cells. The only light in the room came from a single candle on a table next to a haggard old man with a set of metal keys hanging from his belt.

When the guard saw us, he pushed to his feet and shuffled toward the first cell. The door creaked when he opened it. The only place to sit was on the gritty dirt floor scattered with moldy bits of hay.

"Please." I held my hands toward the soldier and the guard, begging for them to remove the shackles.

"Do I look like a fool to you, witch?" snarled the guard. "I'll not have you casting any curses on my watch."

There was no sense telling the man I wasn't a witch. He wouldn't believe me. "What will happen to me?"

"They'll notify the proper authorities of yer trial, and ye will be sentenced."

I pressed the heels of my hands to my eyes and let the tears come. They'd do no good. Nothing would now.

How could I hope to save Rían from the Queen when I couldn't even save myself from this?

Low scratching noises came from the darkest corner of my cell. Were there mice or rats? I scooted closer to the bars. The ache in my wrists eventually went numb.

Everything went numb.

Footsteps shuffled through the dark hallway. I looked up to see a man in a fine black suit standing there, his face an impassive mask. "Remove your glamour and show your true form," he demanded, glaring down at me through the spectacles sitting on the end of his nose.

"What bloody glamour?" I pulled my hair. Scratched my face. Dragged at my bloodstained dress. I was just me. A lady being held against her will.

The searing pain of the poisoned manacles fueled my rage.

He withdrew a ledger from beneath his arm and made a note. "What was your relationship to the victim?"

The *victim*? Robert wasn't the bloody victim, I was! "I didn't know the man."

He stopped writing. "The witnesses claimed he was your fiancée."

I glared at him.

"Why did you attack an innocent man, witch?"

"That monster tried to force himself on me," I hissed, shoving to my feet.

The beginnings of a sneer played on the man's thin lips. "I have two witnesses claiming otherwise."

In that moment, I realized this was a fight I couldn't win.

I could give this man all the proof in the world, but as long as he believed me to be a witch, it would fall on deaf ears.

I pointed at his chest, wishing I *was* a witch. That I could cast curses. "I'm glad he's dead," I spat. "I'm glad I killed him so he cannot prey on anyone else. I'd kill him again if I had the chance!"

The guard launched from his chair, grabbed a metal bucket, and threw a wave of water at the bars.

I screamed, falling to my knees.

Not water. *Acid*, melting the flesh from my bones.

Get it off. I had to get it off. The acid would eat me alive if I didn't *GET IT OFF!*

"What did you do to it?" the haughty man sniffed, looking down his nose at me as if I were a worm.

"Water laced with witch hazel. Keeps the rowdy ones in line." The guard kicked the bars. "You hear that, witch? If ye don't shut yer gob, I'll have ye dunked in a barrel of the shite and sealed inside."

Witch hazel was a harmless herb. It grew aplenty near my father's home. I'd gathered it for years, and it had never burned me like that.

What the hell was happening to me?

I stared at the black ceiling.

If I laid perfectly still, the pain was almost bearable. Something crawled along my arm. I didn't have it in me to check what sort of creature it was.

The man and his ledger went away, leaving me with the guard and his candle. In the flickering light, I could see metal instruments hanging on the wall. Some I knew the names of: Forceps. Dagger. Sword. More chains.

Most were foreign to me. I didn't need to know the names to understand how they were used.

Instruments of torture.

I'd barely survived the manacles and acid water. What hope did I have of surviving those?

Eventually, I dried off. My skin felt tight but there didn't seem to be any lasting impact from the dousing. I must've dozed because the next thing I knew, the guard at the table had changed.

This one looked younger, with a scraggly brown beard and dark, sunken eyes. Like this line of work had sucked the life right out of him.

I managed to sit up. The shifting manacles burned anew. The man's hand flew to the dagger on his belt.

"May I have some water, please?" I croaked.

Muttering under his breath, he pushed away from the chair and limped out of sight. A moment later, he returned. Setting a tiny tin cup on the other side of the bars, he used his dagger to nudge it closer. I scooted forward. He scurried back, colliding with the desk. The candle on top rattled; its flame shuddered.

I reached through the gap, my knuckle accidentally grazing

the bars. A terrible hissing sound erupted. It felt like I'd thrust my hand into a fire.

I tried again, this time careful not to touch anything but the cup. Bringing it to my lips, I drank the few drops he'd given me. It tasted like sulfur but was blessedly cool.

"Thank you."

The man gawked at me as if I'd cursed. I returned the cup to the other side of the bars and settled my back against the stone wall.

Had Charlie been kept in a cell like this one? Had he protested his innocence? Had he lost all hope or did some of it remain until that rope snapped his neck?

Boots thudded down the hall. Two soldiers in red livery appeared. At their request, the young guard unlocked the cell door.

I studied the soldiers' young faces as they hauled me to my feet and forced me up a set of crooked wooden stairs, and into a large, round room.

Finely dressed men filled the gleaming mahogany chairs on either side of a narrow aisle. On a raised dais at the end of the aisle sat a wrinkled man in a white wig. His black robes made him look like the crier who used to spout messages of hate from the gallows back in Graystones.

Dull gray light filtered through the high windows. Cigar smoke mixed with notes of brandy followed me down the aisle to a short wooden stool with no back.

All hope was lost.

These sneering men trading harsh whispers had made up their minds about me before I'd set foot in this room.

Witch.

Monster.

Murderer.

The slurs differed from man to man. The only constant was what followed.

Deserves to die.

The gavel banged. The room quieted. The magistrate in the robes motioned me forward. My sluggish feet stumbled to the stool. Heavy hands settled on my shoulders, forcing me onto the seat. The soldiers remained at my back, swords drawn, prepared to strike me down.

The magistrate's eyes narrowed as his lips curled back. "What's your name, witch?"

"My name is Lady Aveen Bannon. And I am not a witch."

To my right, someone snorted. I leaned around my guards to get a good look.

A man with tousled blond hair and alabaster skin sat on a bench by himself.

A man with piercing blue eyes.

Rían.

Relief flooded my veins. He'd come to save me.

Those blue eyes landed on me, but there wasn't a hint of recognition. Not even a slight wince at the pathetic state of my torn, bloody dress, gone brown from dirt and muck.

What if he was still under his mother's control? What if he didn't know me? What if he hadn't come to save me but simply to oversee another execution?

The magistrate leveled Rían with an irritated look. "Do you have something to say, emissary?"

"The witch's name is Brian." Rían's fingers tapped against his knee. "It delights in taking the form of loved ones who've passed in order to infiltrate their homes and rob their families blind."

"He's lying. My name is Lady Aveen Bannon," I insisted. Didn't he know he was condemning me to death?

Rían reached into a bag at his feet, withdrawing a piece of parchment. "According to this death certificate, Lady Aveen Bannon died last March."

The crowd resumed its whispering. The magistrate motioned for Rían to bring forward the damning document. Rían crossed the floor, his back ramrod straight.

"What are the charges against the witch?" Rían asked, fiddling with his shiny silver cufflinks.

The magistrate set the paper aside. "Murder."

"Murder, you say?"

The magistrate nodded. "The witch murdered a young man named Robert Trench."

Rían's eyes darted to me for a split second before returning to the front of the room. "And how has it pleaded?"

The judge's chair creaked. "How do you plead, witch?"

How did I plead? *HOW DID I PLEAD?* "He tried to force himself on me!" I shrieked. If they wanted to see a witch I'd give them a bloody witch. "He attacked me! He slammed my head against a wall and tried to—"

The crowd started to shout and swear, hurling insults and slurs.

The gavel cracked against the desk. "I will have order!" the judge demanded.

"And I will have justice!" I hurled back at the man. "I have a right to defend myself. I have a right to—"

Soldiers grabbed my arms, ramming me down on the stool.

"The punishment for murder is death," the magistrate announced. "Tomorrow at dawn, you will be brought to the gallows and hung by the neck until dead."

Rían cleared his throat.

The judge shot him an irritated glare. "Yes, emissary?"

"With all due respect, hanging isn't the most effective way to execute a witch."

I always knew Rían would break my heart.

I just didn't think he'd take my life as well.

"And what, pray tell, is the most effective way to execute a witch?" asked the judge.

Rían's eyes sparkled black when he smiled. "Beheading."

34

I IGNORED THE PEWTER DISH OF MOLDY BREAD AND TIN CUP OF sulfur water that the old guard slipped beneath the cell door. My eyes fell closed and I prayed to whoever would listen. I said I was sorry for taking a man's life—that I was sorry for everything. As much as I didn't want to die, I deserved this punishment. I had committed a crime, and it was only just that I suffered the consequences.

At least that's what I told myself.

Because every time I thought of how bloody unfair this was, I wanted to burn the entire prison and everyone in it to ash.

Someone kicked the iron bars of my cell.

My eyes flew open. Rían stood on the other side, arms folded and nose wrinkled as he studied the barrier. The candle's flickering flame reflected off the damp walls and instruments.

"What a mess you're in," he drawled.

Though the guard remained seated on the stool, his head lolled to the side.

"Go away," I croaked, my chapped lips cracking.

"Ah, here now, you're not nearly as fun when you're melancholy." Rían nudged the guard's boot. "Do you care to tell me why these eejits believe you're a witch?"

I shoved my matted hair back from my face, wincing when the manacles slipped to a fresh patch of skin. "They don't think a proper lady is capable of murdering a strong, powerful man."

Fire ignited in his depthless eyes. Blue, not black. Was he in control of himself? Or was this another trick of the Queen's, resurrecting my hope only to dash it all over again?

"And how do you explain this?" In his hand, he held his curved dagger.

I'd given up trying to explain any of it. "I can't." Hugging my knees to my chest, I stared toward the bucket in the corner I'd been forced to use to relieve myself. The final shreds of my dignity faded into the dirt.

Rían's footsteps thumped as he stomped forward. "Let me see your wrists."

With no will left to fight, I held my hands toward him.

"Feckin' hell . . ." He dropped to one knee, reaching through the bars. His fingers connected with the iron, making an unearthly hissing sound the same way mine had. Cursing, he withdrew his hand and flicked his wrist. A pair of white leather gardening gloves appeared. "Take these."

The only way to get them on was to shove the iron bracelets higher. I whimpered when the acid met fresh skin. By the time I managed to stuff my hands into the gloves, I could barely keep my eyes open. The moment I shoved the iron back to my covered wrists, the burning stopped.

A small mercy, but a mercy nonetheless. "Thank you for the gloves."

He reached through the bars, lifting my chin so I met his cerulean gaze. "Anything else?"

"Thank you for telling them to chop off my head."

His eyes began to glow, cutting through the murky haze. "Hanging is a dreadful way to die. Beheading is by far the quickest and most painless."

Rían could take his pathetic excuse for mercy and choke on it. "Just get out."

The bastard didn't leave. He stood and began pacing, from the bars to the guard and back again. At one point, he paused to stick a finger into the bucket of water beside the guard's chair and ended up cursing and scrubbing his hand against his breeches.

"It's witch hazel," I muttered.

He glared at me, his mouth pressed into a tight line. "How do you know?"

"The guard doused me with it." The memory left me trembling. "Felt like they'd peeled the skin from my bones."

"Who did?" He kicked the unconscious guard's boot, eliciting a groan from the man. "This one?"

I nodded.

Rían resumed his pacing, his boots grinding against the gritty stones.

"Don't you have anywhere else to be?"

"I'm waiting."

"For what?"

"For you to stop feeling sorry for yourself and bargain with me."

Bargain with me.

A spark lit in my hollow chest.

Bargain with me.

Rían. Please, please be Rían.

"What are your terms, oh great and powerful prince?"

The moment his dimples appeared, my hollow stomach began to flutter. "If I decide to use my immense power to save a weak, pathetic human such as yourself," he said, his smile slowly fading, "then you must promise to never set foot in the Black Forest."

I knew what he was doing. If I never crossed the Black Forest, I wouldn't be able to save him. I may never see him again. Never see my sister. Forcing me to stay away was as good as giving in and letting the Queen win. And I was having none of it. "I don't agree to those terms. Come up with something else."

He dropped to his knees and clutched the bars, filling the air with a sickening hiss. "The moment you set foot in the Forest, the

Queen will either carve your heart from your chest or she'll force me do it. I would rather see you die tomorrow than watch you become one of her victims."

There had to be a better solution. There had to be a way for us to defeat her and take back his heart. "Please."

He shook his head, his hair falling across his furrowed brow. "Die tomorrow or choose to live far from me and my world. Those are my terms."

When he stuck his hand through the bars, I skirted back. "I won't do it."

"Take my hand, Aveen."

"Rían—"

"When I leave, I will not return. I'm begging you, do not let your foolish emotions get in the way. Swear to never set foot in the Forest and let me save you."

Tears blurred his beautiful face. I would find a way around this. I would spend the rest of my life trying to find a way. But I couldn't find anything if I was dead. Despite everything inside me screaming to refuse, I slipped my hand into his and felt the bargain take hold.

The pain of the iron on my skin was nothing compared to the vicious ache in my heart when Rían let me go. Rose to his feet. And said, "You will always be mine."

I closed my eyes, not having the strength to watch him leave.

A sickening *snap* reverberated off the dank walls. The guard's body slumped to the floor, his head cocked at a wrong angle, unblinking eyes staring toward the mold-blackened ceiling.

Rían was gone.

Boots stomped. Curses flew. Locks clicked. Hinges creaked.

Four guards waited outside my door, iron chest plates and silver helmets gleaming. The body on the floor remained.

One gestured at me with a sword. "On your feet, witch."

My nails dug into the gritty stones as I stood.

I wasn't afraid.

Rían had promised to save me.

I wasn't afraid.

"Try anything, and I'll run you through," the man warned, motioning me forward with the blade.

My heavy feet refused to cooperate. How long had it been since I'd eaten? I chanced a step forward. My knees gave out, cracking off the stones. My hands weren't fast enough to keep my face from slamming against the floor. One of the guards at the back cursed, pushing his way to the front.

"Don't touch the witch! She'll curse us all," another bellowed.

"Leave off. The poor woman can't stand." Two hands clamped onto my elbows, lifting me. Soft brown eyes peered from inside the helmet.

The other guards kept their swords drawn and aimed at me as the one who'd assisted me tightened his hold, helping me down the hall, past torch after torch, until we reached the final door before the exit. Instead of bringing me outside, the man gave the door three swift kicks.

"The witch is here fer her confession," one of the others shouted.

The door creaked open. Two low wooden benches sat at either side of an ancient altar. Shafts of sunlight burst through barred windows, landing on a man in black robes.

"Bring her in," said the man in the robes.

The guard set me on one of the benches. The heavy scent of incense left my stomach rolling and head spinning.

The man in the robes motioned toward the door. "Leave us, my son."

The guard's boots scuffed against the stones. The door closed and the lock engaged.

The priest raised his head. Beneath his hood, his golden eyes glowed.

The moment I'd seen his hulking figure, I'd known who he was. "Hello, pooka."

"Hello, human."

Ruairi withdrew a set of keys from his pocket to unlock my shackles. The metal clattered to the ground. From beneath the altar, he removed a white shift and black robes similar to his own. "Change into these and give me yer dress."

Choking on my tears of relief, I reached an unsteady hand for the garments. "I . . . I don't think I can."

He was over me in an instant, working the buttons free, tugging the dress down my body, and replacing it with the soft, warm shift. "I can't carry ye out of here," he said, wrapping the black robes around my shoulders. "Ye need to walk. Think ye can do that for me?"

I nodded. I'd find the strength somewhere.

"There's a girl. Let's put this up." He drew the hood to cover my hair, tucking the ends inside.

After draping the dress and manacles over the bench, he tugged up his own hood and pounded on the door.

A key scraped the lock, and the door opened. Ruairi yanked the guard in by his iron breastplate, slamming his head against the stones. There was only one left on the other side—his eyes glowing and green.

Tadhg.

He held a finger to his lips. I nodded. I could do this. I could keep silent.

Keeping a hand on my elbow, he escorted me to the entrance and out into the clear sunlight.

A crowd had gathered around a raised wooden platform. The executioner waited, a black mask concealing his face. Tadhg led me in the opposite direction, toward a line of busy shops. I tried to ignore the whispers, the slurs, the speculation, hating every single person who had come to watch me die.

Tadhg didn't stop until we reached the entrance to a pub. Instead of going inside the main bar, he brought me to a skinny set of stairs off the entry, leading to a small, empty apartment with colorful cushions piled on the floor in front of the hearth.

Tadgh hurried to the window to draw the heavy curtains closed, casting the space in darkness. I was in such a sorry state, I didn't want to touch the pristine cushions or the sofas.

"Stay in here," he commanded. "I need to make sure Ruairi gets out before we leave."

"Where's Rían?"

Tadgh's gaze darted to the curtains. "Promise me you'll stay away from the window."

"Tadhg? Where's Rían?"

His expression hardened. "Rían is gone."

Gone? He couldn't be gone. That jail cell couldn't be the last time I saw Rían. It couldn't.

The moment Tadgh left, I dropped onto the rug at the far side of the sofa. A collective roar lifted from the square. I shouldn't look out the window.

What if I peeked? Just to be sure everything was all right? Barely lifting the edge of the curtain, I peered through the grimy pane. The crowd filled the entire square from the cathedral to the pubs. Men and women in finery, servants, and even children waited in the sunshine.

People began to cheer when the door to the jail opened.

I expected to see soldiers pouring out, weapons drawn, desperate to find their fugitive.

Instead, four soldiers escorted a woman in a dirty blue gown toward the dais.

A woman with curly blond hair and blue eyes set in a heart-shaped face I'd spent my life staring at.

My face.

My body.

My hair.

I watched myself kneel in front of a wooden stump, holding my breath as the executioner lifted the axe . . . and let it fall.

A head with mahogany hair landed in the basket.

Bloody hell.

That bastard had just died for me.

The floorboards behind me creaked, but I couldn't pull myself from the gruesome scene.

"I told you to stay away from the feckin' window," Tadhg snapped, ripping the curtain from my grasp. "Do you know what would happen if anyone found out what we've done?"

"His glamour is gone. They already know it wasn't me."

Tadhg knelt, giving my shoulders a shake. "It's not meant to be you, remember? It was a fictional witch named Brian."

The trial.

Rían had told the judge my name was Brian.

Had he been planning on saving me from the beginning?

Would he have saved me even if I hadn't accepted his bargain?

"Let's go." Tadgh helped me to my feet.

He brought me back to the portal in the cathedral's cellar. Instead of emerging from a linen closet, we ended up at the bottom of a dry well and had to evanesce out into the gray day.

The well sat on an incline leading down to the sea.

"Where are we?" I asked.

"About thirty miles north of Hollowshade."

Hollowshade. A town on the north-west coast of Airren.

Nestled at the base of the incline sat a whitewashed one-story cottage. Burnished gold vines swallowed nearly the entire façade, ending at dark slate roof tiles dotted with moss. The sea crashed in the distance.

Tendrils of gray smoke curled from the chimney, yet the four pane windows remained dark. "Who lives here?"

Tadhg withdrew something from his pocket and pressed it into my palm. *A key.* "You do."

35

THE SHORT GATE CREAKED ON ITS SAGGING HINGES WHEN I OPENED
it. Weeds devoured the ground on either side of a stone path
leading to a blue door. A one-horned goat raised its head from the
patch of grass next to a well, oogling us like we were intruders.

"This is mine?"

The cottage, the well, the goat, the weeds . . . all mine? The
crooked door, the hideous rug that reminded me of old striped
wallpaper, and the single-pane windows that would shatter with a
gale.

Tadhg had to duck to fit inside. "It's yours if you want it."

Mine.

The six cupboards, the chipped tea set, the drystack fireplace
burning logs of fragrant turf, the lonely brown sofa and rickety
dining chairs.

All mine.

I'd never owned anything more than dresses and a few jewels
I'd inherited from my mother.

Now I had all of this.

The rest of my cottage took fifteen steps to see. The larger
bedroom had a door leading to a backyard swallowed by bram-
bles. If I pruned them back, I'd have blackberries in September.

Not that I'd know what to do with the things beyond gorging on them raw. But they'd be mine too.

I could plant a vegetable patch along the stone wall. If there was a market nearby, perhaps I could sell a few.

Mine.

Bits of furniture more broken than not cluttered the smaller bedroom and tiny bathing room in between.

Mine.

What was that delicious smell? Bread—two loaves, tucked away inside a basket next to a second one full of fruit and veg.

My food in my house sitting on my table next to my stove.

Tadhg's nose wrinkled when he stuck a finger into one of the holes on the sofa's upholstery.

It didn't matter what he thought.

I loved it. More than loved it.

Far from perfect but beautiful in its mismatched glory, this place was mine. No one could take it from me.

Mine, all mine.

A cottage by the sea with a garden.

My wish.

This place had to be from Rían.

Outside, the orange sun sank toward the horizon. I clutched my black robes to keep them from tangling with my dirty boots, stepping from one creaky floorboard to the next. "Bring him to me. Please."

Tadhg frowned down at his flexing hands. "There's no telling when he'll turn again. You need to let him go."

Let him go.

Now wasn't the time to let Rían go. Now was the time to hold him tighter.

"You love my sister and would do anything to save her, right?"

Tadhg's dark eyebrows came together. "Aveen—"

"Am I right?"

He gave a reluctant nod.

"That's how I feel about Rían. It's my turn now. My turn to save him."

Grimacing, Tadhg scraped his teeth along his bottom lip. "He won't come."

He would come. I wouldn't give him a choice. "You tell your infuriating brother that if he isn't here by sundown, I will throw myself into the sea."

Sighing, Tadhg nodded and turned toward the door.

I waited outside for what felt like hours. The goat continued munching away, not a care in the world.

Rían would come.

He had to.

Unless he called my bluff. Unless he knew I didn't have it in me to go through with it.

My hope fell with the sinking sun.

I turned and stomped back toward the house. If I was going to die, I didn't want to die in this hideous black robe and a shift.

"Throw yourself into the feckin' sea? What sort of shite is that?"

Rían stood by the gate in a spotless white shirt, one arm thrown around the post, his long legs encased in black breeches.

I wanted to jump on top of him and hug him against me. To kiss his irritatingly handsome face. To strangle him for trying to force me into giving him up. "It's how I respond to 'accept my bargain or die.'"

Rían's thumb tapped the wooden post. "I'm here. What do you want?"

What did I want? Wasn't it bloody obvious? I wanted *him*.

I stepped forward. My blasted slipper tangled with the heavy hem of the blasted robe, sending me flying headfirst into his chest.

Rían caught me in his cinnamon-scented embrace. "Dammit, Aveen. When was the last time you had food?"

"I can't remember." Food was the last thing on my mind when he picked me up and started for the cottage.

I ended up on the sofa, watching a prince flit from cupboard to cupboard, collecting plates and bits of food and water from a clay jug with a broken handle.

He dragged over one of the mismatched chairs to use as a small table, setting the feast right under of my nose. "Eat."

As delicious as the bread smelled, my clenching stomach was having none of it. I picked the end of one slice apart and popped a piece into my mouth to appease him. I swore the morsel echoed when it hit bottom.

"I shouldn't be here," he sighed. "I could spin out at any moment."

"Does it happen often?" We'd known each other for months and I hadn't seen it happen more than the once.

A faint blush painted his sharp jaw. His gaze dropped to his boots. "She leaves me alone as long as I don't break the rules."

That evil witch . . . I was going to kill her. And I was going to enjoy it. "We need to get back your heart."

Rían told me I'd lost my "feckin' mind" and stalked to the spare room, returning with a copper tub to place in front of the fire. After collecting a bucket from beside the cupboards, he stepped outside, slamming the door behind him.

The bite I'd taken seemed happy to stay down, so I had another. And another. By the time I finished the plate of bread, smoky yellow cheese, and cured ham, my queasiness had subsided enough to sit upright.

Rían lugged in bucket after bucket of water, six in total. The kettle on the hob started whistling. Water sloshed onto the plank floor when he added the final bucket. With the fire blazing in the hearth, it wouldn't be long before the puddle dried.

I dipped my fingers into the tub, then sucked in a breath. "It's bloody freezing."

The kettle ceased its screaming the moment Rían lifted it from the hob. "That's what this is for."

"That tiny kettle won't make a blind bit of difference to this much water."

He dumped the steaming water into the bath, then stuck his hand in and cursed. "How the hell was I supposed to know that?"

"Haven't you drawn a bath before?"

Brow furrowing, he stared down at the tepid water. "I've never needed to."

With his ability to conjure anything and everything, what would be the point in doing things for himself? "Just do your little flicky thing and warm it up."

His eyes narrowed. "My little flicky thing?"

"You know." I did my best impression of his magical wrist-flick. "Your flicky thing."

Rían folded his arms over his chest. Why wasn't he doing it?

"Is it not working again?" Returning from the underworld must take a considerable amount of magic. If he had any left, surely he would've shifted the bath instead of filling it bucket by bucket.

"My 'flicky-thing' is working just fine," he muttered. "I've warded this cottage against magic, so I have to do this the pathetic human way."

"Why would you do something like that?" He seemed to use magic for everything.

"Our magic leaves a lingering scent, and I never wanted the Queen to find out about you. This was where you were supposed to wake after Tadgh's curse wore off." He turned and started for the door with the kettle.

This place had been his plan all along.

Rían had given me my dream.

How could he think for even a moment that I wouldn't do everything in my power to give him the same?

I checked the tub again. The water wasn't *that* cold.

Did I really want to sit in my own filth any longer? My legs trembled when I stood. I threw another turf brick into the hearth and shed the robe and shift. The moment my toes dipped beneath the surface, goosebumps erupted over my skin.

Cold. Cold. So bloody cold.

I had to do this quickly so I didn't turn into a block of ice.

Holding my breath, I dunked my head. When I came up for air, I found Rían slack-jawed in the entrance, the kettle hanging loosely in his hand.

My trembling lips lifted into a smile. "Do you know if there's any soap?"

He dropped the kettle and ran to the spare room, returning with a fluffy brown towel and bar of soap. I thanked him and went about scrubbing away the remnants of my incarceration. If only erasing the memories and the stain of utter hopelessness were as simple.

Rían left me for the bedroom, making a racket doing heaven-knew-what.

The scars at my wrist were no longer red and raw but silver.

Silver like the scar on my palm.

I blinked.

And blinked.

And blinked.

Silver scars . . .

Iron burned my skin . . .

Witch hazel scalded like acid . . .

Rían's dagger . . .

All those things shouldn't have happened. And yet they had. Why? I'd handled iron before and had no adverse reaction. Same with witch hazel. And the dagger? I'd never been able to conjure an object out of will and desperation.

What had changed?

Why were these things happening to me now?

The answer flashed like a bolt of lightning, sharp and fast.

I had died and come back, not after a year as the curse had dictated but after only a few months.

Not only had I come back, I'd been resurrected with an immortal's life force.

"Rían!" I shot out of the tub, sloshing water all over the floor.

"Rían!" I snagged the towel from the sofa, wrapping it around my waist. My sopping hair felt like ice on my back.

Rían came charging in, a stack of clothes in his arms. "Why are you roaring?"

I held out my wrist. "Look."

The clothes fell to the ground. He took my hand, bringing it closer to the fire, turning it this way and that. His eyes slowly widened.

"You don't think—"

He shook his head. "I don't know."

"I shifted your dagger," I told him. "At least I think I did." There was no other explanation for what had happened that night in the alley.

I didn't have a dagger. I only wished I did.

And then one had magically appeared.

Cursing, Rían let me go to pace the three steps between the fireplace and the cabinet and back again.

"Does this mean I can evanesce?" If I could, then I wouldn't need to cross the Forest to get to Tearmann.

"I don't know."

"Can I do the flicky thing?" I flicked my wrist, but nothing happened.

"I don't know."

"Am I immortal?"

He stopped, tugging on the ends of his hair as if he wanted to rip it all out. "How the hell am I supposed to know?"

"Why are you so upset? This is a good thing."

If I was a true immortal, I couldn't die.

Or rather, I could die, but I would come back.

This was amazing. Bloody brilliant.

I threw my arms around his neck, hugging him close, pressing my cheek to his chest.

A chest that held no heart.

No . . .

His eyes met mine, glistening with unshed tears.

No. No. No.

I stumbled back, ramming into the copper tub. "The dagger . . ." If I was a true immortal, I wouldn't be able to use it. I wouldn't be able to save him.

He cupped my face, stroking my cheeks with his thumbs. "This is brilliant news, Aveen. Brilliant." He brushed a tender kiss to my temple.

I slid my hands over his. "No. No, it's not. Your heart—"

His forehead dropped to mine, and he said with the sweetest smile, "You are my heart."

I pulled out of his grasp, sinking onto the faded rug. This wasn't the way our story was supposed to end. The Queen could take him from me at any moment. She could take him away and never give him back.

I wouldn't let her. I couldn't.

Rían dropped beside me, hugging his knees to his chest.

"We have to get your heart." Our mission remained the same. We'd just have to find a way to go about it without the dagger. There had to be some way to retrieve it.

Rían eased forward, collecting another block of turf and throwing it on top of the fire. Orange flames licked at the brown log.

I could do this. I could save him. But to do that, I would have to give up my own life.

Perhaps the fortune teller was wrong.

Was I really going to give up on the off chance she wasn't?

"I understand you're scared," I said to Rían as much as to myself, "but—"

"You're feckin' right I'm scared. You can't imagine how scared I am. I have watched my mother tear the heart from a woman's chest and consume her life force. I've felt her claws reach into my body to rip out mine. If you're not scared senseless by the idea of entering that Forest, then you are a fool."

I was scared. I was more scared than I would ever admit.

But just because we were scared didn't mean we couldn't succeed. "We can do this."

He nudged the stone chimney with his boot, the corner of his lips crooking into a sardonic smile. "Immortal or not, you can't set foot in the Forest."

Set foot in. I smiled. "Then I'll ride a horse through."

He opened his mouth, then closed it again.

"Or you can release me from the bargain," I finished.

"Not. A. Hope."

He wanted to be stubborn right now? All right. I could be stubborn too.

I tugged his collar, exposing the vicious scar like a silver necklace circling his throat. "Look at this." I traced the smooth bubbled skin where they'd cut him. "You died for me today, Rían. *You died for me.* You don't think I would do the same for you?"

"Aveen, listen to me—"

"No, you listen to me. If you give up now, she wins. If you leave me, you are letting her take away your soulmate. We can end this. Once and for all."

"It's not worth it."

"That's where you're wrong." I rose to my knees, taking his face in my hands, forcing him to look at me. To see me. To *listen.* "You are worth everything to me. And because I love you, I will give you a choice. You help me get back your heart, or you refuse and I do it on my own."

Rían studied me for so long, I thought he wasn't going to respond.

Then he stood and took my hand, bringing me to my feet. "How do you think we're going to take back my heart when you can no longer wield the cursed dagger?"

Right. The damn dagger. The dagger that could kill me if I used it—but only *if* I was a true immortal. How did we get Rían's heart back without it?

I thought and thought. There had to be some way to—

Hold on.

We were looking at this all wrong.

This mission wasn't about vengeance. It was about taking back something that had been stolen.

I smiled up at him and said, "I have a plan."

It wouldn't be long before the candle flickering on the tiny bedside table burned out. The lateness of the hour was the last thing on my mind as I hugged Rían closer. Staring toward the cracked plaster ceiling, Rían traced idle patterns on my bare back.

"I should've let you go," he confessed to the night. "I should've let Tadhg bring you to the Forest the very first day and request safe passage. I just . . . if the Queen had said 'no,' I thought . . ."

"You thought I'd be stubborn enough to go anyway."

His hand stilled, and he nodded.

Would I have been foolish enough to cross the Black Forest? I'd been understandably distraught, but that didn't mean I would've put my life at risk. Then again, it was hard to say for certain. And anyway, there was no point dwelling on the what-ifs.

"I'm glad you didn't," I said, breathing him in, committing to memory the feel of his warmth mixing with mine. "I'm glad you wanted to keep me."

There was a smile in his voice when he said, "I wanted to keep you the moment I accosted you in that shed."

The wind howled outside, whistling through a gap in the sill and sending a chill tickling down my spine. Rían lifted my arm, extricating himself from beneath me. Rolling off the bed, he padded silently toward the room across the skinny hall, returning with a handful of gray putty. He picked off a bit, rolled it between his fingers, and stuffed it in the gap.

The whistling stopped.

The mattress dipped when he came back to bed. I snuggled close, missing his heat. "Watching you do things turns me on." Before bed, he'd banked the fire, made us both a cup of tea, and washed the few dishes we'd used. Domestic Rían was quickly becoming one of my favorites.

"You must be constantly turned on then. I do things all the time."

"I mean handy things. Like boiling the kettle. And filling the tub. And fixing my window."

"I can literally open the earth with a flick of my wrist, and you're turned on by a bit of feckin' putty?" His chuckle vibrated under my cheek. "That's it. I'm asking for a new soulmate. You're defective."

"Stop," I giggled, giving his chest a smack. "It makes you seem more human." I liked thinking of Rían having limitations like the rest of us instead of being all-powerful.

"That is not a compliment."

"It is to me."

He drummed his fingers against my back. "I puttied all these windows."

My stomach fluttered. "Did you now?"

He nodded.

"Did you do anything else?"

He settled deeper into the thin pillow at his back. "Replaced the shite windows with less shite windows. And fixed the hinges on the shite door. And pulled a hundred years' worth of bird and mouse nests from the chimney."

I propped myself onto my elbow so I could see him better. Candlelight flickered on the far side of his face. The side closest to me remained draped in shadows. "You're serious?"

Rían's eyes shuttered. "I was in a dark place when you died. Convinced you'd never forgive me for what happened to your sister. I . . . did some things I'm not proud of."

"Do I want to know?" I was certain I didn't.

"Slept with a maid." A wince. "Or maybe three."

We hadn't been together. I'd been dead. Feeling betrayed would be silly, and yet I couldn't help it. Why would Rían do something like that if he believed I was truly his soulmate? Tears welled in my eyes. I hated that he had been with anyone else. That both of us had.

"I'm sorry. I just . . . I believed all hope was lost." His hands fell open on the faded quilt. "Then I remembered your wish. And that gave me purpose. I thought that, even if you never spoke to me again, you may think fondly of me one day."

I scrubbed at the useless tears rolling down my cheeks. What good would they do? What had happened in the past didn't change things now.

For all his faults, all his mistakes, Rían had wanted me to be happy. Even if it was without him. "So you bought me a shack and some flowers," I said, the words coming out all wobbly and weak.

"I built you a shack and flowers."

Did he say he *built* this?

Rían's frown deepened as he looked around the room from the small armoire to the window and back again. "Probably not something I should boast about."

Rían, a man who hated dirt and was allergic to dust, *built* me a house.

What in the world was I supposed to say to that?

"This grumpy old farmer owned it," he went on, picking at his nails and avoiding my gaze. "Asked for far too much. He showed me what to do. Helped me some days."

"I'd love to meet him." And request stories about how Rían had survived getting dirt on his clothes.

Rían finally looked at me, eyes glowing a faint blue. "We can go tomorrow if you'd like."

"We have plans tomorrow." Plans to get back his heart. "Let's go the following day."

His mouth flattened.

I didn't have to ask to know what he was thinking. What if there was no day after tomorrow? What if tonight was the last night we had together? The thought had crossed my mind more than once. But how could we have any hope of success if our minds were focused on failure?

I held Rían's face between my hands and kissed him. "I love you, my deceitful prince. Despite everything you've done, I will love you tomorrow. And I will love you the day after that."

"And the next day?" he whispered against my lips, slipping his hands to my hips and drawing me onto his lap.

"That depends on whether or not you irritate me."

His reluctant laugh was a burst of warm air.

He brought my hand to cover the scar on his chest, his skin warm and solid and smooth. But also silent and still. "Out of darkness shines a light, bringing day to darkest night. Find your soul's one true mate, for she will save you from your fate."

The chill running down my spine had nothing to do with the howling wind battering my poor cottage. "What's that?" I asked. The beautiful rhyme was like a song of hope.

"A fortune told to me long ago."

Fortunes.

I didn't want to think of the one given to me. Instead, I focused on Rían's.

For she will save you from your fate.

One way or another, tomorrow I would succeed. I took solace in that.

Drawing me into his embrace, Rían pressed a soft kiss to my hair. "You've filled the hollow parts of me, angry, miserable, violent, happy, beautiful Aveen. And now that I've found you, I'll not let you go."

36

WE WOKE AT DAWN'S FIRST LIGHT, MAKING LOVE TO THE SOUND of the sea. Neither of us speaking, letting our bodies tell our truths. Rían held my hand on the short walk to the portal inside the bowels of the mildewy dry well. The linen closet on the other side smelled infinitely better: lavender, vanilla, and fresh air.

The family who lived in the house was nowhere to be seen, but the doors had been left unlocked. Following a path through a forest draped in wintery white, we eventually ended up at a border of shiny black stones. No snow fell on the cursed black ground writhing on the other side.

An icy breeze laced with carrion fluttered my unbound hair.

Rían shifted a pocket watch, staring down at its ticking hands.

"Is it time?" I asked, trying to keep my voice from giving away the extent of my nervousness.

"Yes. But this is a terrible plan," he muttered.

"It'll be fine."

"While I appreciate your poor attempt at optimism, we are depending on a man cursed to tell the truth *lying* to a witch who can smell such things. You'll forgive me if I don't share your confidence."

I had faith in Tadhg. Besides, this wasn't just the best plan we had. It was our *only* plan. "Do you like being controlled by a heinous murderer?"

A smile ghosted across Rían's lips when he sent the watch away. "Ah, here now. I wouldn't call you a 'heinous murderer.' You only killed Robert Trench."

I punched him in the arm. He feigned a wince, rubbing at his shoulder. "I'm being serious, you know. Now, give me the dagger." I motioned toward the glowing emerald hilt sheathed at his waist, which he had retrieved before we'd gone to bed last night.

Grumbling, he withdrew the blade, flipped it over, and offered me the hilt. "What are the rules?"

Rían and his bloody rules. "Surprise is key. Get close. Go for the kill." My sister had killed Fiadh, but the witch had taken so long to die, she'd almost killed Keelynn as well.

"And?"

I rolled my eyes. "And if you turn, I am to kill you before you kill me."

He released the blade with obvious reluctance. I tried to ignore the way it continued to glow as I stuffed it into my skirt pocket.

"Are you ready?" I could only imagine how hard this must be for him, after losing the woman he loved to the Forest.

He scowled down at his boots grazing the onyx stones.

We didn't have time to tarry. I took a deep breath and stepped over the line. My boot landed on the cursed earth, roiling like the sea. "There. That wasn't so—"

Black roots coiled around my ankles. Rían cursed. Flicked his wrist. The roots retreated enough for me to extricate myself. He picked me up and set me on a spot two steps to my right. The ground still roiled, but where I stood remained solid.

I gave him a sheepish smile.

"I know this is your plan," he said, finally taking that step across the border, "but I might take the lead for this part, if it's all right with you?"

We left the glistening white world for one without sunlight or life. Bodies of small birds and rodents in various states of decay littered the writhing blackened earth.

The invisible path wound through dead trees with roots that sat above the ground like the tentacles of some mythical sea monster. Nothing grew here but black trees.

Rían didn't speak, for which I was grateful. Speaking would've forced me to drop my cloak from my nose and breathe in the bitter stench of death. He appeared immune to all of it. The skulls rising to the surface. The femurs. The hand.

A single crow circled the darkening sky, nearly invisible through the twisted tree branches. Then another joined it. And another. And another.

Cursed trees seemed to stretch on for eternity. Then the air grew damp, and the song of the sea replaced the murky silence. Suddenly, we were no longer in a forest but standing at the top of a sheer cliff face, staring down at churning waves. The call of seabirds echoed in the distance. The path wound precariously close to the eroding edge. My foot slipped; Rían caught my arm, dragging me back.

At the top of the next incline sat a large tower house built entirely of black stone. Candles flickered in the arched windows. I tried to ignore the dread swelling in my stomach as we drew ever closer. A gate of sharpened iron pikes topped with skulls marked the entrance to the keep.

"Where are the guards?" I had imagined a line of black-clad soldiers guarding the Queen's castle.

"She doesn't need them. No one in their right mind comes here." Rían shifted the curved dagger and slid it across his palm. With blood welling from the wound, he squeezed his fist, letting it drip into the black lock keeping the gates closed. There was a soft click followed by a rusty groan as the lock fell away and the gates slowly opened.

Rían passed beneath without issue, but when I tried, I hit an invisible barrier. "The old crow is so feckin' paranoid," he muttered.

Paranoid for good reason. I had a weapon capable of killing her.

A weapon capable of killing me as well.

I'd assured Rían the dagger was for defensive purposes only. If the Queen came for me, I needed a way to fight her.

And since there was a chance it would still work, he'd agreed.

A small chance was better than none at all.

Rían took my hand, crossing the barren stretch of earth and stone to the stairs.

What must it have been like for Rían to grow up in this place, surrounded by death and darkness? A lonely little boy accustomed to skulls and human bones rising from the ground and drifting away like ships on the sea.

Looking at the entrance hall on the other side was like staring into a snowstorm. White walls, white marble floor, white staircase. Two guards in black leather uniforms waited on either side of the door, so still and silent I wasn't sure they were alive.

"You know where you're going?" Rían asked.

Nodding, I showed him the crude map he'd drawn on my palm. Up the stairs to the second floor, third door on the left. Simple.

He kissed my temple and wished me good luck.

And then he went back out into the yard and evanesced. Tadhg was currently hosting the Queen under the guise of rene-gotiating the treaty with the Vellanian King. She'd agreed to visit his castle for one hour. Rían's plan was to pop in and out so she thought he was still at the castle, and to make sure she hadn't left.

"She can hear the heartbeats," Rían had explained while we were discussing our plan last night.

If she was in the Forest, she could pinpoint a single heartbeat the moment a person set foot over the enchanted border. No Queen in the Forest meant no one to hear my heart thundering as I climbed the stairs. And no Queen meant no one to control her mindless minions standing guard by every door on this floor. I kept expecting them to shout or stab me with their swords. None of them so much as twitched.

The same white from the hall continued inside the Queen's chambers, where Rían was convinced she'd hidden his heart.

If I were a heart, where would I be?

I would want to keep it somewhere safe, where no one could find it. So not in the armoire or dresser or desk. Beneath the wide, white canopy bed? No. Too simple.

A second door connected the bedroom to a bathing chamber with a sunken tub. Beside a sink rose a large gilt-framed mirror with cherubs peering at their reflections from each of the four corners.

Probably not the best place to hide a heart.

There was a closet on the other side of the room, filled with children's toys. Wooden soldiers and swords, leather balls, a rolling hoop, a set of quoits. All lined along the wall, just waiting for a child to discover them. I ran my fingers through the yarn mane of a little white rocking horse.

Something moved behind me.

I gripped the emerald dagger. Whirled.

Bloody Rían.

"You nearly gave me a heart attack," I breathed, pressing a hand to my pounding chest.

Chuckling, he picked up a stuffed bear to examine its black glass eyes.

"Are all of these toys yours?" It seemed oddly sentimental for the Queen to have kept them for so long.

Rían nodded. "She never let me play with one for more than a week. When I'd get attached, she'd take it away again." He set the bear on the back of the horse. His grin faded, and he turned in a circle. "Do you hear that?"

I shook my head. All I heard were my own ragged breaths.

Rían stilled before stepping to the back of the closet and pressing an ear to the wall. His eyes widened as he drew away. "There's something in there."

His hands slid along the white stones. One, about halfway down, protruded slightly. I nudged him aside and pushed the stone as hard as I could.

Something inside the wall clicked. And then an entire panel slid to the side with a scraping groan.

Rían stepped into a hallway so slender, he had to turn sideways to fit. Floor-to-ceiling shelves stretched into the darkness, lined with silver bird cages.

Only the cages didn't hold chirping birds.

They held beating hearts.

There had to be hundreds, if not thousands.

"Whose hearts are these?" I whispered, dread pooling in my chest.

Rían shook his head, running a hand down the silver bars on the closest cage. "I haven't a clue."

The only distinguishing marks were numbers engraved on each base. Not random numbers. Dates. "Do you remember when she took your heart?"

He touched another cage. The heart inside continued its steady beating. "Not exactly the kind of thing a man forgets."

We continued back and back, traveling centuries into the past.

At the very end of the hall, he froze. "*Shit.*"

I tried to peer around him but there wasn't enough room. "What is it? What's wrong?"

"There are two from the same day."

Sure enough, two hearts sat side by side in silver cages almost at the end of the corridor. "We can take them both."

He reached for the first cage from almost three hundred years ago.

Three hundred years without a heart.

Three hundred years of not knowing when his mother would take control.

The second heart with the same date started beating faster. "Look." I gestured toward the quickening organ.

The moment Rían's fingers connected with the bars, the little door flew open.

Before he could reach in, I stopped him. "Let me do it."

Although his brow furrowed, he turned and let me squeeze past. Bile burned the back of my throat when my fingers wrapped around his warm, wet, and still-beating heart.

We'd done it.

We'd actually done it.

"We need to put it back."

He took my arm, tugging me toward the doorway, which was barely visible at the end of the corridor. "When we get to the cottage."

I dug in my heels, refusing to budge. If the Queen returned, we would both be dead. This couldn't be for naught. At least with his heart back, he could be free. I'd known the moment I walked into the Forest that I may not make it out.

"We do it now," I insisted, cradling his heart against my chest.

"Aveen, there isn't time—"

"Then stop wasting it and put your heart back where it belongs."

I knew he could do it. Last night, he'd explained how it worked. About the reanimation spell the Queen had him under. About the spell he needed to return his heart to where it belonged. But he'd also admitted that he wasn't sure whether or not his mother would still be able to control him if he simply evanesced with his heart and hid it away.

He had said it didn't matter.

I had not-so-quietly disagreed.

Cursing, he dragged me toward the light at the end of the hallway.

When we reached the Queen's bedroom, he tore off his coat, grumbling and cursing about time and women. He ripped open his shirt, exposing the jagged scar to the candlelight.

The heart in my hand contracted wildly.

Closing his eyes, Rían took a deep breath, and the beating slowed.

He began to murmur, his words a hum too low to make out. He was chanting too slowly. He needed to hurry.

As if he'd heard my silent plea, he breathed on his fingertips until they glowed like a branding iron. An unearthly hiss erupted as he dragged them along the scar on his chest.

His face contorted. Sweat beaded on his brow. "I can't . . ."

I had magic. Maybe. Possibly. "Can I help?"

He grasped my free hand. Warmth spread from his body to mine as I became a conduit for his magic. He gestured for the heart, and I let him have it, watching in rapt fascination as my fingertips began to glow too.

"Finish it," he ground through his teeth. Blood dribbled from the wound he'd opened. I brought my index finger to the other side of the "X" and traced the scar, flaying the skin open. My stomach lurched. For all the times he'd saved me, I could do this.

"My heart," he whispered, face ashen and eyes black.

I collected it from his limp hand.

"Against the cut."

I pressed the contracting muscle against the open wound.

Rían rasped out two final words.

And flicked his wrist.

The heart disappeared. The wound closed.

Gasping like a drowning man, Rían's hand flew over the scar.

I held my breath, tears collecting along my lashes. "Did it work?" I assumed it had because the heart had been there and now it wasn't.

"I don't know," he rasped, lips as white as his open shirt.

What if it hadn't worked and the heart had gone back to its cage? What if the Queen had found out and had stolen it at the last minute?

"I . . . I *think* it did."

I refused to let the relief welling in my core settle. Not yet. "How do you feel?"

"Like shite."

Oh no. What if we'd screwed it up? What if he'd done the wrong spell or something had gone wrong or—

Rían brought two fingers to the pulse point at his throat. Blue eyes flew to mine.

And he smiled.

I launched myself into his arms, dotting kisses to his cheek, his neck, his chest.

His laugh was like a song, deep and rumbling. "Can we do this later?"

"Right. Yes. Of course." I scrubbed the tears from my eyes and stood.

Rían remained on the floor.

"Aren't you coming?"

He tried to stand only to collapse again. I helped him to his feet, bracing his arm across my shoulder, taking as much of his weight as I could. "Princes. So pathetic and weak."

He chuckled.

My soul sang as we slowly made our way down the stairs, Rían's feet dragging and face pale. My heart leapt as we trudged into the empty yard, through the gates, and back to the path along the cliff.

And then my heart sank when I saw the Queen.

37

The Queen's feathered skirts fluttered in the salty breeze. The sun on the horizon silhouetted her slender frame.

Nostrils flaring, she glowered at the two of us.

I let Rían go, stepping between my prince and his mother.

Rían had insisted on a contingency plan for if something went dreadfully wrong. We both knew exactly what we had to do.

Her presence just made things a little more complicated.

The Queen's head tilted as she watched me, an impassive expression on her thin face. "You were free and yet you returned. Why?"

Simple.

"I love your son." My love for this heartless prince had helped me find my voice. Had helped me find myself.

She inhaled, long and slow, something flickering in her endless black gaze. "You know the penalty for crossing the Forest," she said, a curved dagger appearing in her hand. "One life."

"Rían," I said without turning around. "I love you."

He chuckled. "I love you too, my little viper."

I whirled . . . and shoved him off the cliff.

The Queen's ear-piercing shriek rattled my bones. "You fool!" She lunged, catching my arm. Black nails bit into my flesh. The black veins beneath her skin pulsed. "You will pay for this!" she snarled, her heated breath sickeningly sweet.

Through chattering teeth, I smiled. "I just did."

One life. That was the price of crossing the Forest.

"I choose which life I take," she snarled, pressing the tip of her dagger against my chest. "*I choose.*"

"Not if the penalty has already been paid."

The law made no distinction over whose life was forfeit if someone were to cross the Black Forest. Rían could die and come back. And Rían had been more than willing to pay my debt.

The Queen threw me aside, lowering her dagger. The fire in her obsidian eyes swelled. I could taste her rage, like sulfur and smoke. "Mark my words, this crossing will be your last."

I didn't need her bloody Forest.

I knew exactly where I belonged.

In a land of myths and monsters. With a prince who had helped me find freedom.

I turned on my heel and started for Tearmann, each step bringing me closer to my future. A future I had chosen for myself. I would miss the cottage Rían had made for me but held fast to the hope that someday I would see it again. If I could shift a dagger, I could learn to evanesce. I had faith in myself—in whatever magic now lived inside my veins. I would find a way.

"Oh, Aveen," the Queen called.

The smile in her voice left my footsteps wavering. Slowly, I turned. Her bloodred lips twisted in a sneer. Wind whipped my hair across my cheeks, stinging my eyes. The Queen stood all alone against a backdrop of death. "Tell my son I look forward to making him pay for what he stole from me."

"You stole his heart first." Returning something stolen to its rightful owner wasn't against Tearmann law. According to the stack of books on the subject that I had found in Gaul's library, returning a stolen item to its rightful owner wasn't a crime.

She shook her head. Her feathered skirts fluttered, yet her hair remained in an undisturbed mahogany sheet. "I didn't steal Rían's heart. He gave it to me."

That wasn't true. It couldn't be. "You're lying."

Her soft chuckle left my heart pounding. "She was a pretty thing for a human, his Leesha. With fiery red hair and green eyes. But his human broke the law."

I didn't want to hear this.

And yet I couldn't move.

"Rían knew his duty was to his people. He knew what needed to be done. He knew and he refused. Begged me for *mercy*." She spat the word as if it were a vicious curse, her black-tipped fingers curling into fists. Black blood leaked from her palms, dripping onto the waving grass at her feet. "I begged for mercy once. Do you know what the humans did?" A heavy pause stretched between us. "They cut out my sister's heart with a cursed dagger and burned her body to ash."

I didn't want to feel sympathy for this monster. For this woman who had taken everything from the man I loved. Who had stolen mothers from their children. Fathers from their families. Daughters and sons.

This Queen who had ripped away countless lives without mercy.

But a monster wasn't born a monster.

A monster was made.

"When my weak, pathetic son refused his duty, I was forced to do it for him. He was a dramatic boy back then, always wailing about one thing or another. He said, 'If you take her heart, take mine as well.'" A smile. "So I did."

No . . .

No no no no.

"So, I would like you to remind my son, that the penalty for theft is death."

"He will come back." Rían was a true immortal. The underworld couldn't keep him unless she used the cursed blade hidden inside my skirts. A cursed blade she would never get her hands on.

The Queen's smile became a sneer. "He won't be coming back from this."

My hand fell to the dagger.

She was too far away. I wouldn't catch her off guard. She'd kill me before I even got close.

The penalty for theft is death.

My mind cleared, the panic in my chest loosening as the fortune teller's words rang through my mind.

For the only way to save him was at her own expense.

I stared straight into the Queen's soulless black eyes and said, "Rían didn't steal the heart. I did."

Then I stepped backward off the cliff and plummeted toward the sea.

38

Pity the girl from Graystones
who loved a heartless prince.
For the only way to save him
was at her own expense.

39

Darkness wasn't cold.

It was warm and comforting. Beautiful in its simplicity.

I didn't mind the dark. It was the light that hurt.

Light burned and scalded, ripping away my darkness, forcing me to move, forcing me to breathe. Boiling oil poured down my throat, surging through my veins like liquid fire.

My peaceful nothing became a pair of blue eyes. My weightlessness became strong hands holding me down.

You're back.

I heard the words but didn't recognize the voice.

"*Aveen? Can you hear me?*" The question swam in my mind.

I could hear but couldn't respond or move my head or my hands or legs—

"It's all right. I'm here. I'm here."

The backs of my eyes burned, but there were no tears. A broken whimper came from somewhere.

"I know it hurts. I know it does. Breathe through the pain."

I opened my lungs, accepting the fire with a choked sob.

Rían held me in his arms, his dark, wet hair plastered to his head. Soft sunlight trickled through yellowed lace curtains, casting a floral shadow over Rían's pale face. I recognized the tiny bedroom in my cottage. So far from Tearmann. So far from him and the castle and my sister. "Why are we here?" I managed, the words sounding garbled and heavy. My mouth tasted awful, like fish and seaweed. Sure enough, a chunk of dark seagrass was stuck between the buttons at the front of my wet blue dress.

"I had to bring you somewhere safe. If she found your body . . ." His Adam's apple bobbed when he swallowed.

If the Queen had gotten my body, she would've had access to my heart.

"When I came back and saw you fall from that cliff . . ." Rían whispered, gathering my gritty hair from my face, moving it behind my shoulder, "I thought you were gone forever."

I thought I'd be gone forever as well.

Although the ten-second fall to my death had been peaceful, filled with memories of the two people I loved. My sister and my prince. The impact had been swift. The darkness that waited on the other side had been welcoming.

"What happened?" he asked, lifting my chin with frigid fingers so I could see into his watery eyes. Flecks of sand stuck to his cheeks.

"It doesn't matter."

All that mattered was that we were both here.

Together.

Alive.

Whole.

He cradled me closer, kissing my forehead. My temple. My hair. My ear met his chest. I heard the sweetest sound in the world.

Rían's heart. Strong and steady. Back where it belonged.

Together, we had defeated the Queen. I knew better than to believe this fight was over. But whatever troubles we faced from this day forward, we would do so together.

And we would win.

A small smile tugged on the corners of my lips. "You said you loved me."

"Only to enrage my mother."

I pinched his arm beneath his wet sleeve, pulling a hiss from the ridiculous prince. "For once in your life, will you please tell the truth?"

Rían smiled down at me, obnoxious dimples on full display. "The truth is, violent Aveen, my heart may beat in my chest, but it has always belonged to you."

The End

PRINCE OF DECEPTION

A MYTHS OF AIRREN NOVEL

JENNY HICKMAN

Prince Of Deception

CHAPTER ONE

SHE DIDN'T KNOW MY REAL NAME.

She'd never seen my real face.

And she wanted me to fuck her in a shed.

Those three things summed up my "relationship" with Eithne O'Meara.

I stepped around the bench and table in the blacksmith's old tool shed, careful not to disturb the layer of dust covering everything. Sneezing and sniffling and watery eyes weren't exactly a recipe for seduction. I'd offered to meet Eithne in her husband's mansion overlooking the seaside. Unfortunately, she preferred our dalliances to be more . . . What had she called it?

Ah, yes. Seedy.

I was a prince in Tearmann, not beloved like my brother but certainly feared and respected. In Airren, I may as well have been the dirt on this disgusting wooden floor.

The misty rain kissing the shed's slate roof fell with a soft sigh. Quick footsteps from the humans outside slapped the cobblestones. The steady *clip'clop* of horses' hooves punctuated each second as time ticked past.

Eithne would want to hurry it on. I had things to do.

Thinking her name made my stomach revolt like I'd guzzled

too much faerie wine. I wouldn't have touched the woman if it wasn't absolutely necessary.

Once again, I put duty above everything else, knowing all too well what would happen if I didn't.

I shifted my pocket watch to check the time. A gift left to me by my father when he passed.

Passed.

A polite way of saying "gutted in his sleep by a cursed dagger." The old fae prince had no more fondness for me than I did Eithne. He'd only left me his watch and prized cufflinks out of guilt for abandoning me in the Forest.

I needed to be in Rosemire by half past if I wanted to make the trial.

Trial.

A polite way of saying "pre-execution."

I could leave without seeing Eithne, except I needed to know when more soldiers were to arrive from Vellana. Something was brewing, I could feel it in my gut. And Eithne was my key to learning what it was.

Her husband, and Graystones' magistrate, served as the Vellanian King's eyes and ears on the East Coast. His wife had a loose tongue. A tongue she liked to jam into my mouth as if she wanted to make sure my tonsils were still there.

A year ago, mass executions were few and far between.

Now, they were more common than not.

I'd tried explaining my concerns to my brother. As usual, Tadhg either had his head buried in a bottle or his cock buried in a woman.

The man blamed his curse for his uselessness.

We were all cursed. Every last one of us.

Drinking himself delirious wasn't going to fix it. Not that I could tell him that when he was in one of his *moods*. That's what they called his month-long binges. All Tadhg had to do was find a woman to love his drunk arse, and he'd be free.

Some of us didn't have that luxury.

Some of us would never be free.

Dammit. Where the hell was Eithne?

The door opened. There was a flash of light. A flurry of skirts. A woman's heavy breathing.

"You're late." I said it with a smile, to keep Eithne from recognizing the hate on my tongue.

Eithne's breathing hitched. I could hear her hammering heart like the beat of a bodhran, no doubt sending a wealth of blood rushing south.

She smelled different today, like raindrops on rose petals. If she weren't so revolting, I may have liked it. I had her pinned against the shed wall before she could give me an excuse for her tardiness. There wasn't time for excuses.

Her hips didn't feel as bony as they usually were. Or her arse.

When she didn't grab for me the way she always did, my chest tightened. The last thing I needed was for her to start showing restraint.

My mouth met her rose-scented skin. And burned.

Eithne whimpered.

The sound was too high. Too sweet. Too nervous.

I jerked back, ramming into the feckin' table, sending whatever was on top crashing to the floor.

Not Eithne. Not Eithne. Not Eithne.

Shit. Shit. Shit.

"Why have you come?" I demanded. "Who sent you?" And where the hell was Eithne? I scrubbed my mouth with my sleeve, still burning like I'd rubbed it across a hot coal.

"No one sent me," clipped a high voice. The woman's posh accent held a hint of Vellana, slight but definitely there. "Next time, plan your trysts someplace with a little more light."

Accosting a woman was a capital offense. If she reported me, I'd meet the wrong end of a hangman's noose. It wouldn't matter that it had been an accident. A misunderstanding. A case of being in the wrong place at the wrong time.

How many times had I heard those excuses cried at the foot of the dais?

How many times had I ignored them?

My mind screamed for me to evanesce. The worthless hole in my chest begged me to stay. The hollowness living inside me almost never spoke.

When it did, I listened.

I flicked my wrist, conjuring a ball of flame in my palm.

Heart-shaped face. Freckles across the bridge of a pert nose. Golden curls that I could imagine slipping through my fingers. Fisting. Pulling so I could taste the nectar living on the column of her throat. Magnificent chest heaving beneath a dark cloak.

Good. Pure. Unblemished.

Forbidden.

Ice-blue eyes reflected my dumbfounded expression.

And my face.

Feck it all. My feckin' glamour had slipped.

No one outside Tearmann saw my true face. *No one.*

"Who are you?" she whispered through full lips that turned down slightly at the corners. Not a frown but a perpetual pout.

"I am whoever you want me to be," I said. Her slave. Her puppet. Her prince. All she had to do was say the word, and I could become the thing she wanted most. My brother may have been cursed to look like a woman's fantasy, but I had the power to become whatever she desired.

Her eyes narrowed. "The only thing I want you to be is gone."

I could do that too. A flick of my wrist, and I could be all the way across the feckin' country. I would've. I should've. Only the hollowness echoed for me to stay.

"I was here first." And since I was here, and she was here, we may as well be here together.

"Fine. I'll go." She walked away, and I had to have a serious chat with my feet to keep from following her.

"Oisin?" a grating voice hissed. "Are you in there?" Something moved outside the door.

Eithne had the worst feckin' timing. I couldn't do what I needed with Eithne if this gorgeous creature was watching.

Well, I suppose I *could*, but I didn't want this woman getting the wrong idea—even though the "wrong idea" happened to be the truth. But it wasn't the whole truth.

The hinges on the door whined open.

Run. Run. Run.

Stay. Stay. Stay.

To hell with the consequences. I grabbed the mysterious woman's cloak and pulled her with me to the other side of a high wooden bench. "Not a word," I whispered, my lips still burning from whatever she'd used on her skin.

Damn, she was beautiful. I'd known plenty of beautiful women. This one, though. This one would be a feckin' masterpiece stripped bare. Curves and softness and pouty pink lips.

"*Oisin?*"

The floorboards creaked. Eithne's footsteps drew ever closer.

The soldiers. The king. I could deal with them another day.

This woman? I wanted to deal with her now.

"Eithne? Where'd you go, pet?" a man called, his voice weak and gravelly. Strong Vellanian accent. He held onto the "o" in "go" a touch longer than most. *Where did you gooo, pet?*

Eithne grumbled a curse. Her boots thumped against the wood when she stomped back toward the door. Sounds of the town swelled, then faded.

"That was close," I said with a laugh, relieved and, for some reason, a little nervous.

Instead of returning my conspiratorial smile, the woman got up, dusted off her skirts, and started for the door.

I jumped to my feet, ramming into the feckin' bench. "You're leaving?" I don't know why I asked, it was fairly obvious when she slipped out the door without another world.

The shed felt empty. The *world* felt empty.

From a crack between the wooden slats, I watched her mount a brown mare and turn toward the road leading out of town.

My fingers grazed my lips.

I should leave and never return.

I should put her out of my mind.

And I would.

But first, I wanted to know her name.

ACKNOWLEDGMENTS

The first people I always thank are the readers who took this journey with me. It still blows my mind that people want to read what comes out of my brain.

My poor, neglected husband is the only reason I'm able to give you so many books. I love you, Jimmy. You're great.

My two monsters, Colin and Lilly, someday I hope you read these and think I'm cool. But if not, that's okay. I love you regardless.

Hi Mom. I LOVE YOU. Remember that when you pick this one up. Megan, thanks for devouring my books and constantly asking for more. Miriam, my oldest friend and my brilliant beta reader, you gave me so much insight into this story's potential. You are a goddess.

Krysten, I really couldn't have done this without you. Thank you for reading this one again and again and sitting down with me to throw around ideas. (He definitely needed stabbed.)

Meg. Meg, Meg, Meg. Where do I begin? Your invaluable input has once again shined my drivel into something worth reading. Don't ever leave me.

Elle and everyone at Midnight Tide Publishing, thank you for giving my stories a home.

ABOUT THE AUTHOR

Jenny is the founder of the PANdom and a lover of books with happily-ever-afters. A native of Oakland, Maryland, she currently resides in County Tipperary, Ireland with her husband and two children. As much as she loves writing stories, she hates writing biographies. So consider this the "filler" portion where she adds words to make the paragraph look longer.

ALSO BY JENNY

The Myths of Airren

(NA Dark Fantasy Romance)

A Cursed Kiss

A Cursed Heart

A Cursed Love (2023)

Prince of Seduction (2022)

Prince of Deception (2023)

The PAN Trilogy

(YA Sci-Fi Romance with a Peter Pan Twist)

The PAN

The HOOK

The CROC

Omnibus Editions

The Complete PAN Trilogy YA Omnibus

The PAN Trilogy (Special Edition Omnibus)

Adult Contemporary PANdom Spin-Off

Never (2022)

YA Fantasy Romance

Married by Fate (2022)

MORE BOOKS YOU'LL LOVE

If you enjoyed this story, please consider leaving a review.
Then check out more books from Midnight Tide Publishing.

A CURSED KISS

BY JENNY HICKMAN

Living on an island plagued by magic and mythical monsters isn't a fairy tale... it's a nightmare.

After Keelynn witnesses her sister's murder at the hands of the legendary Gancanagh, an immortal creature who seduces women and kills them with a cursed kiss, she realizes there's nothing she wouldn't do to get her back. With the help of a vengeful witch, she's given everything she needs to resurrect the person she loves most.

But first, she must slay the Gancanagh.

Tadhg, a devilishly handsome half-fae who has no patience for high society—or propriety—would rather spend his time in the company of loose women and dark creatures than help a human kill one of his own.

That is until Keelynn makes him an offer he can't refuse.

Together, they embark on a cross-country curse-breaking mission that promises life but ends in death.

NOW AVAILABLE

MERCILESS STARS
BY CANDACE ROBINSON

Two sisters. Two loves. And a secret that can destroy them both.

For years, Silver has used her magic to draw the same human soul, Keelen, from the afterlife and place him into a wax raven she created. Each visit, her impossible relationship with Keelen deepened, leading Silver to want more than friendship. Yet it isn't until after Silver and her queen sister, Afton, are forced to defend themselves from an enemy king's guards, that Silver discovers a way to give Keelen human life and become Afton's weapon.

Afton had never given her heart to another ... until she met Ragan. Just when it seems she's found true love, she must temporarily push her feelings aside and accept a betrothal contract from the enemy king to keep her territory safe. But when Afton uncovers a danger that threatens all she has built, the sisters must put a stop to it before everything they love, including their sisterly bond, shatters

NOW AVAILABLE